SINNER'S SIDESHOW BOOK 2

AIDEN PIERCE

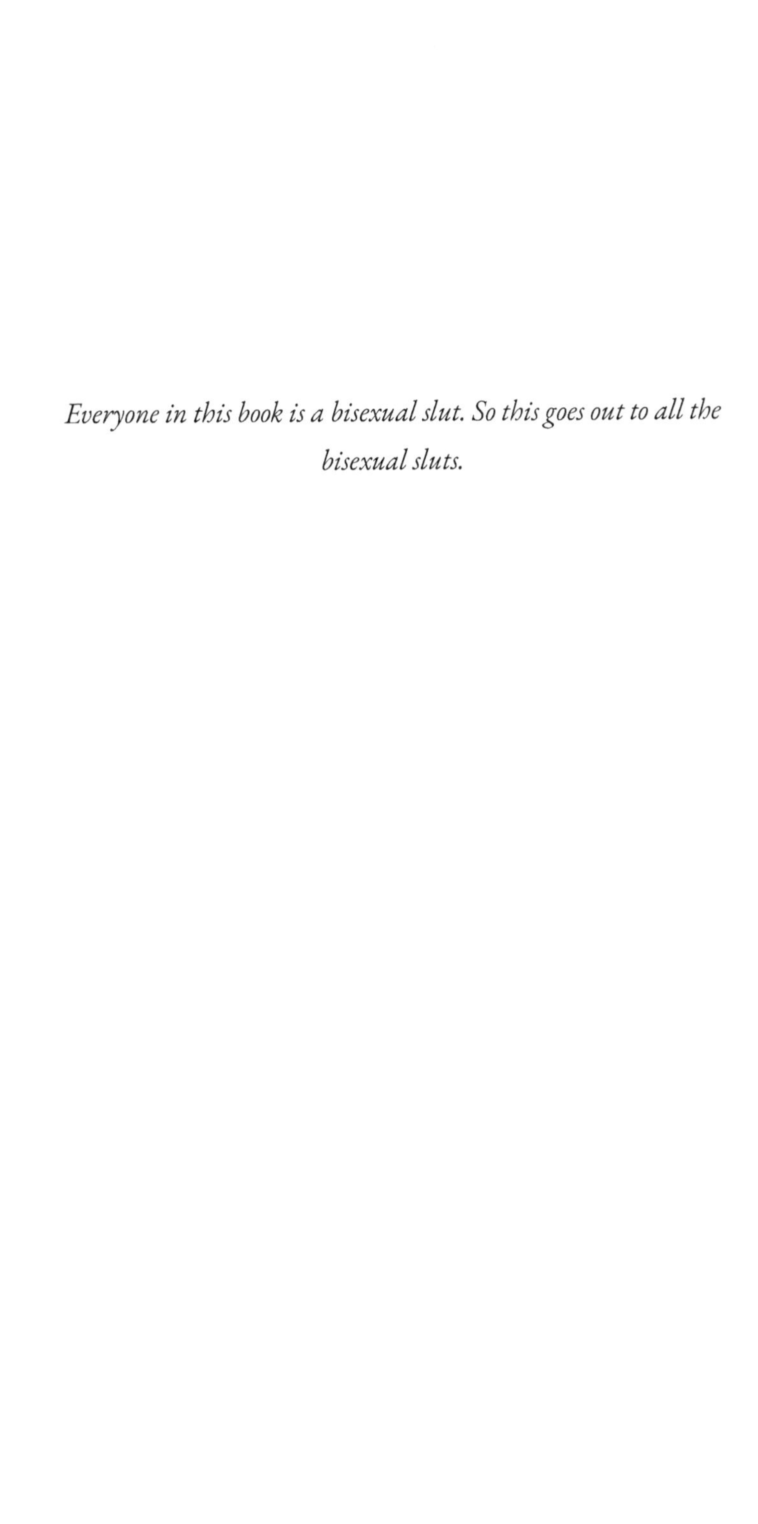

Everyone in this book is a bisexual slut. So this goes out to all the bisexual sluts.

A Word of Warning

CARNIVAL CREEPS IS DARKER AND CREEPIER THAN THE FIRST BOOK. PLEASE READ THIS WARNING CAREFULLY.

This book contains triggering situations such as gore, violence, murder, torture, death of a pet, discussions of parental loss, breath play, fear play, knife play, pain play, demonic clowns, exhibitionism, voyeurism, sadism, masochism, monster appendages, knotting, breeding without pregnancy, sharing, bondage, spitting, snowballing, extreme size difference, DVP, dub-con, consensual non-consent, non-con (not involving the heroine) and other graphic sexual content.

Your mental health matters.

The Thing About Sex Demons

DAEMON

Oh, the dark and disgusting sins I'd commit to stay in bed with Megaera for just a little longer.

I kissed the pink-haired demoness goodbye and stood over her for several moments, watching her drift back to sleep.

I could watch her like this all damn day.

Here she was. Naked, in *my* bed, wearing my collar, her sugary scent entwined with the heavy tang of hellhound cum.

There was a part of me that still hadn't completely processed last night. Meg had shown up at the ringmaster's caravan, desperate to remove her chastity belt. Her plan to seduce Alistair took an unexpected turn.

She'd gotten the belt off, but I'd been the one to remove it.

I'd taken her virginity.

I turned the fresh memory over in my mind, recalling the way she'd felt beneath me—so small and tight and *perfect*.

It had taken every fiber of my will to refrain from shifting and marking her. If I had lost control, I would have broken her. She wasn't built for three hellhound cocks. But she'd taken my human form so beautifully.

Now, she was mine. So long as I paid up.

Alistair had given me the key to Meg's chastity belt on the condition that I kill her mother.

I'd been the devil's pet for centuries, obeying his every whim, fulfilling every twisted task—all without breaking a sweat. His request for me to kill Astrid, who turned out to be Lilith herself, should have been the hardest thing he'd ever asked me to do. But no. Tearing myself away from her daughter was much more difficult.

I put my fist to my mouth, biting my inked knuckles until I tasted blood. She looked like a fucking angel, with her pink hair spread over my pillow like a halo. All I wanted to do was settle down between the cradle of her thighs, slip inside her cunt, and hold her close until Alistair forcefully dragged me away.

My stomach twisted with unease. Too bad murdering Meg's mother was priority number one right now.

What would Meg say if she knew the truth?

That her mom was alive?

That Alistair had lied about killing her, and that now—after all these years—he was sending me to finish the job?

What would she say if she knew her mom and dad had never been in love? That Astrid had charmed her father and conceived her only to be a sacrifice to Discord in a pathetic attempt to secure his mating mark?

What would she do if she knew, after everything I'd done to her, that I was slinking off to kill her mother?

Knowing Meg, she'd want Astrid to die. Still, discovering the truth would break her heart.

She'd don her armor and act as though nothing in the world could penetrate it. But I saw the girl beneath, the one who wanted to be loved and accepted for exactly what she was. It's why she'd sought out Sinner's Sideshow in the first place.

As long as I sent Astrid back to Hell, her daughter would never have to know the truth.

Protecting Megaera was worth keeping up the lie.

I gathered a couple of things for Meg and left them on the foot of the bed for her to find. Scribbling a note, I tucked it beneath the pile and turned to leave. I froze in my tracks when she moaned my name in her sleep.

A soft growl rumbled from my chest as my dick thickened in my jeans. She was dreaming of me.

"You're not making it easy for me to leave you, Pup."

She mumbled something unintelligible, then, in an adorable, sleepy little whine asked, "Why are they booing?"

My heart clenched. Was she dreaming we were in the ring together?

I strode back to the bed and kissed her brow, my fingers stroking over her rosy locks. "If anyone ever jeers at you, I'll rip out their intestines and feed them to my hounds."

Then, with one last lingering kiss, I turned and left the trailer.

I forced my feet forward, trying like hell to ignore the ache that had burrowed under my gut, growing sharper with every step I took away from Megaera. It felt like I was leaving a limb behind. If I had any doubt about her being my true mate before, there was no questioning it now.

It was too early in the day for anyone to be up yet. There was no show tonight, and we weren't jumping to the next town until the weekend, so everyone was taking the rare opportunity to sleep in. Not even the sound of birds could be heard as I strode across the camp toward the animal tents. They knew this place was full of predators.

The hellhounds perked up in their cage when I entered their tent, all whining softly. They always seemed to know when I was about to leave.

"I won't be gone for long." I reached through the bars to rub between each of their ears.

"Where is she?"

I bristled at the two familiar voices behind me, speaking in perfect unison.

Discord's Depths. My mind was so caught up on the half-blood in my bed that I hadn't noticed the clowns sneaking up on me.

Squaring my shoulders, I slowly turned to see Rafferty and Rifton standing in the tent's entrance. They weren't usually awake this early. Had they been up all night worrying about Meg? Their brightly colored hair was sticking up around their horns in every direction, and they weren't wearing so much as a drop of makeup. I couldn't remember the last time I'd seen their bare faces. Even in this disheveled half-asleep state, the twins were attractive bastards, and they knew it.

I stuffed down whatever emotions I could so all they'd pick up on was my annoyance. It was easy to do since ninety percent of the time, all I felt around the twins was irritation.

"Get lost, freaks. My hounds are hungry, and unless you're looking to be their breakfast, you have no business here."

Riff pushed into the tent, his tail lashing the air in frustration. "Are you hard of hearing? We asked you a question."

Raff prowled behind him, his blue eyes narrowing into deadly slits. "Where. The. Fuck. Is. She?"

I busied myself with watering the hounds, turning my back on them so they knew I wasn't threatened. "Your senses are almost as good as mine. You can scent her arousal on my dick, and I'm willing to bet you can smell her blood too. So you know exactly where she is. In my bed, dripping with my cum, wearing nothing but my collar on her throat and my bruises on her thighs."

The tension in the air was thick enough to slice with Larry's rusted cleaver. I waited for them to snap, to take a swing at me.

My eyes were on my hounds, but that didn't mean I wasn't coiled like a goddamn spring, ready for them to try me.

Instead, Riff tossed his head back in my periphery and started cackling.

My hounds growled low, their hackles raised. Even terrifying hellbeasts were put off by a laughing clown.

My irritation morphed into something darker. "Mind letting me in on the fucking joke?" I asked in a tone that would have anyone else retreating. But the clowns only prowled closer, ignoring the cage of snarling dogs behind me.

"We don't give a shit if you fucked Meg," Raff said with a chuckle, his green eyes flashing with amusement. "We're sex demons. We don't do the cagey, possessive bullshit that seems to get your dick so hard."

"Then what the fuck do you want?"

"We heard screaming last night," Raff said, with Riff adding, "That can only mean one of two things. You hurt our girl, or you satisfied her more than we'd figured a non-sex demon could. Either way..."

The twins came to stand on either side of me, so close I could feel their heat, smell the nail polish on Riff's nails, and the faint whiff of lighter fluid that seemed to be permanently embedded in Raff's skin.

"We want to know all about it," they said in perfect unison.

Riff stepped so close that his chest brushed my arm. At the contact, my whip appeared in my hand on instinct.

The twins' attention dropped to the whip. Raff snickered. "Are you trying to scare us or turn us on? Remember, this is Sinner's Sideshow, where fear is pleasure."

That's when I felt it.

This...*tug,* pulling from deep under my gut. The thing about sex demons was that they could feast on more than lust. They had the ability to feed on any emotion and draw power from it.

These creeps were feeding on me.

Something inside me snapped.

My palm slammed into his chest with enough force to send him flying backward. He caught himself, flipping through the air and landing in a crouch.

Before he could stand, I was towering over him, shoving the butt of my whip in his face. "Don't *ever* feed on me again. Not unless you're looking to get torn apart."

Any other man would cower at my feet. This demented incubus *licked his fucking lips* as his manic grin stretched wider. "Uh-oh, leather daddy's *mad*. As fun as you make getting torn apart look in the ring, I think we'll take a rain check."

"Maybe he's not talking about tearing us up in the ring," Riff chimed in, his tone suggestive.

Raff pushed to his feet, running a hand through his electric green hair. "Oooh, a hate fuck. My favorite."

"Not even in your wildest nightmares, imps," I snarled, my upper lip peeling to reveal my sharp canines.

They put up their hands in mock innocence. "Relax. We're just teasing."

"Yeah, messing with you."

"Anyway." Raff gave a shrug. "We wouldn't want you to shift."

"I don't know, Rafferty," his brother offered, canting his head, hot blue eyes running me through. "If he shifts, we'll have five dicks and six holes between us."

Riff nodded thoughtfully as his line of sight dropped to my groin. "I like that math."

They were trying to get under my skin, and Discord save me...it was fucking working.

"Call Meg to check on her if you must, but stay out of my trailer, or I'll be gifting her a pair of still-pulsating clown hearts."

"Try our cocks instead. Meg will like that better. Don't want to kick off your relationship with her thinking you're a shitty gift giver."

There was a reason why I kept my distance from the clowns. They had a way of crawling under my skin. With everyone else, I was level-headed and calm—an obelisk of obedience. Whenever I released my hellish wrath, it was calculated.

Not with these imps.

Before I could do or say something I'd regret, I turned and stormed out of the tent, the sound of their cackling laughter fading away to a maddening hum in the back of my skull.

Alistair's residence sat at the far end of the grounds, away from all the other trailers and tents. I pushed inside without bothering to knock. He would have felt my presence long before I reached the door.

Most mortal stories surrounding the devil were complete bullshit, but they got one thing right. He was a handsome bastard. Especially now with this new skin. Alistair's tailoring skills had improved. You couldn't even see the threads of dark magic stitching the dead flesh together.

My master was stretched out on his bed, shirtless, with his arm tucked behind his head.

A book lay open in his lap. He was always reading—rabidly consuming human texts. Forever fascinated with the world he'd been shut out from for so long.

What was surprising was that he was fast asleep.

Discord didn't need to sleep, though sometimes he'd drift into the cosmic expanse of his mind to escape the thoughts I knew haunted him.

But even the devil had nightmares.

I moved the book to return it to its place and stopped, seeing what lay under it. His pants were slung low, exposing his hips and spent cock. By the sheen on his skin, he'd pleasured himself last night.

I walked to the bookshelf and placed it with the rest of his collection. When I turned around, he was awake, watching me.

My attention dipped back to his cock, which twitched in appreciation under the heat of my gaze. "I see you enjoyed the show."

Alistair, to ensure I didn't shift, had watched every second of my night with Meg through his shadow's eyes.

"I always enjoy your performances, Pet." His hand drifted down to his cock, and in a beat, it was erect, thick and full and begging for my attention. "Now come here to me. I want you to fuck me while the scent of her still clings to your flesh."

I stood my ground while I debated. I had a job to do, a contract written in dark magic and sealed with blood. Every second Astrid remained breathing was more excruciating than the last.

"It can wait," Alistair murmured in that intoxicating timbre that was smooth and dark and sinister all at once.

"Fine. But it's not going to be gentle. I'm not in the mood for that shit right now. Meg has me too worked up."

Alistair's lips quirked into a knowing smile as if he knew Megaera wasn't the only sex demon to blame.

2
Awakened

Meg

I dreamt I was back in the cage with Daemon, but this time it wasn't just Alistair's shadow that watched us fuck…

It was the whole damn circus.

The cage sat in the middle of the ring, with every eye in the house fixed on us. I blinked against the blinding lights, but a firm hand gripped my jaw and forced my gaze to the golden eyes boring into me through a mess of jet-black hair.

"Eyes on me, Little Pup," Daemon growled as he pumped into the cradle of my thighs. The cage rattled with every punch of his hips, and the wet slap of skin against skin could be heard over the crowd's jeering.

"Why are they booing us?" I gasped, my arms banding around his muscled shoulders, claws digging into his flesh as I held on for dear life.

A shadowy figure at the edge of my vision drew my attention back to the bars of our enclosure. The ringmaster hunched down beside the cage until he was at my eye level, his emerald eyes gleaming beneath the brim of his hat. "Because they came to see the *virgin* succubus. We need a new stage name for you."

"How about the Whore Succubus?" Daemon snarled.

Alistair's shadowy form sent me a malevolent grin through the bars. "*The Whore Succubus.* Just like her mother."

I jerked awake, bolting into a sitting position. I shook off the dream with a shiver and forced my attention to my surroundings.

I was someplace unfamiliar. It was a trailer, a new one, larger than most with fancy upgrades. It was clear a bachelor lived here—the place was pretty bare and boring as far as aesthetics went.

Daemon's scent leached from everything. The furnishings. His black sheets. My thighs.

Memories of last night came flooding back. After removing the chastity belt and fucking me stupid, Daemon had carried me to his trailer, cleaned me up, and kissed me goodbye.

I drew my knees up under my chin and wrapped my arms around my legs. This was the first moment I'd had to unpack what had happened with Daemon.

My chastity belt was off, but I didn't feel free. I had still signed my whole life away to Alistair in exchange for a job at his circus. And now, I felt myself tethered to Daemon, bonded, even without his mating mark.

Soon, I'd have his mark and the twins', too. Maybe even Alistair's, if I played my cards right. Then I'd be tied to this circus and the family I'd found within it forever. There wasn't a thing in this world I wanted more.

A buzz at the foot of the bed had me lifting my face from my knees to see my cell phone sitting on a folded t-shirt. I'd left the phone in my trailer, meaning Daemon had broken in to get it for me. Deadbolts meant nothing when you traveled with a group of horny supernaturals with no sense of personal space.

I unlocked the phone to find a few texts from Lollie.

Lollie: Giiirl. Sin was out having a smoke with some of the haunt workers last night and saw Daemon chase you into one of the supply tents.

Meg: Did he hear anything?

Lollie: Oh, girl. Half the camp heard you two screwing. You weren't banshee loud, but you weren't quiet either. Don't blame you. I'd be screaming around that thicc D too. Anywho, congrats on getting the metal undies off.

Fucking fantastic. Everyone was bound to find out sooner rather than later that I was with the twins and Daemon. But it wouldn't be good if the twins found out from someone else. I had to get dressed and find them.

I turned my attention to the clothes Daemon had left me. He'd brought me my cell phone. He could have easily fetched some of my own clothes. Instead, all he'd left me was one of his black t-shirts.

Typical Daemon. He didn't want me to leave his trailer. I was half surprised I didn't wake up chained to his bed. It wouldn't be that much of a stretch, considering I was already wearing his collar.

I got out of bed and pulled his shirt over my head, briefly snagging it on one of my horns. When I pulled the shirt down, a scrap of paper that had been lying under it caught my attention.

> **I want to find you in my bed when I get back. Do that for me, and I'll reward you like the good fucking girl you are.**
>
> **–Daemon**
>
> **P.S. Don't let the clowns in.**

I scoffed, tossing the note over my shoulder. If that asshole thought he was going to keep me to himself, he had another thing coming. The possessive alpha thing got old after a while.

A glance at my phone told me it was too early for the twins to be up yet, so I stumbled to the kitchen and sighed in relief at the sight of a coffee pot and a can of Folgers beside it. Thank fuck. Daemon drank coffee.

I brewed a pot and poured myself a mug.

My phone buzzed, and I glanced at it, expecting it to be Lollie again. I almost dropped my mug when I saw Raff's name—with a green heart emoji—instead.

Raff: We know what you did last night.

I typed out a response and deleted it several times before blanking. Shit. What was I supposed to say to that? They already knew.

What I had with the twins was bizarre, intense, and more serious than any one-month-old relationship had any right to be. But they knew this wasn't exclusive. We were sex demons. Monogamy wasn't our thing. That didn't mean they'd jump for joy when they saw Daemon's collar around my throat.

My phone buzzed again.

Riff: We know who you did last night.

Raff: Naughty little demon. The plan was to seduce Alistair to get the belt removed.

I poured a second cup of coffee, letting them simmer in the suspense for another minute or so before tapping out my response.

Meg: Plan went tits up. Alistair gave Daemon the key.

Riff: Did he hurt you? We can kill him. Not sure how, but we can figure it out.

Raff: Fire won't cut it. Maybe we can hack him up into pieces and feed him to his dogs.

Riff: Ooooh. I like that plan. ;)

A smile crested my face as I read their unhinged texts.

Meg: Sorry guys. No murder today. He was nice.

Riff: ... Yeah, right. Good joke, babe.

Raff: Sure it was Daemon you fucked? Cuz that doesn't sound like our Hellhound.

Riff: He mentioned bruises. Send us a selfie so we know ur ok.

I chewed my lower lip, wicked thoughts stirring in my mind. Daemon must have run into them when he left earlier this morning. What else had he told them?

Knocking back the last mouthful of coffee, I set my mug on the counter and held my phone out above me. I lifted Daemon's shirt to expose my breasts, stuck my tongue out, and snapped a selfie.

I examined the picture, noting how my pink hair stuck up around my horns in a very "just got fucked" style. My pierced nipples and trimmed patch of pink pubic hair were on full display, with a few light hickies bruising my breasts and thighs.

Daemons' spiked collar around my throat dominated the picture front and center.

My thumb smashed the "Send" button before I could lose my nerve. The phone vibrated a few seconds later.

Riff: Fuckin hell, babe...

Raff: So you got Alistair's belt off just to have Daemon's collar in its place.

I couldn't tell if the incubus disapproved or if he was simply making an observation.

Meg: It's not like it's stuck on me. And with the collar, I can still fuck you two.

Riff: So you gonna invite us over? ;)

My fingers froze over the screen. If this was heading where I thought it was heading, Daemon would be pissed. My gaze dropped to the note on his bed. *Don't let the clowns in.*

He had to know by now that I wasn't a rule follower. And I definitely wasn't one of his bitches he could tame.

Meg: He'll kill you both if I let you in.

Riff: He's gonna have to learn how to share his toys. Plus, he has it coming.

I didn't bother asking Riff to elaborate. Whatever transpired between them this morning, I was certain Daemon had gotten shitty with the twins. He always did.

Meg: What's his problem with you guys anyway?

Raff: He doesn't like that we can read him like a book, so he keeps his guard up.

Riff: And he doesn't like clowns.

Raff: If he's taking out the boss' garbage like we think, he won't be back for a while. Plenty of time for us to fuck and suck you until there's no question that you belong to us too.

My thighs clenched, liquid fire tearing through my core. Suddenly, I was starving, and not for food. Now that I was no longer a virgin, it was like the floodgates had been blown clean off their hinges.

I needed more.

My fingers shook as I tapped out my response.

Meg: Here? In his trailer?

Raff: He needs to get it through his head that you belong to us just as much as him. What better way than to fuck you in his bed? Hell, we'd mark you, but Alistair would flip his shit. No shifting into full forms without the boss' say-so.

Riff: As much as we like being watched, we want the first time with you to be just for us.

I swore under my breath as I sent my next message.

Meg: I wouldn't be agreeing to this if it wasn't for the fact that I don't think I can make it across the camp without riding something.

I stuffed the hem of Daemon's shirt between my legs in an attempt to soak up my arousal.

Riff: You're a newly awakened succubus. You need to be fed often if you want to get stronger. Think of us pumping you full of cum as a favor to Daemon. He wouldn't want his new mate all weak and starving.

My heart hammered in my throat as my hand dropped to my apex, smoothing over my center.

Raff: You better not be touching yourself. We're going to sate your ache. How about we make a game out of it?

Meg: What kind of game?

Raff: The kind we've played a dozen times in the ring. But this time, it will be for us. We'll invite ourselves in. You can do what Daemon would want in this situation. Try to fight us off. But you won't win. We'll come inside, no matter how hard you fight. Because we'll know how much you want it.

They wanted to play out one of *those* games. I was fucked in the head because I loved forced play with the twins. And it was the first time we'd be doing it for us. Not for a house filled with the perverted scum of Upside monsters.

Meg: You two are fucked in the head.

Riff: And we know just how wet it makes you.

Meg: Get over here before I change my mind.

Riff: You sure? We're all going to be feeding off each other. It might get intense.

I swallowed a primal noise that tried to crawl its way out of me. I didn't have to stop and think about my answer as I frantically tapped it out. This went past desire. I needed them to make this ache go away. The rougher, the better.

Meg: Oh, I'm sure.

Riff: Remember what to say to end the game? Once we're inside, 'stop' isn't gonna cut it.

Meg: Playtime's over.

Raff: Good girl. We'll be there soon. And babe?

Meg: Yeah?

Raff: You know we love you, right?

I swallowed down the swelling lump in my throat.

Meg: Yeah, I know.

Raff: That's good. Because we're going to fuck you like we don't.

3
Send in the Clowns

MEG

I texted asking how long they'd be. No response. They wanted me to sit here with my nerves eating me alive, drive up my adrenaline and make my heart race with trepidation.

What I needed was a distraction, so I busied myself around Daemon's trailer. I fried myself an egg—the only food he had in his fridge, aside from a few bottles of condiments and a case of imported beer I'd never heard of. After my meal, which did nothing to sate the dull pang of hunger low in my belly, I wandered around his trailer, sipping my coffee.

It was a weird look inside the workings of the demon who was so private about his life outside the ring. Not that there was much to look at. The place was pretty bare compared to the way the twins had decorated their trailer.

Clearly, Daemon spent most of his time working his hounds outside, and most nights he'd turn in with Alistair.

I stopped to admire one of the few touches of personality in his room: A wall decorated with his old circus posters. They featured variations of The Bitch Tamer decked out in his leather, his whip in hand, with his loyal pack of hellhounds at his heel. Below the posters was a display of collars and leashes, all with plaques inscribed with the name of the hound that they belonged to. My mouth went dry, and the thrumming between my legs almost turned unbearable when my gaze fell on the collection of some fetish gear he wore from past shows.

A biker cap with studs on the visor. Sunglasses. A selection of whips and even a riding crop. All the cliché shit that shouldn't have turned me on as much as it did.

My fingers skimmed the straps of a harness—one he'd worn not long ago by the scent of sweat and testosterone embedded into the leather.

I chewed my lip, imagining Daemon in his stage persona.

Then my mind dwelled on what it would be like to share the stage with him in our own act. Now that shit would sell tickets. My stomach flipped when my thoughts drifted to the dream, the nightmare. No. It wouldn't be like that. Alistair didn't care that I was no longer a virgin. He'd said it himself. What would my new stage name be? I pondered names as I wandered to the bathroom to examine myself in the mirror.

I really looked like a hot, just-got-my-brains-screwed-out-of-me mess. My eyes flicked to the shower, debating if I should rinse off the hellhound cum still crusting my thighs. No... I had a sneaking suspicion that the twins would be into it.

A loud knock at the door wrenched me from my thoughts. I padded out of the bathroom, reminding myself not to appear too eager. We were playing a game, a dark and twisted one that was perfect for driving up our lust and creating the perfect, sumptuous, sinful meal for one another.

The clowns loved to watch me struggle.

I eyed a chain lock screwed into the doorframe. I doubted it had ever been used—what idiot would break into Daemon's place? I decided to secure it just for the added thrill of the game before cracking the door and peering outside.

"Who is it?"

"Avon lady. Who the fuck do you think it is?" The twins stood at the door with their hands shoved in their pockets, looking absolutely wicked in their sinister face paint.

Instead of the traditional clown paint, they'd opted for skeleton makeup. The black paint around their eyes made their irises pop, with the white paint thin enough that their brow tattoos—Riff's name under his left brow and Raff's on the right—were still visible. They'd even painted the skeletal spinal column over their throats.

They both wore black and white skinny jeans, black shirts that hugged their lean frames, and steel-toed combat boots with bright laces that matched their hair.

It was diabolical how good they looked.

Riff slowly ascended the trailer's steps and hunched his lanky form so that we were at eye level. He peered through the gap in the door, a chuckle flitting from his lips as he took in the chain lock, almost as if he found my pathetic effort to keep them out amusing.

"We heard the most delicious little rumor."

I glared at him through the gap in the door. "What's that?"

"That you're the alpha's latest toy. Now he's gone, left you all alone..."

Raff pushed in close beside his twin, his cheek flushed with Riff's so two eyes now bore at me—one green and one blue. "Now we want to play with you too."

"Fuck," Riff rasped, his nostrils flaring as he dragged in a shaky breath. "Can you smell that, bro? She reeks of Hellhound jizz."

There was no missing the lust pouring off the incubi in powerful waves. I'd been right. The twins were turned on by the fact that I'd been with Daemon last night and still carried his scent.

Raff's nails raked into the door frame, carving deep claw tracks. His nails were on the longer side compared to Riff's, but he kept the index and middle finger trimmed down for me, a detail that made my mouth water every time I thought about it.

"Unlock the door, fuck toy. It's our turn now."

A blush burned my cheeks, the heat sinking lower until it settled between my legs. "Get bent, fuck clowns."

I moved to slam the door in their faces, but Raff wedged his foot in the doorway, stopping me. I gaped down at his boot and slowly brought my eyes to his, the skeleton smirk I found him wearing nothing short of wicked.

"Let's get one thing straight...we're going to come in one way or the other. You can be a good girl and let us in. Or you can be bad, and we'll *force* our way in. And if we have to force our way in, you're going to be punished."

I could practically hear Daemon's voice in my head, reading what he'd written in the note. *"Don't let the clowns in. I'll reward you like the good fucking girl you are."*

Hmm. I had two options. Be a good girl, follow Daemon's rule, and get rewarded later. Or be a bad girl, let the clowns in, and get punished for it now.

In a perfect world, I'd get both. One of these nights, I was sure I would. For now, the choice was a no-brainer.

Ramming my shoulder into the door, I threw my entire weight into it. But the demon was wearing steel-toed boots, almost like they'd predicted this happening.

Raff leaned in, his skeleton face filling that gap in the door, his lips a kiss away from mine if it wasn't for the chain lock. "We can smell him leaking from you."

"Bet she's so wet we won't even need lube," Riff rasped over his brother's shoulder.

"I want to know how 'The Bitch Tamer' broke in our wild demoness. I bet she made the sweetest little cries for him."

Riff gave a cruel laugh. "I've seen what the alpha's packing. Must have been torture for that tight pussy the ringmaster has been keeping under lock and key."

"We know you bled for him, Harbinger..."

Raff snapped the chain with ease, and his hip slammed into the door, sending me flying back into the wall. My wings shot out, exploding through Daemon's shirt and catching enough air to soften the impact.

I slid down the wall as light from the outside flooded the trailer, and two horned shadows enveloped me. My eyes lifted to find the twins standing over me with all sorts of dark promises etched into the lines of their faces—depraved ones only two starving sex demons could make and keep.

"We can make you bleed too."

4

On Your Knees

MEG

Everything about the twins' presence made me increasingly aware of the growing ache between my legs. Their athletic frames packed with lean muscle. Their mouth-watering scent, a masculine aroma laced with the barest hint of lighter fluid. The skeleton paint.

I shouldn't have tapped into their emotions as much as I did.

Their lust slammed into me like a ton of fucking bricks. It leached from them like acid, eating at my sanity. Poisoning the air and infiltrating every breath I took.

Bleeding into my lungs.

Crawling into my being.

Sinking straight between my legs and making me *feral*.

The spade of Riff's tail snaked beneath the hem of Daemon's shirt and tugged it up enough to give the twins a glimpse of my pelvis. I didn't bother closing my legs. I wanted them to see—to get a good look at all of me.

The last time they'd seen me without the chastity belt, it had been in the haunted house, and it had been dark and murky. Plus, they'd been wearing masks, and I'd still been partially clothed.

"*Discord's cock,*" Riff cursed, his gaze pinging to his brother. "She's got a pink bush. Why is that so hot?"

Normally, I liked to keep myself shaved down there. Sex demons were known for their crazy hair color. Lashes. Brows. Even pubic hair. I loved the rosy locks on my head, but I'd been too self-conscious to rock the pink below the beltline. The chastity belt had gotten in the way of my usual shaving routine. With the way the twins were drooling over the little pink patch of hair, maybe I'd keep it.

"Because she's a sex demon. Everything about her is meant to entice. To lure you in until those pretty manicured claws of hers are hooked deep into your ballsack. I'm surprised she let the hellhound leave the bed."

Raff placed his hand on the wall over my head and arched over me, leering down at me with a demonic smile. "What was so important that it had the alpha running off, leaving his new toy behind?"

Riff snickered. "Yeah. He didn't even leave his dogs to guard you. It's almost like he wanted us to break in and finish what he started."

"Because I can look out for my fucking self." To punctuate, I slammed my foot into Raff's shin. He stumbled back into his brother, buying me enough time to lurch to my feet and grab a knife from the knife block Daemon kept on the counter.

Riff's eyes lit up when I brandished the knife. He tongued the point of his sharp canines. "Now this is foreplay I can get into."

Raff laughed, prowling toward me. These demons were faster and stronger than me. They could overpower me if they wanted. Raff could have, at the very least, moved out of the way when I slammed the knife down in his direction.

He didn't.

I watched in horror as the blade punched into his shoulder, deep enough that when I let go, it stayed there.

Raff's brows kicked up in surprise as he just looked at it for a tense beat.

His brother started to laugh, his eyes lighting up with wicked glee. "Oh my God. She stabbed you. That's so fucking hot."

Raff wrenched the knife from his shoulder, bright red petals of blood peppering the kitchen floor, and *grinned*. "You're going to pay for that, Harbinger."

"What the actual fuck, Rafferty?" I snarled, breaking character at the sheer disbelief that he'd intentionally let me stab him. "Why didn't you move?"

"What, and miss out on getting stabbed by the hottest woman alive?" Riff shook his head. "Yeah right. He's gonna be jacking off to the memory of this for a while."

Registering that the incubus was okay, alarm ebbed, and lust crept back in to take control. "You clowns are fucking psychotic." I slowly backed up, unable to keep the grin off my face as my back hit Daemon's pantry.

"What's with the smile? You're cornered, girl."

"Nowhere to run," Riff sing-songed.

They were within arm's reach. The air between us was hot and heavy. I could barely breathe—the lust rolling off them the most raw, feral emotion I'd ever tasted from someone's aura.

It made sense.

I'd been at Sinner's Sideshow for just over a month. A freaking month of having my pussy locked up in a chastity belt like I was some medieval princess.

As a sex demon, it had been pure torture. There were only so many blow jobs and tit jobs you could give before going insane.

The lust pouring off them crashed over me, wave after intense wave. I drank it all in. Feeding on it, allowing myself to be swept away in the dark, twisted bubble of space that I shared with the clowns and the clowns alone.

It hadn't been all that long ago that I'd come around Daemon's cock. And yet, it wasn't enough.

My freshly freed pussy was on a mission for more, as if I needed cum like I needed air and water. Before I joined the circus, I'd cursed my mom for passing down her insane libido. But at Sinner's Sideshow, I was *living* for it.

I was finally in my element.

Raff prowled toward me with the knife clutched in his hand, his own blood dripping off the blade.

"Now you've done it," I snapped. "You've gotten clown blood all over Daemon's rug. He's gonna kill you for that."

Riff's laugh was dark and manic. "I think the alpha will be less concerned about the clown blood on his floor and more concerned about the clown cum we leave inside his *Little Pup.*"

Riff danced behind me and pinned my wrists behind my back with one hand. The other gripped my jaw, forcing my attention on his brother as he approached.

I was almost glad Riff held my jaw. Otherwise, it would be hanging open.

Raff looked so damn good with his tousled green hair and skeleton face paint, dripping blood. "Let's play a game. Guess which one we're going to fuck you with first. The knife..." He gave it a toss in the air, then caught it and positioned it so the point caught on the button of his jeans. "Or a fat demon cock? Answer correctly and you'll get to carve whatever you want into our flesh."

My heart hitched. "Where?"

"Wherever you want. As big as you want. On our chests—"

"On you're fucking dick is where I'll put it."

I'd thought the incubi would show a flicker of hesitation at my suggestion. Instead, the lust rolling off them was thick enough to choke on.

Raff matched my crazed grin with one of his own. "Is that supposed to scare us? Carve your love note onto our cocks. It will be a pretty sight watching it disappear inside you when we fuck you."

Riff nodded. "But if you guess wrong, and we win, we get to carve our names into *your* flesh."

So. That's what this was about.

Daemon's collar had more of an effect on them than they'd let on. Now they wanted to make their claim too.

It would be easy for them to lie and say the correct answer was the opposite of my guess. It didn't matter.

I wasn't supposed to win. I didn't *want* to win.

Holy fuck. This little game was getting serious, fast.

Sensing my trepidation, Raff took a step back. "If this is too much, we can stop. You know the magic words."

I didn't want it to end.

This was a dark and dangerous path we were taking. I'd heal quickly, but probably not before Daemon got back. They'd probably piss him off. I didn't care. He knew I was a package deal with the twins.

"I'll play your stupid guessing game."

"Good. Now, which one are you about to be fucked with?" Raff gripped his cock, and gave a flick of the knife. "The knife or a demon cock?"

Riff's mouth grazed my ear, his hot breath leaching into my skin and sinking straight to my thighs. "Answer him."

"The knife," I pushed out. "You're about to fuck me with the knife."

Raff wagged his finger at me. "Sorry, baby. The correct answer is *both*."

He threw the knife down with enough force to firmly lodge the blade into the kitchen floor. He pointed to the protruding hilt, his eyes narrowed, radiating dark lust and wicked glee. He licked his lips, smearing some of the paint. "On your knees, baby girl."

Riff shoved me down. I fell to my knees with the knife between the crux of my legs.

Raff's foot nudged against the inside of my knee and slowly pushed my stance wider. They watched me sink onto the hilt, looking like hungry wolves about to pounce with the way their muscles were coiled, their shoulders tensed.

To my surprise, Raff took several steps back and leaned against the kitchen counter. Noticing the pot of coffee, he poured himself a mug as Riff took his place in front of me.

My mouth watered when his hand dropped to his fly, his painted black fingernails drumming the button of his jeans before tugging himself out. I sucked in a breath when his cock sprang free.

It was long and thick, with a Prince Albert piercing at the tip, the sword tattoo along the top of his shaft and a five-bar Jacob's Ladder piercing on the underside.

"Open that pretty mouth and take what I give you," he instructed as he fisted his cock.

My lips parted. He canted his hips and pushed the head of his cock inside my mouth. My lips instinctively pursed around him.

He released a groan and his fingers flexed around my horns for leverage. "By Discord, she feels so damn—*good*."

Raff smirked over the rim of his coffee cup. "Don't unload in her mouth. Save it for her pussy. I want to see how much cum she can hold."

Riff laughed, the sound distorting in my ears as he drew his hips back only to ram back inside me, filling my throat.

His pace turned punishing. Every time he pulled out, he punched back inside, each stroke deeper and harder than the last. Even the slightest movement shook my body, making me twitch and clench around the knife's hilt.

It felt so good I could cry. I *was* crying. Riff fucked my face so hard tears streamed down my cheeks and soaked Daemon's collar. I blinked the tears away to see Riff's painted face twisted with a fierce expression, the cords in his neck taught, beads of sweat streaking a path through his makeup.

His dick throbbed in my throat, and just when I thought he was about to explode, he was wrenched out of me.

"Fuck!" His tail lashed furiously behind him, his nostrils flaring. "I need to fuck her cunt. *Now*."

Raff dragged in a deep inhale and strode over. He set the mug of coffee down on the counter and crouched in front of me. He let out a cruel laugh at the way I writhed on the knife, desperate for friction.

"Look at you. So *cute.* You're not very good at pretending you don't want it. You're too much of a cock hungry slut. Because that's what you want, isn't it? For us to fill you full of cum."

He was taunting me.

A shiver of dark excitement worked through me. If that's how he wanted to play, so be it.

I spit in his face, the glob of saliva sliding down his lips. He didn't so much as twitch. Instead, his expression turned stony, and in the same breath, he was wrenching me off the knife by my hair and dragging me to the bed.

5

Sympathy for the Devil

ALISTAIR

"**I**f they shift and hurt my newest pet, I'll shatter their souls. I don't care how much money they bring in," I muttered beneath my breath as I watched Daemon dress.

The hellhound sent me a pointed look over his shoulder as he buttoned his pants. "What are you mumbling about?"

"Nothing," I said with just enough simulated innocence not to register on the hound's radar as suspicious. "I'm just musing about something my shadow sees."

Daemon's jaw ticked, but he didn't press the matter. Some part of him knew he didn't want to know. He was always perceptive.

The hellhound would have to learn how to co-exist with Megaera's other mates, but now was not the time. He didn't need the distraction. Not when he needed to focus on murdering Astrid.

"Astrid will fight you in her true form. You'll need to do the same."

Daemon tensed at the mention of shifting. He hated his hellbeast with a passion, but he knew its strength was the deadliest weapon in his arsenal.

The hellhound's muscles tightened in his shoulders, making his inked flesh ripple. "Is her monster form anything like the imps'?"

My thoughts trailed back to what my shadow was witnessing, where he lurked in the corner of Daemon's trailer, concern setting in. Concubi were powerful creatures in their full forms. Terrifying skull heads with serrated teeth. Powerful, muscle-packed bodies. Endowed. They could rip Megaera apart if they weren't careful. However, I would have to allow them to mark her as their bonded mate eventually.

Because Daemon would do the same.

If she could survive the twins' mating, perhaps she could survive Daemon after all.

"Yes. Although, Lilith will be stronger. She's far older." I closed my eyes, thinking back to the last time I'd seen Lilith shift. It had been one of her many attempts to seduce me. I could barely recall the memory, either because it was so long ago or because I'd tried my best to completely shove the sight of Lilith making a fool out of herself from my mind.

Maybe I would have felt sorry for her if I believed she truly loved me.

She didn't. That ice harpy wasn't capable of love. Her lust, on the other hand, was a thing of legend, specifically her lust for power. If she became my bonded mate, she'd secure the highest position a demoness possibly could. And as my mate, the bond connecting us would feed her much of my power. Like a magical umbilical cord of sorts.

Refusing Lilith's advances went well beyond my distaste for her. I was doing all man and monster-kind a service by keeping her abilities capped.

The mattress shifted and a strong hand clamped over my throat. I was jerked from the deep mire of my mind to find Daemon straddling me. His golden orbs glowed hot as he leaned down, his hot breath washing over my cool flesh.

"You're not paying attention, Alistair. You were distracted while I was fucking you too. If you were anyone else, I'd snap your neck for daring to take your eyes off me."

His lips twitched with a wicked smirk as he felt my cock start to harden again. I always had a deep fondness for creatures who didn't fear me.

It didn't matter if no one else in my troupe but Daemon and Meg knew what I really was. Survival skills told every living creature to be weary of me. Not them.

They were the only two who could *inspire* this dead flesh of mine in the way they did.

What was the most interesting thing about it was that, for the first time ever, I was attracted to a female. No…It was more than mere attraction. My desire for her deeply confounded me and intrigued me to no end. And as the oldest demon in existence, little struck my wonder these days.

It wasn't even her charm at work. Whatever drew me to Lilith's daughter was something much deeper than simple succubus magic.

It surely had something to do with the fact that Lilith had chosen to conceive her in the first place as an offering to me.

Daemon's grip tightened, and my grin stretched wider. "Careful. Bruise this skin, and I'll wear yours next."

The hellhound rolled his eyes to feign irritation, but I didn't miss the way the bulge in his pants twitched. He had a thing for being threatened since no one else in the troupe seemed to have the balls to do it. Except for our resident sex demons.

"Fine. Do it. Then maybe you could actually fuck Megaera. Since you don't think this body is worthy of touching her."

I nodded thoughtfully. Daemon had been present for my conversation with Meg when she'd come to my caravan last night. She'd attempted to seduce me, and by my depths, it had nearly worked. It was more than her desire to remove the belt. She felt this pull between us, whatever it was. If I wasn't wearing the skin of a sex-trafficking ringleader, I would have taken her virginity for myself.

"When you return from your task, you can find me a host that will be worthy of touching her."

Daemon's fingers loosened from my throat, and his brows hitched. "You won't let me kill innocent humans. So you want me to find someone who deserves to die but whose crime doesn't leave a sour taste in your mouth at the thought of you fucking her with his cock? What, so I'm supposed to hunt down some benevolent billionaire guilty of tax evasion who builds wells in Africa or some shit?"

"No. You'll find me an archdemon. Someone who will be grateful to donate their body to their god. Any one of my disciples would jump at the honor."

A frown thinned Daemon's lips. We were thinking the same thing. Maybe in the past, my archdemons would jump at the honor. But I'd been away from the Downside for twenty years. Loyalty to Discord wasn't what it once was. Even on the Upside, I heard the whispers. The rumors that I was more taken with the human world and the monsters within it than I was with my own kind.

And it was true.

I still had a duty, though. If I wanted to keep my power and my position, I needed to snuff out problematic demons like Lilith before they turned into bigger problems.

I'd done some truly benevolent things over the course of my time as Discord. Anyone else in my position would be far worse.

Keeping my status was in everyone's best interest.

"Fine." Daemon crawled off me, found his shirt on the floor and tugged it on. "You promise not to touch her until we find you a suitable human form?"

I sat up, my eyes narrowing to deadly slivers. The alpha didn't flinch, but goosebumps pebbled his skin as he registered the warning in my gaze. "Would you be able to make such a promise with a creature like that?"

"No..."

I stood up, my clothes materializing around me. Today, I opted for a simple black dress shirt and black slacks. I strode to where Daemon stood and reached to trace his neck where the collar—the one I'd placed on him years ago—had been for so long.

Everyone would notice it around Meg's neck and know the alpha was laying claim to her.

My pets could all mate and mark each other to their hearts' content.

But really, they were all mine at the end of the day.

Daemon knew this. Meg knew it. And soon, the clown twins would too.

"Are you angry that I gave her your collar?" Daemon whispered, his brow coming to rest against mine, his eyes searching mine as if he could see where my thoughts had wandered.

"No. That would make me a hypocrite, wouldn't it? Considering I plan on sharing your true mate with you."

He caught my wrist, held my knuckles to his mouth and brushed my cool skin to his fever-hot lips. He was always so warm. "Remember when we met?"

I cocked one brow, curious that he was bringing this up now. I'd never forget that day I found the feral hellhound, the most dangerous to ever stalk the Downside. He'd killed his mate and had gone on a rampage. I'd always remember it as the day I met my closest, dearest companion.

He remembered it as the day he murdered who he thought was his true mate. Of course, she hadn't been his true mate at all. If she had been, his flames wouldn't have touched her.

I nodded. "I remember. So many of my memories from that long ago have faded in the vast expanse of my mind, but not that one. That one is forever branded into my brain."

Daemon chuckled, his breath tickling my knuckles. "You captured and muzzled me."

I sighed, that particular part of the memory stinging like a hot blade being stabbed into a heart that wasn't there. "I whipped you. Tortured you..."

The hellhound wasn't the only one who regretted the monster he'd been all those lifetimes ago.

"You tamed me and taught me the value of obedience." Daemon's hold on my hand tightened, his grip bruising while his voice came out smooth and gentle, a tone I wasn't even aware he was capable of. "I was nothing but a wild, murderous animal before you."

"You still are."

"Yes, but now it's a weapon I've learned to hone. When you took my muzzle off, and I found enough control to summon my human shape for the first time, I swore all of myself to you. You remember?"

The air between us grew hotter, headier than it had been minutes ago when he'd been inside me. "I remember..."

His other hand curved over the back of my neck, holding my gaze so fiercely that I couldn't look away. "Tell me what I told you that day."

"Everything I have is yours. Always."

"I didn't swear my loyalty that day simply because you were Discord. From that moment on we were bonded, Alistair. Everything I have is because of you. Even Meg. I wanted you to send her away, and you refused. I may not own her completely, but a woman like that can't be tethered to one male. If I can learn to share her with the fuck clowns, I can share her with you."

I could count on my hand the number of times a lesser creature had rendered me speechless. This was one of those times. Daemon wasn't normally this vulnerable with me. Where was this coming from? Was this because of what happened last night? He'd been in his hound form while Meg had been in my caravan, listening in on our conversation. She'd asked if I loved Daemon. Though, she hadn't really poised it as a question. She knew.

I'd confirmed it.

There'd been so many times I'd questioned if it was possible for the devil to love. So many human texts depicted me as some spiteful, vengeful creature. An angel who'd fallen and had shed tears for his father, casting him aside. He'd mourned his loss. He'd grieved. And what was grief but love lost?

That story was nothing but fiction, but I'd studied it countless times over the years until it nearly lost its meaning altogether. I'd read just about every document on the matter of the devil that I could find. Searching for something I knew I'd never find in human texts. Still, I searched.

I'd finally found my answer, and it wasn't in a dusty old book.

It had been whispered from the perfect lips of a half-blood succubus. *You love him.*

"What do you want?" I laughed, shaking my head as much as his hold would allow. "You're only like this when you want something from me. You've already fucked me, so it isn't that."

"I want you to promise me you won't touch Megaera. You won't mate her in your human form, so I'm afraid your monster will take over. If you lose hold over your true shape and you claim her—"

"I'll kill her," I said, cutting him off and finishing the thought for him. "I know."

He was right. The dark urges inside me would take control if I got too close to her. We hadn't been selling that many death seats lately. Everyone was coming to see our newest headliner, and they wanted to live to see her again. Terrorizing the souls and consuming their fear was how I fed—how I stayed strong.

I didn't trust my ability to control myself in this state, and Daemon didn't either.

"So, promise me you won't touch her until I get back. Then I can help you find a new human form."

I leaned close enough to him that our lips were nearly touching, and I knew all he could see was my vibrant, emerald gaze. "I don't make promises, Pet. Not even for you. I make deals."

He went rigid against me. "Fine. You keep from touching her—"

"Be more specific."

"You keep your cock out of her cunt. At least until you properly feed *or* until we get you a new human body."

"And what do I get in return?"

His hands dropped away, and he took several steps away from me, leveling me with a hard look. "I'll give you my mark."

At the mention of his mark, a fire sparked somewhere deep inside me. I held out my hand, and my top hat formed from shadows, dropping out of midair to fall onto the crook of my index finger. I placed it on my head, dipping my chin so the brim hid the maelstrom of emotions storming behind my eyes.

I'd been begging my hound for his mark for centuries. And I was Discord.

I didn't fucking beg.

He was mad if he thought I was going to forge a mating bond simply because he was using it as leverage to guarantee Meg's safety. "I won't harm her. We don't need to make a deal for that. I've told you before I want your mark because you love me. Not because you're selling yourself to ensure—"

I couldn't get another word out. He cut me off, storming forward, his fingers curling into my shirt and slamming his lips to mine in a kiss that consumed all of me.

When he broke the kiss, his eyes searched mine. Pleading with me. "Make the deal with me, Master. Or don't. Either way, I'm giving you my mark. Just so long as you know, I'm giving it to Meg, too."

I nodded, emotion tightening my throat, making speech almost impossible. "Yes. It's a deal," was all I could push out between several gasping breaths that tangled with his.

He kissed me again—this one softer. He had my lips chasing his, then he tore himself away and strode for the door. Astrid's amulet, the one that would lead him to its owner, dangled from his fist. "I hate to think of what the clowns will do to Meg while I'm gone, so I'll be as quick as I can."

I bit back the laugh that burned in the back of my throat. If only he knew what they were doing to her right now, in his bed. Still, I refused to say a word about it. He'd find out soon enough. For now, he needed to direct his anger at Astrid, not the twins.

"Don't rush it, Pet. Remember, Astrid is Lilith herself, the oldest succubus alive. She'll try to take you and Meg and this whole damn circus away from me if it means securing my mark."

"I won't let that happen." His fists clenched until his knuckles cracked. Infernal rage swirled off him, making his tattoos glow and smoke rise off his skin. "I'd sooner burn this entire world to the ground."

6

You Lost the Game

MEG

The demon's touch should have been cold and cruel. It wasn't. There was electricity in the way Raff touched me. We were all perfectly in tune with one another, feeding off our lust, surrendering to our own depravity, and enjoying this kind of game without an audience of skeevy monsters, all whooping and yelling and touching themselves as we fucked.

Still, I couldn't shake the feeling that we were being watched. Somehow, the creeping sensation that someone, some*thing,* was here, spying on us, seemed to push my lust higher.

Raff threw me onto the bed, and I scrambled into a sitting position in time to see Riff wrench the knife from the floor and place the hilt to his lips. His eyes locked with mine as he slipped it into his mouth and sucked my juices clean from the handle.

"I get to carve my name into her skin first," he said around the knife.

His twin prowled toward me, a wide grin cracking his mouth, the skeleton paint making him look completely unhinged. "Fine. But I get to fuck her first."

He peeled his t-shirt over his head and kicked his jeans off to reveal toned muscles straining against his flesh.

My attention dropped to his cock, eyeing the clown shibari tattoo that sat between his shaft and his navel. I licked my lips. The taste of his brother lingered on the back of my tongue.

The demon's brows kicked up when something on the wall caught his attention. I followed his line of sight, my heart lurching into my throat when I saw Daemon's collection of show leashes and collars.

Immediately, I knew what Raff was thinking. I was thinking it too.

"He'll kill you for touching them." I tried to sound hostile, but the venom in my voice was replaced with something more sensual as I watched Raff stride to the wall and lift one from its hook.

He shot me a filthy grin as he stalked back to the bed, his fingers twisting the leash. "No more than he'll kill me for what I'm about to do to you."

He kneed up onto the bed, and even though I wanted nothing more than for him to shove me down and push himself inside me, I scrambled to get away from him.

I wasn't going to make any part of this easy for them. The struggle made the prize at the end all the sweeter.

The demon's arm shot out, his slender fingers closing around my ankle, and he dragged my thrashing body back across the bed. His cruel laughter hooked in my lower belly, molten heat sweeping between my legs and making me drip.

I cried out when his knee pushed down onto the small of my back, pinning my belly to the mattress. "I love watching our toy struggle, don't you, Riff? Fucking Hell. She gets so wet when you hold her down."

Raff wrestled my arms behind my back, ignoring me even as I bucked my hips. He wrapped the leash around my wrists, knotting them so tight that the leather straps cut into my flesh.

The green-haired demon leaned back to admire his handy work and, with a satisfied hum, gave my ass a quick swat. "You look so damn beautiful in a collar and leash, baby."

He put both hands on either side of my head, caging me between his arms and leaned down, his mouth pressed against my ear. "We're going to pump you full of our cum, and you're going to thank us for it. Do you fucking understand?"

All that came out was a strangled moan as his hips began to move, his hard cock grinding against my ass. His knees spread, forcing my own legs wider, allowing him to line himself up with my center. When his head was flush with my entrance, I threw my head back, slamming my skull into his.

He reeled back, clutching his nose. On the next breath, I felt warm, wet droplets pepper the back of my neck. I'd broken his nose.

"Fuck, you're really making me bleed today, aren't you, Hell Bat?" The stark lust and the low stain in his voice had me biting back a moan. His hand smoothed over my wings, his tender touch catching me off guard. "I like playing with fire. I fucking love getting burned. So, your wounds, your fire? Nothing gets me harder. Fuck."

The groan of a male teetering on the edge of sanity ribboned around my ear as he glided the length of his shaft through my folds.

Riff came to stand at the side of the bed, looking down at us with the freshly cleaned knife in his hand. I heated and clenched at the sight of him, standing there watching his brother precious centimeters from penetrating me.

"Make sure to scream, baby."

The words had barely left Riff's tongue when Raff punched his hips forward and filled me with one savage stroke. No gentle easing himself in. No working me up to fit his mass. No warning.

He forced his way in with one shove, but there was no pain. No stretching sensation. Just pure fucking *bliss.*

Raff moaned into my shoulder blades, his breath feathering the sensitive skin of my wings, making me shudder in unholy delight.

For a moment that felt like an eternity, Raff stayed motionless. He was breathing heavily in my ear, with only a single broken curse dropping from his lips.

Riff moved in my periphery, moving his weight back and forth between his feet. Impatient.

"Are you going to fuck her or what?"

"I'm trying not to shift," the demon hissed through clenched teeth.

Riff's blue brows hiked until they were almost in his hairline. "She feels that good, huh?"

Raff didn't answer, but he didn't need to. His clenching muscles and labored breathing were signs enough that he was struggling to keep it together.

"Don't slip into your full form now," Riff warned. "The boss will lose his shit if he finds out. And you never know when his shadow's lurking around."

Alistair's shadow.

That's why I couldn't shake the sensation that we were being watched. We *were* being watched.

The devilish ringmaster had warned me that he'd be around to supervise my intimate time spent with his troupe members to ensure my safety. As a half-blood, my ability to forge mating bonds with them was put into question.

I was still part human, after all. And to seal a mating bond, I'd have to be claimed in their full forms.

"Don't shift, Raff. Not yet," I gasped against Daemon's sheets. "Pull out if you have to—"

Raff's fingers sunk into my hair as he shoved my head down onto the mattress and snarled into my ear, "It would take a wild pack of hell hyenas to drag me off of you. I'm not leaving your perfect cunt until my balls are empty of every last drop of cum I've been saving for you. Got that, Hell Bat?"

His filthy words, along with the new nickname, lured an embarrassing little mewl from my throat, making his dick twitch inside me.

It felt so good, and he wasn't even moving yet. I tried to wriggle my hips, desperate for friction, but Raff pressed his weight onto me. His heavy muscle, paired with the leash binding my arms behind my back, made it impossible to move. I was helpless, forced to lay there and take his dick at whatever pace he decided.

Riff crouched beside the bed, and I twisted my head to find his gaze level with mine. His hot blue eyes were glowing—he was feeding. "You might like torturing your ballsack, bro, but I'm not a fucking fan. You better start screwing her brains out now so I can have my turn, or it'll be me dragging you off her."

Something seemed to snap in Raff's brain.

On the next beat, he was pounding into me so hard that the headboard slammed against Daemon's wall. Above that were the obscene sounds of a male chasing his release, rabid grunts and the clap of bare flesh.

His cock pulsed, and he jerked, his movement stilling for a beat as a hot gush of fluid filled me. There was no time to be disappointed that he'd come so quickly—he was already chasing climax number two, his thrusts harder and quicker than before. When he came again, he pulled out and allowed Riff to crawl onto the bed in his place.

They both flipped me so I was face up, my arms pinned between me and the bed.

Riff pressed the flat of the blade to my inner thigh and gave it a tap. He snickered when I felt the cold metal kiss my blazing flesh. "Ahh, now you've done it, harbinger. You're leaking my brother's cum all over the place."

Raff positioned himself so he was kneeling at my head. I tilted my face to see his cock, a rope of pearly white cum oozing from the tip. He tapped my lips, and they parted to suck him clean.

"The alpha's going to be so angry when he sees what a mess you've made of his sheets."

When I licked every last drop from Raff, I lifted my head to peer at the mess he'd made between my legs.

"Y–you never come this much in the ring."

"It's a breeding thing." There was something in Riff's inflection that had my muscles winding tight. I watched with wide eyes as he arched down and painted a lick over my seam, tasting me *and* his brother.

A low, shameful moan bled from me. Both the clowns—with Riff's mouth still flush against my mound—started cackling. Manic and unhinged peals of laughter filled the room.

"Look at her face," Raff told his brother, his bright green eyes sparking with amusement. "Wonder what has her freaking out, the fact that you just tasted my cum or that our primal natures demand that we mate and breed?"

Riff sat back on his haunches, wiping his face with the back of his hand. A wet sheen of cum or my arousal—probably both—smeared his makeup.

Somehow, that made him look more gorgeous than before.

"Don't freak, babe. You're a succubus. You can't breed unless you want to. But our cum is an aphrodisiac. It's like our balls know to save most of it for your sweet pussy, so you can see how virile we are."

"To tempt you to open your womb to us."

"I–I–I don't even know how," I sputtered.

"Good. We're not asking you to carry our spawn. Last thing this freak show needs is a circus brat running around."

I exhaled in relief.

I'd never thought about kids before, but I didn't have to. I didn't want them, or at least not anytime soon. It seemed the clowns and I were on the same page, just like we were with everything else.

Somewhere along the line, our force play game had turned into something else. We were all too pent-up to pretend that we weren't all slipping into a rabid, deranged feeding frenzy. As sex demons, if we didn't relieve our hunger when our bodies demanded, we'd slip into a wild, animalistic state.

One where all that mattered was spilling as much fluids as possible.

"Fuck me," I moaned at Riff, squirming my hips. Without really meaning to, I activated my charm powers. If he was anything other than a sex demon, he'd be magically bound to obey me.

Instead, he only laughed, the cruel laughter only adding to the infernal ache between my legs. "Not yet. You lost the game, remember? We get to carve our names into your pretty flesh. Discord's Hell, I hope Daemon's back in time to see."

Shit. Demons healed fast. Raff's broken nose was already fusing back together, and the stab wound on his arm was closing up. As a half-demon, I healed slower.

Daemon would probably see the aftermath of my first time with the twins. From the clown blood on his carpet to the scent we'd leave behind in his sheets—which he'd sniff out no matter how many times I was gonna wash them.

The first cut stung. I cried out, and Riff paused, his eyes flicking up to meet mine. "Aw, is playtime getting too rough for our toy?"

"We can stop and dial it down, babe," Raff said softly, his fingers threading through my hair, his claws grazing my scalp.

An unholy shiver worked through me. "I'm fine...Th–the pain is g–good."

Riff's lips kicked up with a cocky smirk. "Let's test that."

A mangled moan caught in the back of my throat as he made a second cut. In the same beat, his twin bowed over my body and suctioned his lips around my clit, his twin slicing his name into my inner thigh inches away.

Riff was working on the second F when I came, hard and fast. Riff kept carving even as I climaxed, and Raff's fingers curled inside me as he kept sucking my clit.

They weren't stopping.

Within a minute, I was coming a second time, and they forced me through the orgasm even as I screamed for them to stop.

They laughed, telling me that "stop" wasn't my safe word.

They fucked me until I was raw, red and throbbing. There was no end in sight to their stamina. Blood and cum and sweat ran together. At some point, they switched places, Raff cutting his name into my other thigh while Riff stuffed his cock in my mouth.

"Don't forget to feed, baby," one of them urged. "Take as much in as you can."

"I'm too full," I moaned, my eyes drifting shut as I rode through yet another orgasm.

"Time to call it quits, bro. She's about to pass out."

They pulled me up, untying the leash and freeing my arms. I could barely move them. I was so spent but so fucking satisfied I could cry...

Then I realized I *was* crying.

"I'm sorry," I muttered through my tears. "I don't know why I'm crying. That was great."

"It's okay, baby. Come down however you need. You did so good for us."

I wasn't usually a crier. But these tears weren't sad or bitter. They were cathartic.

So, I let them fall, allowing myself to be vulnerable as the twins cradled me between them. Riff kept his forehead pressed to mine, telling me how perfect I was as Raff pressed slow, soft kisses to my shoulder.

I wasn't sure how long we'd been like that when Riff brushed my hair out of my eyes and pinned me with a concerned look. "Have you eaten yet? Real food?"

My stomach grumbled at the mention of food. "Um...Does coffee count?"

"Come on," he said with a small smile that had me heating all over again. "Let's get those cuts cleaned up and get you some breakfast. Afterward, we can claim the ring for practice and teach you how to use stilts."

"But I know how to use stilts."

Raff gave one of my horns a playful tap. "Do you know how to use them while fucking?"

"You can do that?"

"Oh, baby. You haven't seen *anything* yet."

7

Monster Rager

MEG

The twins carried me back to their trailer and insisted on cooking me a breakfast of fried eggs and maple links. We all showered, which inevitably turned into another meal with sausage of a different variety. By the time we were fed and clothed, and the twins freshly painted—they opted for their signature "acid" harlequin look this time—the sun was starting to set.

"Shit..." I stumbled out of their larger trailer, shielding my eyes from the glaring golden light of the sunset. "We fucked the whole day away."

"We'll fuck the night away too." Riff punctuated his statement with a slap on my ass. "But we should make an appearance at the party."

Raff nodded, lighting a joint and inhaling, the smoke swirling around him making my heart thump. "Yup. Lollie will have our horns if we don't prove that we haven't fucked you to death soon."

Plans to screw all night and maybe squeeze in work between breaks fell to the wayside when Lollie texted that since there was no show tonight, the troupe was partying in the big top.

As we neared the black and white striped big top, I knew this "party" was a full-on monster rager by the heady emotions laying thick over the tent like a dense fog.

Lust. Awe. Excitement. Paired with the weed, the mixture of my favorite smells had my mouth watering.

Riff dragged in a deep exhale, his nostrils flaring and his tail lashing in excitement behind him. "Fuuuck. Taste that? This is gonna be *fun*."

Raff passed the joint to his brother. "Keep it reigned in a bit tonight, bro. The boss wasn't happy with the shit that went down at the last one of these."

"What happened at the last one?" I perked up in interest. I'd heard the parties that the troupe threw on the very occasional off nights were a thing of legend and that the twins were a big cause of that.

"Turned what was supposed to be a poker game and a few drinks into a full-blown orgy."

"It was totally lame before I spiced shit up with a dash of charm magic."

"This is why the ringmaster doesn't trust us to shift. You can barely control yourself as it is."

Riff's brows gnashed with frustration, and a not-too-subtle wave of anger rolled off him. "Whatever."

"Do you think Daemon will be back in time for the party?"

"Doubt it," Raff answered, his tone dripping acid. "He's usually gone for a couple of days when he's off doing the boss' dirty work."

"Thank fuck for that." Riff sighed in relief, releasing a plume of pungent smoke. "It's pathetic watching half the troupe drool over him when they know they have no freaking chance."

"Speaking of, prepare for some cold shoulder tonight, Hell Bat. Word's out that you're with us *and* Daemon now."

Christ. News spread like a medieval disease in this troupe.

"We fucked, so what? It's not like we're bonded yet."

"With his collar around your neck, you're as good as marked. Plus, people are going to be curious as fuck to see how well the ringmaster is gonna share his favorite pet. The dynamic is gonna be..." Raff made a shrugging gesture. "Who the hell knows?"

"It's gonna be weird," I said with a contemplative murmur.

Body heat, muted stage lighting, and Rob Zombie's *"Living Dead Girl"* poured from the tent's back entrance.

"The fuck clowns are here!" Someone shouted over the din. Everyone raised their drinks in the air and cheered.

Most of the troupe was crammed into the ring, dancing, drinking, but there were monsters scattered through the seats chatting, fucking, and blowing off steam from a week of back-to-back shows.

"That crazy bastard's gonna do whatever it takes to get into the main show, huh?"

I followed Riff's line of sight up to see Roach, "the-more-metal-than-mothman," who was, as his stage name suggested, a mothman with heavy body modifications. He had a bit act in the weekday shows where everyone would ogle the insane amount of hoops and rings and gauges he had all over his body, especially his wings. It was a miracle he could still fly, and that's exactly what he did in the ring to warm up the crowd.

Apparently, he'dbeen trying to wiggle his way into the main show for years by practicing new crazy acts and pitching them to Alistair.

Dozens of ropes and pulleys were attached to the scaffolding above, keeping Roach suspended horizontally over the ring.

This wasn't my first time seeing a suspension act. At Walker's, there'd been a guy who'd suspended himself with hooks through his nose.

"There isn't supposed to be this much blood," I muttered to the twins, my stomach twisting at how thick and jagged the hooks were. And there were so many, punching into his back and pulling it into fleshy peaks covered in matted moth fur.

"No, but Sin looks happy." Raff gestured to the ground beneath Roach, where Sinclair—Lollie's vampiric boyfriend—stood with his head tipped back and his mouth wide open, catching the dripping blood on his tongue.

We moved into the stands and leaned against the half-wall separating the ring from the first row of death seats.

Roach took notice of us, and his antennae twitched as his pierced lips split with a shit-eating grin. "Look at me, Rafferty!" He held out his arms. "No hands!"

The mothman and the green-haired demon were close friends. Roach was the troupe's resident tattoo and body mod expert, and the two had grown close when Raff had gotten his tattoo.

Raff hopped over the divider and into the ring, shouting at Roach to be heard over the thumping music. "Real cute, dude. Shove a hook through your junk and hang yourself by the nutsack, then I'll be impressed."

His blue-haired brother turned to me, pressing a kiss to my temple. "We're gonna make sure Roach doesn't flay his entire back off. Have fun. Mingle. Get trashed. Just don't do anything we wouldn't do."

I snorted. "That list isn't very long."

With a mischievous wink, he was gone, and on the next breath, Lollie was at my side, leaning against the divider with a plastic red cup in hand. Today, she wore a pink tank top that showed off her colorful tattoos and a short black mini-skirt that she'd borrowed from me.

"He's a fucking idiot, isn't he?" The gorgon gestured to the ring where Sinclair still stood under Roach, now on his hands and knees, licking up the mothman's blood.

"Yeah, but you love him."

"I do," she sighed, almost sounding annoyed, but there was no hiding her smile. "Speaking of boyfriends, I'm surprised you can walk, considering the collection you're amassing."

"Honestly, me too. Must be all that sex demon stamina."

"I'll toast to that." She raised her cup into the air, brought it to her lips and took a sip before passing it to me.

I eyed the mysterious blue liquid and wrinkled my nose. It smelled like lighter fluid and an energy drink, but I knocked back a mouthful with a shudder anyway and pushed it back into her hands.

When I turned my attention back to the ring, I noticed people's heads frequently turning in our direction. "Everyone's staring..."

"Can you blame them? Our virgin succubus has been set free of her shackles." She turned to face me, one arm propped on the divider and the other clutching her cup as she gave me an appraising look. Even the mass of snakes on her head seemed to consider me.

"You aren't marked yet. I mean..." She shrugged a shoulder—the one with the medusa tattoo that Roach had inked and styled to look like it was watercolor. "With Daemon's collar around your throat, you're almost as good as marked. Smart move on his part. If anyone fucks with you now, they got a death wish."

Lollie collapsed into one of the seats with a sigh. "So, deets girl. Does 'The Bitch Tamer' have as big of a dick as those pants he wears in the ring advertise? He's gotta stuff. No unshifted monster is *that* big."

"Yeah, well, my sore cooch begs to differ."

The gorgon's eyes rounded. "Really? Damn. That had to be one Hell of a hate fuck. Where is he anyway? Off brooding because he has to share you with the twins?"

"No. I think he's doing something for Alistair. He didn't say what—"

The conversation was interrupted by a sudden explosion of cheering. We looked into the ring to see Larry, the boar-headed giant, standing in the center of the mass. It was the first time I'd ever seen him in the ring, fully clothed. He wore a t-shirt that said "VEGAN" on it that was struggling to keep in the giant's mass of muscles as he bent and picked up a keg. The huge metal container looked small in his hands. He gave it a few pumps over his head as the troupe chanted, "Chug, chug, chug!"

Even Roach joined in from above, though he was starting to look pale in the face from all the blood loss.

Larry snapped the spigot with his bare hand, a geyser of frothy beer spewing everywhere, and he opened his snout and chugged as much of the liquid as he could catch while the rest mixed with the mothman's blood on the floor.

"Idiots." Lollie chuckled, the obvious fondness she had for her fellow troupe members stark in her eyes.

"You call me, Lollie-pop?" Sinclair asked, appearing almost from thin air beside me. His chalk-pale face—along with his white t-shirt—was streaked with Roach's blood.

"Licking blood from the floor, Sin? You're fucking disgusting."

"Jealous I'm licking up other blood and not yours, Lollie-pop?"

By the emotions bleeding into the gorgon's aura, she was a tad jealous—and a little turned on. Sinclair seemed to know it too, by the smug smile on his face.

"So…" The vampire swung his blood-red gaze on me. "The virgin succubus ain't so virginal anymore. Half surprised the boss didn't sell tickets to your deflowering."

Lollie threw her cup at Sin, who dodged just in time for it to go sailing past his head and into the ring. The sound of it making contact with someone's head followed up with a curse in Infernal, rose over the music.

"What? It's true! The whole troupe was talking about it!"

Lollie's snakes hissed with the clear displeasure carved into their mistress' face. "You and the rest of the troupe need to learn to keep your mouths shut about Meg and her sex life."

"It's alright, Loll. I'm not offended. Can't really blame everyone for being in my sex life when half of the time it's broadly advertised in the ring. Besides, I'm a succubus." I shrugged. "Everyone's perverted curiosity just feeds my powers and makes me stronger. That way, I can be strong enough to beat the shit out of anyone who crosses the line." I sent Sinclair a too-sweet smile. By his awkward laugh, he got the picture.

"Careful, girl. This one gets off on threatsss," Lollie hissed. She kicked him in the shin, sending him to his knees so that he was kneeling in front of her, then placed the heel of her boot on his forehead.

His blood-red eyes dropped to her center and, judging by his expression, he had a full view of what was under her skirt. "Yes, Daddy."

"Right..." I chuckled. "That's my queue to leave."

"T–t–talk to you later, Megs! *Oooh!*" I turned around, but not before catching a glimpse of Lollie fisting Sinclair's hair and pushing his head beneath her skirt.

I shot a glance into the ring to see that the twins had lowered Roach to the ground and were carefully pulling the hooks out of his back and wings one by one. Knowing they'd be busy for a while, I decided to dip out of the big top and into the smaller entrance tent.

Since we still had a couple of days before our jump to the next town, the haunted house hadn't been torn down yet. The red lights were on but dimmer than usual, and the fog machines were still churning out smoke that stirred around my heels as I walked through the haunt's wandering pathways.

I stopped in my tracks, a sudden wave of uneasiness slamming into me. If I'd been drinking, I would have blamed it on that, but I'd only had one sip of Lollie's alcohol. No, it wasn't that. It was a sudden, sickly-sweet, overpowering flavor of lust spiking the air.

It occurred to me that I wasn't alone. Someone—several someones judging by their clashing auras—had followed me into the haunted house.

"I know you're here. Fucking show yourselves."

My pulse accelerated with every passing second of silence as I waited for them to appear. After several beats, two men in terrifying rubber clown masks stepped out from behind some decorations, blocking my path.

I breathed a sigh of relief. "*By Discord's fucking dick*, guys. What the hell are you doing? Haven't we played this game before? I mean, I'm down, but I thought you two were more creative than this."

Barbed silence stretched between us as I waited for them to respond. A joke. A witty retort. Something sinisterly sultry to make my panties melt. Anything but silence.

A foreboding sensation hooked under my gut, making me take a step back. "Uh, guys? You're starting to freak me out. Playtime's over. I'm going back to the party."

Whipping around, my heart plummeted when I found two more men in masks had snuck behind me to block my exit. One wore a grotesque scarecrow mask with rotting burlap and fake maggots filling the eye sockets, and the other a creepy gorilla mask.

My unease morphed into instant panic. The two in clown masks weren't Riff and Raff at all.

"What's the matter?" a rough voice from the scarecrow mask asked. "I thought our whore succubus liked demon cock? Isn't it fair we have our turn too?"

8

Hunt in the Haunt

MEG

There were four of them. Too many to charm at once. I didn't have my sword with me to defend myself, either. And the music was so loud in the big top that if I screamed, chances were good that no one would hear me.

"Touch me, and it will be the last thing you do."

"Why?" he taunted. I couldn't make out any of his features through the screen mesh of the mask's mouth, but I could picture the leering grin on his face. "You think the sex demons are gonna give two fucks? All they care about is each other. You're just another hole to fuck."

My throat swelled with anger. "You're wrong. They'll set you on fire and dance around the flames. Then we'll fuck on your ashes. You better pray they get their claws on you first because that will be child's play compared to what Daemon will do to you."

They all laughed, and Scarecrow answered, "But he's not here, is he?"

I sprinted off the path and into the maze of decorations, winding around the Styrofoam tombstones and taking as many sharp turns as I could. I had no idea where I was in the haunted house, and there was no time for me to slow down to gain my bearings. If this were a human haunted house, there'd be glowing exit signs. Then again, if this were a human haunted house, there wouldn't be monsters in rubber masks chasing me.

When I came too close to one of the animatronics—a skeleton with blinking red eyes and an electronic cackle that could be heard through the entire tent—one of them shouted, "She's somewhere over here!"

I took another turn, an angry sob lodging in my throat when I found myself at a dead end.

Fuck, fuck, fuck.

I whirled around, shrinking back into the shadows to try and make myself as small as possible, and pounding footsteps neared.

What was I gonna do? Scratch their eyes out? Draw as much blood as possible? Maybe I'd offer to suck one of their dicks, and once I got it in my mouth, I'd bite it off and spit it back in his face. I wasn't going down without a fucking fight.

I looked around for a weapon. My chest soared with hope when I noticed a butcher knife sticking out of a foam section of fencing, and I snatched it up to discover it was plastic. Perfect.

One of the masked men rounded the corner. "*There* you are. You're a very naughty bitch, making us chase you like this. Then again, you like being chased, don't you?"

Oh, my God. Was he one of the haunt workers who'd seen Daemon chase me into the supply tent last night?

"Don't worry. I can knot you too, baby." He reached up and pulled his rubber werewolf mask off to reveal he was a real-life werewolf.

I brandished the most poisonous smile I could muster. "Wow. Plot twist. What, am I supposed to clap now?"

His black eyes gleamed with malice beneath his too-bushy eyebrows. "You're supposed to scream."

I rolled my eyes, refusing to show even an iota of fear. "For you? I don't think so."

He prowled toward me, shifting as he came close. Fur exploded over his body, his snout grew, his spine arched, and his legs morphed into haunches. Fuck. He knew it would be harder for me to charm him in his monster form.

He reached for me, claws extended. Then, there was a shift in the light, a shadow passing over him. If my eyes weren't playing tricks on me, I could have sworn I saw something slither inside his nose.

He froze. His eyes widened with horror. A bead of blood trickled from one of his nostrils.

Then he exploded in a spray of blood and bits of flesh. I didn't even blink as I was splattered with werewolf guts. I couldn't tear my eyes away from the horror of what was happening in front of me.

I'd been with Sinner's Sideshow for over a month. Monsters died at every show, usually by beheading, stabbing, and, in the most extreme circumstances, disembowelment.

This monster hadn't simply exploded. He'd been totally obliterated. There one moment, and nothing but a fine mist of blood and flesh the next.

My jaw dropped as I watched the shadow take the form of a tall, slender man. Slowly, he turned from shadows to flesh. The ringmaster was dressed in a perfectly tailored black dress shirt and slacks. He was so handsome. So stylish. Even covered head to toe in the blood of my would-be rapist.

Especially covered in his blood.

"You stay here, Little Demon. I'm going to take care of the rest. I'll be back for you."

He turned to leave, but I snatched his sleeve, and he turned back toward me with a cocked brow.

"Are you going to kill them?"

"Naturally. I won't have filth like this in my troupe, terrorizing my favorite pets. I'll make the others suffer. This one—" He gestured to the puddle of blood beneath his feet. "I acted quickly out of anger. The others won't be so lucky."

"Let me help you kill them."

Alistair's lips bent with the ghost of a smile, and his gaze dropped to the plastic knife still clutched in my hand. "With that?"

A blush burned my cheeks. "No."

The shade considered me for a moment, debating. "It's nearly impossible saying no to you, Little Demon. How do you do that?"

"Do *what* exactly?"

"Wrap the most jaded demons around your horns?" He heaved a sigh and pulled me to him, slowly picking a piece of flesh from out of my air and flicking it away. "Even me."

"So does that mean I get to torture those fucking assholes?"

"Megaera." The way he said my name had my heart clenching. "You're shaking. You need to clean up and calm down."

"But—" Suddenly, arms wrapped around my middle and pulled me backward into someplace cool and familiar. I looked up to see the blurred shape of curling horns.

I was inside the ringmaster's shadowbeast.

"Take her to my caravan," the shade instructed his shadow.

"But Alistair—"

He leaned close to his shadow, his glowing emerald eyes narrowing into deadly slivers. The intensity I saw within them had me shivering. They warned me not to disobey him like the night Daemon lost control of his hellbeast and burned the chapel tent down. "Do as I say, Megaera."

The urge to fight for my right to wreak revenge burned like bile in the back of my throat.

But I kept my mouth shut.

He'd instructed the shadow to take me to *his* caravan, not mine.

Seducing the devil was objectively a bad idea, no matter how you turned it, but it wasn't just the forbidden nature of the whole idea that had me in a chokehold. I couldn't shake that moment I'd shared with Alistair in the illusions. He'd tried to scare me away, but he'd only intrigued me more.

There was something darkly intimate surrounding the devilish enigma that drew me to him like a moth to a flame, flocking happily to her own destruction.

It was like nothing I had with Riff, Raff, or Daemon.

So, I didn't fight the shadow as he carried me away. Unholy cries of agony rang out behind us as we left the tent. I shut my eyes, imagining I was in the ring with my sword down my throat and my audience cheering and roaring their delight to drown out the dying men behind me.

I needed a distraction from the fact that I wasn't the one making them scream.

9

The Devil's Surprise

MEG

The moment the shadow set me on my feet, the old oil lanterns in Alistair's caravan sprung to life and bathed everything in a muted golden glow.

Alistair's residence wasn't like the shiny new RVs that the rest of the troupe lived in. His was an old traveling caravan stuffed with every kind of trinket you'd expect an ancient malevolent wizard to own. Books on demonology, creepy monster specimens in bottles, yellowed portraits of renowned circus actors and rolled-up posters that had more energy to them than inanimate objects should. Even the shadows had a life of their own as they danced in rhythm to the flicker of the lantern flame.

I should have found the whole place foreign and creepy. Instead, I found it oddly familiar. Maybe because it had once belonged to my mom back in the day.

The human part of my brain told me that washing off the werewolf guts should have been priority number one, while my succubus half didn't give two harpy fucks about the carnage crusting my flesh. If anything, there was a smug little part of me that was all too happy to walk around covered in my attacker's innards as if it was some primal instinct that warned other predators not to fuck with me.

I poked around Alistair's collection of books, marveling at how old some of them were. Like *Gutenberg Bible* old. "Who knew the devil collected antique bibles?" I snickered, half to myself and half to his shadow who trailed behind me. It rumbled in quiet acknowledgment.

My heart rammed into my ribs when I rounded a stack of books that was almost as tall as me to see a door in the corner.

"That wasn't there before." I cast a glance at the shadow, who only grunted in response.

I approached the door, twisted the crystal handle, and pushed it open. The hinges creaked loudly, and I stepped into what looked to be a very long hallway, with countless books stacked almost to the ceiling on either wall.

This was the part where I'd shut the door and pretend I never saw it....*if* I was anyone other than myself. But this was me we were talking about. So, I snuck inside.

The hall went on for longer than what was physically possible, given how small the caravan was on the outside. It went on and on.

I turned around to look behind me, seeing Alistair's shadow had followed me.

"He's been having you follow me ever since last night in the supply tent with Daemon, hasn't he?"

The shadowy beast made another grunt and bobbed his head.

"I knew it. That's why he knew I was in trouble. You know, I don't need a bodyguard."

The shadow stepped closer, and my pulse accelerated when he reached for me. His dark fingers plucked a wad of werewolf flesh from my hair, just as his master had minutes ago. What he was saying was clear.

"Okay, I see your point. I did need rescuing today. But the whole damsel thing isn't usually my bag. This was just a one-off. Next time, I'll be carrying my sword. Pepper Spray. Taser. Silver stake. Holy water. You know, lady stuff."

Other than his red eyes glinting through the murk of the corridor, the shadow had no reaction.

"Nothing? Wow, okay. Tough crowd."

We wandered deeper down the hall until the caravan's main room was a small square of light behind us. Soon, we arrived at the end of the hall, where several doors sat. I knew better than to go opening random doors in Discord's personal residence. Still, curiosity had me reaching forward and twisting the knob.

I braced myself for the worst. It wouldn't be that far of a stretch to find myself staring into some hellish corner of the Underside.

I was thrown for a loop when I opened the door to find a linen closet that smelled of cedar and lavender.

The next door was the coziest bathroom I'd ever seen, complete with plants and all sorts of curios hanging from the ceiling, a round window with crystals lined up in the curved sill, and a wooden tub at the center of it.

I glanced at the shadow. "You know this is pretty weird for the devil's house. What's next, a candle-making room?" I opened the next door, and my jaw dropped.

It was a fucking candle-making room.

I promptly shut the door. "Okaaay, now I'm creeped out."

This time, the shadow chuckled. Or I thought I surmised a chuckle. The sound was deep and strangled. Guess that was to be expected from something that didn't have vocal cords.

"There's a spell on the caravan that makes the rooms and halls shift to cater to the inhabitant's needs and desires."

I whipped around to find Alistair in the doorway, leaning against the doorframe with a hand in his pocket, tapping his cane against the side of his polished shoe. As he raised a hand, shady tendrils exploded from his palm to wrap around the door that had been the linen closet. Blood-curdling screams, flames, and the gut-punching scent of sulfur shot from the doorway, making me jump.

He promptly closed it with a smirk. "See?"

I forced an awkward laugh. "That's good. I was starting to think Discord was secretly an old lesbian woman with a candle-making side business and a subscription to *Better Homes and Gardens.*"

He pushed off the doorframe and came to stand in front of me. My heart rate lurched into hyper-speed at his closeness. His aura was a dead zone for me, but I didn't need my succubus powers to feel his dark presence dancing over my skin and making my hair stand on end like electricity.

"Don't do that." For once, his words were pleading, not commanding.

I quickly looked away in a failed attempt to keep my pulse under control. It made me uneasy how well he could see through me and my armor. Uneasy and vulnerable and *seen.*

"Megaera, look at me." He took my chin in his grip and guided my gaze back to his. "Don't pretend that you're okay when you're not."

There was no hiding anything with Alistair. When he looked at me, he saw everything. Which made the fact that I couldn't read him worth a damn that much more frustrating.

"I'm fine." A twisting sensation in my gut called me a liar. "I'm mostly fine," I amended. "You warned me that this isn't a place for half-bloods. There are gonna be monsters who don't see me as one of them. There are going to be monsters who are monsters in the same way that some humans are. I think the thing that bothers me most is that you had to rescue me."

"I didn't rescue you. I was protecting my property."

His words should have pissed me off. But I was the one who'd sold my soul to the devil for a job at this circus. And I'd happily do it again. Plus, Alistair's possessive streak appealed to that fucked-up part of my brain that had me chasing his demented creep show in the first place.

"Well, your property is feeling a little crusty. I think I'm gonna use your bathroom to wash up."

"Before you do that, I have a gift for you. The kind that will only make you filthier."

At that, my wings perked, and my tail lashed the air in excitement. "Well, color me intrigued. Should we find a bedroom or...?"

"Close your eyes and hold out your hand."

I blinked at him but did as I was told, my palm heaving between us. I don't know what I was expecting him to put in my hand. This wasn't a normal man. Flowers and chocolates weren't his vibe.

My lip peeled when several round, wet little balls were placed in my hand. "These better be peeled grapes."

The shade laughed, the sound rich and melodic and sinister all at once. "You can look."

My stomach flipped when I found six severed eyeballs with the retinas still attached. "Wait...Are these—?"

"Through that doorway, you'll find the rest of your gift." He pointed with a claw-tipped finger to a door behind me. With my heart in my mouth, I opened the door to a huge industrial space. The magic caravan had created a creepy warehouse, complete with flickering fluorescent lighting and racks of tools bolted to the walls. From rusty railroad spikes to old-school bone saws. In the middle of the room there were three steel tables, all with a body chained to them.

They screamed and writhed as they heard us approaching. Heard, not saw. Their eyes had been brutally wrenched from their sockets, leaving the pits hollow with blood and hacked-up tissue.

"I thought you killed them," I muttered, my tone a ragged rasp. I pivoted to face Alistair, who was watching me with an expression I couldn't parse. Before I could let the sensible part of my brain convince me otherwise, I threw myself into his arms.

There was a beat of silence, where he didn't do anything, but a moment later, his arms wrapped around my waist. He arched down to bury his face in my neck and press a kiss on the edge of my jaw. "It's only right that you be the one to send their wretched souls back to Hell."

He pulled back, and his eyes, hot and full of hellfire, locked with mine. "I would have let you do it in the haunt, but I couldn't stand the thought of you being the last thing they ever saw."

10
The Horsemen

DAEMON

I stood beneath the rusted motel sign, the "No Vacancy" casting me in a red glow. I'd been staring at the shitty, flea-bag motel for almost an hour. Scoping the place out. Making sure my nose hadn't led me astray. No. It never did. Lilith's necklace had led me here.

An abandoned motel in the middle of nowhere. There were no cars in the parking lot, trash everywhere, and most of the windows were either boarded up or smashed in. The only sign of life was a dim light leaking from the tattered mini blinds in one of the few intact windows.

This enforced my theory that Astrid wasn't interested in seducing Alistair for his mark. If that were her game, she wouldn't be in this dump.

I pushed the dark thoughts swirling around the succubus to the back of my mind. None of it mattered. She'd be dead within the hour. Then I could get home to Meg and Alistair.

I approached the door to room four and drew a deep breath, inhaling the demoness' strong scent.

She's here.

Normally I'd kick the door in, tear the scum's throat out, and call it a day, all in the span of a minute. Since this was an ancient archdemon, I needed to have more tact. I'd broken into the lobby and managed to find the spare key for room four. The sun was only just starting to set, so there was a chance she'd be sleeping since demons were commonly nocturnal.

Before the key hit the lock, a feminine voice called from inside, "It's open."

My muscles tightened, and I bared my teeth on instinct. *Fuck.* So much for sneaking up on her. I threw the key into the parking lot with a curse and pushed my way inside.

Astrid lay in bed with her folded wings propped against the headboard, a cigarette pinched between her fingers. She was naked, wearing nothing but the bedsheets tangled around her thighs. She was beautiful, with her dusky purple hair and soft violet eyes. Tanned, tall, with the curves of a goddess. I could see how the myth of her being too beautiful for Discord to touch had started. I also understood that was bullshit, and how Alistair simply couldn't stand her.

In spite of her beauty, there was a foul stink that clung to her. One that couldn't be washed away no matter how many showers she took or gallons of perfume she bathed in. Even a soak in a tub of fluoroantimonic acid wouldn't strip the odor. No, her stench was that of a rotten soul. Lilith was gorgeous on the outside but putrid and blackened on the inside.

"You're a day early," she said, her voice tight with displeasure.

My attention wandered to the mass on the bed beside her. She was with a man.

Poor fuck.

"You're fucking crazy if you think Alistair was going to show up here and mate you in this dump, reeking of some other man."

She brought the cigarette to her mouth, and her lips pursed into a bitter smile as she took in a drag. A plume of smoke coiled through the air, winding around her horns. "You stupid mongrel. Don't you think I knew he wouldn't show?"

"Then why come to our camp and blackmail him into mating you, using your own damn daughter as leverage?"

"Because I knew he'd send *you*." She flicked her cigarette over the ashtray on the nightstand and sent me an arrogant grin. "And when you don't come home, he'll come looking for you."

I summoned my whip, my knuckles cracking as my fingers flexed around the leather grip. "I don't know what your plan is, and I don't care. I plan on being home in time to crawl between your daughter's thighs tonight. But not before dropping your corpse off on my master's porch as a thank-you gift for giving her to me. Maybe I'll throw in your lover as a bonus."

With that, she threw her head back and laughed. The man beside her stirred. I bristled when I finally picked out his scent from the mass of strange smells around the room.

He wasn't mortal, and by the magic energy rolling off him, he wasn't some bottom-feeder monster either. Astrid was in bed with another archdemon.

"Perhaps his corpse will make for a very nice gift for my master. Actually, as luck would have it, we're looking for an archdemon to donate his skin to make Discord a new suit." I approached the male demon's side of the bed and pulled the blankets back. "Pray you're pretty. Otherwise, Discord will have no use for your carcass."

The male's eyes flew open, and a meaty arm wrapped in a complex network of veins snapped out to seize me by the throat. I jumped back, and before my feet made contact with the ground, he was out of bed.

He was huge, with enough muscle packed onto his frame to make me look small in comparison. He hadn't a single hair on his bald head, and instead, his skull was covered in ancient tattoos. Flames danced behind his eyes, and I knew in an instant that I was outmatched.

Lilith's lover was the Horseman of fucking War.

"What are you doing here?"

"Waiting for you, hellhound," he rumbled in a hellish baritone deeper than even my own. "You're going to be the perfect bait for luring Discord."

"You're betraying your god. And for what? Her cunt can't be that good."

"Our god has been more interested in playing around in this pathetic excuse of a realm. It's time to end this world so he can return to our own."

"That's right, mongrel." Astrid took another puff of her cigarette, watching us from the bed with that smug smile growing by the second. "In exchange for helping me claim my crown, I'm granting the Horsemen permission to bring about the apocalypse."

Every sinew in my body strung taught. I'd been right about one thing. She didn't love Alistair. She loved the power he offered. What I hadn't seen coming was the Horsemen of the Apocalypse.

"You're willing to end all of mankind so you can worm your way into becoming Discord's mate?"

Lilith's perfectly arched brows stooped low on her face. "Yes. I am. I never liked this trash realm. I never understood Discord's fetish for it. He doesn't even feed on humans. He'd prefer to squeeze fear from his own kind. No wonder he's grown so weak. When he comes looking for you, it will be oh-so-easy for the Horsemen to hold him down while I forge our mating bond."

Blistering fury raged inside me like a maelstrom, making my skin heat and my tattoos glow. "Are you fucking kidding me? You can't rape a god. He can destroy you with a single goddamn blink."

The succubus laughed again. "Not after he's been playing Circus in the human realm for two decades. He needs fear to make him strong. Why do you think I slayed all those humans when I was running Sinner's Sideshow? To keep him strong."

I hated how right she was. Alistair was but a shadow of the eldritch monstrosity he'd once been. These days, he only feasted on the fear of the willing, and because of it, he'd grown weaker. He was still stronger than all the monsters on the Upside combined, but if he was to go against The Four Horsemen in his current state...

He'd lose.

I had to hand it to Astrid. She was a clever bitch. She'd seduced the Horsemen by offering them the one thing they'd been after for an eon—with some tail thrown in—and had lured me here. Now, I was to be the bait, and eventually, Alistair would come looking for me, where the Horsemen would be lying in wait.

The whole using me as bait thing was where their plan would fall apart.

I turned and slammed my knuckles square into War's crooked nose, which had clearly been broken countless times before. The power in my punch would have crushed the skull of any mortal and knocked a lesser demon off his feet. The Horseman barely recoiled.

His mouth stretched into an unhinged grin, the blood trickling from his nose, staining his jagged teeth. "You think you can take me, hound? I'm not even shifted yet."

I had no intention of letting this fucker shift. Everyone knew the Horsemen were dragons.

There was no chance in Discord's Hell that I'd beat him in a fair fight, monster to monster. And summoning my hounds was out of the question. He'd kill them, and I'd rather die myself and wait for Alistair to collect my soul in the Downside than let this demon harm my pack.

One moment, he was staring at me, blood pouring down his face, and the next, he was hitting me with the force of a semi-truck. Lilith's manic laughter hit my ear before I slammed through the wall, busting into the next motel room with an explosion of drywall dust and shards of wood.

The bed broke my fall, my mass smashing it to pieces.

War's brawny frame appeared in the hole in the wall. "Let's take this outside so we can fight in our proper forms, Hound."

"Fuck that," I groaned. "Humans will see."

"Then we'll kill them. Oh, that's right. I forgot. You're a filthy mortal lover. I can smell the cream of Lilith's half-blood bastard crusting your cock. She as good a fuck as her mother? Guess you wouldn't know. You don't know what it's like to bed a demon worth a damn."

I was on my feet in an instant, raising a huge chunk of the bed frame and smashing it into his chest. He faltered just long enough for me to summon my whip and snap it in his direction.

It wasn't just any whip. It was the same one Alistair had used to tame me back when I was wild. It could shatter forms and force monsters to shift to their lesser states. War was already in his weakest shape, so when the lash made contact with his chest, he roared in pain and collapsed to one knee.

"Get up, War!" Lilith screeched from the next room.

I strode over to the demon with a cocky smirk curving my lips. "You're the brawn, but you sure as hell aren't the brains of your outfit, are you, War? She's playing you like a goddamn fiddle."

The smoke began to ebb, giving me a clear view of the black pattern my whip left on the swells of the Horseman's pectorals. It looked like he'd been struck with lightning.

"So what?" the Horseman growled. "We help her mate Discord, she becomes a goddess and forces him back to the Downside. Our kind get their god back with a new mate to keep him in line, and my brothers and I end this sad excuse of a realm. Sounds like a win-fucking-win to me."

"Of course, it does. You're a power-hungry idiot. But I've been Discord's companion for ages, and I can scent a shit deal from a mile away. Trust me. Working with Lilith gets you screwed in more ways than you bargained for."

His eyes blazed with infernal rage. I recognized that gleam embedded within them. He'd like nothing better than to bury his hand in my gut and ease my intestines out like hand-pulled taffy. So when his hand snapped out, I was ready.

I sidestepped, moving my feet so I stood behind him, and wrapped the cord of my whip around his throat, yanking it like a leash.

"Well, well. Look at that. No wonder you wanted to shift. My human form is stronger than yours." It looked like years of holding in my hellbeast had paid off. I was more powerful than I'd given myself credit for.

I placed my boot between his shoulder blades and pushed. His muscles strained, and his thrumming veins bulged as he fought me, but slowly, his strength began to give, and he bent at the waist.

One swift kick was all it took to get him to fall face-first into the filthy carpet. I stepped on him, resting my arm on my knee. "I do this in my show all the damn time. They call me The Bitch Tamer. You know what this makes you now, War? My bitch."

A yelp wrenched from my throat as pain tore through me. I looked down to see a glowing spear sticking through my stomach, the pointed tip glistening with my blood.

It wasn't Lilith who'd snuck up on me and stabbed me.

There was only one demon known to wield an adamantine spear.

"I told you not to underestimate him, War," the Horseman of Conquest seethed. He gave a jab to the spear, and I bit back a whimper of pain.

Adamantine was the strongest material known to demonkind. I couldn't snap or bend it with my bare hands like I could with other metals, and it hurt like a bitch. Shitting a medieval mace would have made for a more pleasant experience.

"You're not supposed to kill him!" Lilith shrilled at Conquest. "If you send him back home, Alistair will go looking for him there. He'll be most vulnerable on the Upside."

"Stop screaming like a fucking banshee, Lil," Conquest muttered. "I missed all his vital organs."

With a yank, he dragged me backward into the next room. Blinding pain shot through my skull, my vision going blank for a beat as he rammed the spear—with me still attached—into the wall.

A smack cracked across my cheek. "Stay conscious, mongrel. I want you to watch this."

I opened my eyes to see Lilith's naked form standing over me.

Fuck. I was sitting on the floor with my back to the wall, the adamantine keeping me pinned in place. Lilith sauntered back to the bed where War and Conquest waited.

"Maybe we should let him join too," War rumbled. "With that spear wound, it would be an extra hole to fuck."

"And let him bleed out so he can die and ruin the plan? I don't think so."

The demoness placed her hand on War's chest. I didn't miss the way he winced as she traced the fresh wounds, lighting a pattern with her claw. Then she gave him a shove, making him lie down, and climbed on top of him.

She fisted his cock, lined his tip up with her pussy and lowered herself onto him. Conquest positioned himself behind her, curled his fingers around the base of one of her wings for purchase, and slowly began to fit himself into her ass.

War's cock was big, but from someone like War, I'd expected bigger. Conquest's cock was the more impressive out of the two.

I'd kill them before Alistair could come looking for me. Somehow.

It would be Conquest's body I'd gift to Alistair. He was blond and blue-eyed, which wasn't my thing, but the shade never used those parts of his victims. His emerald eyes and shadowy hair were the two features that he always kept his own.

But his slender frame, with surprising muscle packed on, that thick and veiny cock? It would be as much of a gift for Alistair as it would be for Meg and me.

All I had to do was wait. Bide my time. And not bleed out before I came up with a plan.

As unconsciousness took me, the obscene noises coming from the demonic threesome just feet away faded.

And the last conscious thought I had before I passed out was the hope that the Horseman of Death didn't show up.

11

Candy Sweet Fear

ALISTAIR

I'd known what had happened the first night Megaera came to Sinner's Sideshow. This wouldn't be her first murder. But charming that ghoul into running himself through on her sword was to protect the honor of another. Now, she'd be killing three men for the sake of her own... Not that there was much honor in a place like Sinner's Sideshow.

She knew taking the lives of these men would have a different effect on her than the ghoul had. It was plain in the way her soft pink eyes swept over the tables where the three haunt workers were chained. She hadn't taken any pleasure in killing that ghoul. But this? Oh, she was going to *enjoy* this.

"P–please. We're sorry," one of the monsters cried out weakly, his chains rattling as he struggled on the table.

Another thrashed harder against his bindings. "The hell we are. All this for the half-blood whore? She's a succubus. She's supposed to be fucked!"

Ancient, infernal rage bubbled inside me like hot acid, and I had to resist the urge to reduce them to red puddles of goo as I had with the werewolf. If I killed them, their souls wouldn't go back to Hell. Death by my hand was final. Absolute.

But I'd let these souls rot in Hell for a few eons if it meant their deaths would be teased out. Not to mention, I'd get to watch Megaera take pleasure in their last, anguished breaths. The thought of her covered in their blood sent a pulse through my body.

Meg gritted her teeth as she moved closer to the table where the least apologetic of the three was chained. "You're going to burn in Hell for a very long time."

The monster let out a hysteric laugh rife with pain as his gaping eye sockets wept with blood. "I am a faithful disciple to Discord, bitch. My dark god loves me. He'll watch over my soul. Not that a mortal whore like you would understand."

My lips curved slowly.

Meg's gaze flicked to me and mirrored my grin. "You're right about the watching you part. But I don't think he loves you as much as you think."

Her tail lashed the air behind her as she moved to the wall filled with every kind of tool that would turn even the most depraved torture master green with envy. My caravan had a personality of its own. It had been a long time since it had catered to anyone other than Daemon or myself, and seemed to be taking the opportunity to spoil Meg.

She opted for a bone saw and walked back to the table with an extra spring in her step. The monster froze when she started to undo his pants. Confusion carved his face. "W–what are you doing?"

"What? Isn't this what you wanted?" She pulled his cock out and gave it a few strokes. He was rock hard and panting within seconds.

Since he was blind, he couldn't see her bringing the saw to his ballsack.

With the first cut, a piercing scream filled the warehouse. The monster begged for Meg to stop, but of course, she didn't. Filth, like him, didn't deserve her mercy. The sawing motions were deliberately slow while her other hand kept pumping his shaft.

"You like that, baby?" she asked in a sultry purr, loud enough to be heard over his screams.

Hearing what was in store for them, one of the other monsters tried to shift in an attempt to escape but found the chains forged from my shadow magic kept him confined to his human shape. The other one sobbed quietly and, judging by the dark stain on his pants, had wet himself.

Meg's eyes glowed, and the air vibrated with her arcane energy. "You're going to come for me."

Ejaculating while getting your dick sawed off with an antique bone saw seemed improbable, but Meg was using her succubus magic. Under the influence of the charm spell, his body was bound to her will.

She stroked him at a maddening pace, the blood from where she cut into him acting as lubricant. He jerked violently against the shadowy chains, and as he started to release a torrent of pearly white fluid, she severed his cock completely.

"Open up."

His jaw unhinged on her command, and she held the cock over his mouth, allowing the rope of his own cum—mixed with bright beads of blood—to dribble all over his lips, his chin, his tongue.

"Good boy," the demoness practically sing-songed. "Now *swallow*."

There were few sights that could bring an ancient manifestation of darkness like me to his knees.

This was such a sight.

I watched in dark awe as my little half-blood goddess went to work. As a shade, I didn't have a heart, but fuck me, something inside me was aching as I watched her. I'd only ever felt this way with Daemon, and even then, it wasn't as strong as what I was feeling now.

I wanted to protect her, both from the brutal world that revolved around me and from myself, which would be a difficult task considering I wanted nothing more than to crawl inside her and never fucking leave.

It was little wonder Daemon had made me promise not to fuck her. I didn't want to touch her with the mortal flesh that had belonged to a sex trafficker, but ancient urges were stirring to life, and I found myself caring less and less what I fucked her with. So long as I fucked her.

However, if I got too carried away, my true form would come bursting free. And I hadn't been feeding enough to keep it under control. So, as Meg hacked away at her victims, I stood in the corner with the rest of the shadows and quietly fought a war within myself.

When the final monster of the three breathed his last breath, the bone saw dropped from her hand and clattered to the floor at her feet. Her face turned ghostly white as she appeared to come down from her bloodlust, the carnage—and the fact that she'd caused it—fully sinking in.

"How do you feel?"

"I... I feel..." Confusion flashed across her face. "Good. Too good."

I knew the look in her eye all too well. She'd fed on their fear, which had my cock hard and my balls aching. She was stunning. And she was shaking. I wanted to hold her close, but I didn't trust myself.

"They had every intention of raping you, Megaera. They deserved their fate."

"I know that. But that doesn't make me any less of a monster."

"Yes, you are. However, don't mistake that with thinking you're the same kind of monster as them."

Her chin bobbed with a series of small nods. "You're right. Fuck them. They can rot in Hell with their werewolf friend."

"They won't. He's gone for good."

"What do you mean?"

"*I* killed him. When I do the killing, regardless if they're mortal or immortal, their soul is destroyed forever."

Her eyes rounded. "Oh. Well, shit."

A fresh wave of candy-sweet fear radiated from her, coiling tight with her succubus pheromones. How could I forget my little demon got off on fear, especially her own?

Fuck.

My hunger for this audacious little half-blood was something dangerous indeed. I wanted to devour every bit of her, and lick the fucking plate clean.

A hot, simmering silence stretched between us. There was a lingering hunger in the room, and I couldn't stop picturing myself ripping her clothes off, cocooning her in my shadows, and burying my cold, dead flesh within her heat.

I was a dead zone for her powers. She couldn't detect my lust, but she saw it written all over my face by the way her smile turned smug. "You're looking at me like you want to eat me."

I took a step toward her, unable to help myself. "I do want to eat you."

She pushed the grizzled remains to one side of the table to give herself room to hop up, perching on the table's edge with her legs hanging over the side. She parted her thighs and lifted her skirt, showing me that she was wearing nothing underneath. "Then eat me."

She was so blissfully unaware of the monster that lurked beneath my surface. That, or she could sense the danger she was in and was that much more intrigued. Sex demons had a tendency to be most attracted to other demons. The more lethal, the more alluring the prospect of mating them.

What a dangerous instinct for a *mortal* succubus.

"I can't."

A frown crested her lips. "Why?"

"You know why. I told you last night. If I fuck you with my monster form, I'll kill you. I have to feed more before I can even entertain the idea. And I refuse to mate you with this unworthy mortal flesh."

"Who said anything about fucking me. All I want is a kiss."

She wriggled her hips, indicating which set of lips she wanted kissed.

Fuck. Gods damn me if I wasn't already.

I was in front of her in a blink. I shouldn't touch her. Shouldn't give into temptation should my dark urges break free. But all I promised Daemon was to keep my cock away from her until I either fed or found a more powerful human form that would do better at keeping my darkness in.

So, I slowly lowered to my knees. I was so tall that my head was perfectly level with her center. My hands cupped her knees and slowly trailed up until I was gripping her plump thighs. I could see traces of her flaming circus tent tattoo between my spread fingers. My touch dropped to her inner thighs, and her breath hitched when I traced the healing wounds where the twins had carved their names.

"You saw them do it, didn't you? Your shadow was there."

"I saw."

She searched my expression for any trace of anger. "You're not pissed at them?"

"How could I be angry with them when it clearly brought you so much pleasure? Besides, you'll heal." I bent forward, enjoying the way she tensed as I brushed my mouth to the scabs. I pressed a series of slow, teasing kisses to her thigh, each one coming closer to her apex. I laughed against her when goose-bumps burst over her skin, and I flicked my tongue out to feel their texture.

Her head dropped back on her shoulders, and a breathy "fuck" dropped from her lips when I finally painted a lick over her seam. Her hands flew to my head, her fingers burying in the shadowy locks of my hair.

This was the first time I'd ever tasted a female, yet somehow, I knew she was special. No other woman tasted like her. No cunt would be as good as hers.

I cursed lowly in Infernal, making her thighs tremble around my head as my heady breath swept over her center.

I looked up at her to find her staring down at me with dark reverence. Or maybe that was my own devotion to her reflected in the rosy depths of her eyes.

"You look so goddamn gorgeous covered in the blood of the damned, Little Demon."

Her pulse kicked up. Her breathing turned ragged. She nodded, urging me on. Not everyone would be so eager to be eaten out by the devil himself, but here she was, so eager for my mouth that her pussy was weeping with desire. Her juices slicked down her folds and dripped onto the table, mixing with the blood of the body that still lay inches away.

Shadowy tendrils appeared from the dark corners of the room, snaking over her skin like writhing snakes and curling around her arms, her horns. One hooked under her shirt and lifted it to expose her breasts. A delicious whimper slipped from her when two more coiled around the soft mounds, the ends of the tentacle-like tendrils suctioning onto her nipples. The metal of her nipple piercings could still be seen glinting through the shadows.

My tongue circled her clit, and I marveled at how sensitive the bud of flesh appeared to be by the way she writhed and cried.

Oh, I was going to have *so* much fun with my female pet.

My lips suctioned over her hole, and I could taste the lingering traces of the twins and Daemon, too.

It was almost funny how possessive I used to be over my things. I still was, in a way, but the moment Megaera pushed her way into our troupe, things changed. Tasting my other pets inside her did dark, wicked things to me.

I sunk my tongue inside her, and her walls clamped down on my invasion as if trying to pull me deeper. What would it be like to slip my cock inside? No wonder the twins and Daemon were obsessed.

Her sweet cunt was as close to Heaven as demons like us could ever get.

"Oh fuck!" She panted. "Alistair. Fuck me now. Fucking do it!"

Her tone turned sharp and demanding, her claws gouging into my scalp.

Oh. How cute. My little pet thought she was the one in charge here.

I snapped to my feet, and too much pleasure showed in the shock and fear that quickly spread across her face. My hand gripped her throat just above Daemon's collar, and for a moment, I admired how my fingers made almost as pretty of a necklace around her delicate neck.

Perhaps, if I ever marked her, I'd place the scar right on her throat where everyone could see. If I could do it without killing her. If I wasn't careful and I accidentally snapped her neck, it's not like I could fetch her from the Downside. If I killed her, that was it. She'd be gone forever.

The thought had my chest aching all over again.

My fingers loosened, allowing her to suck in a gasp. "Alistair—"

"Let's get one thing straight, Pet. I don't take orders from anyone except for Daemon, and only when he's eight inches deep inside me. And while I'm between your thighs, you will refer to me as what I am. Your 'master.' Understand?"

Her pink lashes fluttered, her pulse lurched in pace, and her pheromones grew more potent.

My little demon loved being dominated.

"Y–yes."

I cocked a brow. "Yes, what?"

She licked her grinning lips, the little flash of her fangs sending me into a dizzying whorl of lust. "Yes, Master."

12

Shadow Banged

MEG

"**T**hat's my good girl."

My toes curled, hearing those words drop from Discord's lips. I knew he had control over shadows outside his shadowbeast, but I'd never seen him do this—warp and shape them into tentacles. I lost count of how many of them there were, and I was too drugged on the pleasure they brought to try and keep track. They suckled my nipples, coiled around my waist, my wrists. Two of them curled out from beneath the table and encircled my ankles, pulling my legs further apart. Another took the place of Alistair's hand on my throat as he returned to a kneeling position between the crux of my thighs.

On the next breath, his tongue was back inside me. He wasn't warm like the twins or Daemon, but his subtle coolness was bliss

on my hot skin. Even though he'd never been with a woman before, he was familiarizing himself quickly. There was something
deeply intimate in the way he took his time mapping my body
out, memorizing my pleasure points.

He was clearly the one in control, but his brand of dominance
was slow and sensual. Unhurried. Teasing.

Not what I expected from the devil. But everything about the
ringmaster was unexpected. Especially the part about death by
his hand being final. That meant that if he lost control over his
true form and he did kill me, that was the end of the road.

Being privy to that little fun fact should have had me running
for the door. Not spreading my legs and inviting him deeper.
But if Sinner's Sideshow had taught me anything, it was that my
succubus side was a perverted adrenaline junkie.

The murder and torture of my attackers, the eyeballs—which
were tucked in the pocket of my mini skirt as I had plans to jar
them and keep them as a memento—making the haunt worker
swallow his own cum from his severed dick? It was all just an
extreme form of foreplay, and my succubus hunger ate it the
fuck up.

As Alistair tongue-fucked me, another of his shadows suctioned over my clit. My back bowed in pleasure, and a swollen
moan rose up from my throat.

Other than his tongue inside me, he was barely touching me.
The shadows were his hands. I knew why. He was afraid to lose
his grip on the monster lurking beneath his surface. I was a bit
afraid, too, and that just pushed my pleasure all the higher.

His shadows swept the remains of my victim off the table, and they fell to the floor with a sickening *plop*. Next thing I knew, they were tugging me down so my spine was flat against the table's surface. My head hung over the side, and I saw Alistair's shadow approach.

He growled, the guttural sound almost a purr that immediately had my muscles relaxing.

His dark claws combed through my hair. I didn't yet fully understand exactly what the shadowbeast was. I knew he was a part of Alistair, but beyond that, it was a mystery. Whatever part he was, I liked him. I felt safe with him.

I wanted him.

My mouth opened in invitation, and the beast hummed with approval. His cock emerged from the shadowy place between his muscled thighs, and he slipped it inside my mouth. I didn't expect him to feel so solid.

Alistair's tongue pumped into my pussy while his shadowbeast fucked my mouth.

My vision went blurry around the edges, my mind splintering from the pleasure.

"Death by Discord," I moaned, my voice coming out strangled due to the shadowbeast's cock stuffed in my mouth.

Alistair laughed at me—or rather, laughed *inside* me. He pulled out for a moment, giving a quick little spank to my pussy. "That better not be a request, Megaera."

I should have come by now. My climax loomed over me like an impending tidal wave. My muscles clenched as I waited for it to crash over me. It didn't.

The ringmaster's ministrations were diabolic in their pacing. I was used to quick, hard, unhinged fucks. This was slow, agonizing, torturous ecstasy.

"If you want to come, beg your god, girl."

I waited for his shadow to pull himself from my mouth. He didn't. If anything, his pacing increased.

"Leph me come, Maphter."

A blush seared my cheeks at how ridiculous I sounded. I couldn't even get the words out correctly. My ability to articulate was robbed by the massive shadow cock rammed down my throat.

The tentacles tucked and probed and pawed at me while Alistair's tongue lapped and licked and danced over my pussy. Pleasure mounted.

He pulled from my center, nipping the flesh where Raff had carved his name. "I don't care whose collar you wear or who cuts their name into your body. Never forget that you are *mine*, Little Demon."

The possessive words pushed me into a brutal orgasm. A cry clawed up from my throat just as the shadowbeast pulsated against my tongue and unloaded a torrent of cum. It tasted smoky, but the flavor evaporated on my next breath.

The shadows slid back to the far corners of the room. Alistair rose to his full height, a wild look in his gaze that had my stomach knotting and my thighs clenching.

Then I saw it. Something dark peeked out from behind his eyes.

Maybe he saw the naked terror on my face because he promptly turned away. "Come. Let's get you cleaned up."

Alistair looked out of place in the bathroom the caravan had created for me. The room was warm and cozy, with floral wallpaper and candles that bathed everything in gold, while the shade stood in the corner with the rest of the shadows, watching as I approached the tub in the center of the room.

It was already filled with water.

My attention flicked to Alistair, acutely aware of the way his intense emerald eyes burned into me. I started to pull my shirt over my head, but his shadow materialized in front of me and took over, stripping me out of my clothes.

"So, what is your shadow, exactly?"

"I already told you, it's a facet of myself. I can't contain all of my shadows to one mortal body, so the rest of me takes another form outside the flesh I inhabit."

I stepped into the tub and let out a long sigh as I sunk down into the steaming water. The shadow knelt beside the tub, his clawed hand hovering over the variety of soap bottles the caravan had selected on the edge of the tub. All of my favorite scents.

The shadowbeast opted for the strawberry-vanilla body wash, squirted a dollop into its palm and started smoothing the soap over my skin with his tentacle hands.

"So, um, I guess that means he doesn't have his own name since he's you?"

"Have you named your shadow?"

"No, but mine can't do—*fuck*!" The shadowbeast's hands worked my shoulder muscles, easing tension I hadn't even known was there. "Mine can't do that. Do you mind if I name him? If he's going to be, um, doing shit like this to me, I want to know what to call him. What about Al?"

The shade's brows furrowed into a scowl while his shadow rumbled its approval. Now, that was interesting. Alistair claimed that he and his shadow were one and the same, but that didn't appear to be completely true as the shadowbeast appeared to have his own set of opinions.

Al continued to lather me in soap, though it became clear cleaning me wasn't his primary goal. His hand roamed from my collarbone down to my breasts, kneading and massaging them until I was moaning beneath his fingertips.

He plucked at my piercings, hard enough to wrench a cry from my lips, and rumbled a chuckle at the way I leaned into his palms in a silent request for more. His hands slipped lower, down my belly, past my navel, and dipped into the soapy water between my thighs.

I expected to feel the sting of his claws, but I knew he'd retracted them into his fingertips when I felt the smooth pad of his index finger glide through my folds.

My head dropped onto the lip of the tub, and a low "fu-uuuck" left my lips.

Alistair approached, his strides devouring the distances be-tween us in no time. He arched, his hands gripping the edge of the bathtub at my feet. "Spread your legs, Little Demon. Let him in."

My thighs parted on his command, and the moment they did, the shadow was inside me. Al's fingers were much larger than Alistair's. They were the size of a mortal man's cock, and put most of the ones I'd seen to shame.

I moaned as he stretched me, my eyes glowing as I started to feast on the shadow's desire.

My head started to swirl from the heady concoction of lust and steam, but a buzz from my phone, where it lay in my skirt pocket, pulled me out of the fog wrapping my brain.

I started to reach for it, but Al pushed me back into the water with one hand while his other pushed a second finger inside me.

Alistair moved to where my skirt lay on the floor in a heap, crouched down and extracted my cell from the skirt pocket. I opened my mouth to tell him the code to unlock it, but I already knew he was inside when his face was aglow with the color of my wallpaper: a picture of Raff dressed up as the Joker and Riff as a gender-bent Harley Quinn.

"W–who is it?"

By the smirk curling the corners of Alistair's mouth, I already knew who it was.

"The twins. Wondering where you slipped off too."

"T–tell them I'm with you...Getting banged by shadows."

Alistair tapped out his response, and a few beats later, the phone buzzed again. His brows slowly rose.

"What did they say?"

Alistair's gaze darkened. "'Prove it.'"

"Perverted fucking clowns..."

"Lift her up," Alistair instructed his shadow. "I want them to see all of her."

Before I could make sense of what he was saying, Al pulled his finger from my pussy and slipped his arms beneath me. With my back against his chest, he pulled me up so I was hovering over the water, and his hands cupped the underside of my spread thighs.

Alistair positioned himself so he was standing at the foot of the tub once again, directly in front of me. Shadowy tendrils—like the ones from the torture room—snaked out from the darkened corners of the room. One curled around my breast, another around the base of my horn, two around my wings, stretching them out.

Alistair snapped a picture, just as another pushed inside my pussy.

It wasn't more than a few seconds later when the phone started to buzz.

"Oh, look," the ringmaster mused on a dark purr. "They're FaceTiming you."

13

Little Charmer

MEG

A white face, with black diamonds over the eyes and the tip of his nose painted black, filled the small screen. Green hair fell over the demon's forehead in pieces. "There you are, Hell Bat."

My cheeks flamed. With how Alistair angled the camera, they could see everything. "H–hey guys. How's the p–party?"

"We followed your scent, and it led us to a pile of werewolf guts. We figured you were fine. Our first guess was that you'd gone back to your trailer."

A hand came from off-screen and pushed Raff out of the frame. "Ow! Fuck off." The phone shook in the wake of the brotherly scuffle, and on the next beat, a mop of blue hair came into view. "Yeah, getting fucked by shadow tentacles was guess number two."

Raff shoved back into the frame, his cheek flush with his twin's. The hunger was written all over their faces.

"You look so damn good with your holes filled," Riff rasped.

"Yeah." Raff licked his lips, smearing his painted smile. "Especially when we can see through the tentacle, straight into your pussy."

"Yes. It is a pretty sight," Alistair drawled. His emerald orbs churned with thought. "Pretty enough to put on a poster."

My heart lurched in my chest. "*My* poster? A–as in the bill for my act?"

"Perhaps. We'll need a new act for you now that the chastity belt's been removed. No more Virgin Succubus. Rafferty?"

The incubus made a strangled noise that was somewhere between a "hmm?" and a grunt. By the pleasure etching his face, he was touching himself to the show.

"What did you call her? Just now?"

"Uh, Hell Bat, Boss."

"I like that. 'The Hell Bat.' Has a ring to it, as the humans say. What do you think of that as your new stage name, Megaera?"

The shadow wrapped around my horn, tugged my head to the side, and Al dropped his mouth to my neck, lapping up some of the suds and sweat while the rest slicked down my body and dripped into the bathwater below. The water was still hot enough that steam rose up, curling around my spread legs, snaking around me as the shadowy tendrils prodded and poked and *sucked* me. All while the ringmaster stood over me, holding the phone up so the twins could pleasure themself to the scene.

My senses could barely process everything that was happening, let alone articulate an answer to his question. "I–I…"

"The ringmaster asked you a question," both the twins managed to say in perfect unison, in that creepy yet endearing way they sometimes did.

"I l–love it…" My voice came out strained and swollen with pleasure.

I wasn't sure what I was referring to exactly, the new stage name or the fact that I had a freaking *tentacle* made of shadows stuffed up my pussy and my ass. Either way, it was an appropriate answer.

When Alistair chuckled—the sound dark and dangerous—and leaned forward, muttering, "Good. I fucking love it too," I knew he, too, was referring to more than the stage name. "Now come for us, Little Demon. My clowns and I want to watch you fall apart."

That's exactly what I did. All it took was a few more thrusts from the tentacles, and I was screaming my release. The twins had to be coming too by their staggered, distant grunting.

The climax was brutal bliss. I loved being watched. There was no better meal than the lust I took from those watching me, especially the ringmaster and my favorite males among his troupe.

When I went limp in Al's arms, the shadows dissipated, leaving me with an empty sensation, but I didn't care. The afterglow swallowed me like the rising tide and pulled me into a peaceful, floating sensation.

Al gently lowered me back into the tub and continued washing me as Alistair flipped the phone around and explained to the twins what happened in the haunted house.

The twins fell quiet when he told them that the scare actors had planned an attack. Then Riff piped up, "I'm going to pluck out Sinclair's fangs and cut his throat with them."

"He couldn't have known," Raff said before I could.

"Bullshit. He's been working in the haunt the longest. He's friends with most of them."

Alistair's lips slanted with a frown. "He wasn't the mastermind behind the attack, and I don't believe they would have told him either since he's mated to Megaera's best friend."

"So where are the rest? Need help 'firing' them?"

Alistair's lips curved. "No. Megaera's already seen to that. Just tell the troupe they've been let go. We'll be short-staffed in the haunt house until I can source replacements."

He hung up the phone and tossed it to Al, who caught it and stashed it back into my skirt pocket. Then he set to washing my hair while the ringmaster stood there, looking as ominous as ever. Watching. Plotting.

What I would give, the things I'd do, to read this bastard.

It would make seducing him a hell of a lot easier.

There was this primal little part of me that demanded I mate. Mortals wouldn't do. My body had physically rebelled wherever I'd tried back before I joined Sinner's Sideshow. Only the most powerful, protective, virile of demons would do. And Alistair was the king of them all.

It didn't matter that he had an inherent wickedness that left me on edge. It didn't matter that this was the sly monster who'd bargained for my virginity in a ploy to keep my pussy locked up like a medieval nun.

It didn't matter that he was the devil himself.

He was going to be mine.

I knew I had him on the hook. Otherwise, he wouldn't have let me join the circus in the first place. He wouldn't have his shadow watching my every move. He wouldn't be so possessive, like how he tore out the eyes of the scare workers just so I wouldn't be the last thing they ever saw.

And he wouldn't be standing there, looking so fascinated by the simple act of me taking a bath.

Yeah. I had him wrapped around my horns. All I had to do was seal the deal.

"When you have better control over your true form, will you mark me?"

The ringmaster's brows shot up at my sudden outburst. Admittedly, it was an audacious question. I didn't care. Everything good in my life right now was because I demanded to have it. If I just waited around for shit to happen, I'd still be living in my Volkswagen, creeping around scummy truck stops in search of my next meal.

"Perhaps."

"Perhaps? What the hell does that mean?"

"Even if I feed and can better control my hunger, it doesn't mean you can survive me."

I sunk deeper into the bath until the waterline came up to my chin. I made a mock pouty face through the mountains of bubbles. "I survived Daemon's heat from his true form. His fire didn't burn me at all."

The shade gave a thoughtful nod. "That's because I believe now that you're true mates. I was speculative before, but after seeing what happened in the chapel tent... There's no denying it."

"What does it mean to be true mates, exactly?"

"Simply that you are more biologically compatible than any other partner. It doesn't mean you and he can't have other marks and mates, simply that the bond you share will be far more sensitive. Once you carry each other's marks, you'll be connected to him on a far more intimate level. And it is permanent."

"Is that why he killed his old lover? She didn't survive his flames because she wasn't his true mate?"

Alistair canted his head to the side, some of his long hair spilling over his shoulder. "I suspect so, yes."

"So...That means I'm built to survive my mates, then, right? So, if I can handle Daemon's true form, I can handle yours."

"It's entirely different. You and I aren't true mates. Simply because there's no such thing between shades and sex demons." He walked around to the side of the bath and knelt on the ground, his forearm resting over one knee.

"Do you want to know the truth?" he asked, his low tone sending a chill through me.

"Always."

"For the last two decades, I've been the paragon of self-restraint. Until you came along. Now, I feel myself slowly ripping at the seams…Returning to the monster I once was."

He leaned over the edge of the tub, his cool lips brushing the shell of my ear as he whispered, "The darkness inside me is desperate to taste you, Little Demon."

Goosebumps exploded over my skin. The human part of my brain screamed at the feel of this predator's skin against mine while my succubus half melted into his touch. I gave into my succubus urges—I always did—and turned my head to capture his lips in a kiss.

His mouth was warmer than I expected. He tasted of man and dark magic. The simple, innocent kiss had my blood singing and my body heating. When I pushed my tongue into his mouth to deepen the kiss, he pulled away.

I chased his lips, a whimper slipping out of me at the loss of him. "Please. You won't hurt me."

He sighed as he ran his fingers through his shadowy locks of hair. "I will. I wasn't made for mating mortals. My monstrous form is…quite large."

I blinked and perked up at the words 'monstrous' and 'large.' "How big are we talking here? Like pornstar big? Or like, Godzilla big?"

He chuckled. His laughter always caught me off guard as the sound was so inhuman. "Too big for that little hole between your legs, Pet."

"You're supposed to be the best mage in the Upside and the Downside, right? Can't you just—and I can't believe I'm saying this—make it smaller?"

"I can keep my darker urges caged so long as I'm fed. It was why Sinner's Sideshow was created in the first place. To harvest terror and fear, all to keep me strong. I feed on the death seats. Morally speaking, I feel good about feeding on those who wish to die, but it doesn't make for a robust diet."

"That's why my mom killed innocents. The circus was open to anyone, right? Humans and monsters. There was no such thing as death seats back then."

Alistair went rigid at the mention of my mom. "The entire house was death seats. She even allowed children into the circus. And not a single soul ever survived a show."

"It sounds like she deserved to die."

A barbed silence settled over the room. I waved Al off, who disappeared in a fizzle of shadows. I sat up, pulling my knees to my chin. "I'm scared of being like her."

The ringmaster rose to his feet and looked down at me with a look that had my heart twisting into knots. "You are nothing like her."

"You know what's funny? My father didn't talk about her much, but when he did, it was clear he was in love with her. He was convinced she was a good person."

Alistair's shoulders visibly stiffened. It seemed as though something was burning on the tip of his tongue, and a war waged inside him whether to say it or not.

I glared up at him. "Whatever you're thinking right now, just say it."

"Your parents weren't in love. Your mother charmed him."

"What?" The spade of my tail slapped the surface of the bathwater in surprise. "No. No way. Fake news."

Alistair's eyes narrowed. "Are you calling me a liar?"

The little hairs on the back of my nape stood. "No. It just doesn't make sense. My dad was a nobody, a sword swallower in a traveling circus. What would she have to gain from charming him into loving her?"

"Security. A place to lie low while I hunted her."

"My kind breed only when they want to. There's no such thing as an accidental pregnancy with a succubus. So why would she have me if all she was looking for at Walker's was a place to hide from you?"

"I don't know, Megaera."

I couldn't parse Alistair's expression. His poker face was too damn good. Even without the ability to read his body language or pick up on his emotions, I couldn't shake the uncomfortable feeling blooming in my gut.

He was lying. He did know.

"What are you not telling me?"

"I'm an ancient culmination of darkness and woe. I have many secrets. You'd die of old age before I could tell you even half..." His tone was clipped, icy. I'd pushed too much. Which was total bullshit because it was *my* mother we were talking about. "Finish your bath. Then see yourself out."

I got to my feet and stumbled from the bath. My wet feet slipped on the tile, and I stumbled for him, my hand gripping the back of his shirt to catch my fall.

He whipped around, his eyes wild with rage. "Touch me again without my permission, and you'll regret it."

My jaw fell open in shock. I couldn't help it. This cold came from nowhere. I hadn't even meant to touch him. It was an accident. But me, being the raging brat I was, only held on to him tighter.

He was clearly at the end of his patience, but I didn't care. I needed answers. "What are you hiding from me? Does this have anything to do with Daemon? And where is he? What dirty work are you having him do? Why all the secrecy?"

"So many fucking questions. I will be the death of you if you keep pushing my buttons. Do you forget what I am?"

"What's wrong, *'Master?'*" I flashed him the sweetest smile I could muster. "Pissed off that I'm the one demon you can't cow around in your freaky little menagerie of monsters?"

He gave me a shove that was hard enough to rip his shirt from my grip and flung the door open so hard I'm surprised he didn't rip it off his hinges. Moving quickly, I dashed into the hall and planted myself in front of him, blocking his exit.

"Tell me what you're hiding from me, dammit!"

I wasn't asking. I was demanding. And I was doing more than that...

I was using my succubus powers on him.

It had been another slip. I hadn't meant to do it. In my anger, the spell had been cast. Normally, I was better at controlling my powers, but since I'd fully awakened, everything was a little out of whack. The twins had been right. I needed to fuck, and often if I wanted to gain a better hold over my concubi abilities.

My magic made the air itself shiver. Alistair's mask shattered. For the first time, I could easily read his expression.

Shit. He was fucking *furious.* The slits of his eyes glowed with rage, his jaw set. His hand snatched out, seizing me by the throat. "Are you trying to *charm* me, girl?"

14
Discord's Wrath

ALISTAIR

My fingers gripped her throat, vice tight, over Daemon's collar. She whimpered, the pained sound—laced with pleasure—going straight to my cock.

Fuck me. She was so beautiful. Naked and wet, her skin glistening from her bath.

This half-blood was fucking with my head. I'd told myself I wouldn't touch her. Her bratty tongue might as well have been a battering ram for how it shattered my resolve. She deserved more than this filthy sinner's flesh between her legs. If I wore an archdevil's body, I'd feel better about fucking her with it, *and* it would do a better job containing the monster inside.

But she had to push me.

I wanted to keep her safe from me, but how could I when she defied me like this?

She was a naughty little pet. And naughty pets needed to be punished.

I pulled her against me, crushing her chest against mine. Her pierced nipples pressed into my stomach, sending a bolt of heat through my core. "Before, I didn't want to fuck you with this stolen flesh I wear. I got it from a sinner, you see. One of the worst kinds. But now... Now, I think you deserve to be punished."

At the mention of punishment, her candy-sweet arousal grew stronger, and I realized the more I made it hurt, the more she'd enjoy it. This little sex demon didn't care where my skin came from. It was mine now, and that's all that mattered to her.

What an insatiable little slut. So bold. So bratty. So perfectly fucked.

How *dare* she try to command me with her succubus magic? Did she have a death wish? Or did she get off on the idea of mating a primordial demon who would either make her bow or break? Either way, I'd have her shivering in unholy ecstasy before I shattered her to pieces.

Defiant fire flared behind her dusky pink gaze, and there was no missing the cocky smirk lurking at the corner of her mouth. "What are you gonna do, Master? Spank me with a rolled-up newspaper? Put me on a leash? The twins already did that last one.... Spoiler alert. I liked it."

Just like that, all desire to be gentle and keep her at arm's length for the sake of her safety disappeared like shadows at high noon.

I promised Daemon I wouldn't fuck her cunt. She had other holes, though. And my shadowbeast wasn't beholden to my agreements.

"This isn't going to be like before. This is for my pleasure, not yours. Though I have a feeling you're going to like this too, considering what an audacious little whore you are for demon cock."

Her pink lashes fluttered, and her lips parted under the wash of my breath. "W–what, no safe word?"

I laughed, and it took me by surprise how much I didn't sound like myself. "If you were interested in safety, you wouldn't have joined a monster circus. You wouldn't have willingly sold yourself to the devil."

Keeping my hold on her throat, I guided her a step back, opened the door behind her and pushed her inside. The moment the door opened, the caravan's magic took shape of the room. It was a grand bedroom with a large four-poster bed with a canopy and various other opulent details I didn't bother looking twice at.

It was perfect for a monarch of Hell. I preferred the caravan's front room. Simple, crammed with all my favorite books. But this room would do for its purpose.

"If you wanted safety, you wouldn't have tried to force information from me."

I walked her back until her legs hit the edge of the bed, then pushed her down onto the mattress.

"You don't want to be safe with me, Megaera. All you want at this moment is to be my toy. Even if I play with you until you break."

Shock, outrage, and pure, unadulterated lust glazed her face. She was so furious that I was hiding something from her. She was too perceptive for her own good and too damn stubborn. So this was the price for pushing me, and she was ready to pay it.

She leaned back onto the bed, propped on her elbows with her legs spread.

Fucking *hells*. She was so beautiful and oh so wet.

"Look at you," I snarled at her through a savage grin. She shuddered in delight as I bent over her with one hand braced on the bed beside her head and cupped her soaking center. Just the sight of her pretty pink pubic hair beneath my spread fingers was enough to drive an ordinary man mad. "I'm almost sad the twins and Daemon aren't here to see what a pretty little slut our mate-to-be is. With her greedy slit weeping all over my fingers."

I knew she was desperate for all four of our marks, so calling her "ours" and not "mine" had her heart beating so hard I could feel it on the tip of my tongue—and feel it pound through her pussy, drumming a delicious beat against my fingertips.

She licked her smirking lips. "What happened to my possessive god? I didn't think he liked sharing his toys."

"Even ancient demons can change." I *liked* watching her with them. Lusting after a woman and dominating her in bed might've been new territory for me, but I've always been something of a voyeur. "Anyway, it's unnatural for succubi to have only one mate. You need more than my cock to keep you strong. A newly awakened succubus needs all her holes filled."

She gasped when she registered at least a dozen writhing tentacle-shaped shadows curling up from beneath the bed. They blindly probed at the black bed coverings, searching for her. She bared her teeth and made a show of swiping at one of the tendrils with her manicured claws as it wandered close.

I kneeled on the bed and stretched my arms out as a manic laugh rose from my throat. A couple of the shadows unbuttoned my shirt for me, slipping it off my form. "Come on, Little Demon. Don't you ever dream about the monsters under the bed crawling out to fuck you stupid?"

Two more shadows shot toward her. She could have dodged them, but she didn't. She allowed them to wrap around her wrists—giving an adorable little scream of frustration, even if it was fake as hell. She knew what was coming, and she couldn't have been more excited.

The shadows pulled her up until she was on her knees and secured her arms into a stretched-out position over her head. Two more encircled her thighs and slowly pried her legs open at the same pace they forcibly extended her wings.

What a lovely sight this made. I had to take a picture of this and send it to Daemon. I pulled out my own phone from my pants pocket and snapped a picture. I admired the way her head sagged a little, hair spilling over her eyes as they glared at the camera. She was still wet from her bath, and the flash from the camera lit her up.

"You're so beautiful, Little Demon," I groaned, pushing "Send" before tossing the phone away and placing my hand back over her apex. Her face tipped to the heavens, delicious sound crawling its way from her throat as I sank two fingers inside her. She clenched around me, her internal walls fluttering from the invasion.

"I am not a praying demon because who the fuck would I pray to? Me? Lesser gods? But I'm going to pray that I don't ruin you."

Her rioting pulse kissed the tips of my fingers from where they were buried deep inside her. I curled them, watching her jerk against her tethers as I found the ultra-sensitive spot within a female's body Daemon had told me about. "Ah. So this is where you like it."

"Alistair, please..." I wasn't sure if she was begging me to stop or to keep going. I had a feeling that she didn't know either. I rubbed my thumb in circles on her clit as I pumped into her. With my free hand, I took her by the horn and forced her to look me in the eyes as I finger-fucked her. Her pupils dilated. Her lips opened to release a series of breathy pants. Her arms shook, and sweat and arousal slicked a path down the interior of her thighs.

By my depths. She looked like an obscene goddess, all strung up and shivering with pleasure.

I extracted my fingers, held them between us at eye level and gave them a wiggle. My balls ached at the way she glistened on my dead flesh. "Fuck, Little Demon. The way you cream for me is so..." I trailed off. I couldn't think of an appropriate word to properly justify how damn intoxicating her pussy was, at least not before the urge to taste her gripped me. I popped my fingers into my mouth, tasting her. I groaned around my digits as I sucked her flavor from my skin.

I leaned back on the mountain of pillows with my back propped against the elaborate headboard and frantically ripped the fly of my pants open. "Fuck her."

Her chest hitched with the frozen breath in her lungs. "Wha—?"

My shadowbeast—Al, as she'd named him—appeared on the bed behind her. His meaty arms banded around her waist, and he positioned her so I had a clear view of them both. His claw-tipped paws kneaded her breasts hard enough to knock a whimper from her. He'd probably even leave a bruise or two.

"You'll have to forgive him," I smirked. "He's normally such a gentle giant, but you can't blame him for being eager to take your pussy."

His paws dropped to her hips, and he yanked her ass against his erection. Her eyes shot wide, feeling the massive cock she was about to take.

With a brutal punch of his pelvis, he filled her. He growled, and she screamed. He rutted her hard and fast, his paws finding her horns and using them for purchase as he slammed into her hard enough to bring tears to her eyes.

My hand dipped into my pants and pulled out my cock. My fingertips traced the stitching of where I'd sewn the flesh back together. Daemon had been particularly brutal in slaying this one.

"What's the matter, Megaera? If you can't handle Al's cock, you certainly aren't going to be able to handle mine."

Her gaze dropped to where I fisted my base. I gave it a stroke, some of my shadows leaking through the seams.

"Doesn't seem that big to me."

The words were barely out of her mouth by the time I was repositioning myself behind her, with my shadowbeast evaporating and reappearing in front of her. He pushed the tip of his cock into her pussy, waiting for my go-ahead.

I reached around and forced my fingers into her mouth. "Drench them, Pet," I gritted in her ear. "Sex demon saliva makes for fabulous lubricant. The more I use, the less this will hurt."

She bore back on my dick, grinding her ass against me in search of more friction even as I pushed my fingers deep enough into her mouth to make her gag.

"Gods, I love to watch you choke on me."

She sucked in a breath when I pulled from her mouth, spreading my fingers wide to see the thick ropes of spit connecting them. "This will do."

I wedged my fingers between her ass cheeks, finding her tightest hole, and sunk them both inside.

"Fuck," she moaned, the sound soft, sweet and swollen with hunger.

"Now," I instructed Al, who gave a rumble of understanding as he pushed the rest of his length inside her pussy as I pressed into her backside. I had to strengthen the hold the shadows had on her arms for how much she shook. Another looped around Daemon's collar like a leash with the end securing to the bedpost.

She twisted her head to lock her eyes with mine. "Y-you're in my ass. Discord is fucking my ass."

My lips twitched with a smile. "That's right, Pet." My fingers bit into her hips, and I pushed and pulled on her so Al slipped in as I slipped out, fucking her in perfect tandem. She tried to rock her body to follow our rhythm within a few pumps and fell limp in her restraints, surrendering fully to us.

"Good girl," I praised and dropped my head to paint a lick along the backside of her wing. "Such a perfect little slut for me. Such a perfect offering for your god."

Within seconds, I pounded an orgasm from her. She jerked violently, screaming as it took her. But I didn't stop. I doubt I could have, even if I'd wanted to.

Technically, I wasn't breaking my promise to Daemon, but it was still a mistake burying my cock within her heat.

She felt better than I could have ever imagined. I clutched her tight against me as I fucked into her ass.

Her pants turned sharp and short, and her heart beat much too fast.

The room filled with her pained winces laced with breathless gasps of pleasure. "It h–h–hurts. B–but I... I don't want it to stop."

"Good," I snarled low against the soft juncture of her shoulder. "Because we're not done until I say we're done."

I dragged my tongue up the smooth column of her throat, lapping up a bead of sweat streaking down her flesh. She was a drug to my senses, far more powerful than the shit Mollie peddled to the death seats. Stronger than anything known to mankind. A drug potent enough to bring a god to their knees.

Lost to my baser urges, the blackest of thoughts wracked my body, hooking into me and taking control—driving me into a primal frenzy.

I tried to get a grip on my monster, but I was too weak to contain it. An unholy, ancient hunger was slowly shaking itself from its two-decade-long slumber.

Any second now, I'd shift into my true form.

It was too late to stop it.

It was too late to do anything but pray to whatever forces were stronger than myself that I didn't kill her. Because it would destroy Daemon and the twins, too.

I knew they loved her. And in that moment, I realized I loved her too. I opened my mouth to tell her before I lost myself to my other side.

It was too late.

Shadows exploded from my skin, robbing me of the human form I'd created for myself, stealing my words and my thoughts, tearing away my final vestiges of control.

15
Death

DAEMON

"Hey, get a load of this."

I lifted my head to see War lounging on one of the beds, leaning over to show Conquest—who was on the next bed—the phone stolen from my pocket.

Conquest practically swallowed the cigarette he was smoking when he registered the screen. He swore in Infernal and snatched the phone from War to get a better look. I figured it was a text from Alistair. He always texted me when I was away doing his dirty work.

Judging by how Conquest's eyes lit up and his bare cock stiffened, I knew this wasn't one of Alistair's usual messages.

"Well, would you look at that. It seems our Lord knows how to treat a succubus after all."

"Keep it down. Lilith will have an aneurysm if she sees," War mumbled as he shot a weary look toward the bathroom where Astrid was taking a shower.

With a scoff, Conquest got out of bed and trudged over to where I was pinned against the wall. I hated how much effort it took to lift my head as he approached. I hadn't been trapped here for a full twenty-four hours, but it felt like I'd been here for days. The adamantine was sapping my strength and making me weak.

Conquest crouched in front of me and snuffed his cigarette out on my throat. If he was looking for a reaction, he'd be disappointed.

"I'm immune to fire, shit for brains." I forced out a dry laugh, even as the slight movement shot white-hot pain through my body. It was worth crawling under Conquest's skin.

His blue eyes darkened. "Are you immune to this?"

He smashed his fist into my jaw. I recoiled and lifted my head to spit a gob of blood on his face. "Blond hair and blue eyes aren't normally my thing. But it's not so bad when you're covered in my blood. I'll keep that in mind when I'm fucking the skin I rip from your corpse."

The Horseman's bloody lips pursed into a malevolent smirk. "To give to Discord, right? Admittedly, it would improve his humanoid form. Better than the mortal flesh he wears now. But I think he's too busy playing with his new toy to rut with you. See?"

He held my phone up. My dick went hard in an instant, despite the fact that I'd lost so much blood already.

Alistair had sent me a photo of Meg. She was in a strange bedroom, probably one of the magical rooms in the caravan. She was kneeling on a lavish bed with her arms tied over her head, secured by Alistair's shadows. Naked. Tentacles of darkness coiled tight around her tits, her horns, stretching out her wings.

"Looks like you're no longer your master's favorite pet," Conquest said with a mock frown. "Let's hope he can pull out of her pussy long enough to realize you've gone missing. Otherwise, we'll have to go to him."

War shook his bald head. "No. That will be too ugly of a fight. We have to get him away from anything he can potentially feed on. If he kills his entire freakshow, he can fuel his true form for days. We won't be able to force Lil's mark on him then."

Conquest rolled his eyes. "We wouldn't have to wait around in this shit-hole if we just went to him. Face it, our god's gone too soft. He won't kill his precious circus. Not when he forsakes his realm and his entire people for it."

"You're wrong," I rasped, drawing Conquest's attention back to me. "He'll kill them all if it means protecting her."

I wasn't lying. Alistair did love his circus and the wayward monsters he'd taken in. But I knew him, and I recognized that look in his eye when he looked at Megaera. Because I felt it, too.

We'd both burn the whole world down for that girl. Circus and all.

"What are you doing?" Lilith stood in the bathroom doorway, a towel wrapped around her wet hair with her full body on display.

I looked away with a growl, and she laughed. "Aww, what's wrong, mongrel? This was the body that birthed your little half-breed circus brat. You should be worshiping me."

She laughed as she strode toward us. "I suppose once I'm properly mated to Discord, you will."

When the demoness caught sight of my phone screen, all the amusement drained from her face. She ripped the phone away from Conquest. Her eyes narrowed, hellfire blazing behind them. She crushed the device with a deadly smile that was too tight to be genuine.

"She charmed him."

"He can't be charmed," I seethed. "Face it. He didn't mate you, not because you're too beautiful to touch or because he doesn't like women. Or whatever bullshit reason demonkind has come up with over the years. It's because you're a cold bitch with a rotten soul, and you make him sick."

"You better stay on my good side, mongrel. I need you alive so that your master comes looking for you. Doesn't mean I won't tear your dick off and use it as my personal toy."

She pushed Conquest out of the way and straddled my lap, shoving the spear in my gut in a new direction to make room for her to lean in and consume my gasp of pain in a brutal kiss.

I bit her, and she recoiled, only to laugh as she tasted the blood on her lip. "Or maybe I'll keep it attached after all. You're *fun*."

"Touch me, and I'll burn your pretty flesh off, and even Famine won't want to stick his dick inside you." My skin started to steam, my tattoos glowing. She blinked in confusion, then bolted off my lap with a scream. "Mongrel!"

She kicked the spear, and I bit back a cry of pain.

She whipped around, falling back into bed with War. "Anyway. What do I care if he fucks her? He won't mark her. He hasn't been feeding enough to hold his true shape for more than a few minutes. When we're finally bonded, he'll forget about everything he experienced in this miserable plane. Including her."

Conquest's brows hiked. "You're not taking her back home with you?"

She snorted. "Why would I? Mortals belong in the mortal plane. Play with her all you want, then let her burn in the ashes with the rest of this trash world when you bring about the apocalypse. Besides..." Lilith's eyes flicked to me, cold and scathing. "When I bring Discord home, he's not going to keep pets anymore."

I opened my mouth to fire off a retort, but a deep chill in my bones froze the words in my throat. My skin pricked with goosebumps, and the hellbeast within me whimpered at the sensation.

Discord was awakening. *Why was Alistair shifting?!* Had he broken his word? Fucking Hells. I should have made him promise not to touch her altogether and have him draw up a contract in blood, so he was magically bound to honor it.

Lilith was right about him not having been fed enough to hold his form for long. Maybe not long enough to kill the Horsemen if he walked in on their ambush days from now when he eventually came to look for me.

But he could hold it long enough to kill Meg.

I had to get out of here.

Even if it meant summoning my pack and risking their lives.

As the gears whirled in my head, the motel room's front door slammed open. A tall, pale figure stood in the doorway. He was bare-chested, with a black trench coat and long raven hair.

His thin lips peeled in disgust as he looked around the room. "We couldn't have picked a better place to ambush Discord? A cemetery would have been less disgusting."

Lilith grinned at the new arrival, her tail flicking like a cat, happy to see their master. "About time you showed up, Death."

Fuck.

16

Finger Puppet

MEG

My heart thundered in my chest as Alistair's shadows exploded in all directions and filled the room like smoke. *He's shifting.*

The shadowy tethers unwound from my wrists and legs, slithering away to join the mass of dark energy starting to take shape. Even Al's form slipped into the smoke.

I wasn't tied up anymore. This was the part where my human survival skills were supposed to take over. *"Run,"* they were supposed to scream. Instead, that voice was a whisper that could barely be heard over the feral curiosity running rampant inside me.

The darkness swelled and shimmered with potent energy, morphing until it took on the vague shape of something huge and monstrous. It filled the entire room and pushed against the ceiling until the illusion shattered. The walls, the furniture, and even the bed dissolved, leaving us in pitch-black nothingness.

When the creature took on a recognizable form, he was a dragon, but not just any dragon.

I craned my neck to see two heads. One was hornless, with a large snout and glinting emerald eyes, while the other had curling horns and red eyes, just like Alistair's shadow.

He was a two-headed hydra, with shadows and ancient magic emanating from him like dark, radiant fire.

The shade hadn't been kidding when he'd said Al was a fragment of his true self.

The monster stooped to pick me up, his hand so huge his fingers engulfed my waist.

I'd known his true form would be big, but the word hardly did justice for the creature before me. I fit perfectly in his fist. It was like a scene out of King Kong, but instead of a gorilla, my captor was a two-headed dragon made out of primordial darkness.

It held me in front of its two heads, examining me with hungry eyes, blazing bright with red and green fire.

My hands clutched at one of his enormous fingers, claws digging in as I registered how high I was from the ground.

"Do I terrify you?" the hydra asked, both his mouths moving to spit out a gut-scraping voice as deep as hell itself. The faintest hint of Alistair's melodic cadence seeped out from beneath the hydra's guttural baritone.

"A–Alistair?"

It chuckled, revealing deadly teeth that were almost as large as me. "Barely."

"What do you mean, 'barely?'"

"He is but a shadow of the entity you see before you, mortal. Don't you understand what you've done? What you've released? *I* am the demon monsters worship as their god. I am ruin. I am darkness incarnate. I am Discord."

I froze, going catatonic in his palm. I didn't know what to do or say. Normally, I had a sarcastic retort to fire off, but this was a god. Alistair's lesser form possessed an intimidating demeanor, but it was nothing like the raw violence and dark magic rolling off this beast.

I was literally in the hands of a god. He could crush every bone in my body with a twitch. The notion scared me.

And being the fucked in the head sex demon that I was... *fear made me wet.*

"Look at the little mortal. See how she squirms..." the hydra rumbled. "Making such a mess all over her master's fingers."

He turned me over in his huge hand, and, with a thumb, pushed me down so my back was flush with his palm. He took the index finger of his other hand and ran it down my length. My heart thundered as my gaze followed his razor-sharp claw, terrified that he'd cut me without meaning to.

He laughed—and gods, the sound was terrifying. "You taste so good, little mortal."

It took me a beat to realize what he was talking about. Discord was feasting on my fear.

Fuuuck me.

Knowing this demonic deity was enjoying my terror only made me wetter.

"What...? Weren't you so sure you could 'handle' me?" He lowered me until I was level with his groin. I tipped my head to see the mass of flesh he was comparing me to, and my eyes nearly popped out of my head.

Discord's cock was easily twice as big as I was. The rest of him was covered in black, shady scales, but his dick was deep purple in color and almost tentacle-like, with its tapered tip oozing a thick rope of pre-cum.

"Still think you can take me, Little Demon?"

No. Obviously, the answer was "hell no." So why in the ever-loving *fuck* was I licking my lips and nodding "yes?"

I was insane. That was the only explanation. As a newly awakened succubus, there was an animalistic part of my brain that demanded I mate with the most virile, powerful of demons. Common sense be damned.

There was no demon more powerful than Discord.

My body knew it—and *wept* for it.

Both sets of the hydra's nostrils flared at my enthusiasm. "Cocky little slut."

He dropped his hand lower and moved it so that I was under his cock. His eyes cast a green and red light on the giant appendage, which, in turn, cast me in its shadow.

"If it's seed you need, Little Demon, your god will provide."

He positioned me so my face was directly below his tip. My mouth instinctually parted to capture the large pearl of pre-cum oozing from the slit at his head. A purr-like growl rattled the air around my ears as he lifted me until I was so close to his member that I could feel its head bleeding into my own flesh.

"Kiss me, little mortal," he encouraged in that hellish voice that warned me not to disobey. I raised my head and pressed my lips to the slit. It was *wet*. What was a few drops of pre-cum to him was like taking a shower for me.

The beads of cum oozed over my face and gushed over my hair. He rubbed my body up and down his shaft, smearing the cum everywhere. In seconds, I was completely covered in it. He dropped me lower, pulling me out of his cock's reach.

With bated breath, I watched as he started to stroke himself with his other hand.

I was watching Discord himself jack off.

Even if I could tell the twins about this moment, I wondered if they'd believe me.

The fat veins in his cock pulsed. The muscles in his arms and thighs bulged against his skin, straining as he started to come. Then I realized how much fucking trouble I was in as torrents of hot, milky cum gushed out into the cradle of his palm...with me in it.

Was this how I was going to die? Drowning in a pool of demon cum?

I guess it was no worse than choking to death on clown cock, or getting split open by three flaming hellhound dicks. His groans of pleasure were muffled as I was completely submerged. I couldn't lift my head for air. My wings were pinched firmly between his middle and pointer fingers.

My lungs screamed for air. My little legs thrashed, and my heart dropped to my stomach when I heard both his heads laughing at my pathetic struggles. When there were only a few precious seconds left before I passed out, he plucked me out of his palm and held me up in the air before his two sets of eyes.

"If you're going to kill me, you better be more creative than that." I snarled between gulps of breath.

"So bratty," the hydra mused to himself. "Even on death's door."

Me and my stupid mouth. Daemon had warned me it would get me killed at Sinner's Sideshow. If only I'd known that he hadn't been exaggerating. But the cum was like a drug to me. I felt more powerful than ever. Powerful and completely deranged. "Give me more."

Discord's green-eyed head swapped looks with the red-eyed one. A silent, wicked thought seemed to pass between them.

The tip of his claw flicked one nipple, then the other. He purred a soft growl at the way my nipples peaked. He pressed the pad of his thumb down over my chest and rubbed it around in small, circular motions, smearing his cum into my flesh until my skin was red and stinging.

"You will smell like me for a very long time, Little Pet."

"So, you're going to let me live?"

My heart skipped a beat at the way he seemed to pause to consider my question. "Yes. You have become one of my most precious play-things."

The word "precious" came out as a hiss, and as he spoke, he dragged the point of his claw-tipped finger down my navel toward my apex. He applied just enough pressure to leave an angry red welt down my torso.

"I'm going to test your limits. See just how much of me you can take."

His claw raked down the pink patch of hair between my legs, and a moan fell from my lips as it skimmed through my folds. The bite of pain had my thighs clamping shut, but his thumb and pinky finger pinned my legs in a spread position.

"Let us see…" With his free hand, his fingers drummed up my thigh. One by one, they nudged against my exposed center. "Which one of these can you fit…"

They were all too big.

But when his pinky finger prodded my apex, managing to fit against me easier than the others, I knew he wasn't teasing.

He was going to do it.

Discord was going to take finger-fucking to a whole new level.

Hellfire spread through my core, making my center drip with arousal. My succubus pussy said, "*Yes!*" while the rest of me screamed, "*Um, no. The math ain't mathing.*"

His pinky claw faded into shadows and disappeared completely before pushing harder against me. Tears pricked my eyes as he sunk the first few inches of himself inside me.

How in Discord's Hell was this going to work? His freaking *pinky* finger was bigger than any cock I'd ever seen.

"No," I shook my head. "It won't fit."

"Your body says otherwise, Little Demon," he purred. The sound seemed to relax my muscles as he sunk another inch or two inside me. The stretching sensation was so painful that my vision blurred. Tears welled in my eyes. My nerves felt like they were being torn apart and fused back together on the next breath.

I was taking him. His cum mixed with my arousal, made me slick and pliant. It seemed to numb some of the pain. The rest was washed away in the sudden surge of pure bliss that crashed over me in brutal waves.

With one last push, the tip of his finger was fully seated inside me. Hitting every nerve ending. Leaving me fuller than ever.

Instead of pumping his digit in and out, he lifted me with the hand that clutched me, pulling me up and then pushing me back down onto his pinky finger.

Drool gathered at the corners of my mouth. My eyes rolled back in my head. My legs shook.

It felt better than it had any right to.

I was also scared shitless. Who wouldn't be? I was a tiny doll in comparison to his god-like size. And even with his cum making me feel strong enough to survive whatever it was he threw my way, I was still powerless to do anything but take it.

If he wasn't careful, if he pushed too hard, if he went too deep, I could die. There was no afterlife for those who died at the hands of Discord. And yet, knowing the stakes only seemed to intensify the pleasure.

The size difference was insanity, but my body seemed to be going into overdrive to ensure I could take him. Everything was impossibly tight, yet he slid in and out with ease. Arousal and cum gushed down my thighs, the lewd sounds coming from my stuffed pussy driving us both into a frenzy.

"Look at you. What a perfect little finger puppet you make."

The head with the red eyes and curling horns hunched down, his tongue flicking out to taste me. The muscle twitched and throbbed over my naked flesh, making my nerves flood with sensation. It dragged back down my body, the tip teasing my breasts, my belly button, my clit.

The tongue didn't leave so much as an inch of my skin untasted.

Pain and pleasure ate me alive.

"Beg," he hummed against me.

Beg? *Beg?* Had I heard him right? Was this weird cocktail of fear and lust shooting through my system, scrambling my hearing? No, I was sure I heard him right.

Discord was commanding me to beg. What was I supposed to be begging for? For him to stop, or to keep going?

I hated him for making me choose.

I'd goaded him into this, but I'd never asked for *this*.

It was too twisted. Too weird. Too dangerous.

And it was too fucking good for me to want it to stop.

"P–p–please," I barely managed to choke out. "Pl–please, Master. Please. *Please.*"

Over and over, I repeated the word. My arms clutched one of his fingers, holding on for dear life as he forced me through a violent orgasm. When I screamed my release, he didn't stop.

Discord's pinky finger kept pounding into me. The pain never receded, but neither did the euphoria.

I lost count of my climaxes. My vision blurred. My head swam, and all my thoughts turned to mush. The only things I could pick out from the chaos were the obscene sounds of his body slapping into the cradle of my cum-soaked thighs, and the four eyes of this god watching me.

Those shining orbs of red and green were the last thing I saw before I went limp, and darkness rushed in to take me.

17
Visitor

MEG

I opened my eyes to find myself in the twins' bed, snuggled safely between their sleeping forms. I was tucked into the cradle of Raff's body, his tail coiled around my ankle, while Riff's arms were wrapped around my middle with his head buried into my stomach, snoring softly against my navel.

Alistair must have washed me again before carrying me to the twins' trailer. My hair was still a little damp, with no traces of hydra cum. I gathered the twins had dressed me for bed since I was wearing one of their merch shirts. It had an illustration of them on the front, flipping through the air on the trapeze. In faded lettering, it read "The Demonic Duo."

Riff shifted, grumbling softly in his sleep. Then he cracked an eye, blinked sleepily at the shirt, and mumbled, "Gotta change it to...hrm...the demonic trio," before promptly falling back asleep.

A smile touched my lips.

Every muscle in my body was on fire. My vagina was seriously second-guessing its choice in our latest male conquests, and my mind was turning over what Alistair had said about my mother, which brought everything I thought I knew about her into question. But all it took was one moment with my incubi clowns, and everything slipped into the background.

I heaved a contented sigh and settled back into my pillow.

My eyes started to drift shut, and then two glinting gems of red at the foot of the bed had them snapping back open.

It was Al, standing there in the darkness as still as a statue, watching us sleep.

Just like that, my night with Alistair came slamming back. I pulled myself into a sitting position, as much as I could, with Riff wrapped like a boa constrictor around my waist.

"Tell me the truth about my mother," I whispered to the shadow, knowing the ringmaster could hear me. "After what you did to me, I deserve to know the truth."

Only a few seconds passed when my phone—which had been plugged in for me on the nightstand—buzzed, lighting up the room. I grabbed it, careful not to wake the twins and unlocked it with a swipe of my thumb.

Alistair: Don't pretend you didn't love every second.

Alistair's words on my screen had my heart beating like a war drum. My thighs clenched, and my aching pussy throbbed. I was so tender, so sensitive. My night with the devil had been downright sinful.

Instead of roses, he'd gifted me the eyes of my attackers. He'd laid out the rest of them for me to torture. He'd fucked me with his shadow tentacles in the bath while the twins watched on FaceTime, then when he'd taken me up the ass, he'd lost control, shifted, and turned me into a cum-covered finger puppet. It had been seriously fucked up. Like some twisted Peter Pan x Tinkerbell fanfiction shit.

And he was right. I loved every depraved second.

After everything that happened, I still wanted his mark. But that didn't change the fact that I wouldn't tolerate a mate who kept shit from me.

Meg: Tell me what you're hiding, or I'll tell Riff and Raff who you really are. They should know anyway. Unlike you, I don't have a fetish for keeping secrets from my future mates.

When minutes passed with no response, I placed the phone back on the side table and lowered myself onto my pillow to sleep. My eyelids started to drift shut when two emerald eyes had me shaking myself awake.

Alistair now stood at the foot of the bed in place of his shadow.

He had his dark hair tied back into a low ponytail. He'd changed his shirt—a white lantern-sleeve shirt with a plunging neckline that exposed much of his pale chest, leaving a glimpse of the fine stitching holding his dead flesh together. The shade was dressed to the nines as always.

What was new were the dark circles underscoring his eyes. He looked more corpse-like than ever with his death-pale flesh, and he leaned against his cane with both hands as if the simple task of standing was a strain.

He'd expended almost every ounce of his power shifting.

"Alright, Megaera. You have my attention." His voice came out cool and calm, but there was something in his eyes that had my pulse racing.

"Tell me why my mother conceived me. You say she was never in love with my father, that she charmed him into having me. Why? You say you don't know, but you're lying. I don't need to read your emotions to see the guilt in your eyes."

He tilted his head, neck cracking and eyes glinting. "You really want to do this now? We'll wake the twins."

"Good. If I think what's coming out of your mouth is bull-shit, I'll tell them—"

He dissolved into smoke, and in a blink, he was on top of me with his hand clamped over my mouth. "First, you try to charm me by force. Now you threaten me?" He tutted under his breath. "Such a *naughty* pet."

He looked up, examining the portion of the wall over the bed's headboard where much of the twins' mask and sex toy collection was on display. He reached up and pulled one of Riff's throwing knives from the drywall and removed his hand from my mouth—tapping my lips with the flat of the blade.

"If you didn't have my dick wrapped around that bratty little tongue of yours, I'd cut it out. Then I wouldn't have to worry about you spilling my secrets."

Maybe it was the knife against my mouth that had my veins pumping with dark excitement.

Or the fact that the twins were nestled close on either side of us, a too-loud whisper or a nudge away from waking up and seeing the ringmaster on top of me with his knee wedged between my thighs.

My hands fumbled for his hips while taking care to avoid the twin's limbs.

"By my depths, Megaera. What's it going to take to tame you?"

I wetted my lips, grinning up at him. "You can't tame hellfire, Alistair."

He moved the knife lower to tap its point lightly against the spikes on Daemon's collar. "I've done it before."

"Are you going to muzzle and whip me too?"

Both his brows hiked. "No...Things like that only make you more feral." He dropped the knife onto my pillow and trailed his hand down my torso. I held my breath when his knuckles grazed Riff's arm, but the incubus only snorted softly in his sleep.

Alistair's eyes flicked from Riff to me, and the look behind them had jolts of electricity shooting through my core. His hand slipped beneath my shirt and wedged between my thighs. "Are you sore?"

I nodded and held back a whimper as his fingers stroked over my aching slit. My hips shifted up, searching for more of his touch.

"So swollen. I stretched you to your limit." A beat later, he held his fingers up. Even in the dark, I could see they were soaking wet. "Yet you're still dripping for me, Megaera."

Watching him pop his fingers in his mouth and suck off my arousal only intensified the ache between my legs.

"You don't act like you've never been with a woman before," I said in a ragged whisper.

He kissed along my throat, pausing to inhale the leather of Daemon's collar. His hot breath washed over the sensitive skin, making me shiver.

"You may be my first female mate, but don't ever forget, Little Demon..." Alistair painted one long lick up the column of my neck, his lips brushing my ear. "I created sin."

Something darkly intimate passed between us—like in the illusion the night he'd tried to scare me away. He must have felt it, too, because he gripped me by the horn and captured my lips in a heated kiss.

"Tell me your secret," I murmured against his lips.

He paused, breaking our connection with a sigh. His hands cradled my head as he pulled back and leveled me with a pained look. "You'll hate me for it."

"You're the devil," I whispered. "You should be used to being hated."

He stroked the side of my temple with his thumb, his touch achingly tender. "I am. But not by you. Not after everything I've done. Now, there is no escaping me, Pet. You'll be mine forever."

"Because of the deal I struck with you?"

"No." He sat back on his heels, his hand snaking back under my shirt. I swallowed a wince when his fingers danced over a sensitive patch of my flesh. "Because you are my bonded mate."

Every inch of my body went cold, save for the place over my thigh where his fingers lingered—it throbbed like a fresh burn. "What are you talking about?"

He tugged my shirt up, and my gaze followed his line of sight.

My breath froze in my lungs when I saw it.

A bite mark so huge it wrapped around my entire upper thigh. He must have marked me while I was passed out.

I was now Discord's bonded mate.

"I'll tell you everything you wish to know once Daemon returns."

"And when is that going to be?"

"A day or two. Maybe three. If he takes any longer than that, there's a problem. I'll have to go looking for him."

"What kind of problem?" When the twins started to shift in their sleep, I dropped my whisper lower. "Is he in danger?"

"He's fine." Alistair tried to assure me, though the shadows behind his eyes did fuck-all to ease my worry.

The shade carefully climbed off the bed and started to fade back into the shadows. "As for telling the twins who I am, do it. You're right. They should know."

With that, the ringmaster disappeared into the night.

18

The Devil's Mark

RIFF

I woke up to the sound of voices. Whispers. Cracking an eyelid, I found the ringmaster in our bed.

On top of Meg.

The shade had one hand gripping her neck and the other wedged between her legs. He was inside her by the way her lashes fluttered, and her lips parted on the tiniest wisp of a gasp. He pulled his fingers from her center and held them up so she could see how wet she was for him.

My dick hardened when he slipped his fingers into his mouth and sucked her juices clean.

When he tasted his tongue, his face set with a fierce expression that had goosebumps exploding over my skin.

"Don't ever forget, Little Demon, I created sin."

Alistair had it *bad* for our little half-blood.

He'd marked her. He hadn't even exchanged mating marks with Daemon yet, and those two had been screwing for-fucking-ever.

This pink-haired she-devil had cast her charms on all of us without so much of a lick of actual magic.

We knew he'd bonded with her the second he'd carried her through our door. Her scent was still hers, sweet and mouth-watering like cotton candy. But now there was a new layer to the aroma—masculine and darkly cloying, like brandied fruit and infernal magic.

He'd ridden her hard. She was covered in bruises—he'd tied her up at one point. And something huge had clawed her torso, leaving an angry welt that stretched from her clavicle to her rosy patch of pubic hair.

Other than Daemon, no one in the troupe had seen the ringmaster's true form. Whatever shape he took, it had to be huge. His bite encircled her entire thigh.

I squeezed my eyes shut and was careful to keep my breathing even so as not to tip off the boss that I was awake. Normally, the shade's senses were too acute to be fooled, but tonight, he was too focused on his new mate to notice.

They spoke of secrets.

Something he was keeping from her and something they were both keeping from Raff and me.

Whatever it was, it had to be a real bombshell with the way they whispered.

When he tugged her shirt up and gestured to her fresh mark, her heart beat so hard I could feel it against my own chest. Her emotions were so strong it was like a punch to the gut.

Surprise.

Delight.

Exhaustion.

And a dash of anxiety—but mostly surprise.

She hadn't known he'd marked her. How the fuck could she not know? He'd carried her to our trailer unconscious... Had he fucked her in her sleep?

When he was gone, the bed shifted as she carefully crawled out from under the tangle of incubi limbs and padded out of the bedroom.

I didn't miss the limp in her step.

"Hey, wake up." I tried to shake Raff awake, who only turned over in his sleep and swatted at me with his tail as if I was an annoying fly.

Rolling my eyes, I climbed on top of him, wrenched his head off the pillow by the horn and delivered a sharp slap to his cheek.

The incubus jerked to consciousness. His hand went for one of my knives sticking out of the headboard, and in a blink, he had the blade at my throat.

First, recognition flooded his eyes, then annoyance. "What?"

I pointed to the empty spot beside him on the bed. I could sense that familiar tide of unease rising inside him. He felt it, too. The need to keep her close.

Neither of us could explain why, but something huge seemed to be hanging over Sinner's Sideshow lately. Something dangerous, like an impending doom. Maybe it had to do with the secrets Meg and Alistair were muttering about.

"Where is she?" Raff demanded.

Before I could answer, there was a clatter from the kitchen followed by a string of curses. Raff bucked his hips and I went flying off the bed. I landed in a crouch. He stood over me with his arms crossed—looking at my boxer briefs and the bulge the thin material struggled to maintain.

Meg was a particular fan of the pair I was wearing since you could make out the shape of my dick piercings.

I rose to my full height and grinned at Raff. "What's that human saying? Oh yeah, take a picture, it lasts longer. Fuck head."

"That's not the saying."

"Yeah, well." I shrugged. "I added my own little flair there at the end."

"Put something on that makes you look ugly. Last thing she needs right now is more cock, even if her freshly awakened hunger doesn't understand that."

I pouted. "But I look good in everything."

He opened our dresser and rifled through our clothes. He tugged on a pair of baggy black joggers. Then he tossed me an identical pair.

"At least put on pants."

"Fine."

He charged out of the room, and I hopped after him while simultaneously shoving my legs through the sweats.

We found Meg in the kitchen, on her hands and knees in front of a cabinet, wrestling a frying pan from the shelf.

Raff folded his arms over his chest and leaned one shoulder against the wall, watching her. "You need help waking up the whole camp there, Hell Bat?"

"I'm sorry—fuck—" She gave another tug to the pan's handle, and it came flying out in a spray of random pot lids. She shoved to her feet, holding the frying pan up with a victorious look on her face. "I didn't mean to wake you guys up. I'm on a quest for sausage."

When she turned for the refrigerator, my mouth opened to fire off the obvious innuendo, but Raff buried his elbow into my side before I could. "There's some in the back. Don't tell Larry. He's trying to get everyone to swear off pork."

She nodded and started pillaging the fridge in search of the meat.

Raff and I swapped a look. He must have sensed the powerful wave of apprehension radiating from her.

"Hell Bat..." He pushed off from the wall and joined her by the fridge, snatching the package of sausage from her hand. "Here, let me cook that for you."

"I can do it myself," she huffed.

"You should be resting. After what you've been through—"

Her angry glare cut to me. "You don't know what I've been through."

"No, we don't. Not exactly. But we do know Alistair marked you. That couldn't have been–er, *comfortable*. Assuming his true form is bigger than ours or Daemon's."

Her lower lip warbled. She was putting on a brave face, trying not to show any weakness. When would she understand that she could step out of her armor with us? That she could be soft and vulnerable, and we'd only love her more for it?

"Did he hurt you?"

She shook her head. "No. Kinda. I don't fucking know. It didn't hurt then, but now it feels like I'm on fire."

Raff plopped the meat in the skillet, taking over the task of preparing her a real meal that didn't consist of lust and cum. I took her by the hips and lifted her onto the counter so her legs dangled off.

"Let me see."

"It's not like you guys didn't see it already when you dressed me for bed."

"We saw it, yeah. But our priority was getting you dressed and in bed. Now stop being a brat, and let me see it, Harbinger."

Her jaw set, but she didn't protest when I pushed the hem of the shirt we put her in up to her hips. She sucked her bottom lip between her teeth as I gripped her knees and slowly guided her thighs apart.

Raff gave me a glass-sharp side-eye through the steam rising up from the skillet. I returned the look, one that said, *"Can't you see Alistair ripped her up bad? I'm not a fucking animal."*

His glower said it all without the need for words. There was a part of me that didn't care how sore she was.

The monster inside me always thirsted for her.

Taking in a deep breath, I turned my attention to the bite mark encircling Meg's entire upper thigh. My fingertips feathered over the puncture wounds. She winced—the sound turning to a moan as my touch drifted to her inner thigh, my knuckles grazing her bare pussy lips.

"This is gnarlier than any archdemon mating mark I've ever seen." I couldn't hide the curiosity, or the hunger, lacing my words. "These fang marks are insane. Just how big was he, Meg?"

A blush stained her cheeks. "Uh... Big."

"How big?" My brows rose at the bend in her tone. I held my hands up with my palms facing each other and slowly pulled them further apart. "Tell me when."

When my arms were stretched out as far as they'd go on either side of my body, I laughed. "Okay, now that's just scientifically impossible, babe. Not even Lilith herself has that stretchy of a vagina."

"I-it wasn't normal sex, okay? It was...weird. I..." Her voice wavered and broke. She started to wring the spade of her tail between her manicured fingers, her gaze boring straight through me, lost in thought.

Tension simmered in the sausage-scented air. Fucking Hells, what I would have given to be a fly on the wall when Alistair mated Megaera. Something went down. Something fucking huge.

A thousand questions burned in the back of my throat.

What did the shade's true form look like? What did he do in bed to make a sex demon speechless? And what were they whispering about earlier? What secret was he keeping from her?

What secret were they keeping from *us?*

As feral as I was for answers, I pushed my curiosity down and took her hand gently in mine. "Are you happy you have his mark?"

She nodded.

"Good. That's all that matters, right?"

She nodded again, this time seeming less sure of herself—which wasn't like her at all.

I opened my mouth to pry a little bit more into whatever it was she was keeping from us, but Raff was giving me the evil eye from the corner of my vision, warning me not to push her.

He'd be singing a different tune if he'd overheard what I had.

Raff turned off the stove, plopped the sausage onto a plate and passed it to Meg along with a fork and a napkin. I held back my smile. Look at him, being all domestic and shit. This girl was changing us.

She was changing all of us.

"So, um, tell me about you guys."

I blinked. What a weird question. Sure, we'd only known her for just over a month, but it sure as hell didn't feel like it. She could read our every emotion and had memorized every inch of our bodies. She'd seen my truest form, and eventually, she'd see Raff's, too. Soon, our marks would join Alistair's, making her ours forever.

"What else is there to know, Hell Bat?" Raff asked, his tone tender and amused all at once. "We love pizza and horror movies."

"Knives and fire," I added.

"We love you and this circus."

I dropped my head between her spread legs, my face so close to her molten flesh that I could see her clit twitch beneath my stare. The scent of Alistair's cum oozing from her slit had me weak in the knees. "And this pussy. We fucking *love* this pussy."

Heat radiated from her beautiful pink eyes, but I rolled her shirt back over her thighs and took a step back before I went back on my word not to touch her tonight.

"Er, what I meant was, tell me about your past."

"Well, uh..." Raff scrubbed the back of his skull with his palm, making his apple-green hair stick out in every direction. "Alistair recruited us into Sinner's Sideshow about five years ago."

"Before that, there isn't much to tell," I added. "We were entertainers, basically court jesters for a pompous bastard of an archdemon named Conquest. One of the four Horsemen of the Apocalypse."

"Wait, The Horsemen of the Apocalypse are real?"

"Yup. Discord created them to destroy the world."

"Why haven't they yet?"

Raff and I shrugged in perfect synchronicity. "He changed his mind. They're all horrible, ancient, unfulfilled bastards. Supposedly, they've tried just about everything to get him to change his mind since they can't do it without a monarch of Hell's say so. All they care about is destroying the Upside. Guess you can't blame them since that's what they were created for."

"So, what made you decide to leave your home and work for Alistair?"

"Well, you don't have much choice when you're sold to the highest bidder."

Meg stopped chewing mid-munch on her sausage. Her eyes rounded. "*Sold?* Wait. You were slaves? I thought you guys said Alistair recruited you."

"Bought, recruited. Tomato, tomatoe."

"No, *not* tomato tomatoe. There's a huge difference. Free will and autonomy being the big key difference."

She finished with her breakfast, and handed her empty plate to Raff. He took it, giving her a stern look before placing it in the sink. "Don't forget, you were bought too, Hell Bat."

Her blushing cheeks deepened in color, and frustration bloomed from her aura. "That's different. I sold myself. It was my choice."

"Trust me, babe. Alistair buying us for the show was the best thing that's ever happened to us. If we hadn't joined Sinner's Sideshow, we would have never met you."

"Even if we are still slaves, Alistair does a damn good job hiding the fact. We get paid. We can wander the Upside on our nights off. We don't have to have sex with anyone we don't want to anymore."

Raff shot me another poisonous glare. Shit. I should have left out that last part.

Her lips opened in a soundless gasp of horror. "Wait. Conquest *forced* you into sex?"

Taking her by the hips, I plucked her off the counter and set her on her feet between Raff and me. She was wedged so tightly against us that our thundering hearts beat as one, and our lungs seemed to entwine.

"Don't," I said, breathless, as I found myself lost in her pink gaze. Don't go feeling sorry for us. We're fine."

Raff arched down, whispering into her ear, "Especially now that we have you."

Her pupils dilated, and her lashes fluttered as the words seemed to sink deep inside her, hooking their way into her soul. "I'm starting to think I don't deserve you two."

Raff radiated offense at the sentence, but I met her statement with a knowing smirk. "Why? Because you've been keeping secrets from us?"

My twin sent a confused look over Meg's head, but I ignored him.

Meg's mouth morphed into the shape of an "O" as realization set in. "You were awake."

"That's right, Harbinger. I got front-row seats to your filthy little tryst with the boss. So…"

I pressed a finger beneath her chin, lifting her gaze to mine. "What's this secret about Alistair?"

19

Three Days Later

DAEMON

As Discord's favorite pet, I was no stranger to pain. Back before the surface softened him, he'd been a brutal master. He'd tempered me into something stronger than I'd been before. He'd taken my chaos and forged me into the perfect tool. I could suck cock, I could kill. I could even work in a circus and have the crowd begging to eat out of my hand.

Withstanding torture was, how did the humans say it? Oh, yeah. A fucking cakewalk.

The more they hurt me, the more I bled, the more cathartic it was.

Because even the Horsemen didn't know the true definition of agony, not until they suffered the full extent of Discord's wrath. Alistair would bring a hellstorm down on these bastards once he learned of their twisted plan.

I just had to summon the balls to free myself.

I couldn't shift until I got the adamantine spear out of my gut, which was impossible with them watching me every damn minute, day and night. What I needed was a distraction.

Summoning my hounds was the only plan I'd managed to come up with. I sat here trying to figure out a way to free myself in a way that didn't involve putting my pack in danger. I'd come up with fuck-all. It was the only way, and knowing that hurt more than the gaping hole in my side.

My pack were ferocious beasts that had seen their fair share of war and carnage. But these were The Horsemen of the fucking Apocalypse. My pack was no match.

Withstanding torture was easier than putting my dogs in danger.

But I loved Alistair more.

I'd be damned all over again if I was going to sit here and allow The Horsemen to force Lilith's mark on Alistair so the power-hungry bitch would be nudged high enough on the demonic food chain to orchestrate the end of the mortal plane.

I wouldn't let her drag Alistair to the Downside as her bonded mate.

Time was running out. Soon, he'd come looking for me. And I'd be damned all over again if I was going to allow him to walk into the ambush.

"Time to wake up, mongrel. It's a new day."

I hadn't been sleeping. I'd hardly slept a wink. I'd only pretended to sleep to catch bits of their conversations. Mostly they just fucked, and gloated about how they were doing right by Discord's "memory." As if he was dead.

To them, he probably was.

I cracked my eyes open just in time to see Death's black boot hurling forward, giving a hard kick to the grip of Conquest's spear. I gnashed my teeth as pain savaged my system. A fresh flood of blood gushed from my wound.

I'd been stuck here for three days. No food, no water. No place to piss except for right here on the motel's filthy shag carpeting.

My body didn't care. It didn't give a single fuck.

Death's gaze dropped to my lap. His brow furled, and he noticed the bulge. He took his scythe and hooked the blade beneath the waist of my pants, cutting the fabric. My erection sprung out, and everyone in the room turned to take it in.

"He's…He's got a hard-on," Death said, his nose wrinkling in disgust. "What in Discord's Hell is wrong with you?"

I peeled my lips back to reveal my canines. "Clearly, you've never seen one of my shows. If you had, you'd know pain is kinda my thing. Normally, I prefer to inflict it, but mixing shit up is a nice change of pace."

Death's beady eyes narrowed into slivers. "You sicken me."

"*I* sicken, *Death?*" I rested my head against the wall, my tongue running over my parched lips—the dehydrated skin splitting and bleeding as it stretched with my manic smile. "What an honor."

Astrid lifted her head from War's chest, who had her tucked against his side. "If it bothers you, just cut it off. We can use it as a toy."

Death didn't bother turning around from where he was seated at the end of the second bed where Conquest was stretched out. He kept his hate-filled glare on me. "He's a hellhound. Do third-degree burns on your cooch sound like your idea of a good time?"

"I say we send it to Discord in a pretty box tied with a bow. Then he'd come running, and we could finally get on with the plan."

Astrid sat up, her wings popping out as she snarled at Conquest from the next bed over—much like a cat raising its hackles. "Right, and alert him that it's us who's holding him? If he has any reason to suspect that his strongest archdemons were holding his favorite pet hostage, he'll come prepared. He'll feed. The only hope that this plan will work is if he comes unprepared. He hasn't fed properly in decades, and he won't unless he's given reason to."

Death nudged the blade of his scythe so its edge curved around the base of my cock. I hissed between clenched teeth as it sliced through the first few layers of skin.

For the first time since he'd entered the motel room, Death cracked a smile. "I say we chop it off anyway. We can give Discord a nice new hole to fuck."

At his words, my cock thickened, standing straighter. My brows slid up in surprise, considering how much blood I'd lost. "Damn. Don't you go taking the credit for that, Death."

The Horseman's eyes flared with dark fury. "You're making this whole intimidation thing uncomfortable. You're supposed to be pissing yourself with fear."

"I am Discord's assassin. His bodyguard. His lover. His show monkey to do whatever tricks he asks of me. I am whatever he needs me to be. The list of shit that can actually intimidate me is shorter than that pathetic lump of flesh between your legs, Death. Your threats don't scare me."

Another brutal grin savaged my dry lips, and I spit—it was more blood than saliva—at his feet. "A for effort, though."

"You fucking—"

I gripped the blade, uncaring that it was ribboning into my flesh and spilling crimson I didn't have to spare. Not that it mattered. Death was here. He had the power to keep me alive if that's what he willed. "Touch my cock, and I promise you, Discord will be wearing yours as his next prized skin suit. He tends to go for sharp jawlines and lean muscles like yours."

The air between us was electric and filled with hatred.

My heart pulsed hard as I watched him with wild eyes, daring him to fuck with me. He wasn't going to do shit. His hand shook too much, its tremors causing the blade to slice deeper into my hand.

I intimidated him.

It was disappointing. Death was supposed to be one of Downside's biggest badasses. I'd get no satisfaction from killing him. It was probably just as well. That was the annoying thing about Death. Only Discord could kill him.

Astrid appeared behind him as if out of thin air. Her lavender hair spilled over his shoulder as she planted a seductive kiss on his ear. He went corpse still the moment she touched him.

"Come on, Death baby. You've made the mongrel bleed enough for now. Come to bed. I'll take your mind off the waiting."

Her hands skimmed over his bare chest and dipped toward his beltline, but he captured both her wrists in one hand before they found their mark.

"No, thanks." His answer was cold and clipped. "The rancid scent the mongrel is putting off isn't really doing it for me."

Bullshit. Since when did the smell of filth put off Death?

Lilith didn't seem to suspect his obvious lie. That or she didn't care. With a feline flick of her tail, she turned and crawled on top of Conquest. Irritation flickered across Death's pale features as the bed started to gently rock, heated moans and the wet slap of flesh on flesh filling the room.

My line of sight drifted to the bite mark peeking out from the collar of his duster jacket. That's why he didn't want to fuck her. Death was a lot of things, but his loyalty to his mate was the only thing I found tolerable about the bastard.

When the demon noticed me staring at his mark, he leaned forward and dropped his voice to a whisper. "Too bad you didn't exchange marks with your master, mongrel. Otherwise, he would have sensed you were in trouble, and Astrid's plan would have crumpled before it could even walk."

I hated how right he was.

If I hadn't been such a stubborn asshole and exchanged mating marks with Alistair, he'd sense I was hurt and would come prepared to fuck shit up.

Now, I had to bail myself out.

"How *is* Famine?" I asked, low enough to go no further than Death's ear.

A vein ticked in the Horseman's jaw. Of course, I knew. I was a hellhound. I could smell what he'd eaten in the last week, let alone who he'd been fucking. I'd never met Famine, but there was no other demon this stretch of misery and despair could belong to. "Where is he anyway?"

After an awkward silence filled with the creak of old mattress springs, I took a shot in the dark and murmured, "He doesn't want anything to do with this, does he? He's still loyal to Discord. That or he's the only one among you with sense enough to fear him."

"Why would I fear an old god's faded shadow?"

"He still has the power to—" I lifted my arm and opened my hand to simulate an explosion. "Obliterate you."

There it was again—that flicker of hesitancy. But it was gone on the next beat as his lips spread into a mocking smirk. "Once Lilith forges her bond with Discord, we'll have no more use for you. You'll die, and your soul will return home. Whatever happens to you, that's Lilith's prerogative. But as for Lilith's half-blood brat..."

Anger siphoned into my lungs as the conversation shifted to Megaera.

"She'll stay with us," Death said quietly. There was a gleam of satisfaction in his eyes, knowing he'd hit a nerve. He threw a glance over his shoulder at Astrid, who was now on her hands and knees with Conquest's dick rammed down her throat while War's hips pounded her ass, fucking her from behind. "As you can see, my brothers have a thing for succubus pussy."

My rage was so thick in my throat I could choke on it.

The final thread of my restraint snapped.

My tattoos glowed hot, and I started to steam as I summoned every ounce of my remaining strength to summon my dogs. Hela was the first to come, exploding from thin air in a burst of flames with one of my whips clamped in her jaws.

Landing beside me, I took the whip from her and cracked it. The tail whistled through the air so fast, it was wrapped around Death's throat, all in a blink. Before he could react, I yanked on the whip and jerked him off the bed.

My fingers snapped around his throat, and I surged forward, teeth bared, and sunk them deep into his nose. My cock twitched harder than ever as the taste of him bloomed over my tongue.

His muscles jerked as his body registered what was happening, but he didn't scream. He didn't seem to feel pain whatsoever. Even though I'd bitten off his nose. All that was there was a gaping pit of glistening sinew and jagged cartilage.

My other dogs appeared and launched themselves at War, Conquest, and Lilith. Lilith shifted into her true form while War and Conquest were forced to fight in their human shapes—or they risked bringing the whole building down.

I spat Death's nose back in his face, flecking his pale skin with blood. "You don't fear death by my hand. But it's gonna take a while for your nose to regenerate. So unless you want to be walking around with a second 'new hole' for Famine to fuck in your goddamn eye socket, you'll pull the spear from my gut."

20

The Show Must Go On

MEG

"Are you sure you want to do this?"

Raff's voice sounded distant, even though he was standing right beside me.

"I want to do this," I answered mechanically while keeping my attention glued to the ring.

"Then why won't you look at us?" Riff asked. "You've barely glanced in our direction since we got into costume."

I tore my gaze off the stagehands who were setting up for our performance and forced my eyes to take in the panty-obliterating sight of Riff and Raff in their new costumes.

Blood-red paint had been smeared over their eyes—making their white contacts pop. They wore black leather harnesses over their otherwise bare chests.

The red paint had also been smeared on their nipples in an X pattern.

Thick iron bracers hugged their forearms, with little loops on their wrists where the chains would attach.

They were barefoot, and the only other item of clothing they wore was a chain belt loosely over their hips, leaving much of that delicious V running from their hip bones to their pelvis on display. A single piece of long black fabric was draped in the front and the back of the chain, exposing their muscular thighs.

Apparently, these were the typical garb of royal courtesans to high-ranking archdemons in the Downside.

I hated how much seeing them dressed up like this turned me on. *Knowing* that they were once forced to dress like this all the time—what they were forced to do while they were in costume.

Riff tweaked a brow at me, his tattooed name wrinkling. "How are you feeling?"

How am I feeling? Normally, that would've been a silly question for an incubus to ask. But I was purposefully holding back my lust as much as I could.

"Fine," I answered in a clipped voice, turning my attention back to the ring. "I'm just nervous."

We were standing behind the big top, peeking in on the ring from the back entrance flap. It was intermission. The stagehands were moving furniture into the ring, making it look like a hellish bedroom similar to the one in Alistair's caravan.

It was a full house tonight.

They'd all come to see my first performance as The Hell Bat.

It shouldn't have been anything special. Like our other act, this one was depraved, taboo. The typical debauched-fuckery you'd find in the center ring of our black and white big top...

Except with one little twist.

"Fucking look at me." Strong fingers pinched my chin and wrenched my gaze to Raff's. "You're a circus brat. Performing in front of an audience is as easy as breathing for you, and your succubus blood doesn't give two harpy shits about doing live fuck shows. They're cake for you. So don't pass this off as normal stage jitters."

"I..." The words I wanted to say froze in my throat.

Riff leaned back on a stack of crates with his arms crossed over his chest. "You know you can tell us anything, right? So how about you stop being so stubborn and just talk about your feelings?"

Maybe it was the warmth of his genuine eyes melting the ice in my throat. Maybe I was so tired of keeping everything in. It was probably both.

"I miss Daemon so much it hurts. Alistair still won't tell me where the fuck he is, and I feel helpless. I need this distraction."

Raff's thumb stroked the edge of my jaw while his tail curled around my thigh and slipped under my skirt. A moan caught in my throat as his tail grazed my opening. "There's a lot of other ways we can distract you, Hell Bat."

"I want *this* distraction," I insisted, my cheeks burning. "I meant it when I said I wanted to help you guys heal from your past."

The twins pretending they were sex slaves in the ring was their way of taking power over what had happened to them in the past. This was by their terms. They seemed especially insistent after learning that they were still another demon's property.

Being prized pets to a literal god was, of course, a major improvement to being sex slaves to the Horseman of Conquest, but still, knowing you weren't completely free had a way of fucking with your head.

Making a joke out of their trauma and hamming up a pain point from their past life was their therapy.

I was all for this.

What I didn't expect was how fucking turned on I was by the whole concept—how excited I was to flip our usual roles.

Riff and Raff exchanged one of their looks. Several silent seconds passed as they seemed to have an entire conversation with their eyes alone. When they looked back at me, identical grins stretched their mouths from ear to ear.

"Oh. I get it now," Riff snickered. "Our twisted little half-blood is embarrassed by being *so* turned on by the thought of our little reverse force play."

A wicked smirk tugged at Raff's lips as his tail slid through my fold. "So that's why she's soaking wet."

"What did we tell you about shame?" Riff tutted.

I huffed. "That there's no place for it at Sinner's Sideshow."

"That's right. Given our pasts, it makes sense that you're a little embarrassed to want this. Don't be. There are hundreds of sex-starved monsters who are excited, too. And trust us..."

Raff bowed his spine, the point of his tongue sweeping over the seam of my lips and mimicking the motions of his tail beneath my skirt. "No one wants this more than us."

Just like that, all my reservations about the act were gone. This whole thing was their idea anyway.

This was for them more than it was for anyone else.

Besides, force play was our usual go-to act—with some knife throwing, trapeze stunts, and sword and fire swallowing thrown in for flavor.

The only difference now was that I was playing the dominant role.

"Meg!"

I turned to see my best friend pushing her way through the backstage troupe members. The bounce in her step had the nest of snakes on top of her head flopping and hissing with displeasure.

She came to a halt just a few feet shy of us with her arms behind her back as if she was hiding something. "Tail where I can see it, Rafferty."

At Lollie's voice, the incubus gave a begrudging grumble and slipped his tail out from under my skirt. "Lollie, it's intermission. You're supposed to be running the concession counter."

"Mollie's watching it. I had to come back here and give you a little good luck charm—Oh, my Discord. Look at you! You're one hot Hell Bat. Damn!"

I was wearing next to nothing. My breasts were bare, and Roach had fitted me with fancy nipple piercings to replace my old ones. They were topped with dainty metal chains that had little obsidian charms shaped in the obelisk of Discord dangling at the ends.

The skirt was like chain mail, delicate metal hoops all woven together to create something sheer and feminine, yet it was menacing and masculine all at once. Something fitting of a succubus queen of hell.

On top of my head, nestled between my horns, was an iron tiara fitted with obsidian gems.

"You look like a queen," Lollie mumbled, her eyes widening.

"Queen of the sluts, maybe," I said with a laugh.

"See? She hates the crown," Lollie said to the twins in an *"I told you so"* sing-song voice.

"I don't hate it. I'm just not much of a 'crown' girl."

"I figured. So, I got you this..."

Both of the twins cleared their throats, and she corrected, "Sorry, *we* got you this."

She brandished the item she'd been concealing behind her back.

My heart squeezed as I registered Daemon's cap dangling from her finger. "How did you get this?"

The gorgon shrugged. "I had the twins sneak in and nick it. But it was my idea, so I wanted to be the one to give it to you."

Riff plucked the crown from my head, and Lollie stepped up to replace it with the cap. She fussed over my hair before stepping back to admire me.

"There. That's better. Don't you think, boys?"

"Perfect as always. But yeah." Raff nodded slowly as he eyed Daemon's Bitch Tamer hat. "It looks good."

The leather smelled like my hellhound. Dark and leathery, with traces of sweat and blood. There was that ache again, the one that made every cell in my body burn with need.

I was beginning to miss the grumpy alpha to the point of pain.

The house lights dimmed, and Alistair's velvety voice carried through the tent. "Spooks and specters. Creeps and cunts..."

"That's our cue, Harbinger." Riff kissed my left cheek and dipped into the big top to take his place.

Raff kissed my right cheek with a "See you in a few minutes" and disappeared after his brother.

"They really love you, you know?" Lollie said after they were gone. Her gaze roved down to my exposed thigh, where Alistair's mark permanently marked my skin. She never asked which of my men it belonged to, but I had a feeling she knew. "They all love you."

I reached up to idly thumb the dull spikes on Daemon's collar. "Yeah. I know."

"He's going to come back, you know. He always does."

"U–um, sorry I'm late, Miss Meg," Larry's guttural voice, with its faint lick of an Irish accent, rumbled behind me. I turned to see the boar-headed giant approaching.

Tonight, our lovable Fomorian wasn't dressed as The Butcher. He was making an appearance in our act, and instead of his blood-splattered apron, he wore a tiny little loincloth that barely managed to hide his "pork roll," as the twins called it.

His tusks were decorated with iron bangles with more delicate chains similar to my nipple jewelry, which clinked with each heavy stride he made.

With a sharpened halberd clutched in his hand, he looked pretty menacing. Though his faint scent of kale took away the edge a bit.

"Larry, how many times do I have to tell you? It's just Meg."

He shuffled his weight from one foot to the other. "I'm sorry, Miss Meg—Shit!" Twin stains of red bloomed beneath the coarse fur of his cheeks and spread to his snout. "Meg," he corrected. "Just Meg."

Lollie propped a hand on her hip and shook her head in disbelief at the giant. "Larry, baby. You really are too good for this place."

Alistair finished announcing the act, and the din of applause was our cue to enter. Lollie told me to break a foot, or "whatever the human showbiz saying was," and Larry guided me into the ring.

The moment we passed through the tent's opening, Larry's demeanor shifted from awkward and sweet to cold and domineering. He was one hell of an actor.

His steps were quaking, and the butt of his spear clanked against the ground with every step. My nipple piercings gently clanked as I trailed behind him, following him to the center of the ring.

The butterflies in my belly turned to hornets when I took in the scene waiting for us beneath the spotlight's glare.

The bed was one of the largest I'd ever seen, made of crude iron and fitted with sheer red curtains that were tied back so every seat in the house would have an unobstructed view.

Riff and Raff were in the middle of the bed, kneeling side by side with their heads bowed and their wrists bound together.

Metal collars were fastened around their throats, each one secured to the bed's canopy by a heavy chain.

Black Hannibal Lector-style masks were strapped over their faces, with metal bars covering their mouths and thick straps buckled over their hair and behind their heads. The red-painted portion of their faces looked so brutally gorgeous, peeking out from the black leather.

The basic story was that The Hell Bat was Discord's newly claimed mate and queen. The obvious mark on my thigh was all part of the costume. Little did the audience know, it wasn't makeup.

"A gift from your mate, My Queen," Larry growled in his stage voice. "They are brothers and well trained in the art of pleasure."

I caught Alistair's emerald gaze burning into me from the shadows, where he lurked at the far side of the ring. Beside him were the two gleaming red eyes of his shadow. The mark on my thigh had healed into a silvery scar, but it stung like it was new every time the ringmaster looked in my direction.

Now that he'd marked me, I figured we'd become closer. *Wrong*.

Over the last few days, we'd hardly exchanged more than a few words.

In truth, I was pissed at him. He told me he'd come clean about what he was keeping from me in regard to my mother and her reasons for conceiving me once Daemon returned.

So where the hell was he?

"They're waiting for you, My Queen," Alistair mouthed.

My eyes narrowed in as deadly a glare as I could manage with my rosy pink eyes.

I had every reason to hate being this dark god's pet. But I didn't.

No matter how much he frustrated and confused me, I loved being his. I loved that he seemed to have an obsession with sharing me with his other prized pets.

I'd willingly sold my soul to the devil and his little sideshow of sin. And I was so fucking thankful I had. I'd found my family, my mates. My purpose...

So why couldn't I shake the sickening feeling that I was on the verge of losing it all?

Was it just PTSD after what happened to Walker's? Even if doom was on the horizon for Sinner's Sideshow, what was I supposed to do but hold tight to my new family and keep on smiling for the audience? Because even if the world started to crumble around us...

The show had to go on.

21
Milk the Crowd

MEG

The only things I hated about being in the ring at Sinner's Sideshow were the disgusting noises. The grunting, the heavy breathing, the lewd sounds of rutting monsters in the audience. Usually, they fucked themselves, but occasionally they'd screw each other, sometimes people they'd come with or sometimes complete strangers. We'd even started an orgy or two.

I liked being watched.

What I wasn't a fan of were the noises of other men who weren't mine. Especially when they catcalled and shouted at the twins about how they wanted to see me fucked. Whenever that happened, my incubi would invade my every sense so that all I saw, all I felt, all I heard was them.

I looked back at the bed where Riff and Raff were chained and muzzled.

Tonight wasn't going to be like that.

I closed my eyes for a moment and thought back to the breathing tips my father had given me when the jitters flared up.

Breathe in. Breathe out.

"That's right, angel," his voice echoed somewhere in the back of my memory. *"Just like that. Always focus on your breathing. And don't lock your knees."*

I opened my eyes, tempered my nerves, and strode toward the bed with my head held high. I wrinkled my nose at them in mock distaste, which was hard considering they looked so fucking hot my succubus urges demanded I throw myself in bed with them now—the show be damned.

"If they are well trained in the art of pleasure, why are they chained up like rabid dogs?"

"They may be resistant to serve you, My Queen," Larry answered from where he stood diligently beside the bed—far enough to be respectable for a guard and close enough to respond should his queen need anything. "They are among your new subjects who are not pleased that their god has chosen a human mate."

"Half human," I corrected on a dark purr as I sauntered to the foot of the bed and slowly unfurled the wings from my back.

The audience—mostly the males—hollered and whooped in delight. Thankfully, that's when the music started. "Monsters" by Ruelle drowned out most of the noise from outside the ring, allowing me to slip into a world all our own.

As I approached, the twins tensed, and their fangs bared from behind the metal bars covering their mouths. Their animosity was so convincing it had me pausing to feel out their auras. All I could parse was lust so thick I could barely breathe.

I allowed the desire and the music to roll through me, my hips moving to the beat as I stepped up onto the bed.

A bar suspended over us ran from one end of the bed to the other, where their chains were hooked. I held onto the chains for balance as I strode across the plush mattress and slid them up the bar as I walked.

I felt sexier than ever, feeling the twins' eyes track the motion of my nipple jewelry as the chains and charms swayed back and forth.

I placed my bare foot on Riff's chest. The corners of my mouth curved at the way his heart thundered beneath my sole. Slowly, I pushed him back into a lying position on the bed. He didn't fight it. For a moment, I kept my foot planted on his chest, enjoying the way the thin fabric covering his pelvis started to tent.

He liked being stepped on.

"You may not like that I'm a half-blood…" My tail snaked beneath the fabric and swept it back to reveal his erection. His cock piercings gleamed under the spotlight, making my mouth water. "But your bodies don't give a fuck. You're hungry, and you must feed."

Taking the chain, I looped it around Raff's throat and, with a jerk, yanked his head over his brother's cock.

"Spit."

The house went grave quiet as everyone held their breath in anticipation. Then, the loud hawk of Raff spitting a mouthful of salvia echoed through the big top.

My God, did he ham it up. Fat tendrils of spit dribbled from the hole in his mask and coated Riff's cock. I crouched down to get a better look at his glistening shaft. I loved how beads of spit streaked down the pronounced veins and over the metal barbells.

"Good, little fuck toy," I praised Raff, following it up with an unhinged laugh.

I'd been so nervous about this scene, but now that it was happening, it felt natural. And it made me feel powerful.

I took more slack from Raff's chain and looped a section of it around his neck, then around the base of Riff's cock. The chain was only so long, and since I still had much of it wrapping Raff's throat, it forced his face close to his brother's balls.

If he pulled back, he risked bruising his brother.

I looked down at Raff, whose cheek was pressed against his brother's upper thigh.

Fucking Hells. They looked so good in those leather half-masks—muzzled like feral dogs—and draped in chains.

"Stay just like that for me, boys."

Stepping over Riff, I straddled him and slowly lowered myself down onto his hips. His muscles strained in anticipation, but a hissing breath of frustration and pleasure whistled through the grate in his mask when I lowered my ass onto his stomach with his cock barely nudging my folds.

"You think you get your queen's pussy that easily?" I laughed again. "Oh, sweet little fuck twins. You're going to have to earn that."

Bracing my hands on the bed beside Riff's hips, I started to grind my clit against his cock. My mouth went slack, watching the sword tattoo on top of his shaft glide up and down, looking like it was disappearing inside me with the angle I was at.

I knew we were giving a spectacular show with the level of lust and excitement that settled over the crowd. Even Alistair was completely fixated because he wasn't even narrating or commenting on the act, which he always did.

Everyone was hypnotized, including ourselves.

"Fuck. Please, I need to be inside you," Riff whispered from behind his mask, his voice ragged with need.

"You heard me," I whispered back. "You're going to have to be a good boy for me and earn it."

Both of them hissed out a broken curse in Infernal tongue.

I bobbed up and down on Riff's hips, bringing my body down hard so my ass made a hard smacking sound that carried to the back of the ring and into the house. It was little details like that that made us pros.

When Riff's breathing turned into short, barreling huffs, and his cock started to twitch and throb, I set a harder pace. I pulled on Raff's leash, which cinched the chain around his throat and his brother's balls—choking them both.

I licked my lips, imagining the collar of bruises that would mark Raff's throat. Too bad they'd heal within the hour. Oh well. Soon, I'd mark them both with something a little more permanent.

Riff came with a masculine groan, and a torrent of pearly cum oozed from his tip. I canted my hips and smeared his cum over my seam.

"Look what a mess your brother's made. Clean me."

Raff blinked at me, trying to process how he was supposed to lick me clean with the leather mask still strapped over his head. A beat later, his eyes darkened as it clicked. The mask made it impossible for him to properly lick.

He'd have to suck.

Our eyes locked. One of those silent looks he usually shared with his brother passed between us, the kind where we could have a whole conversation without saying a word.

This was a force play scene, so it was my move.

"Fuck you, whore queen," he seethed. "You're lucky your pig muzzled me. Otherwise, I'd tear your pussy to fucking shreds."

I jerked again on his chain, which knocked a strangled scream from both of them as the chain pulled tighter around Raff's throat and Riff's balls. My other hand gripped his horn and moved his face so he was a kiss away from Riff's cock.

"I said *clean me*. If I have to repeat myself again, I'll make you eat your brother's dick. And I'm undecided on whether I'll leave it attached or not."

The demon seemed taken aback for a moment, then quickly recovered with a dark little laugh.

Like he was impressed with how well I was pulling off this evil succubus queen thing.

He took his brother's cock and swept it out of the way, then fitted his masked face against my center.

A shiver worked through me as his breath came out harsh and heavy from behind his mask. Beads of perspiration streaked a path through the red paint smeared over his eyes, and strands of electric green hair clung to his brow.

I took him by the horn and guided his mouth closer, the space between us shrinking at an agonizing pace. Teasing shit out like this was torture. We were sex demons. Sometimes we were so hard up for it we needed a quick, hard fuck.

But that wasn't what this was.

Alistair was very particular with how his show ran. He wanted his audience to walk away as sated and satisfied as we did. So it was our job to drag out this filth and milk the crowd for every drop of cum they had.

I sucked in a breath when Raff's mouthpiece wedged between my thighs. The bars covering the little hole over his mouth were warm from his breath and felt surprisingly good. From where I sat, I had a perfect view of his round ass with his tail swishing back and forth. He gripped his brother's knees for purchase, the muscles in his back shifting, and he got comfy between the cradle of my thighs.

Anticipation thickened the air. The twins were dragging this out more than usual. Then, when I caught Raff's line of sight darting to the side of the ring where Alistair watched us, it all snapped into place.

Tonight was a lot of firsts for us. My first show as The Hell Bat. My first time topping the twins.

And this was their first time performing with the knowledge that their god was watching.

I tugged on his horn, guiding his attention back to my center. "Eyes on me, fuck toy. While you're in my bed, between my legs, *I* am your god."

My words seemed to have a magical effect on Raff. He smashed his face into my pussy, and *sucked* like his life depended on it. Intense pleasure shot through me, making my thighs tremble.

Raff's eyes darted up to peek at me through his mess of hair. "I fucking love the taste of my brother on you," the incubus rasped, his voice so muffled by the leather and my pussy that there was no hope for anyone outside the bed to hear.

"Oh, Discord, *yes.*"

The bars of his mask glided over my soaking flesh with ease. They were close enough together that they prevented him from slipping the entirety of his tongue out. He could only manage the tip, but fuck, it felt good as he swapped between suctioning my clit into the narrow hole of the mask and prodding my swollen flesh with the point of his tongue.

My head tipped back on my shoulders, and Larry came into view. A diabolical idea bloomed in my mind.

I liked the sensation of the mask between my legs so much…

"G–guard. Put my new pets on their knees."

Larry stomped forward and reached up to the bar over our heads, unfastening the chains and clutching them in his hand. He tugged at their chains and pulled them off the bed. "You heard your queen. On your knees."

"We're not kneeling for some half-blood whore queen."

I crawled off the bed and prowled over to where they stood. I held out my claw-tipped hand, and Larry placed their chains in my waiting palm. "You will submit to me…On your knees. *Now!*"

My eyes glowed pink as my succubus charm shimmered through the ring's heavy atmosphere. A look of pure shock flashed across Riff and Raff's faces as they crumpled to their knees suddenly. My hand slapped over my mouth.

They weren't acting. I'd forced them to their knees with my charm powers. Which made no sense. It wasn't supposed to work on other sex demons.

The mark on my thigh was burning up, and the warmth spread through me like a fever.

My eyes scanned the dark for Alistair, and I found him, looking not the least bit surprised.

Like he knew all along that my powers were stronger now because of our mating bond.

It made me wonder: what else was the devil hiding from me?

22

Every Twisted Girl's Dream

MEG

"We'll unpack this later, Meg." Riff hissed beneath his breath. "Keep the show going."

With the tiniest nod, I took a breath and snapped back into character.

I slowly circled them, winding the chains around their necks. "Once you get a taste of me, you'll submit."

They looked so good on their knees, glaring up at me with mock hatred. Most girls wouldn't have found the creepy masks as fucking hot as I did. They were like something straight out of Silence of the Lambs. Something only dangerous asylum inmates and rabid animals wore. Plus, the leather strap. The buckles. The chains.

It was every twisted girl's dream.

I planted myself between them and turned so Riff was facing my front and Raff my back. I lifted my skirt, revealing my bare pussy. "Now be a good pet and eat. I know you must be starving."

Riff's eyes bulged. His lust spiked the air. The strip of cloth covering his cock peaked with his thickening erection. He pushed his masked face into my center and inhaled. The little hairs on the back of my neck stood at his sucking breath, breathing in the fine coils of my pubic hair.

He slid his head lower, angling his neck so his cheeks were flush with my inner thighs and the mask's mouthpiece hovered over my clit. My eyes rolled back as he started to suck, just as his twin had.

I craned my neck, tossing a glance back at Raff. My tail twisted, lifting the back of my skirt to expose the globes of my full ass. "Two of you, two holes."

Raff's glower faltered. I could see the wicked glee in his eyes. We'd shared an act for a little over a month now, and there weren't a ton of things we hadn't done on stage.

Putting anything around my ass other than a cock was on the short list of shit we hadn't tried.

He gripped my ass cheeks, the chain manacling his wrists together cold against the back of my legs. His face pushed between my ass cheeks, and the small portion of his tongue that fit through the mask painted a lick over the tight ring of muscle.

These two were pros in the art of oral sex, but the mask added an extra challenge. Everything was sloppier. Sucking and licking as much as the cages over their mouths would allow.

My hips writhed in slow, undulating motions, grinding against the metal bars on his mask.

The crowd started to cheer and jeer, chanting "make her cum" over and over.

This seemed to egg the twins on, driving their pace into a frenzy.

The pleasure was so intense that I could barely keep myself upright. I reached down and took their horns, one in each hand for purchase.

The bliss consumed me. My awareness of everything slipped into white noise. The only thing my senses could process were the twins and what they were doing to me. It was hard to keep control over the sensation when all I could do was hold onto them for dear life as they ate me alive.

My hips writhed in slow, undulating motions, grinding against the metal bars of their masks, searching for completion. I tried to scream, but no sound came out as my brutal climax crashed over me, stealing the breath from my lungs.

I blinked down at Riff, who'd angled his head to catch the arousal dripping from me. There was so much—was I squirting? I could barely make sense of what was happening. The noise from the audience was disorienting. The air smelled of sex and strange monsters. Raff pushed between my legs, his tongue sliding and slipping over the bars and licking up every drop of my cum he could capture through his mask.

There was so much of it dribbling into the mouthpiece that he sputtered and coughed, struggling to breathe. They didn't care. They acted as though they'd never tasted anything sweeter, like two men who'd been stranded in the desert and were fighting over the last few drops of water.

"That's it, fuck toys." I grinned down at him, loving the way the cool metal bars felt against my burning flesh. "Drink me in. Take every drop your queen gives you."

As the afterglow started to ebb, I became all too aware of the crowd. They huffed and hollered, throwing food and other random shit into the ring. Demanding more.

We'd gotten carried away, our influence driving them past orgy levels into full-on monstrous mob territory.

"Make them fuck each other!"

"Cut off their dicks and make The Butcher eat them!"

"Fuck their corpses!"

My stomach heaved, and bile burned my throat at their dark suggestions.

Sometimes, I forgot how horrible our "fans" could be. We traveled all over, so depending on the area, the kind of monsters that frequented the shows were hit or miss. Some were great. Others were rowdy and straight-up evil pricks. Tonight, we'd gotten the latter, and the lust that always leeched into the air when we fucked was like giving bath salts or some other mind-melting narcotic to psychopaths.

This was the part where I let Alistair control the crowd. He was the ringmaster; that was his job. That would have been the reasonable thing to do.

But fuck that shit.

With a growl, I stomped over to Larry, plucked his halberd from his hand, and pointed it menacingly at the crowd with my teeth bared and my wings spread. I felt like the eye of the storm, and my fury raged around me like a maelstrom.

"What makes you pathetic filth think this is an audience participation act?"

I stabbed the weapon into the first death seat that came into focus—a troll who was touching himself.

The deadly point plummeted straight into his throat, severing his head. The crowd fell silent just in time for the smack of his head hitting the floor to echo through at least the first few rows.

Even as his body slouched over, his hand gave one, two more pumps to his cock before falling out of his seat beside his head with his bare ass out, blood pooling around him.

23

Homecoming

DAEMON

I woke up to a wet tongue licking my face. I blinked up at the night sky, one of my hounds coming into my field of vision. She whined, and I reached up to scratch her behind the ears, hissing as pain flared through me. "G–good girl. Ow—Fuck."

I pulled myself up into a sitting position, my arm clutching my gut wound as I took a headcount of my dogs with my heartbeat in my throat.

Hela.

Jax.

Juno.

Lilith.

Guts.

Kali.

I blew out a great breath of relief even as a jagged knife of pain ripped through my insides. All six of my hounds were alive. Bruised and cut up all to Hell, and Guts seemed to have a broken leg. But they all lived.

I'd done it. I'd escaped. But my mission had failed, which was a first.

Killing Lilith would mean taking down The Horsemen of the Apocalypse, too.

Everything came rushing back.

I'd successfully intimidated Death into removing the spear, allowing me to shift. My pack's distraction had been enough to snatch up one of the Horsemen as a gift to Alistair. If I couldn't bring back Astrid's body, I sure as fuck wasn't coming back with my tail between my legs, empty-handed.

Conquest was passed out in the grass beside me, with his own spear protruding from his shoulder. My lips twitched with the ghost of a grim smile. What was that saying? Something about the taste of one's own medicine?

The adamantine would prevent him from shifting, at least long enough for me to present him to Alistair. I lifted my gaze to the black and white striped tent on the horizon. I must have shifted back to my human form when I stepped onto the circus camp.

Using Juno for leverage, I hauled myself to my feet. Shockwaves of pure agony racked my system, and my stomach wept tears of red—leaving bloody footprints in the grass as I started for Alistair's caravan.

Hela took the end of the spear in her mouth and dragged Conquest along beside me.

There was a show tonight, so Alistair would be in the big top with everyone else. Good. I'd have time to clean up.

I couldn't go to Meg and Alistair looking the way I did. Crusted in filth. I'd been away from them for so long that it would be hard not to throw one of them down and bury myself inside. Gaping stomach wound or not.

The moment I entered the caravan with my pack, the room shifted into a warehouse with all sorts of twisted torture tools. I sighed. "Just the usual front room will do."

The caravan hadn't completely misread me. Conquest was in for a lot of hurt, but it would be Alistair doing the torturing, not me.

The room shifted back to the trinket and book-stuffed space that was Alistair's bedroom. The only difference was that the caravan had made the room a little larger than usual, as if it knew my dogs would be staying to guard our new guest.

I picked Conquest up by his spear and stabbed the spear into the mattress, the weapon sticking straight up. I stood at the foot of the bed for a few seconds, admiring the way his blood bloomed over the white sheets. Humans left rose petals on their lover's bed. I left the bodies of bad men to be turned into suits of flesh for his shadows to inhabit.

I instructed my dogs to stand guard and trudged into the back room for a shower. The caravan never created anything for me with frills. Just a serviceable bathroom, this time with some basic medical supplies.

The wound would heal on its own, but the adamantine would slow the process. It'd probably scar. A chill spread through me like ice even as I stepped into the shower's scorching water.

I was lucky I'd gotten away.

But they'd be coming to us this time…Especially after we killed Conquest.

We'd have to come up with a plan to get Alistair fed and fast. He'd need to wreak more terror than what the Circus did alone to fuel his powers and grant him full control over his true form.

I got out of the shower, dressed my wound, and pulled out a fresh change of clothes, a form-fitting black t-shirt and pants. I considered going to my trailer to get into my Bitch Tamer costume, but Alistair wouldn't want me performing tonight.

When I approached the big tent, the tell-tale signs of a wild-fucking show invaded my senses. The pungent scent of sweat and blood and cum burnt my nostrils, and screams and cheers and grunts deafened my acute hearing.

It had to be the sex demons act. No one else could excite the crowd like this.

I slipped through the backyard where we kept the dressing rooms and ring stock tents, ignoring the stunned looks on the troupe's faces.

"He's back."

"Who do you think he's killed this time?"

"Wonder what he'll say when he sees Meg's new mating mark?"

I stopped dead in my tracks and slowly turned my heated glare on the monster who'd whispered that last line. It was one of the clowns from the harpy milking act.

"What did you just say?"

His hands wrung the straps of his overalls. "Uh...um...uh."

Clowns weren't exactly my thing, at least not this kind of clown. But there was something about pure terror on a face slathered with an exaggerated smile that I found hilarious.

My arm shot out to seize the gangly fuck by the throat. "Who marked her?"

He sputtered and choked, and his face started to turn purple beneath his white face paint. I leaned closer so all he'd see was my twisted sneer and razor-sharp canines. "I could snap your neck, and no one would bat an eyelash."

"It was the boss! The ringmaster claimed her the night you left."

My brows contorted with confusion. Then my glower deepened as rage set in. "If you're lying to me, if this is just troupe gossip, I'll be back to feed you to my dogs."

I released my grip on his throat, and he crumpled to his knees at my feet. I turned and charged off, leaving his pathetic wheezing and the murmurs of "he's fucking psychotic" behind me.

Slipping through the big top's back entrance, my eyes went straight to the spotlight that illuminated the giant bed at the center of the ring.

The sight that greeted me had all the blood in my body sinking straight to my dick.

Fuck. Me.

In one month, our little half-blood had become the shining star in our filthy little creep show. It was easy to see why.

Meg was perfection incarnate.

She was wearing the sexiest outfit I'd ever seen on her. If it could be called that, with how much of her milky skin was showing. She was topless, with custom nipple jewelry—Roach's work, no doubt—that incorporated the obsidian charms marking her as a follower of Discord. She was still wearing my collar, and on top of her head, almost a little too big for her, was my Bitch Tamer cap.

But the best part of the whole scene was the fact that she had her little chainmail skirt pushed up over her hips with the twins on their knees on either side of her, eating out both her holes as best as the leather masks on their faces would allow. They were dressed similarly, though there were a few details to indicate that they were much lower on the demon food chain. They were royal court sex slaves, to be exact, complete with collars and manacles.

I ground my teeth at the way my cock ached, seeing them like this. *Worshipping* her.

The fuck clowns got on my nerves for a lot of reasons, but I couldn't deny how good they looked with my pup. How good they made her feel. How much she loved them.

She had a hand on each of their horns, her knuckles going ghost white with how tightly she held onto them. Her face tipped to their heaves, her features twisted in pleasure as she mouthed their names between breathless little huffs.

There was something hypnotic about these three in the ring. They were in their own little world, and I found myself wondering what it would be like to be a part of it all.

When I found my attention settling on a scar so large it wrapped around her entire upper thigh, it was like a bucket of cold water had been thrown over my head.

So it was true. Alistair had marked her.

I desperately searched the darkness for the ringmaster. Sure enough, he wasn't far off. Even he was transfixed by the trio's performance. He was sitting down in one of the death seats when he was supposed to be commentating, but then again, a show like this didn't need any embellishments.

The moment I stalked near, his attention flicked up to settle on me, and the world around us seemed to freeze.

I'd known Alistair for most of my life. It had been so long that I'd lost count of how many years we'd been together. Centuries. When he'd found me shortly after I murdered who I thought had been my true mate, I'd been nothing but a wild hellbeast.

He'd made me so much more. My master, my god, my lover. For so long, he'd been my everything until she came into our lives.

Now, I had to figure out how to walk the line of being a loyal, obedient servant to my master and protecting Megaera.

Unlike him, I kept my promises. So, I had every intention of giving him my mark. They'd both be mated to me.

But if I was forced to choose, I'd pick her every single time.

"You fucking lied to me. You told me you wouldn't fuck her." My voice was more than a whisper, but no one seemed to notice. Everyone was too fixated on the debauchery unfolding in the ring.

I wanted to be angry. I *was* angry, to the point where smoke started to rise off my skin. But the expression on Alistair's face was like another bucket of ice water being dumped on me, putting out the flames that burned within an instant. He wasn't smiling or giving me that smug, smooth-as-sin look.

The devil had tears in his eyes.

I'd never seen him get emotional. *Ever.*

"Daemon." Relief flooded his voice. "You're alive."

24

Filthy Things

DAEMON

Just like that, the miasma of emotions raging within me turned to nothing but a bitter numbness that spread through my body, leaving me frozen as I stood there, gaping at my master in disbelief. "You thought I was dead?"

Had Alistair really spent the last three days thinking I was gone? No wonder he looked like he'd never known a day of sleep, with dark circles lining his eyes.

"I didn't know what came of you. You were taking so long. You weren't answering your phone, and I almost came looking for you, but...." His voice trailed off as his eyes shifted back to Meg. "I couldn't shake the feeling that somehow, that's what Lilith wanted."

"It *was* what she wanted."

He nodded as if he wasn't the least bit surprised. "She meant to use you as bait the whole time. She knew I'd come looking for you eventually. And I almost did—I *should* have. What kind of master am I to just leave you to your fate?"

His voice was normally so strong, steel wrapped up in silk. But his tone was coming out so fragile and vulnerable.

Like he hated himself for leaving me.

I took a seat beside him, trying not to wince from the simple movement. I didn't want to give him any more reason to worry. "I'm so fucking glad you didn't come."

"I know you hate when I interfere. You don't like me questioning your ability to complete the tasks I give you."

"Master. I failed. Lilith lives."

The silence was filled with the beat of the music accompanying the demonic trio's act. The beat was so loud I felt it in my body like it was trying to beat right out of my chest. Or was that just my heart?

Alistair's demeanor turned so cold I could see my puffs of breath hanging in the air between us. "Explain."

"She has The Horsemen of the Apocalypse on her side. Except for Famine, I think."

Alistair's knuckles cracked as they tightened on his cane, which was planted between his feet, always looking like a supervillain with that thing. "They wouldn't betray me for that harpy. They wouldn't be that stupid."

"Think about it," I growled. "She's been after your mark for eons. Sucking up to you hasn't worked, has it? So now she's resorted to blunt force. In exchange for the Horsemen's help in securing your mating bond, she's promised to use her new authority to permit them to—"

"To bring about the apocalypse to the Upside," he said with a weighted sigh.

My lip curled thinking of the last three days I'd spent watching her fuck Conquest and War. "Plus, other incentives."

The shade's hand lifted from his cane to massage his temple. "I'm disappointed in their betrayal, but I suppose it's not all that surprising, is it? They wish to fulfill their purpose. After all, I created them for destruction back when I was nothing but a vengeful young god."

"You've changed. You're better now."

"Not according to them. To them, I'm weak." His lips pressed into a thin line. "They're right."

I swallowed, wishing I could lubricate the dryness in my throat, but the only liquid I seemed capable of producing was blood. So much blood. Luckily, Alistair hadn't yet noticed the hole in my gut. "We just need to get you fed. This circus produced enough terror for you to fuel your hydra form for weeks."

"Yes, back when it was nothing but a slaughterhouse. Why do you think people hate clowns so much? Why do they appear in so many mortal movies wielding knives and splatter in guts and blood? Sinner's Sideshow birthed that delightful little trope, Pet. This is all fine and well, but who are we going to kill? I won't kill innocents. I refuse to go back to what I was."

I looked back at Meg, my dick tightening against the restraints of my pants as she came against the twins' mouths with a silent scream. "We should tell Meg. We have to tell her everything."

To my surprise, the ringmaster nodded. "I agree. I'm done with all the secrets."

Thank fuck. I was done with the secrets, too. It felt so fucking wrong lying to her. I hated having to walk that line between following Alistair's wishes and being the best mate I could be for Megaera.

"I am curious, though..." Alistair's words were tight and shadowed with something that had the hairs on my nape standing. "How exactly were the Horsemen planning on aiding Lilith in her mission to mark me?"

I tensed. "How does one rape a starving god? Get three other well-fed archdemons to hold him down."

He chewed his bottom lip in thought. The air around him was so cold now that frost started to accumulate on the armrests of our chairs. "Straight forward, I suppose."

There was a lot of shit we had to work out. We'd probably have to get the entire troupe in on it. Meg—and probably the twins, too—would have to be let in on certain details. Because the Horsemen would show up, and she'd have questions. With her stubbornness, she'd never let up until everything was out in the open. Hell, by how exhausted Alistair looked, she'd probably done nothing but berate him with questions on where I was and when I'd be back.

Maybe he'd fucked her just to fill her mouth with something other than a million questions.

"I kept my promise. You asked me to keep my cock out of her cunt, and I did just that. Not that wriggling my way inside her via a loophole makes things any better. I still lost control." The corners of his mouth quirked into a sly grin befitting of the devil. "And I can't say I'm sorry, either."

"Alistair. I asked you not to. You can't control your other form as you are. You could have killed her."

"Well, I didn't," he said, his tone clipped.

I shook my head, trying to imagine how such a hydra could mate with a five-foot-tall half-blood succubus without stretching her out like an overused rubber band. To forge a mating mark, a demon had to enter their partner in true form and bite.

As if he could sense me trying to puzzle it out, he laughed and twirled a lock of his dark hair around his pinky finger. "I was *creative.*"

What was that supposed to mean?

A dozen other questions burned the tip of my tongue. This would have been his first time with a female.

The shit I would have done to see that. Had he dominated her?

With me, he was usually submissive, but I knew how he could be. Alistair loved being in control, especially these days when he was slowly losing his power, which was all a side effect of going against his true nature.

Had he made her beg for his mark? Knowing Meg, it had probably been her idea first. I bet the brat had been rethinking her decision when she saw just how big Alistair's monster form was.

Seeing that mark on her thigh had pissed me off when I'd first seen it. I thought he'd broken yet another promise. I mean, he was right. Worming his way through a loophole didn't make things much better. He'd lost control, which was exactly why I'd wanted him to keep away from her little holes in the first place, but hadn't hurt her. And seeing our master's mark on her thigh—knowing she was just as bound to him as I was—did dirty things to me.

Soon, she'd carry my mark, too.

And the twins'.

I waited for jealousy to set in. It didn't.

The more we marked that gorgeous skin, the more she'd be ours. Each mark was like another collar clamping around her gorgeous body, chaining her to us. The more we marked her, the more obsessed we'd all become. The more obsessed, the harder we'd fight for her. The harder we fought, the safer she'd be.

And her safety was more important than the alpha urge to keep her all for myself.

Alistair inhaled his fingers drumming impatiently against the golden hellhound's head that made up the grip of his cane. "Now that we've gotten that out of the way, I think a kiss is in order."

I gave him a dark grin, captured his chin between my fingers and pulled his lips to mine in the sweetest kiss we'd ever shared.

As if we were in love. As if creatures like us were capable of such things.

After a beat, I broke the kiss and leaned back to flash him a grin. "I may not have brought back Lilith's body for you, but I did bring you a souvenir from my travels."

His perfectly arched brows hiked high on his forehead and disappeared beneath the brim of his ringmaster's hat. "A souvenir?"

We all spoke fluent English, even though Infernal was our native tongue. Sometimes, though, certain words were lost on us. We traveled all over, but few of us ventured far from the circus grounds. He struggled to find the word, but then his eyes brightened with understanding. "Like a magnet or a keychain?"

I chuckled, thinking back to the way Conquest's body looked. "Something like that, yeah."

Before he could ask me to elaborate, the crowd went wild from the strong doses of pheromones leeching into the air. Sometimes this happened. Being around sex demons, especially three incredibly hot sex demons, wasn't something every monster could handle.

They started to jeer and shout for more, even tossing in disturbing suggestions that had Larry and the sex demons tensing in discomfort.

This was bad. Sinner's Sideshow was a monster circus. Our customers were vile, cutthroat, bloodthirsty beasts. This had to be nipped in the bud before it got out of hand.

I started to stand and held my hand out to summon my whip, but Alistair's shadow was in front of me, pushing me back into my chair.

"Sit, Pet. Let's see what our little demon does. She has my mark, after all."

I blinked at him. "You haven't told her yet, have you?"

Alistair sent me a sharp look which was the only answer I needed. No, of course, he didn't tell her. But telling Meg about her mother was a huge step for him. That conversation would lead to why Astrid was so hard up for a mating bond with Discord.

The power that came along with being mated to a demon of his stature.

Megaera was quick to react to the rioting crowd. She grabbed Larry's weapon and stabbed some random fuck in one of the death seats.

I groaned, my hand finding my dick over my jeans and squeezing as I imagined it was her cunt wrapped around me instead of my fist. "She just slayed her first death seat."

Alistair chuckled. "Beautiful."

Fucking *Hells*. Seeing her standing over that corpse did filthy, wicked things to me.

She turned back around with the most sinister smile I'd ever seen her wear. A smile that went straight to my dick.

"Guard, clean that up." The little pink-haired, five-foot-tall demoness was a pro at ordering around demons three times her size. Her voice had all the confidence of a queen. No, a goddess.

My mouth began to water with the urge to get on my knees before her and worship her.

Larry swung the corpse over his meaty shoulder, sending a spray of blood across the ring. Some of it spattered onto the twins, who didn't so much as flinch.

I hated to admit it, but the clowns looked good, covered in the blood of our girl's victims.

Four days. It had been four fucking days since I'd been inside her. It was too long. And she looked too damn good wearing my collar and cap for me to sit this one out a second longer.

She needed to wear me too.

I snapped to my feet, moving a little too fast. White hot pain spiked through my system, and I stumbled. Alistair's shadow caught and steadied me. Dread chased away the pain when I felt Alistair's glare burning into my back. "Pet. Turn around and remove your shirt."

Slowly, I pivoted to face him. Holding him glare for glare, I peeled my shirt over my head and dumped it onto the ground at his feet.

Alistair's pale features hardened as his eyes traveled down my torso. I'd done a shotty job at dressing my wounds. It's not like I was used to it. I usually walked off most injuries, but this was the first time I'd been stabbed with a metal meant for killing demons.

The bandages were already so clogged with blood that tracks of crimson streaked down my stomach and matted the fine trail of hair stretching from my navel to my groin.

"You look like you had an erotic rendezvous with an adamantine weapon."

"Yeah, well, Conquest did kind of fuck me."

His lips slanted with a frown. "You need to rest."

I resisted the urge to laugh in his face. "Right. Rest. What's the worst that can happen? I bleed all over the sex demons? They love that shit."

Alistair's brows knitted together when he realized what I meant to do. "They'll eat you alive."

I stepped in front of Alistair's seat and leaned over, bracing one hand on his arm while my other hand quickly worked to undo the buttons of my fly.

His eyes gleamed as I released my cock, then darkened when he took in the deep cut running along the base. "Who fucking did that to you? Who touched what's mine?"

My stomach tightened at the calm rage embedding his words, sending a fresh wave of stabbing pain into my gut. If we weren't in the big top, holding a show right now, he wouldn't bother reigning in his wrath.

"Your old friend Death. He came this close to cutting off my cock." I held up my fingers in front of Alistair's face to demonstrate. "*This* close. So, if you don't mind, Master, I'm going to go celebrate the fact that it's still attached."

I dropped my hand to Alistair's lap, my fingers working quickly to free his cock. It sprung out, long and thick. With delicate stitching made out of the finest threaded magic, holding the dead flesh together. I'd miss this cock. But the human form of a demon would better contain his shadows.

I stepped to the side and reached for his shadowbeast, taking hold of its horn and guiding it to take my place in front of Alistair. I brought the toe of my combat boot to the back of his knee and applied enough pressure to make him fall to his knees. Shoving on his horn, I pushed his head down into Alistair's lap.

Since his entire body was translucent, I could see the shade's cock slipping into the mouth of his own shadow.

Alistair's head tipped back onto his chair's headrest, and a delicious moan dropped from his perfect lips. "*Oh*. Daemon...I've missed you."

There was a tightening feeling in my chest, a warm, tingling sensation that seemed to numb some of the pain. He'd never spoken so sweetly to me before.

I couldn't help thinking that this was Meg's doing. That bratty little five-foot half-blood was changing us. She had a way of peeling back our layers and exposing humanity we'd never known we possessed. She was, after all, the one who'd gotten Alistair to admit that he loved me the night he'd given me the key to her chastity belt.

A slow smile took over my face. "I missed you too. Now, all I want you to do is sit back and enjoy your favorite pets, all together, on stage for the first time."

25

Fever Dream

MEG

For a moment, time stood still inside the black and white big top. Every eye in the tent was fixed on me. The air thickened with an intense cluster-fuck of emotions that had my head spinning. Fear. Lust. Shock. *Respect*—That was a new one.

I'd just murdered someone. It wasn't the first time. I'd killed the ghoul in the haunt for assaulting that poor bunny shifter, and I'd cut up the three haunt workers for trying to do the same to me until they were nothing but puddles of piss and blood. But this was different. This monster had been an innocent.

This was the part where guilt was supposed to kick in.

I waited. Nothing. Not so much as an iota of regret. Maybe because he'd purposefully bought a death seat with the intent of being sent to Hell in style.

No. That explained the lack of guilt, not the wicked glee I'd felt seeing his blood bloom from his body and spread between my bare toes.

I pushed off the troubling thought; just another thing to unpack later.

Riff and Raff were still on their knees, looking so damn delectable with their leather masks drenched in my arousal. I crouched in front of them, pretending I was just gathering their chain leashes in my hand, but I was getting close enough to hear their muffled praises.

"That was so fucking sexy," Riff groaned.

Raff nodded his agreement. "First death seat kill. That's a cause for celebration."

I swallowed back a laugh. "Celebrate how? A party? Weed? More sex? We do that all the time anyway."

Raff's attention darted to the edge of the ring, and his green brows shot up in surprise. A breath later, the wrinkles at the corners of his eyes betrayed the smile beneath his mask. "I can think of something the three of us haven't done together yet."

Riff followed his line of sight, a curse in Infernal falling from the hole in his mask.

I turned to see what it was that had the incubi so speechless.

Daemon strode across the ring, looking like some kind of feral demon who'd just fought his way out of Hell. He was shirtless, his dark, wet hair slicked back behind his ears, wearing black pants that were undone and slung low on his hips. He'd been hurt badly. The gauze wrapping his abdomen was working hard to keep his guts in, and still, that didn't stop the cocky stride in his step as he approached.

Blood seeped from the bandages, streaking the defined V of his hips in blood. A thin sheen of sweat made his tattooed flesh glisten under the lights, and his citrine eyes burned like freshly smelted gold as they met my stare.

The atmosphere in the ring buzzed with his brutal eminence.

He was...fucking beautiful.

I wanted to throw myself into his arms and kiss him. I had a hundred questions ready to fire off. Where had he been? How had he gotten so hurt?

Now that he was here, Alistair needed to follow through on his promise of telling me all his secrets. Especially the ones about my mother.

I didn't follow any of those urges. We were doing a show. Hundreds of monsters were watching us with bated breath, waiting impatiently to be thrilled.

I fought my instincts to run to him and instead took several steps backward with my teeth bared and my claws extended in a defensive stance. "Who are you? What do you want?"

He took a step forward, then another, his pace set purposefully slow to build tension with the audience. He rolled his head to the side, his thick neck cracking. I licked my lips at the way his veins strained against his inked skin.

Before he'd even said a word, I knew he intended to fuck me in front of all these people. By the amount of blood he was losing, it wasn't exactly a smart idea. But this would be my first time with the alpha in the ring. Plus, the twins were here. There was no way they wouldn't get involved.

How could I say no to sharing all three of them? Especially when the pressure of everyone watching would force them to play nice.

His eyes slid down my body as he took me in, piece by piece. His cap on my head. His spiked collar around my throat. My bare tits and the way the chains draping from my nipples started to sway with my heaving chest as I took in breath after ragged breath.

"I'm here to free your slaves," he said in a dark voice that sank straight to my pussy.

My tail whipped the air in mock outrage. "Don't you know who I am? I am Discord's chosen! I am your queen!"

His expression was so severe, his gaze so heavy and intense that I battled the urge to squirm. "What you're about to be is my royal whore."

A shot of lust was injected straight into my core, sending sparks into my nerve endings. "Guard! Guard!"

"Oh, I slaughtered your pig. Made him squeal." Daemon laughed, the sound harsh and cruel and oh so sinful. "Now it's your turn."

My breath hitched.

My pussy clenched.

I was so turned on that arousal dribbled down my inner thighs.

I turned to run, but the last thing I wanted to do was escape.

"Catch her," Daemon commanded in a hell-deep baritone.

The twins snapped to their feet, and in the span of the same heartbeat, Riff grabbed me by my hair and shoved me face-first onto the bed. He slipped the chain of his manacles under my throat and pulled, forcing my spine to arch off the mattress.

I turned my head enough to see Daemon's combat boots come into my frame of vision, and he stooped to pick up his hat, which had fallen off my head. My heart hammered so hard against my ribs that it felt like it was going to explode out of my chest. Blood rushed to my cheeks. My head swirled with anticipation.

Daemon's heavy footsteps rung in my ears like the peel of a church bell, calling all sinners.

A moment later, there was a crack of metal and the clank of chains dropping to the ground.

Daemon snapped the padlocks off the twins with his bare hands. The chain was removed from my throat, and the weight of heated muscle lifted off me. I darted across the bed, trying to make a fake getaway. As I expected, Raff was already on the other side of the bed, pushing me back into the mattress.

His collar, mask, and manacles were gone. In their place were yummy indentations where the metal had pressed into his skin.

"What's the matter, My Queen?" he snickered, crawling onto the bed. "Didn't you want to screw us? That's why we're here, isn't it?"

"I don't want to fuck you anymore."

I scrambled backward, and my wings hit a warm, hard stomach. My head tilted back to find Riff—mask and collar free. His blue hair spilled into his eyes, and he grinned down at me with devilish intent. "Too bad it's you who doesn't have the choice now."

Raff grabbed my ankles and slid me across the bed so my back was flush with the mattress. Riff bent over the bed and pinned me down by my wings as his brother crawled on top of me.

"No!" I denied with a scream so every seat in the house could hear me.

Daemon closed the last distance left between him and the mattress, his stance wide at the foot of the bed. His hands gripped the footboard as he leaned over so his mouth was just inches from my ear and whispered, "We're gonna fuck you so hard, those screams are about to be real, Little Pup."

Raff pried my thighs apart, one hand biting into my thigh over my tattoo of the flaming circus tent and the other digging into Alistair's mating mark. He settled between my legs, his hand rubbing over my center and pushing a testing finger inside. He grinned down at me. Even without the clown paint exaggerating his smile, it was manic and too wide for anyone but twisted girls like me to find attractive.

"Oh fuck, she's dripping for it."

His finger pulled from my pussy, and he offered it up—to *Daemon.*

The Hellhound considered the digit, then, after a solid second of driving my pussy crazy with anticipation, he slipped

Raff's finger into his mouth and sucked it clean. He growled around the digit as my flavor hit his tongue.

While I was held captive by the dark sight that was Daemon's lips pursed around Raff, Raff used the distraction to drive his cock inside me. My head slammed back on the bed, and my mouth opened to unleash a scream, but Riff was waiting. He'd gotten himself out and rammed his erection past my lips and straight into my throat. Tears pricked my eyes as he fucked my mouth, setting a hard pace that matched his brother's.

I purred around his girth, knowing the audience couldn't hear my sounds of delight. Not that anyone bought the fact that I wasn't enjoying getting spit-roasted by the twins, with Daemon's shadow engulfing us.

He leaned closer to the point where his metallic, masculine scent tickled my nose. He smelled so good I could cry.

"You want to know a secret, Pup? Why I haven't shared the ring with you since the night we met?"

My eyes widened. It was the only movement I could manage as Riff and Raff pistoned in and out of me in perfect tandem.

"It's because I can't stand the thought of all these strange monsters drooling over you. Seeing your naked body, seeing how well we fill your pretty little holes, and knowing they're touching their unworthy flesh at the sight of you...It makes me feral with rage."

His eyes blazed with all the heat of the Hells. His fingers gripped the iron footboard so hard it started to bend under his brute strength. "It makes me want to crush every last one of their skulls. And knowing what I do and how badly our master needs to feast on their terror, I'm seriously considering doing just that."

26

"This Is Gonna Be Good"

RAFF

The hellhound was back.

There was a time, not that long ago, when I would have been more than happy if he'd gone off to do the boss' dirty work and never come back.

It was funny how much things could change, how much *we* changed. How one little half-blood had gone and fucked it all up.

And how we loved her for it.

Riff and I were happy to see the bastard. Fucking happy. And it went beyond feeling Meg's nerves ease now that she knew he was safe.

Hell, maybe I just had more respect for the hound altogether, knowing that he'd survived being Discord's favorite pet for all these years. Knowing he topped our literal god? Yeah, the guy deserved props for that.

He was the embodiment of domination. And by Discord's cock, did he look fucking good drenched in blood. We'd been stunned when he'd walked into the ring. It couldn't have been Alistair's idea, not with that gut wound. Daemon was ready to mate his little pup again, knowing that in the ring, the three of us were a package deal.

The four of us put on a show that had the entire house as still as the grave. Enraptured by the way we owned our Hell Bat. Because she was fucking perfection.

I hissed through my teeth, my fingers biting into her flesh hard enough to leave marks as I fucked into the crux of her thighs. "Such a good little whore. The perfect royal fleshlight."

At my words, Meg's pussy clenched tighter around my dick. As if it was trying to suck me in deeper, like it couldn't get enough even as Riff and I plunged inside her, giving her every inch of flesh we had to offer. Riff's hands palmed her tits and plucked at her nipple piercings, making her moan around his cock as he pulled her nipples to the point where little shivers of pain and pleasure had her muscles shivering.

"You want my brother to come in your mouth, don't you, *whore queen?*"

Riff pulled out of her mouth just long enough for her to manage a scream, crying out for the guard who wasn't coming. We shared a dark cackle, his hands wrapped around her throat over Daemon's collar before ramming himself back into her mouth.

"What's the matter, My Queen?" Daemon asked, leaning over her with his golden eyes cutting through the shadows the stage lights cast. "Isn't this what you wanted? To break in your new fuck toys? Well, they love playing in your holes."

Riff picked up his pace, shoving inside her so hard she started to choke and gag on his pierced cock as it rammed down her throat in a series of savage thrusts. He pulled out, fisted his base, and unloaded a spray of hot cum onto her face. Thick ropes of pearly white streaked her flushed cheeks, and her pink lashes batted, lids going heavy as her tongue snaked out to taste a few drops that had fallen on her lips.

It took every ounce of my willpower to pull out of her pussy. She whimpered at the loss, and I gave her a cold laugh in response. "What a filthy half-blood slut you are, so thirsty for demon cum."

Daemon ordered us to reposition her on the bed, and his steely commands had us racing to obey.

I took her by the hips and lifted her while Riff lay down on the bed. I lowered her onto his lap and crawled behind her, bringing my chest flush with her adorable little wings.

Daemon moved to the side of the bed and ran his inked knuckles over her cheek. "Is this the first time you're going to have two men take your ass and your pussy at the same time?"

Her rosy eyes rounded as she realized what we were about to do to her. She gave a nod, and his smirk turned feral.

"That's what I thought."

His thumb stroked her bottom lip, wiping up a bead of Riff's cum. "Open for me, Pup," he cooed in a tight and husky whisper.

Her lips parted for him, and he pushed the cum inside her mouth. "Now, open up wider, show him how pretty his spunk looks on your slutty little tongue."

Again, she obeyed. How could she not? His tone was hard steel coated in honey, making you too scared to disobey and too turned on to even consider it.

No wonder they called him The Bitch Tamer.

"Good girl," he praised. He wedged his hand between us, his fingers curling around the base of her tail, and with a tug, he guided her down on Riff's cock. "Now, be a good little whore queen and sit on your throne."

Riff's eyes glowed behind his contacts as he watched himself slowly disappear inside her. "Fuck. So tight."

"It's about to be so much tighter." Daemon got up on the bed behind me, so close I could feel his heat seep into the pores of my backside.

"Ooh, is this one of those things where I fuck her in the ass, and you fuck me, and your thrusts only push me deeper inside her? Cause I can get into that." I turned my head, flashing him one of my unhinged smiles that always seemed to piss him off.

This time, he only grinned back. "Yeah, I'm sure you'd love that, fuck clown. I'm not going to fuck you. But I am going to touch you unless you say the magic words, 'playtime's over.'"

My cock twitched at the way he held my eyes with that severe glower of his, giving me the safe word we had for Meg. I licked my lips. "Oh, this is gonna be good."

He reached up to grab my horn, wrenching my head around. "Eyes on me. I want you to watch this, Rafferty."

My lungs smacked together at the way he said my name, with the faintest hint of resentment etched into his face. Like he was tasting something he didn't want to like. I could feel Riff and Meg's eyes drilling into us, not daring to speak or even move for fear of breaking whatever spell this was binding us together.

I wasn't sure what I expected him to do. I was a perverted sex demon who worked as a clown for a living. There wasn't a lot of shit that surprised me.

But fuck me sideways, this motherfucker threw me for a goddamn loop when his free hand dipped into his bandages and pulled back out oozing blood—dripping it all over my cock.

He gripped my cock and gave one, two pumps to smear his blood around. The way his thumb tracked one of the veins rendered me speechless.

This was Daemon. He was supposed to hate us.

But he was touching me as if all that had been an act. As much a production as our over-stated fuck show.

He lined me up with Meg's ass, and she stiffened at the first kiss of my tip against the tight ring of muscle.

I smoothed my palm between her wings and pushed, gently guiding her to lay chest to chest with Riff. "Relax, baby. We got you."

Pleasure glazed her eyes as my brother's eight-inch dick shifted inside her, and the muscles in her little frame visibly unclenched.

"You've worn a lot of shit in the ring. So many costumes I don't know where you keep them all. But this right here..." Daemon canted his hips, slowly pushing my body into hers. "Wearing *her*. You imps have never looked fucking better."

27

Hell of a Show

MEG

I was so full.

I'd taken big dicks—among other things—before, but having one in my ass and one in my pussy at the same time was a sensation that had me seeing stars. It wasn't just the way they felt inside me that had my head spinning.

The fucking mouths on these men.

They knew exactly how to tweak and tease me. How to punish and praise.

And they were getting along!

No, they were more than just getting along...Watching Daemon with Raff was like witnessing a dark miracle unfold before me. The obscene things he whispered into his ear, the way he used his own blood to lubricate the clown's cock—working it up and down his shaft with his own hand.

If I'd known I was the bridge that would bring them together, I would have thrown myself between them a lot sooner.

The blood had Raff slipping inside my ass with ease. The alpha guided him in slowly, his pace torturous.

I glanced over my shoulder to see Daemon leaning over Raff, his mouth twisting into a sneer against his green hair. "Can you feel your brother's cock inside her?"

Raff gave a drunken nod, his grip on my waist tightening. I'd have bruises in the morning.

"Can f–feel his p–piercings."

"Oh my *God*," I moaned.

"He's not coming," Riff said, grinning up at me—a kiss away. "We're your gods now."

He took my horn and, with a tug, consumed the distance between us with a rough kiss. His tongue plunged inside my mouth, and our teeth bashing together every time Raff thrust into me from behind.

Fuck.

It felt so good.

Every savage thrust from Raff just angled Riff deeper inside me, making him hit a spot that had my eyes rolling into my head. When I thought the pleasure couldn't climb any higher, Daemon worked his hand between Riff and me—which in turn had Raff's chest pinning me tighter against his twin—to rub my clit.

The pressure in my belly tightened, and my insides fluttered around the clown cocks inside me.

I ripped my lips away from Riff's and bit out, "I'm going to come!"

"Scream your release, whore queen. Scream so loud your god can hear what we're doing to you."

A swollen, strangled scream wrenched from my throat. Someone—I wasn't sure who—jerked my horn and forced my attention to the ringside where Alistair sat. His emerald gaze burned bright enough to shed light on his face, which was contorted with pleasure.

Al, the shadowbeast, was on his knees in front of the ringmaster's chair with his head bobbing up and down in his lap. His own shadow was sucking him off.

Our eyes locked together from across the ring. An emotion I couldn't quite place flashed across his face. But then his lips parted on a silent moan, and he mouthed the words, "My Queen."

That was enough to send me hurtling over the edge. As I fell apart, Raff tensed, and he bore down on top of me, crushing me against his brother as he released a hot wash of fluid inside me. While Raff came, Riff held my stare, muttering quiet praises on how pretty I looked milking his brother's cock.

I slumped against Riff, our chests sweaty and knocking together with every labored breath we took. The bed shifted as Daemon climbed off and strode around to the side.

"It's time to go, sex devils," he told the twins, gesturing toward the exit with a nod. "You're free now."

The twins exchanged a look, understanding banked in their eyes.

Daemon wanted time on the stage alone with me.

Riff gave me one last kiss while Raff delivered a hard smack to my ass before they dumped me on the mattress and scrambled out of the ring, making a hasty exit with their signature unhinged laughter as they slipped out of the big top.

My attention turned back to Daemon as he stepped closer, his shadow falling over me on the bed. Even wounded, his intimidating presence was thick enough to choke on. He took his bloody fingers and stroked them over his onyx hair, slicking it back with his own life force.

"That was beautiful, whore queen..." His thumb hooked into his pants and slipped them down his hips. His cock sprung out, giving me a clear view of it for the first time. "But you're not done yet."

My mouth wet slack as I took in the alpha hellhound's girth.

I knew he was packing since he'd been the one to take my virginity when Alistair's chastity belt had come off, and I'd caught several glimpses of it through the dark.

But now I was face to face with it, and *holy mother of god*. The spotlight fell on him, lighting him up like a statue in a museum. He was beautiful. Hash lines and glistening skin. With a thick and full cock covered in a complex network of mouth-watering veins.

His body was covered in tattoos, some faded and ancient and some more modern human styles—probably Roach's work. Out of all his tattoos, one in particular captured my attention.

The black obelisk of Discord inked at the base of his shaft.

My gaze slid a little lower, and my stomach churned when I registered the gash curving beneath his cock, as if someone had tried to slice it off.

What the hell had happened to him in the last three days?

"Daemon," I whispered, my voice rife with concern. "You're too hurt for us to do this."

He chuckled—as if what I said was some hilarious joke—and his golden orbs glittered with amusement. "I'm fine, Little Pup."

My brows pulled together in a scowl. "No, you're not fucking 'fine,' you dick. If you were fine, I would have gotten a text over the last three days. Anything to let us know you weren't dead. You had Alistair worried sick."

His lips twisted into a dark smile. *Goddamn.* He was beautiful when he smiled. "Is that your bratty way of telling me you missed me too?"

"I did miss you! You fucked me and took off."

"Because Alistair told me to, not because I wanted to. Now, we're supposed to be putting on a show, Megaera," he scolded me with a growl that had my skin exploding with goosebumps. "If you're pissed at me for disappearing for three days, fucking let it out. It will just make the show better."

He didn't have to tell me twice.

I lifted my hand, my pink manicured nails growing into deadly claws, and I struck him across the face. They ripped into his flesh, raking deep ribbons of red along his sharp jawline.

Oops. I hadn't meant to slice him up so badly, he was already losing a lot of blood.

Daemon laughed lowly to himself and his deranged grin sent a chill through me. "Vicious bitch."

I sent back an equally manic smile. "What are you waiting for, *Bitch Tamer?* Isn't this the part where you break me in?"

He slapped me across the face—not hard enough to hurt, but it created a sound that rang over the house. The crowd erupted and bile burned my throat at how excited they were at the mock abuse.

They'd probably be more than happy to see the alpha actually rip me to pieces.

Daemon's hands flattened on the bed on either side of my head, creating a protective cage around me with his body. "Shut up!" He growled, breaking character for a moment to reign the audience in.

They quieted down in an instant. Even without his whip and his pack, the monsters in the crowd feared him.

He slowly turned his attention back to me, locks of hair coming loose from the crust of blood, casting his face in strips of shadows and strands of gorgeous black hair.

I gaped up at him with rounded eyes. My heart beat so fast, I knew he could feel it. He knew what his sudden possessive outbursts did to me. When he threatened to murder them all...

A delicious swell of heat swept through my core, and at that moment, I felt more like a monster than ever before.

I lost myself in the molten gold pools of his eyes. Drowning in him.

The music switched over to a new song, *"Closer"* by Nine Inch Nails.

The energy between us was electric, heightened by the fact that we missed each other to the point of pain—and that our reunion was being closely watched by our colleagues, our lovers, and hundreds of strangers.

We were going to put on one hell of a show.

Keeping his stance wide with his feet firmly planted on the ground, he pulled me closer to the edge of the bed. His hand curved under my knee and lifted my leg in the air—spreading my pussy. His grip tightened painfully on the backside of my thigh as he took in my flushed and swollen flesh.

"Look at your royal little holes, dripping with sex demon seed. They made you so nice and wet for me."

I thought he'd slam into me—the twins usually did during our force play shows. But no. He was slow—torturously so—feeding each delicious inch of his cock into me to the slow and steady beat of the thumping music.

"Daemon," I gasped on a flayed whisper as my hips tried to buck up to take more of him. He held me down, his muscles crushing me into the bed and holding me captive. I was forced to stretch around him at the pace he set.

"Fuck," he cursed beneath his breath. "You feel so fucking good, Pup."

"Stop! I can't fit you," I cried out for everyone to hear. My hands flew to his back, and my claws shredded his muscled shoulders. His jaw clenched, and his eyes flickered with fire, but there was no other sign that the pain even registered.

With one last thrust, he was all the way inside. His fingers found Alistair's mark, and he traced the silvery scar with surprisingly gentle—almost adoring—strokes. "If you can fit any part of Discord, you can fit me. You don't have a choice."

His thrusts were slow but harsh, pulling out and pausing for dramatic effect, then slamming back inside me. His timing to the music was perfect. He teased every moment out, leaving the audience on the edges of their seats. When he thrust in, the clap of our flesh fell in line with the song's rhythm.

Clap.

Beat.

Clap.

Beat.

He bent down, his hair spilling over to frame his face as he mouthed with the music, "You get me closer to god."

Even though this was his first time doing a fuck show in the ring, he was such a showman. But I knew it wasn't for the monsters in the audience. It was for Alistair.

I reached up, my fingers tangling in his hair. "I love how you love him. He's your everything, isn't he?"

Daemon froze for a second, caught off guard by the tenderness in my words. His features softened, and he arched to brush a kiss on my lips. "No, Pup. He *was* my everything. Now he has to share me with you. And he knows that. He wants that. It's why he let you into the circus even though I begged him not to. We fucking need you."

He looked up, something capturing his attention off-stage. I twisted in his arms, tracking his line of sight to where the twins had poked their heads in through the tent's canvas flap, watching us.

"All four of us need you," he admitted. "And you'll have all four of us. No more fighting. No more secrets. No more lies."

His words stole the breath straight from my lungs. I gave a wobbly nod, trying to bite back tears of happiness. "Thank fuck for that."

"I wasn't the first to mark you...but if you decide you ever want children, I *will* be the first to breed you."

My vision blurred as tears of pleasure and pain set in. While his words were sweet and loving, his body was brutal and unforgiving in its assault on my core. "I won't open my womb to you," I pushed out between gritted teeth. "Not ever."

He laughed breathlessly. "We'll see about that. What you are going to do for me is bite me."

I blinked up at him. "What?"

His lips peeled back in a snarl. "Fucking *bite me!*"

There was something about the force behind every word rolling off that tongue that demanded obedience. Obey. It was in my nature to make my men work for my submission. Especially Daemon. But my teeth went slamming home into his shoulder because I knew what would happen.

He whimpered and his body jerked, his arms tightening around me and pulling me flush to his body, holding me so tight I could barely breathe. Then his muscles strained against his flesh, and bones snapped and fused together to create something larger and far more monstrous.

He was shifting into his hellbeast form.

28

Three-Headed Hound

ALISTAIR

"**D**on't my two favorite pets look perfect together?" I asked Al, my fingers tightening around his horns as his head bobbed up and down in my lap, sucking me with more skill than a shadow ought to.

It hummed in agreement, sending vibrations through my body. Pleasure thrummed through me, hot and heady.

The shadowbeast drew me deeper inside him as my orgasm started to claw its way from my depths.

I came hard, panting each breath even though I had no need for oxygen. I waved my shadow off, who licked down a few drops of my cum slipping down his chin before disappearing in a swirl of shimmering magic.

My attention refocused on Megaera and Daemon.

One of these days, I'd join them in the ring. But not tonight.

Tonight was for Daemon. He needed to reconcile with the twins or at least take a step in that direction.

And he needed to mark Megaera as his bonded mate. I knew that he had every intention of doing so the moment he'd stepped into that ring.

I didn't try to stop him.

There was no doubt in my mind now that she could survive him. After what she'd endured with me, she could survive anything.

When she'd first appeared at one of my shows, demanding I give her a job, I didn't think she'd last a week. Even with Lilith's blood in her veins, she was still half-human.

Who knew that made her perfect for us?

Her supernatural blood made her capable of enduring the harsh realities of life among monsterkind, while her humanity helped us find our own. She gave us a softness we all desperately needed while challenging us with that bratty, beautiful mouth of hers.

And she was all ours.

Daemon, in his true form, was terrifying to behold. He had the head and haunches of a monster and the torso of a man. His skin was dark, like a black crust over molten lava and glowing embers for eyes.

And, of course, his claim to fame among the humans. His three heads—although, unlike Cerberus, Daemon's three heads were located between his legs.

The king of all hellhounds.

The crowd sucked in a collective gasp. This was their first time seeing The Bitch Tamer in his true form, and his virility which was literally legendary.

Meg, on the other hand, was clearly all too delighted. She'd been wanting this moment, lusting for his mark long before the chastity belt had come off.

After a beat of drinking in the hungry monster before her, a look of mock fear snapped into place. She shoved at him. He let her go. She bolted across the ring, trying to get away.

There was no chance she'd escape, even if she wanted to. Either way, Daemon wasn't going to turn down an opportunity to chase her.

The beast caught up with her in one bounding leap, landing on top of her. His clawed-tipped hand wrapped around her tiny waist and lifted her from the ground.

His other hand ripped off her skirt, finally bearing her completely to the crowd. She thrashed and cried out in fear...

What a good little actress she was. Then, her scent hit me. Vaguely sweet and bitter, like ultra-dark chocolate. That's what Megaera's fear tasted like. That's when it clicked.

The screams. The struggle. It wasn't all for show.

She was, at least in some small part, truly afraid.

I suppose it made sense. Who wouldn't be terrified to be in the clutches of a wild dog monster who was seconds from finding a place within your body to bury his three enormous cocks?

But this was Megaera. Fear, especially when it came to me and my pets, turned her on. The aroma of mortal fear permeated the tent, making me salivate. I drank it in, the monster inside me inhaling like it hadn't known a good meal in years. Because, well, it hadn't. I could only control my hydra form when my magic was at its peak, and my magic didn't just occur. It was to be fed with fear. Preferably the fear of humans. They put off the most of it. Over the last two decades, keeping my shadows stuffed inside this human vessel had somehow created a moral compass I'd never had in the Downside.

If Lilith were truly on her way here with the Horsemen, I'd have to feed. And the little fear that Daemon was squeezing from Megaera wouldn't come close to sating me.

I'd need to terrorize hundreds, if not thousands.

Forcing the thought from my mind, I turned my attention back to the ring where Daemon was slowly working his way inside her.

"The twins have stretched you for me," he rumbled.

My brows shot up in surprise at the guttural voice. I hadn't heard him speak in his true form in centuries.

Then again, before Meg had come to our circus, I hadn't seen his true form for almost as long. It was as if she was waking up this part of him, the part that had fallen into a deep self-loathing after he'd killed the last female he'd tried to claim. The poor woman he'd left burnt to a crisp. Meanwhile, Megaera wasn't succumbing to his flames. Other than the full-body blush that spread from her cheeks down to her dripping cunt, there was no sign of any reaction to the heat whatsoever.

Daemon had his feet planted on the ground, both his hands wrapping Meg's waist as he guided her down on top of him. Her legs kicked, and her upper body squirmed, but her struggle ceased as he began to work himself deeper inside her—one fitting inside her ass, one in her pussy, and one grinding her clit.

Her tail wound around his wrist, almost as if trying to pull him closer to her lips, as she mouthed his name with little breathless huffs. *"Daemon, please. Daemon. Fuck. Fuck!"*

The hellhound was right. The twins had stretched her out for him, allowing him to slide in with ease. "Look at you," he praised. "Taking me so well. Finally, a hole that doesn't split when I fuck it. You'll do nicely as my mate."

Fake shock, mingled with disgust, contorted her features. "What? No! I'm Discord's mate!"

One of his claws traveled from her waist to squeeze her throat over his collar. "And now, you'll be mine too."

Seeing his huge fangs sink into her delicate shoulder had me hard all over again.

Daemon started to thrust into her with a pace that had her eyes crossing in pleasure and drool streaming down the corners of her mouth.

Just like it had when I fucked her on my finger.

Abruptly, he stopped and slowly slipped out of her. Everyone in the audience waited with bated breath—eager to see what he was going to do.

His show of control impressed me. My pet had come so far from that wild mongrel I'd found curled up beside his ex-lover's corpse in the Underside all those years ago.

Back then, his hellbeast hadn't been able to stop himself even as she burnt to death. Now, he was lying down on his back and settling her on top of him so she could control the pace. All so that she would be more comfortable.

Well, well. He was no longer a slave to his appetites.

I envied him.

"Try to run from me again, and I'll catch you. I'll make you take all of me in that tight little ass. Understand?"

Her face drained of all color, and she gave a frantic nod.

"Good. Now ride me, Little Queen."

She placed her hands on his chest, and her eyes went wide as she seemed to marvel at the way her fingertips remained unscorched even as they splayed over his skin.

He was a masterpiece of jagged rock with magma-filled cracks running in between and a set of teeth that would scare even the most savage of prehistoric Upside creatures. She reached down to feel his three heads, curiosity lighting up her pink eyes.

Everyone was held in complete rapture at the way she touched him. Like Beauty, realizing her love for the beast.

It took both her hands and her tail to line herself up with all three appendages, and slowly, she lowered herself down onto him. One in her ass and *two* in her pussy.

She shook as she pushed herself down onto him, and a low, animalistic sound curled up from her throat. "Oh, God—" She caught herself, her gaze latching onto mine. "Oh, Discord."

My ancient name in her mouth had me smiling and mouthing, "Good little demon. Come for him. Come for Daemon."

She sucked her plush bottom lip between her teeth and gave me the cutest little nod in understanding. Then, just a handful of thrusts later, her head tipped back, and her wings spread with her release.

Daemon growled his approval, his claws encircling her waist once again. They were so big and her so small, he could crush her with the slightest twitch. But that knowledge only seemed to push the little monster fucker's pleasure higher. No wonder she'd come so savagely when I'd been in my hydra form. She'd been terrified for her life.

And terror made my pet wet.

Daemon fucked her hard, and within seconds he was coming. He surged into a sitting position and sank his teeth into her shoulder. She screamed—the sound painful and flayed. My fists clenched on the armrests of my chair as I battled the primal urge to rip him off her and protect my mate.

He held her steady as her body started to convulse. Tears welled in her eyes. Riff and Raff started to head toward them, overcome with the same instinct to shield her from pain. Even if they weren't mated to her yet, they were so protective. They'd make good mates for her, too.

My shadow appeared in front of them, blocking their path.

Their attention shot to me from across the ring, eyes burning. They knew what I was, yet they didn't fear me. They were ready to defy Discord, all for the sake of Megaera. At the end of the day, it was her they worshipped, not me.

Yes, they would make good mates.

I shook my head and motioned for them to stay back. It was too late now. The mark had been made, and the pain was unavoidable. It would soon pass, anyway.

Daemon unlatched his jaw from her, and her body sagged in his grip. Her eyelids drifted shut as if he'd sapped her of so much strength she couldn't keep her eyes open.

He lowered her gently against his chest. He remained inside her, but the shift in angle had cum gushing out, pooling beneath her, and rolling off his hips and down onto the floor.

The crowd erupted into an explosive round of applause and cheering, along with the occasional satisfied grunt of a monster satisfying themselves to the show.

I rose from my chair and made the usual closing show spiel, hardly paying attention to my own words.

"You heard him," one of the gorgon sisters shouted from somewhere near the concession stand. "Show's over. Get the hell out!"

Megaera's eyes shot open when she felt what was happening next. A taste of what happened on their first night together. "Uh, what's happening?"

I entered the ring, the metal butt of my cane ringing with every stride as I approached. "He's knotting you, darling. To hold all that cum in so that it might take root."

I stared down at her, loving the way her bare body looked, molding to Daemon's true form.

She was spent and stuck on three engorged cocks. Yet, by some dark miracle, she had the strength to raise herself up on her arms and lick her smirking lips. "Was that a good show, Daddy? Sorry—*Master?*" she amended with a snicker.

"So sassy," Riff snickered as he came to stand on one side of me.

Raff appeared on my other side a beat later. "Even when she's dripping with hellhound cum."

I smiled. "You did such a good job, Little Demon."

She purred her delight. "What now?"

"Now we wait for Daemon to shift back. Until then, you're going to be stuck on him for a while. But after that, I think you've earned yourself some answers."

Conquest

MEG

"So, wait. Are we just supposed to let him bleed to death or...?"

There was a blond-haired man speared to Alistair's bed, and when we'd first walked into the room, the shade hadn't seemed the least bit surprised. Then again, why would he? This was Sinner's Sideshow, home to all things creepy and freaky and straight-up weird. Like Daemon leading us to Alistair's caravan to present a "souvenir" from his travels, which just turned out to be a beautiful man on the brink of death, whose destiny was to be turned into a suit for our shadow daddy to wear.

Alistair had taken Daemon to one of the backrooms of the caravan so he could create some supplies to redress his wound, leaving the twins and I alone with the strange man and Daemon's pack, who diligently stood watch.

"Let him fucking bleed," Riff said from across the room where he was eyeing trinkets and curios from Alistair's shelves.

Raff sat criss-cross on the floor, thumbing through some ancient tome written in Infernal. He had the book propped in one hand with his other patting one of the hound's heads, who was lying beside the incubus with her head in his lap. Usually, the dogs weren't fans of the clowns. Today they seemed unfazed. Maybe because the twins carried their master's scent.

"That would be too good for the bastard," Raff said with a shrug, feigning indifference as he flipped the page.

I frowned. Something was up.

The moment we'd stepped into the caravan, their auras darkened. I couldn't decipher anything but hatred for the man on the bed. Contempt rolled off them in powerful waves, making me wonder how exactly they knew him.

Other than the fact that he'd been stabbed with what I ventured was his own weapon—judging by the gems encrusting the handle that matched some of the stones adorning his clothes—he was an attractive man. Tall and lithe, with a strong chin and a long nose. He was passed out from blood loss, but I ventured a guess that he had light eyes, probably baby blue. He had that "blond hair and blue eyes" kind of handsomeness about him.

Handsome, and aside from the jewels and fancy clothes, unassuming. He didn't seem like anyone the twins would hate so passionately. Then again, monsters came in all shapes and sizes, especially around here. I got up off the floor and approached the bed. The dogs seemed antsy at my proximity to the man, one going as far as to bite at my skirt and drag me back a few steps.

"What's the big deal? He's passed out."

"He's dangerous, Meg. You should keep your distance." Riff looked up from one of my mother's old specimen jars, his unpainted face warping in the glass. "He's an archdemon. Specifically, a golden dragon with the power to harness the sun."

"Why would a demon have the power to control the sun? The Downside doesn't have a sun."

"Not usually, no. But that archdemon was specially created by Discord himself to end the mortal world as we know it. And the real bitch is that there are four of them."

"Wait." My mind stretched back to the conversation I'd had with the twins when they'd told me about the Horsemen of the Apocalypse and how one of them had been their previous owner. Now, their tangle of dark and maleficent emotions made sense. "This is Conquest, isn't it?"

The answer was written on their faces. Yes. This was Conquest, their previous owner, and if I hadn't misconstrued the small amount of information they'd given me about their past lives, their rapist.

I glanced back at the blond man, and revulsion snaked through my veins. I didn't find him attractive anymore. It was like jerking off to weird porn and, in the wake of the afterglow, being disgusted by what you'd found attractive only moments before.

He needed to die.

Before I fully processed what I was doing, I bolted over to where Raff sat and pulled out the knife I knew he kept in his boot. "Let's kill him!"

The sex demon's tail ensnared my ankle and sent me hurtling to the floor. In the same second, he was on top of me, pinning the hand wielding his knife with a vice-like grip.

"Ow, what fucking gives?" I spat.

The dogs didn't move. They didn't so much as growl at the twins.

Did this mean...Did this mean that Daemon was okay with Riff and Raff now? At the very least, it was probably safe to bet that he trusted them around me.

"We can't kill him, Hell Bat," Raff gritted, his hand ghosting over the bloody stain in my Bitch Tamer t-shirt, where Daemon's fresh mating mark lay below.

Riff strode over to us, his Doc Martens with their blue laces coming into my field of vision. Crouching down, he smoothed my hair away from my temple, then plucked the knife out of my hand. "He's a gift to Discord. You don't go stabbing holes in a gift intended for a god. That's how you get smited."

I rolled my eyes. "Alistair isn't going to smite you. And he isn't going to accept the present. He knows what Conquest did to you guys, right? There's no way he'd wear his face around you."

Just then, the door to the caravan's back rooms opened and out strode Daemon and Alistair.

Daemon was shirtless, his stomach freshly wrapped. There was a warm feeling in my belly when I took in the bite mark on the pronounced muscle between his neck and shoulder.

A V formed between his brows when he looked at Raff and me on the floor. "My dogs in heat hump less than you guys."

I scrambled up. "Alistair, you can't make Conquest into your next suit."

The shade shifted his attention to the bed. "I didn't plan to."

Daemon's gaze cut to Alistair. "Why not? I thought you said you wanted an archdemon's human form for your next skin. So it would be worthy of being with Meg."

"And this one doesn't check those boxes, Pet. Though I do appreciate the gesture."

Daemon's eyes narrowed, and his jaw set. Something told me he'd gone through a lot of trouble to get the Horseman here. "What's wrong with this one?"

"It would be bad form to wear him, love. Considering the things he did to the twins."

Riff and Raff looked just as surprised as Daemon.

"Wait." Daemon's gaze flicked between the twins before whipping back around to face Alistair, his shoulders tensed like a dog raising his hackles. "Conquest is the demon you bought them from?"

Alistair's expression took on a hardness that had Daemon stomping over to the twins. He pointed a finger back at the bed without turning around. "That's the bastard that owned you?"

Riff shrugged. "Yeah. Conquest owns lots of shit. Jewels. Gold. Slaves."

A vein ticked in Daemon's jaw. "This isn't a fucking joke. Aren't you pissed?"

The clowns swapped a quick look, the kind where an entire conversation seemed to unfold in a short breath without any words said.

When they looked back at the alpha, their smiles were gone. "No shit, we're fucking pissed. That asshole made our lives hell. But what are we supposed to do?"

"You could torture him. You can do to him the shit he did to you over the years." Daemon nodded to the door leading to the back rooms. "You can take him back there, keep him as long as you want. Do whatever the fuck you wanna do to him."

It was the first time I'd ever seen the clowns speechless.

"What is this? Some kind of peace offering?" Raff's tone was hopeful but guarded at the same time.

"It's a gift," Daemon said simply, his own inflection not betraying a single emotion even though the three of us could read him like a book.

He was enraged on their behalf.

Riff shook his head. "You brought him here for Alistair."

"Yeah, and you heard him. He doesn't want him. So I'm giving this sack of shit to you. Do whatever you want with him, then send him back to Hell. Or have Alistair make the last blow, and you can sleep at night knowing he's never coming back."

My throat swelled with emotion. Daemon was doing something nice for the *twins*.

"What's the catch?"

The amber flecks in the hellhound's irises smoldered and, for a moment, he looked feral with rage. "There is no fucking catch. I dragged this motherfucker all the way here, and it's not going to be for nothing."

Pained grunts drew our attention to the bed. Oh, goodie, Conquest was waking up.

The twins exchanged another look. Wicked smiles slowly curved their lips. In a blink, they were on the bed. They stood on the mattress, looming over Conquest as his eyes blinked open.

"Wakey, wakey. Remember us?"

"What the—" Conquest's eyes stretched wide when they took in the twins. Then he looked around the room, desperately searching. "My Lord!"

Alistair remained in the back corner of the room, dangerously quiet, an unsettling smile the only distinguishable feature thanks to the shadow of his hat masking his face.

"My Lord! P–please. Help me."

Alistair said nothing. Raff rapped the spear's handle with his knuckles. "We're going to play a game. Let's call it..." The demon scratched his head for dramatics.

"Torture?" his brother chipped in.

"Yeah! Torture. And in this game, *we're* going to be the devil. And you're going to be the rapist we punish."

Conquest released another pathetic sound as Raff wrenched the spear from his shoulder. Daemon snapped at his dogs. "Juno, Jax." Two of the hounds perked up. The rest of the command was issued in Infernal and must have been an order to help the twins drag Conquest to the back room.

The door swung open—even the caravan seemed eager to help the twins get their justice. They disappeared into the background, practically skipping as they went.

Alistair strode over to Daemon, his smile wry. "That was sweet of you."

"Can we not make a big deal about this?" he growled low in his chest. "We need to tell Meg the truth about her bitch mother."

30
Twisted Appetites

RAFF

We didn't want to be here. We didn't want to be doing any of this shit.

After three years as an "entertainer" in Conquest's court, I thought we'd grow numb to this place and the things they did to us within it.

It was almost funny thinking back on how desperate we'd been for this life.

Before we knew better.

Every demon that grew up in the Brimwastes stared up at the castle that loomed on the horizon, daydreaming about the lives of the higher-ranking demons inside. The feasts they had, the beds they slept on. Even being a servant in a place like that was the ultimate pipedream for low-born nobodies like us. But if we could bag a job there? No more scavenging the Brimwastes for food, knowing next to nothing grew out of the craggy, sulfuric rock that stretched on forever. No more breathing in the scent of rotten eggs day in and day out. No more sleeping on hard ground.

In Conquest's service, we'd have our own room, with a bed and furniture and regularly scheduled meals on plates. So, when we heard they were looking for court entertainers, it sounded too good to be true. We'd practiced our routine for weeks. Simple acrobatics. Juggling skulls. We'd painted our faces with exaggerated smiles—using blood for paint.

Those rich upper-crust demons ate it the fuck up.

It hadn't been so hard in the beginning. We performed for the court during the day, and at night, we were made to sleep with whoever took a liking to us during our show. Then Conquest took notice.

That had been exciting at first. A rich, powerful archdemon who had access to the surface. Kissing up to him seemed like a no-brainer at the time.

I felt so stupid for being so goddamn naive.

Conquest was one sadistic fuck. The dark and twisted things he made us do. Almost every night, we ended up in his chambers. Eventually, we stopped performing altogether. Nights in his room turned to days, weeks, months. When we tried to leave he had chains installed to his bed.

Like fucking dogs.

No, even dogs were treated better than this.

We were sex slaves.

When the sound of flapping wings filled the room, I grabbed my brother's arm and shook him awake. "Riff, wake up. Conquest is back."

Riff let out a groan and stuffed the pillow over his head. I frowned at all the bruises on his back that hadn't yet healed from last night. He was always the defiant one, the "Feisty Fuck Hole" Conquest had taken to calling him.

What might become of my brother when Conquest inevitably stopped finding it amusing haunted my nightmares.

The glass doors leading to the balcony rattled under the gust of wind, announcing our master was home. Through the glass, there was a flash of golden scales. Several moments later, Conquest appeared in his lesser form.

He turned to face us. I sucked in a breath and steeled my nerves.

My hatred for this bastard ate me from the inside out like some lower-crust parasite. But I couldn't betray that on my face and thank Discord for the fact that he wasn't a sex demon with the power to read our emotions. Then he'd know I got hard to my fantasies of torturing him.

Because death for demons wasn't like what it was for mortals. When a demon died, they'd be separated from their body, but their soul would be released and eventually find a new form. That would be too good for Conquest.

We braced for him to undress, or command us to do it for him. Instead, he brandished an item from his pocket that we'd plotted to steal a hundred times over. The key to our chains.

"Tonight is a special night, boys. Tonight, the other Horsemen are joining us for dinner. You will be performing for them."

With that, he left, leaving Riff and I reeling.

"We haven't performed in months," I said, blinking at the door where he made his prompt exit.

"Maybe this is our chance to get our old jobs back. Or at least get out of this fucking room every once in a while, and suck a different dick for once. Or a female. By Discord's cock, do I miss pussy," Riff whined, falling back into his mountain of pillows.

The air felt lighter than usual as Riff's hopefulness seemed to break up some of the uncomfortable tension that always hung heavy over Conquest's chambers. I, on the other horn, couldn't shake the uncomfortable, foreboding feeling pulling under my gut and worming into my marrow that, somehow, we were better off staying in this bed.

Too fucking bad we didn't have a choice.

Conquest loved the "arts" so much that he'd had a theater built in his castle. Eerie orchestral music played from beyond the heavy curtain, separating us from the audience on the other side.

By the din of chatter coming from the other side, Conquest had invited more than just the Horsemen for dinner and a show.

I turned to Riff. We were both in our full forms. Muscular and tall, with thicker tails and fuller horns than our half-shapes. Our heads were fleshless, monstrous skulls that we'd painted so much that the bone had stained. We weren't allowed to wear any of our face paint, but we still had the faded diamonds over our eyes.

We hadn't been allowed any of our old props, either. Not our costumes, our stilts, or anything else we'd used in our shows before.

When Conquest approached us backstage, his blue eyes swept over us in quiet appraisal. "Time to go on."

Riff and I exchanged a side-eye before I looked back at Conquest and asked, "Uh, what exactly do you want us to do, Master?"

"Knock her around a little bit. Terrify her. Fuck her. Entertain my guests, and I'll free you both."

Before we had time to process the information, the curtain drew, and the stage lights blinded us. A deafening round of applause greeted us, and all we could do was move toward the sound in a daze.

My heart lurched to my throat when I registered the bed in the middle of the stage. If it could even be called a bed. It was a slab of hard cushion on a raised platform, with no blankets or pillows of any kind. It definitely wasn't a bed designed for sleeping.

And it wasn't empty.

In the center of the mattress was a young woman, completely naked and shivering. Her legs were tucked under her body, and her arms were wrapped around her chest in an attempt to hide her breasts.

Even from here, we could get a read on her emotions.

She was terrified.

Her terror only spiked when the curtain drew to reveal us.

"What kind of demon is that?" Riff muttered under his breath. "Her lesser form seems off."

I nodded as I took in the small woman, trying to puzzle it out. She smelled different and seemed so timid for a demon. Even one who was forced here against her will. She was shaking uncontrollably, and her heart was beating so hard I could practically feel it roaring in my ears. I'd never heard of a demon's heart beating so fast.

I considered her for a few beats longer before turning to Riff. "I think she's mortal."

The demon's eyes flickered with glowing blue light. "No...Mortal souls don't take shape after they die."

"I think she's still alive."

There were stories of archdemons and kings of various regions with access to the Upside dragging mortals down to our realm, but I'd never seen one for myself.

I caught Conquest's glare from off stage where he stood behind the curtain, positioned so that he was hidden from the audience but would have a front-row seat to the horrible shit we were about to do.

All for the sake of freedom.

Clenching my fists, I replaced my unease with resolve and strode toward the bed with Riff tailing behind me.

The girl started to scoot backward, her eyes swiveling desperately around her as she seemed to search for an exit. All the while, hopelessness permeated her aura. She knew there was nowhere for her to run.

"D–don't hurt me p–please."

Her voice came out so soft, so fragile, just like the rest of her. She had the prettiest blonde hair that fell around her shoulders in silky waves. Her flesh looked to be the most supple I'd ever seen, and freckles peppered her cheeks and shoulders.

"We're not going to hurt you," I told her, hating how the statement felt bitter and heavy on my tongue. Like a lie. With my hand extended, I slowly approached as one would with a timid animal.

Her doe-eyes rounded. "You understand English!"

"Some," Riff answered, coming to stand beside me. "We've picked it up from archdemons who frequent your world. Mostly phrases you'd say in bed—"

I elbowed Riff in the side, and he released a growl.

"How did you get here?"

Her brows scrunched together as she tried to remember the details. "I–I don't know."

"What's your name?"

Her blonde lashes fluttered with several consecutive blinks, taken aback by the fact that I cared enough to ask.

"Ellie."

"Ellie. I'm Rafferty, and this is my brother Rifton."

Her aura lightened some as she started to feel more comfortable in my and Riff's presence. But my efforts to relax her were undone in the next instant when Conquest snarled from offstage, "I said screw her. Terrify her. Ruin her little pussy. Or you can kiss your freedom goodbye."

Every muscle in my body tightened, and Riff's discomfort with the situation was so intense I could barely breathe. But what other choice did we have?

Whoever had brought her here sealed her fate, not us. If we refused to do this, she'd still be in Hell, and we'd still be slaves.

"I'm sorry about this, Ellie. We're just as much prisoners here as you are."

The apology didn't make it better. In a way, the familiarity of her name in my mouth just soured everything all the more. I pushed her down onto the bed and pried her legs open.

She screamed and thrashed and cried as she tried to push me away. "No!"

I knew Conquest would be pissed if we charmed her into submission.

They wanted to see her fight. They wanted to see her suffer. They wanted to hear her screams.

I didn't care.

After three years of enduring Conquest's twisted appetites, I could do just about anything in front of an audience. But not this. Not while she was screaming and begging me to stop.

I cupped her cheek, wiping away her tears with a gentle swipe of my claw and reached out with my charm magic. "It's okay. I'm not going to hurt you. Just lay back and be quiet, Ellie. It will be over soon. Just don't fight it. It will only make this worse for everyone."

Half-lidded and dazed, she stopped her struggles and allowed me to work my length inside her.

She was so tight, our size difference making it a struggle to get it in.

"It hurts," she whimpered. "You're too big."

I shifted to my half-form, and her eyes opened when she registered my human features. Her hand reached up, her trembling fingers threading through my green hair and brushing over my horn. "You're a nice monster."

Guilt stabbed me in the lungs, making every breath I took painful. "No. I'm not at all, Ellie. I'm tricking you with magic. You don't want to be doing this with me..."

She started to weep, and the most unadulterated misery I'd ever tasted permeated her mien.

Fuck.

I bit back the urge to vomit and promptly pulled out, flipping her around so she was on her hands and knees so I wouldn't have to look at her face. At Conquest's cruel direction, Riff got up on the bed in front of her and charmed her into opening her mouth for him.

What was worse than fucking a frightened mortal girl and fucking her from both ends while she cried, feeling her body grip us with every sob that racked it? Doing it while a theater full of demons watched, cheering and jeering for us to tear her apart.

"I'm sorry. I'm sorry," Riff kept whispering to her. That's all he could say as he thrust into her against her will. "I'm sorry. I'm sorry. I'm sorry."

My brother's voice broke under the brunt of guilt.

But all I felt now was hatred for Conquest, strangling me in its unforgiving grip.

The entire time, I tried soothing her. "It's okay, Ellie. You're doing good for us, baby."

It didn't help.

When Riff came inside her mouth, his muscles bunched up. There was an odd look in his flickering eyes. Then he pulled out in a hurry as her body started to heave. Thick chunks of whatever meal she'd eaten last spewed all over the mattress. Riff managed to dodge it, all while holding her hair back for her.

That was it. I couldn't go any further.

I pulled out of her and rose off the bed. "There. We're done. Entertained?"

Conquest's lips curved into a maleficent smile. "Not quite. Slit her throat."

My heart beat furiously in my chest as if trying to escape its cage of bone. "What?"

"You heard me. Kill her." The way he said it sent a chill through me.

So indifferent. So evil.

I gritted my teeth. "You never said we had to kill her."

"Well, I'm saying it now."

A war raged inside me. They were going to kill her anyway. If we were the ones to make the blow, at least there was something to be gained.

I turned toward her, each step more difficult than the last. My claw trailed over her throat. I was a fucking demon. This kind of shit was supposed to come easy to me.

It didn't.

I couldn't.

I looked up at Riff, who, as always, was on the same wavelength as me. We couldn't do it because being slaves to an archdemon was an escapable situation. But slaves to self-hatred would be forever.

"No." I shook my head. "I'm not doing it."

Conquest's smile only spread wider at my disobedience. As if he'd been secretly hoping that we'd rebel. "You know, I've been thinking about selling you. I was going to let you walk free if you put on a good show. However, that was pathetic to watch. So, I'm going through with selling you. I already have two interested buyers."

My blood turned to ice in my veins. Buyers? He was going to sell us?

Like livestock.

Like property.

Of course. To him, that's exactly what we were.

"The first buyer is a demon who rules one of the lower crusts of the Downside," he continued with a cheery lilt in his voice that was only for the purposes of digging the knife that was this information deeper.

"She's looking for an incubus concubine to warm her bed since she has no time to take a mate. Sadly, she's only interested in you," *he said, his blue eyes drilling into me.*

The chill in my body spread, numbness taking over my nerve endings. He was going to separate us? My brother was the only thing I had in this steaming pile of hellhound shit realm.

"Or..." He held up a finger and paused for dramatic effect.

We didn't rattle easily. He'd never managed to scare us before despite his best efforts. Until now.

"I can sell you to the second interested buyer. One of Discord's most prized disciples. He lives on the Upside and runs a sideshow circus to harvest fear in offering to our Lord. And he wants both of you."

Taking his extended finger, he pointed to the incapacitated girl. "Slit her throat, and I'll sell you to the second option. Disobey, and one of you will serve the demoness in the lower crust, and one will stay with me."

His attention slid to Riff. "You. I'll keep you. I like the color blue better."

I stood back, admiring my and my brother's handiwork.

The boss' magical caravan had created the perfect room for us. The stage perfectly mimicked the one Conquest had back home. We'd stabbed the archdemon to the bed with his spear before he could shift and cut off all his clothes.

Now, he was a blank canvas. Ready to suffer as we'd day-dreamed about for so long.

"You pathetic demon scum." He tried to spit at us, but he was low on fluids, and the tiny gob of saliva he'd managed to gather just landed on his own face. "Brimwaste filth!"

"Aw, is the rapist swine angry that he's finally getting what's coming to him?"

"You're sex demons. You're meant to be used and fucked. That's your purpose. Discord has created us all for a purpose, and it's our duty to fulfill it."

"Discord is in the next room, and he knows what we're about to do to you. We don't know why you're here, but I'm taking a wild guess that it's because you don't actually give a fuck about Discord. He protects those loyal to him."

The Horseman's nostrils flared with outrage. "Discord is old. He has many evolutions. Once he's mated with Lilith, she'll have the power to allow my brothers and me to fulfill our purpose. The mortal world will burn to ash, and Discord will be forced back to the Downside, where he will return to his old self. The very air in this realm poisons him against his own kind."

"I think that's just called having a conscience," Riff snarled.

"Speaking of burning the world to ash..." I dug my lighter from my jeans pocket and flipped the lid. The flame sprung to life, reflecting in my brother's eyes. "Do you think Conquest is fire retardant?"

The archdemon thrashed and screamed against the bed, making more blood gush out as the blade of his spear dug deeper into his tattered stomach. "Wait, please!"

Riff clapped his hands in glee. "Oh, goodie. That's a 'no' if I've ever heard one."

31

"We Get Off to Weird Shit"

MEG

"**S**o let me get this straight…" I sat with my legs criss-crossed on Alistair's bed, uncaring that it was still wet with Conquest's blood. "I want to make sure I have the story straight before I completely flip my shit. You're saying that my mother is Lilith herself. The oldest succubus in existence. She founded Sinner's Sideshow as a means to fuel Alistair's creepy primordial magic since it needs terror and fear to run. But then she went a little crazy and decided to kill people willy-nilly. So, Alistair came down to nip that in the bud by killing her and sending her back to the Downside."

The ringmaster nodded from where he stood beside one of his bookshelves, flipping through a dusty tome on demonology in hopes of finding something useful on the Horsemen. "Yes."

"Okay. Here's the part where you start to lose me…" I held up my hand and spread out my fingers, counting the items to keep track. "My mom took off and joined Walker's as a place to hide from you."

Another nod. "Yes."

"And she conceived me with my father, not because they were in love, but because she charmed him. All so she could use me as a blood sacrifice to get back on your good side?"

"Yes."

I wrinkled my nose, not because I was disgusted or horrified but because the whole thing sounded…stupid. Why not opt for a more traditional "I'm sorry I fucked up" gift, like flowers or a mixtape or some shit? Then again, Alistair didn't really seem like a mixtape kind of guy.

I searched his face. "And she thought that was the key into your pants? Baby murder?"

Alistair's emerald eyes gleamed with amusement. "Astrid always had a flair for the dramatic."

"Apparently, she has a thing for archaic Downside traditions," Daemon said from where he lounged in a chair on the other side of the room. He looked like a crime boss from a romance novel with the way he sat shirtless, his inked flesh still splattered in blood, and his dogs standing guard around him with their menacing spiked collars. "Back in the old days, mother demons used to slaughter their firstborn and release their souls, all in the name of Discord."

Alistair grimaced as he licked his finger and flipped the page of his book. "I always hated that. Even back then."

I shoved off the bed, walked over to Alistair and plucked the book out of his hand, slamming it shut in a puff of dust. "You lied to me. You told me that when you found my mother, you killed her."

The ringmaster's eyes narrowed to deadly slits. Daemon shifted in his chair. I refused to flinch, look away, or even blink under the devil's scathing glare, but I didn't need to see the alpha's face to taste his emotions.

Seeing us together fascinated him.

Alistair gripped my hips and spun me around, shoving me against the bookcase hard enough to make the old wood rattle.

"No, darling. You assumed I killed her, and I didn't correct you. I believed it was better for you to think her dead. I thought I was protecting you." His hand lifted from my hip, making a sensual ascent up my side, ghosting over my collarbone to press a finger beneath my chin. I lifted my eyes to his. "I'm sorry I didn't tell you the truth."

I blinked at him, and my heart thumped wildly against the book I clutched to my chest. I wanted to be furious. I *was* furious. But his tone was dripping in sincerity, making it hard to hold onto my rage.

"You're not supposed to be apologetic right off the bat. You're supposed to be defensive and let me yell at you. We fight. Then you realize you were wrong, and *then* you apologize. Maybe you even grovel a little."

Alistair's brows lifted in surprise, and his lips curved into that devilish smile. "Oh, is that how it works? I already understand I'm in the wrong. But if a fight will make you feel better..."

"Don't take him up on that," Daemon warned, leaning back in his chair with his chin resting on his fist. "He'll win. Why don't we just skip right to the groveling part? Get on your knees for your new mate, Master. Show her just how sorry we both are. Would you like that, Pup?"

Would I like that?

Here? *Now?*

There was something about Alistair and Daemon's sexual power dynamic that had me dying to get into the middle of it. So, naturally, before my sensible side could butt in, my succubus urges sent a storm of hunger swirling inside me.

I nodded.

Daemon grinned. "Kiss her, Alistair. Kiss your mate."

The look Alistair gave me stole all the breath from my lungs. His hand tightened on my hip as his finger kept my chin tilted, lining our lips up. His mouth lowered over mine in a filthy kiss that had my entire body aching for more. His tongue slipped over my lips, tasting me. I sighed against his subtle heat, breathing in his taste of dark magic, loving how it danced across my tongue with little zaps of electricity that had goosebumps exploding over my skin.

"Good," Daemon praised with a dark purr. "Now, her other lips."

Keeping his eyes fixed on mine, Alistair slowly lowered himself to his knees. He lifted my skirt, and he flashed me one last smile before disappearing beneath and burying his head between my thighs. My breath hitched, and I nearly dropped the book on his head when his thumbs slipped between my folds and spread them. Cool air hit my exposed clit, then a rush of warm breath. When the tip of his tongue feathered across the sensitive bundle of nerves, my knees trembled, and my legs threatened to give out.

Daemon shoved to his feet and made his way over to us. He took a wide stance directly behind his master, towering over both of us. His gaze took its time savoring all the details. My back pressed up against Alistair's bookshelf. My Bitch Tamer t-shirt was all askew, still stained with the blood from his mark. Our master was on his knees between us, his head shoved under my skirt.

"Daemon... Alistair... I— I still need answers."

Both of them chuckled, Alistair's sending a delicious vibration through my core while Daemon's breath whispered over my flushed cheeks.

The hellhound took the book from me and slotted it back into its place on the shelf over my head. He leaned in closer, his arms bracing against the shelf on either side of my head, caging me between his arms.

"You'll get your answers, Pup. First, hold onto me to keep yourself upright. Otherwise, I'll be telling the story to a puddle of cream on the floor."

My arms looped around his neck. He hissed when I brushed against the fresh bite on his shoulder. "Oops. Sorry. Does it hurt?"

He shook his head, his chest rising with a ragged breath. "No. It feels good."

I frowned, though the frustration on my face was all twisted with pleasure as Alistair's tongue painted long licks over my slit. "No fair. M—mine hurts like a bitch."

"Yeah, well…" He pushed two fingers inside my mouth and pried my jaw apart while his thumb rubbed over one of my canines. "My hellbeast's teeth are bigger than these adorable little needles."

I bit down on his thumb—I couldn't resist. A single bead of blood hit my tongue, and my eyes glowed pink as I drank in the sudden wave of lust rolling off him like a tsunami. "Are they adorable now?"

His hand captured my jaw and squeezed. Goddamn, his hand was so huge his spread fingers swallowed most of my face.

"Fucking brat," he snarled, his golden glare turning ravenous. With his one hand still clutching my jaw, his other reached down to Alistair and pulled his mouth off me with a tug of his hair.

I cried out at the loss of heat, my hips canting forward in search of the lost friction.

"Are you going to behave and let me tell you the rest of the story? Or do I have to fuck some obedience into you?"

Both. I wanted both.

"I–I'll behave. Finish telling me the story."

The hellhound's finger hooked under his collar and dragged my lips to his in a kiss that ate me alive. "Good girl," he purred.

A second later, Alistair's mouth returned to my center. His tongue circled my clit, while he sank a slender finger—it had to be his middle by how long it was—inside my heat.

My lips ripped away from Daemon's, and my head knocked back against the shelf as euphoria shot through my system. But I refused to let my libido get in the way of getting the answers I desperately needed, so I forced my brain to clear from its lust-drunk haze.

"S–so why did Alistair let my mother live?"

It was weird talking about the shade like he wasn't here. As if he wasn't on his knees, with his long hair still gripped in Daemon's hand like a leash. As if *he* was the pet.

Daemon's brows quirked. By the emotions bleeding off him in powerful ripples, he was impressed by my composure...given what Alistair was doing to me beneath my skirt.

Admittedly, it was hard to hold myself together.

His finger pushed inside me with a pace that had me clenching in response around him. And his tongue was doing this *thing* with my clit, which had me stunned with the fact that I was his first woman.

His words from the night we'd mated rang in my head. *"You may be my first female mate. But don't forget, Little Demon...I created sin."*

I shivered against his ministrations and used every ounce of willpower to focus on Daemon's answer to my question.

"Alistair let your mother live because she was heavily pregnant with you when he found her hiding out at Walker's. He made a deal with her. She was never to harm you, and in exchange, he'd never harm her in return. Now she's back. Her goal has always been to secure Alistair's mating bond. His mark means power."

"Power?" I repeated, my tone breathy and laced with a moan. "Is that why my magic is stronger? I can charm the twins now, and I couldn't do that before."

"Yes. In the Downside, demon hierarchy is based on power—magic. When you mate an archdemon, you gain some of their strength as well as their rank in the overall food chain. If she's mated with a primordial demon like Alistair, she graduates from archdemon to basically a demi-god."

"Wait. What does that make me?"

Alistair appeared from under my skirt while plunging a second finger inside me. "That, my darling, makes you an archdemon. A half-blood archdemon without a full monster form."

An embarrassing noise clawed up from my throat as Alistair's mouth latched back onto my clit, making my spine arch and my arms tighten around Daemon's shoulders. "S—so another woman is after one of my mates. And it's my mother, who was supposed to be dead but isn't, because she used me as a bargaining chip to save her hide."

"Yes. And now she's switched her tactics in wooing Alistair. After seeing that he's taken with you, it finally hit home that he's never going to accept her. Now, Mommy Dearest is working with the Horsemen. She's promised to use her new authority to finally allow them to fulfill their original purpose of ending the world."

I ground against Alistair's hand, chasing the building sensation in my belly. My legs were jelly now, and Daemon's arms banded around my waist to keep me upright. "Th–this is a weird thing to come to," I panted.

A sly smile slid across my alpha's face, and I felt Alistair's lips curl into a grin against my folds.

"This is Sinner's Sideshow," Daemon rumbled, the hunger in his eyes paired with that cocky smile sending me hurtling over the edge. "We all get off to weird shit around here."

"You Had Us at Funnel Cake"

MEG

My orgasm tore through me, heightened by the fact that Alistair was still fucking me with his tongue and fingers and forcing my sensitive nerves to overload with shockwaves of pure pleasure. Daemon's mouth was on mine again, devouring the animalistic noises gurgling up from my throat.

Alistair rose to his feet, Daemon's arms now bracketing the both of us.

The shadow demon held his glistening fingers up to the alpha's mouth, who licked them clean without a beat of hesitation.

Daemon swept me off my feet, stepping over his dogs as he carried me over to the bed. His lip curled at the bloody sheets. "I don't want that rapist's blood touching her."

Alistair glided toward me, his shirt melting away from his pale flesh in a swirl of shadows. "Is the skin of a sex trafficker better?"

"While you wear it? Yes. Lay down. Take everything off."

Alistair's veridian gaze glittered with excitement. His clothes were just an illusion, but he took the time to strip out of his pants, soaking in the way we watched him. When they hit the floor, they evaporated just like his shirt. He got on the bed and stretched out.

He was a fucking masterpiece. With his lithe frame, lean muscles, and long hair splayed out over his pillow. Dark, thick eyelashes. Pale flesh so pretty against the shock of crimson beneath him.

Daemon got on the bed with me in his arms. He laid me down on top of Alistair, with my back to his chest. His one arm ensnared my waist, keeping me locked in his embrace while another hand clasped around my throat.

Daemon's mouthwatering shoulder muscles shifted under his inked flesh as he crouched between our tangled legs and took Alistair's cock into his mouth. Seeing his lips stroke over the shaft, saliva gathering at the fine seams where he'd stitched the dead flesh together, had my clit pulsating.

It was almost as if Daemon was hardwired into my nerves because he lifted his mouth off Alistair and stoked his tongue over my pussy. I groaned and squirmed on top of Alistair, his hold on me tightening.

Daemon's tongue pushed into my body, and he gave a maniacal chuckle when I clenched around him with a gasp. He gripped the undersides of my legs, keeping them spread as he savaged my center with his tongue.

Just as I was about to come for the second time, he dropped his mouth back to Alistair's cock. I couldn't be mad. Watching his lips glide up and down the shadow demon's dick, framed so prettily between my legs, was one of the most erotic things I'd ever seen.

Alistair's muscles bunched beneath my back. His breathing turned harsh in my ear. "I'm— Damn. I'm coming."

Daemon shoved Alistair deep inside his mouth as he unloaded inside him, but he didn't swallow. He rose up on his knees and splayed my pussy open with his fingers...and spat Alistair's cum into my hole.

It was so filthy. So obscene. So wrong. *It was so fucking hot.*

Daemon's mouth twisted with a grin as he pushed the cum inside me with two fingers, making me moan in unholy delight. Fisting his cock, he lined himself up with me and speared me with one sharp punch of his hips.

He fucked into me with quick, deep thrusts. "Our master's cum makes such perfect lube, doesn't it, Pup?"

My mouth opened to answer, but all that came out was a pathetic little whimper. I was still sore from mating his hellbeast earlier. I couldn't summon the will to care. The pain gave the pleasure more flavor.

"Fuck," Daemon moaned. "She's still so tight even after taking two of my hellbeast cocks."

His dick—slick with my arousal and Alistair's cum—pounded into me with unforgiving force.

The wet, sloppy sound was embarrassing, but that only seemed to send me hurtling faster toward completion.

Daemon's hand came to rest over Alistair's on top of my throat. They held hands while simultaneously choking me.

"Are you going to come for us, Little Demon?" Alistair whispered into my ear. His voice was cool steel swaddled in sin and honey.

"Y–yes. Oh, *God*."

Daemon captured my chin and wrenched my head sideways. "When you cry out to your god as you cum, you fucking look him in the eye."

Alistair's lips quirked. Something I couldn't put my finger on shone behind his beautiful green eyes, something that had me *shivering* in ecstasy. Obsession? Love? Adoration? Hunger? It was a dangerous cocktail of all four.

The burning knot throbbing in my belly finally burst into an explosion of sensation. Daemon's cock twitched, spilling hot semen into me as we came at the same time. He pulled out of me, and my heart plummeted at the loss of him. But his hands were on me again, lifting me off Alistair and twisting me around so I was sitting up with my back propped against his hard chest at an angle.

I turned my head to get a good look at the alpha. His pupils had expanded, eclipsing his golden irises. He was in his human form, but his eyes had never looked so demonic. And he wasn't looking at me.

"Suck me out," he demanded. I wasn't sure what he meant until Alistair crouched between my legs and brought his mouth back to my dripping center.

Oh fuck, he was going to— "*Oooh!*"

My hands coiled around Daemon's wrists. My wings expanded, and he captured the base of one, pulling on it hard enough to send electric sparks through my veins. My wings were an erogenous zone, and Daemon knew just how to touch them to make me scream.

My moan came out all garbled, an overload of sensation sparking through me as Alistair's mouth suctioned over my pussy.

Daemon hummed in approval as his arm swooped under my legs and spread me wider. "Get every drop."

Alistair's cheeks hollowed as he sucked out the copious amounts of hellhound cum. When he rose, he smiled, squeezing a pearly bead of cum past the seal of his lips.

Daemon's fingers tapped my chin—not hard enough to be a slap, but there was just enough force to stroke my masochistic streak. "Open for him, Pup. Take what we give you."

I obeyed.

Alistair spat Daemon's cum into my mouth and wiped his own with the swipe of his hand, then reached for me and tucked a sweaty lock of my hair behind my ear. "Beautiful. I've lived a thousand lives, and I've never seen anything so beautiful in any of them."

I smiled, although it was a small and vulnerable one. "Well shucks, My Lord."

He gave a soft laugh. "Do you forgive me for keeping my secrets from you?"

"Yes." I blew out a sigh and leaned my head on Daemon's chest, grinning up at him, then back down at Alistair. "That was a really good apology."

We laid back in the bloody bed with me tucked between the devil and his dog, simmering in the peaceful quiet until it was shattered by the agonizing screams of a man coming from deeper in the caravan.

Alistair looked up from his idle task of twisting a strand of my hair around his finger. "It seems the twins are having some fun too."

With that, the situation with the Horseman came slamming back into my brain.

I bolted up, smoothing my skirt back down. "So, Conquest is taken care of, or he will be very soon. What about the other Horsemen?"

"Oh, I'm certain they're planning to come to us now that their little plan to catch me off guard was foiled."

"But that's okay, right? You'll just shift into your hydra form and kill them all?"

By the way Daemon stiffened and Alistair's demeanor turned icy, I knew the solution wasn't that simple.

The ringmaster got out of bed and held his arms out. Dark energy swirled around him, and in a blink, he was once again clothed in a black lantern-sleeve shirt that left most of his chest exposed and black form-fitting pants. His dark hair had fallen out of the ribbon he usually used to tie it back and hung loose around his shoulders.

"Darling. I'm starving."

I stared at him with a vacant look as I tried to make sense of the words. "You're the Downside's oldest demon. You can't starve."

"Not conventionally, no. I won't die. But my magic is almost drained. I'm running on fumes. While I exist in the mortal plane, I need magic to fuel my true form. I used up a significant amount of energy mating you."

"Then restore your magic."

Daemon scoffed from behind me. "It's not that easy, Meg. Alistair must feed on fear to keep himself strong. Mortal fear, preferably. But he's developed a properly functioning moral compass at some point in the last few centuries, so now we only terrorize monsters who want to die."

"Why don't you just go back to killing humans? Bad ones, that is. I mean, you are the devil, right? You source your skin suits by having Daemon hunt down the scum of the earth. You know where they are. So why not just lure them here? Can you do that?"

The shadow demon rubbed his chin in thought. "That would use a lot of magic. We would need to lure quite the crowd to make up for lost energy. Even if we manage to fill every seat, we'd need that and then some. We could do multiple shows, of course, although that doesn't seem economical."

"What if we expand the haunted house? Only, it needs to be something that can cater to huge amounts of people at the same time, right? So, something outdoors. Like...Like..."

A light bulb flipped on in my mind.

"Alistair, remember that illusion you made me see the night you were trying to put me off from joining the circus? The horror carnival. We can do something like that."

Daemon turned on his side and placed his hand on my hip. "Alistair would have to work hard to conceal our campgrounds from innocents while luring in dirtbags. The whole point of this is to replenish his magic, not bleed him dry."

"No, I think she's onto something, Pet. It's true, it would be exerting for me. But with something like this, every member of the troupe could help terrorize our guests."

"Yeah. We can run around in creepy costumes and put out scary decorations. Murderers, rapists and serial killers. Plus, there will be food and rides. Oooh, and a house of mirrors! Imagine setting Riff and Raff loose in that. They'll go crazy."

It was as if the mere mention of their names invoked some ancient summoning spell because, at that moment, the door opened, and they appeared in the doorway, covered head to toe in blood. "What are we doing now?"

I jumped out of bed and skipped over to them while taking care not to step on all the sleeping hounds. "We're turning the circus into a horror carnival!"

"Alistair still hasn't agreed—"

I cut off Daemon with an enthused giggle. "There's gonna be games, carnival rides, funnel cake, and murdering bad guys."

Diabolic smiles broke out on the twins' faces. I was dying to see them in their clown paint again. "You had us at the murdering bad guys bit. Oh, and funnel cake. We love funnel cake."

33

Eyeballs, Undies & Guts

MEG

I froze when the front door to my trailer creaked open as I was halfway through getting dressed for work. All I had on was a ruffled mini-skirt, my face paint, and my hot pink stockings pulled up one leg. "Who is it?"

When no answer came, I went straight for my pink guitar case propped against the side of the dresser and ripped the clasp open. I brandished my father's sword just as a figure appeared.

Daemon stood in the doorway of my bedroom, his brawny frame taking up most of the space as he leaned a shoulder against the doorjamb. He was in his Bitch Tamer uniform of leather pants and huge steel-toed boots that were probably half my weight. He didn't wear the cap tonight, though.

His black hair was slicked back, and his face was painted to resemble a skeleton's. It was just like what the twins had worn that day we'd fucked in Daemon's trailer.

I shoved down the urge to drool over the dark visage in my doorway and instead threw my sword on the bed and resumed wrestling into my pink stockings. "What the fuck, Daemon? Don't you know how to knock?"

His eyes made a slow descent down my body. "Knocking means I'm asking for permission."

I flung him a glare. "Yeah, well, I was about to give you an impromptu sword-swallowing lesson."

"Once you've gotten used to your mark, you'll be able to sense when I'm close."

"Super. Until then, I'll look forward to you popping out of nowhere like some stalker pervert."

"You look fucking beautiful."

"I'd look better if I was fully clothed."

The quiet look on his face told me he didn't agree.

I grabbed for the bodice I'd laid out on my bed and pulled it on. Daemon's eyes swept around the room, bright with curiosity. "That's right. You've never been in here before."

My room was small, but to me, it might as well have been a five-star hotel. My trailer at Walker's had barely been big enough for a bed, let alone a whole bedroom. Daemon pushed off the doorframe and strode inside. His hand skimmed over the various things on my dresser. He picked up my vibrator. It was so tiny in his hand that it was almost comical.

"Why is it so small?"

"Because sometimes I'm not in the mood to get my pussy destroyed by giant monster dicks."

He placed it back down with a chuckle and moved to my bed. A pair of panties hung off the post. It was one of my favorite pairs, with a little biohazard symbol on the front. He picked it up, brought it to his nose and *inhaled*.

"Oh my god, *Daemon.*"

Daemon ignored me, stuffing my panties into his pocket as he moved to my little bookcase. He reminded me of a dog sniffing around a new place he'd never been before.

"Care to explain why you have a jar of eyes?" He turned around, holding up the glass jar containing the six eyeballs of the haunt workers who'd planned to assault me the night Daemon left.

"A gift from Alistair," I said with an innocent smile. "He gifted me other parts of them, too, but keeping those would have been weird."

"I don't think it's weird."

"Coming from the guy who gifts Alistair entire bodies for him to turn into skin suits."

"What else am I supposed to give my lovers? Cheesy human shit?"

I let out a little laugh as I zipped up my bodice, got to my knees and crouched low to the floor, my hand probing under the bed for my pink high-top sneakers. "I guess the severed body parts of our enemies are more our style than chocolates and teddy bears, huh?"

He chuckled. "So, whose eyes are they?"

"Don't ask."

"Am I not supposed to ask about the clown blood I found in my carpet, either? Or the clown cum on my sheets?" His gravelly tone did nothing to help me decipher if he was angry or just amused.

I glanced over my shoulder to find his gaze on my ass, which was on full display with how short the skirt was. Good. My outfit had distracted him from the eyeballs and the fluids the twins and I had left in his trailer.

Or rather, the lack of what was under my outfit had distracted him.

"You're not wearing panties."

"Why bother?" My fingers hooked into the laces of my shoes. I dragged them out from under the bed and plopped myself back onto the mattress to pull them on. "You or the twins are just going to end up stealing them or ripping them off me." I reached for the last piece to complete my outfit, a white ruffle collar.

I moved as if to remove Daemon's collar—even though I had no intention of doing so—and he growled. "Don't you dare take that off."

There was a part of me that loved his possessive little flexes like that, so long as it didn't involve getting jealous of the other guys.

I stood up and gave a twirl before examining myself in the mirror. I was a slutty, pink harlequin clown, complete with three pompoms on my bodice that jingled when I walked. I'd painted my own face. Riff and Raff had taught me how.

I had a white face with pink lips, a pink circle on my nose, and thin brows shaped into a somber position. The only other color I wore were the diamonds over my eyes. One green, one blue.

I winked at Daemon in the mirror and stuck out my tongue. "How do I look?"

He considered me for a moment. "Like a fuck clown."

"And do you like it?"

The gravity of his stare was like an anvil pressing on my chest, making breathing next to impossible. Finally he nodded. "I like it, Pup."

I whirled around, taking in his face paint. "Riff and Raff did your makeup, didn't they?"

"Yes," he answered with an indifferent expression.

"When?"

"While you were getting ready."

I frowned, furrowing my brow. "You went over to their RV?"

"I did."

"They let you inside?"

"No, I broke in and played in their makeup," he said with a sarcastic lilt to his words and an eye roll. "Yes, they let me in."

I prowled toward him, the smile on my lips slowly growing. "They touched you, and you didn't threaten them?"

"I didn't."

I closed the last bit of distance between us with a little hop and pressed my hands against his chest. He was so warm. "Not even once?"

"Not even once. Threatening them for touching me would be pretty shitty considering it was my idea for them to paint me for the carnival."

My smile broke out in full force. "Really?"

Daemon really was making leaps and bounds as far as getting along with the twins went. First, he'd shared me with them in the ring. Then, he'd given Conquest to them. Now, he was going over to their place and getting ready for shows with them?

At this rate, I wouldn't be surprised if Larry sprouted wings and took flight.

"So, what's changed between you guys?"

A V formed between Daemon's brows. "A lot has changed. For one, you told them Alistair's real identity, and so far, they've kept it secret. The imps usually blab shit to everyone."

"No, they don't. They won't. Not when it concerns the five of us."

The five of us. It sounded so right to say. We were a part of the troupe, one big happy family. But Alistair, Daemon, Riff, Raff, and myself were our own shit. I didn't even know the word to describe it. But the hot gossip around the camp was that we were all together, and we didn't correct them.

"So, you've hopped on the clown-fucker bandwagon?"

A vein in Daemon's temple ticked. "I tolerate them."

"Why? Because one day you might actually come to love them?" I asked in a teasing, sing-song voice.

He put his hands on my hips and leveled me with a glare that demanded I come back down to earth. "Because I love you. *We* love you. We happen to share the same mate. So, we have to play nice."

"I'm not their mate yet," I said, trying to keep the disappointment from my voice.

Daemon's face remained unreadable. His poker face was almost as good as Alistair's. It was his aura that betrayed him.

"You know something!" I bounced on the balls of my feet. "Oh, oh! Are the twins going to mark me tonight?"

"I didn't say anything." He turned to leave my room and threw a glance back at me over his shoulder. The ghost of a smirk flitted over his lips. "Act surprised."

I followed him out of the room and lit up at the hellhound curled up in the middle of the floor. His tail wagged when he saw me.

"Guts!" I crouched beside the hound and scratched between his ears. This was the one who'd broken a leg saving Daemon. He had a cast on. Lollie had signed her name in metallic purple pen. It took up most of the cast, and she'd doted her "I" with a heart.

"He's going to stay behind tonight," Daemon explained from the doorway. "Mind if I keep him here? I'll come back for him after the show."

I nodded and glanced out the window. The sky was starting to turn dark, the lights from the carnival lighting up the night. "First night of the carnival."

Daemon came to stand beside me, peering out the slatted blinds to get a good look at Alistair's handiwork. If this was a normal mortal carnival, it would have taken months to order all the equipment and get it set up. Our carnival was made entirely out of illusions, the kind that felt real, just like the ones he'd pulled me into the first night we'd met.

Daemon shook his head. "I still can't believe you got Alistair to agree to this batshit plan."

"It's the perfect plan. The scum of the earth comes to us, and the entire troupe participates in sending them to Hell. No one's going to miss the kind of people Alistair is pulling in. We're doing the Upside a favor. And now that all the work is done, all Alistair has to do is sit back and feast on the terror in the air. Plus, there are snacks and stuff. Don't tell me murder doesn't make you hungry for a deep-fried Twinkie?"

Daemon looked down at me, a devious smile on his face. "You impress me, Pup. When you first came into our lives, I really thought you were just a starry-eyed girl who didn't understand what kind of nightmare circus you were getting yourself into. Turns out, you did every goddamn thing you set out to do. You found your home."

My heart raced at his praise. A warm, tingling feeling spread through my chest. "I've found a lot more than that."

His arms banded around me and drew me close to his chest. I expelled a happy hum when he kissed my brow. "This plan is going to work. I can feel it."

The bad feeling from before—the one that had hooked in my belly like a stubborn thorn was gone now. Which was funny because now that I was in the loop with what was going on, I had every reason to freak out.

My mother was coming to take Alistair away from me, and she wasn't coming alone. There was no telling when she'd show or if we'd have enough time to run the carnival to restore Alistair's magic before she did. There was a chance this would all be for nothing.

Still, I had a good feeling. Maybe it was wishful thinking or Alistair's mark on my thigh inflating my confidence. Whatever it was, I was ready to fight for what was mine. I'd fought too hard to get it.

No one was going to take it away from me.

Not War.

Not Famine.

Not even Death.

And most certainly not my own fucking mother.

34

Cotton Candy

MEG

"**M**egs! What did you get?"

Lollie elbowed her way through the crowd of troupe members, waving the paper scrap drawn out of Alistair's hat. Her sister, Mollie, was two steps behind her. Like Riff and Raff, the gorgon sisters were twins. They were almost identical. The only differences were that Lollie's snakes were green while Mollie's were a dusky violet, and Lollie's tattoos were bright and zany, while Mollie's were colorless and macabre. Their personalities matched their appearances perfectly.

Lollie had painted her head green, with ropes of red beads draped around her neck to look like Medusa's severed head.

"Oh my god, you look great!" I gushed as she approached.

"Not very politically correct, I know," she said with a shrug. "But it's not like any of our guests tonight are getting out alive, so who am I going to offend? Anyway, what job did you draw?"

"I didn't draw. I'm a scare actor tonight."

Not that there was going to be much acting involved. The rides and the games were an illusion, but the spooks and the scares were going to be very real.

"Aw, shit." Lollie glanced at the scrap of paper, then balled it up and tossed it over her shoulder. "Concessions. What in Discord's Hell did I do to get landed with concessions? I *always* work concessions. How did you land the best job without drawing for it?"

"She's fucking the boss, that's how." Mollie's snakes hissed with their mistress' quiet resentment, which bled off her in powerful, pungent waves.

Daemon, who'd been standing quietly behind me like a bodyguard, turned his heated glare on Mollie. "She's the ringmaster's mate. When you speak to her, you'll do so with respect. Or you won't speak at all."

She flinched, and her gulp was so loud it could be heard over the chatter. When the gorgon fled into the crowd, I snapped around and poked Daemon in the chest with a pink manicured finger. "Stop scaring people, or I'll muzzle you."

"Don't threaten me with a good time," he muttered, his smile devious.

"It's okay. Mollie's always standoffish," Lollie laughed nervously. She swept her snakes over her shoulder, and my attention landed on two little dots scarring her throat.

"Oh my god. *Loll.* Did you and Sinclair—"

She giggled and bobbed her head excitedly. "Yeah! Last night. I thought it would hurt like a bitch, after seeing you with, er—" Her eyes flicked up to Daemon before dropping back to me.

I blinked, taking a second to process the look on my friend's face. "Loll, are you blushing?"

"Well, do you blame me? That show was scorching hot. You had everyone screwing and even bonding."

She leaned toward me, her eyes darting around to make sure no one was listening. Thanks to Daemon's five hounds sitting at his feet, looking all menacing—even though I knew what cuddly sweethearts they were when no one was looking—everyone gave us a wide berth.

"I saw Moll slip into one of the supply tents with Larry after your show. And I think it was more than just a fuck. She won't stop talking about him."

"Really? Mollie and Larry? Wow."

It was hard imagining them together, but then again, maybe his shy sweetness would complement her dower hardness. Before we could discuss the topic further, the ringmaster appeared in front of the entrance.

The gate looked just like it had in the corpse carnival illusion; it was a big red devil's face with his gaping mouth as the entrance. Alistair stood just so, the creepy mouth framing him perfectly.

Tonight, he'd foregone his ringmaster attire for a more traditional Carnie look, only instead of a red and white striped waistcoat, he'd opted for a rich maroon and gold one. He wore a black collared shirt underneath, topped with a black bow tie.

His emerald eyes burned brightly from the band of shadows his hat cast on his face. He swept an appraising look over his troupe. The hairs on my nape pricked, and the scar on my thigh ached when I felt his attention settle on me.

"He approves of your costume," Daemon mumbled with a smirk in his voice.

"How can you tell?"

"I just know."

A second later, Alistair's tongue slithered out from the shadows to lick his lips.

Daemon chuckled smugly. "See?"

The troupe waited with bated breath for the ringleader to speak. He paused a few moments, basking in the tension before addressing us. "As all of you should know by now, for an undetermined amount of time, Sinner's Sideshow is going back to its roots. For the first time in two decades, we're welcoming mortal sinners back into our midst. And tonight, every ticket sold is a death seat."

Excited murmurs spread through the throng of monsters.

"Guests will be given tags labeling them with the sin they've committed, so you all can entertain them according to their sin." He gestured a gloved hand to the black and white big top. "We'll still be running our nightly shows for our supernatural patrons, but the acts will be limited."

"He's finally letting Roach perform," Lollie whispered into my ear.

"Really? What's his act?"

"I don't know. It's Roach, so something to do with piercings or needles. Something gross and creepy. He's been spoiling the audience with you lately. So, it's back to horror-fueled night-mare stuff all of a sudden." Her brows wrinkled. "Do you know why?"

"Uh, looks like Alistair's opening up the ticketing booths, so we should get to our stations."

I quickly excused us and padded off in the opposite direction from where Lollie was heading.

Daemon snickered. "That was smooth."

"It's not like we can tell her the truth."

"They're probably going to find out when the Horsemen eventually crash the party."

"Well, until then, it's hush hush."

Guests started to pour in, lumbering through the rows of food stalls and game booths like zombies. Alistair had told us they'd be lured with a strong hypnosis magic—they'd hear his whispers in their ear, and in a trance, they'd come.

"It's kind of like that movie *Hocus Pocus*," I observed from the bench we'd found beside the Ferris Wheel to watch mortals stumble into the carnival in a daze. "The hot witch lured all the children with a song. But instead of a witch wanting to suck the youth from children, it's an ancient shadow monster who's basically the closest thing to Satan we have, wanting to suck the fear from sex offenders and men who tell women they don't know to smile."

As the sinners filtered in, the carnival came to life. The rides whirred, the games buzzed and beeped. Unhinged laughter and screams started to fill the air.

A man approached us, his steps mechanical and his eyes wide. Confusion and mild amusement radiated from him. He had a cone of cotton candy clutched in his hand. As he came close, I saw the paper name tag stuck to his shirt. "Hello, My Name Is" was scribbled out with a marker and written in a shaky script were the words, "Beat wife to death. Got away with it."

He took a seat on the opposite side of Daemon, staring up at the Ferris Wheel's swaying pods with a vacant expression.

The hounds growled at the man's proximity, but Daemon quieted them down with a command in Infernal. "Good doggies," the man said, his speech slurred.

"Do you want me to get you some cotton candy, Pup?"

I perked up at the mention of a snack. "Fuck yeah."

The last word had barely left my tongue when Daemon's hand shot straight into the side of the man's head, his claws busting through his skull with a sickening crunch. With a yank, he pulled his hand from the man's head and in his bloody palm sat a brain.

Daemon plucked the cotton candy out of the man's clutch with his clean hand before the body slumped off the bench. When he turned toward me, my heart fluttered. Half of his skeleton face was splattered in blood. He offered me the cotton candy in one hand and the still-twitching brain in the other. "Better than chocolates and teddy bears?"

His dark smile stole my breath away, but I managed to pant out, "Yeah. Better than chocolates and teddy bears."

35

Carnage Carnival

RIFF

"**A**ll this fear in the air is making me hungry," I said, clutching the golden bar of my carousel horse. Though, it wasn't much of a horse at all. It had wings and horns, and its body was gaunt, its ribcage pronounced against its skin, which was painted to look like it was decomposing.

The carousel played a creepy, off-key carnival tune and went round and round.

Raff sat on one of the benches in front of me. He was stretched out, with the crook of his arm tucked behind his head, staring up at his reflection in the mirrored panels that lined the underside of the carousel's canopy.

He was picking his canines with one of his claws, grumbling about how he'd never tear out the throat of a bearded man with his teeth ever again. His lips curled in revulsion. "How can you be hungry? Everything fucking stinks here. All these parasites and their disgusting emotions are poisoning the air."

I hopped off my horse and propped my arms on the back of Raff's bench, leaning over him with my painted nails, impatiently drumming the wood. "That's exactly it. Tasting all this rotten despair and pity in the air is making me hungry for something sweet."

Raff blinked up at me, then a smile slowly broke out over his face. Our face paint was a little sloppy tonight since we'd rushed it. We'd taken most of our time making sure Daemon's face was perfect. But the rush job added to the horror aesthetic. The patchy black diamonds over our eyes bled into the white base, creating a mixed look that was somewhere between corpse paint and classic clown makeup.

The only color on our faces was the little red dot on our noses and the smear of red that created our freaky, overly pronounced smiles. It looked like blood, and that's because it was. Conquest was long gone now, but we'd saved some of his blood and mixed it with beeswax, making a perfect addition to our cosmetic collection.

We wandered through Sinner's Carnival in search of our favorite she-devil, excitement thrumming in my veins. We'd texted her, but there was no answer; she was probably busy wreaking vengeance and looking hot as sin doing it.

The carnival was a chaotic playground of carnage and death. At first, the troupe was a little on edge. None of us had been a part of the circus in the "old days" when Astrid ran the show.

We'd all taken turns clearing out the death seats, but we weren't accustomed to this level of slaughter and violence.

It only took an hour or two for us to get nice and comfy, disposing of all the sinners. We were monsters, after all.

A clown—an Unseelie female by the name of Daisy Doom—was dressed in a yellow coat and oversized red galoshes. A string of girlish giggles spilled from her as she stomped around in a puddle with a deflated red balloon clutched in her hand, dragging on the ground behind her. It would have been cute if it wasn't for the fact that the puddle was blood and the balloon was a severed head.

"Hey, Daisy!" Raff approached her with his hands in his pockets and let out a low whistle when he spotted the head's body tucked behind a trash can. "Nice kill. Have you seen Meg?"

She pointed us in the direction of the Ferris Wheel. It was only a few steps in that we knew she'd steered us correctly when we heard the sounds of screams and barking dogs and caught the sweet scent of candy coming from that direction.

We rounded a corner, and I nearly swallowed my tongue at the sight that greeted us.

Meg was dressed as a slutty harlequin clown with a ruffled skirt that barely covered her ass and a top so tight you could see the indentations of her nipple piercings. Pink stockings hugged her plump thighs, and I couldn't help but wonder if she was wearing any panties underneath them.

Her makeup was perfectly done, with diamond eyes. One green. One blue.

Fuck. Seeing her in our colors always made me rock hard.

She was standing over a pudgy, middle-aged man who was thrashing on the ground. Fat tears streamed down his cheeks. "Don't know why I'm here! Who–who are you people? No! Stop! *Stop! Arrrgh!*"

His pleas turned to screams of pain while everyone around them just went on with their business. The other guests were so deep in their trances that they barely looked in the dying man's direction.

Daemon loomed over the man with a boot planted on the small of his back, keeping him pinned to the ground. He looked so threatening, which made the fact that he appeared to be holding Meg's cotton candy for her while she stabbed the man in the ass with her sword oddly cute.

"What's wrong? You rape women all the time. They beg for you to stop, and you don't. So why should I give you the courtesy?" Her voice jumped with her fury, and she thrust the sword deeper into his ass.

This reminded me of the day we'd met her when Raff and I had been working in the haunt before the show. We'd watched her kill that ghoul who'd forced himself on that poor girl.

My brother's lust threaded through the air, mingling with the scent of popcorn and the rotten aroma of fear and pity.

The list of our freaky kinks was pretty extensive, but watching our Harbinger of Justice stab a rapist up the ass with a sword while she made the biggest, baddest alpha in the troupe hold her snack? This had to be top three, easy.

A primal noise wrenched from Raff's throat as he watched her. I was right there with him, exerting every last iota of self-restraint I had—it wasn't a lot—in keeping myself from shifting and marking her right here and now.

There was no way she was going to escape this night without our marks on her body to join Daemon's and Alistair's. We'd waited long enough, and with Discord's blessing, there was no reason to wait any longer.

With a few more stabs, the rapist convulsed violently. Pungent terror bled from him like the pool of blood spreading beneath his body. Then he fell limp beneath Daemon's shoe.

Megaera stared down at the body in silence, her chest heaving with heavy breaths. Her knuckles tightened around the hilt of her sword. "Fucking bastard. Who's cleaning up these bodies, anyway? All this blood and guts everywhere is a serious tripping hazard."

My heart stuttered for a few beats as I saw through her act. She was feigning anger to cover up the fact that murdering that man hadn't been as fun for her as she'd probably anticipated.

The hellhound lifted his boot off the corpse, his huge hand clamping down on her shoulder. He pulled her tight against his body and dropped his mouth to her neck, pressing a kiss to the column of her throat.

"He deserved it. All these people deserve it, remember?"

Even Daemon could glean the mild guilt radiating from her.

She bobbed a nod and visibly relaxed against his heat. "Sorry. Sometimes I get these human emotions that just flare up out of nowhere."

"You're still half human. You're allowed to have human reactions to things every once in a while."

She turned around and searched the radiant gold of his eyes. I had to admit, they looked good against his white and black skeleton paint. "You weren't exactly a fan of my humanness when I first joined the troupe."

"Because I thought it made you weak. It doesn't."

She blew out a breath, her eyes closing as she bobbed a nod.

Deciding it was time to break up the sappy scene, I stepped out into the open and cleared my throat to announce our arrival. "Aw, wasn't that *so* sweet, Raff?"

My brother let out a sinister laugh even though his eyes were glittering with adoration as he looked at Meg. "Picture perfect." He created a frame with his thumbs and forefingers and held it up. "Would make the perfect Hallmark card. The rapist with his ass blown out and his innards hanging out really ties it together."

"Fuck off," she said, unable to keep the grin off her face. "Where the Hell have you guys been?"

I shrugged. "Oh, you know. Enjoying the creepy festivities. Raff tore out the throat of a priest who likes to touch little boys. That was pretty cool. Oh, and Lollie gave us a free pretzel. She seems to be in a good mood."

I loved the way Meg's eyes heated as she took us in. She worked her bottom lip between her teeth. I wasn't sure if it was her intention, but she often did it when she was hungry. The kind of hunger that Lollie's concession stand wouldn't remedy.

"So, you guys already ate?"

"Oh, we're still hungry."

I shifted my attention to Daemon, ready to fire off a question I already knew his answer to. We'd told him what we planned to do to her tonight. He really had changed because he hadn't been pissed by the idea.

He'd been turned on.

"Mind if we borrow her for the rest of the night?"

36

Tunnel of Sin

MEG

"I'm surprised you two aren't in your full forms. Alistair's given everyone permission to walk around in their scariest shapes for the carnival."

I looked to the twin on my left and then my right. Each one held my hand as we walked through the carnival. They shared a look over my head, then looked back down at me.

"We were waiting for you," Raff said, and Riff added, "We thought we'd celebrate by kicking it off with a bang."

"Oh." My tongue went dry in my mouth as all the moisture in my body seemed to sink once I got their meaning. "*Oh.*"

I stopped abruptly when I saw Sinclair stationed at the "test your strength" game.

"Hey, Sin! Congrats on the bond with Lollie!"

The vampire's expression lit up as I approached, his blood-red eyes glittering in the carnival's flashing lights. At the mention of Lollie, a rosy hue stained his cheeks. He must have fed recently. "Thanks. I'm still surprised she let me."

Riff chuckled. "I'm surprised you're still in one piece."

"Ha! Right?" Sinclair gestured to the hammer leaning against the metal meter with a bell fixed to the top. Next to that was a sign with an illustration of a buff gargoyle flexing his muscles. "You guys wanna take a swing? Win a head!"

My attention shifted to the prize rack. If this was a human carnival, it would be overflowing with brightly colored teddy bears, inflatable mallets, and light-up wands that strobed in the dark. This was a carnival birthed from Alistair's macabre imagination, though, so the prize rack sported nothing but the severed heads of sinners.

I grimaced. "Uh, no thanks, Sin. I'm all set in the severed limb department."

We said goodbye to the vampire and wove between game booths and food stalls, coming to a stop when we noticed the head of a boar towering over the throng of people.

Larry was in his Butcher persona, which meant he was pretty much nude save for the little apron tied around his waist that barely managed to cover his, er, "meat." His sausage fingers clutched the cleaver propped against his shoulder. Surprisingly, the blade was clean.

"What's your kill count at, buddy?" Raff asked as we approached.

His hog snout wriggled with a snort. "Zero. Boss said I don't have to kill anyone. Just gotta scare 'em and help pick up bodies."

Alistair was an enigma that I doubted I'd ever fully figure out. He was complicated, devious at times, and completely infuriating at others. And not so deep down, he was kind to the people who deserved it. He knew Larry was too gentle-hearted to kill anyone, even the cockroaches of humankind. So, he didn't make him.

We stood with Larry for a moment, wondering what held his attention rapt. It dawned on me that we were standing a few booths down from the concession stand the gorgon sisters were running.

He was staring at Mollie.

Roach the mothman was lounging against the pickup counter, chatting up the gloomy gorgon. By the irritation carving her face, she wasn't enjoying the conversation.

"They would make good mates, wouldn't they?" the giant rumbled, almost more to himself than to me.

Roach was a Death's-head mothman with piercings and tattoos, handsome for sure. And by the way Larry's hand roved over his big belly, he was feeling a bit inadequate.

"I don't think she likes him," Riff said, taking note of Mollie's expression as I had. "Go do some recon, Meg."

He gave a gentle push to my back, nudging me toward the booth. I sent him a sharp look, but curiosity kept me moving closer.

There was a sign taped to the booth reading "Deep fried Twinkies, hotdogs, popcorn." Beneath that was scribbled in marker, "Ask about our secret menu."

"You know, Moll. If you advertise your secret menu, it's not so secret. I'm surprised the boss is allowing you to push your shit here. These fucks don't deserve to numb their pain."

Mollie's brows gnashed. "Don't you have a flame to go fly into or something?"

Roach's antennae twitched, and he scratched the brown fur collaring his tattooed neck. "The show doesn't start for another hour."

"Roach, there you are."

The mothman glanced up at me and shifted uncomfortably at my approach.

Alistair's mating claim on my thigh put a large majority of the troupe on edge. No one had solid proof that the four haunt workers who disappeared last week were tied to me, yet it was the same night Alistair marked me.

People put two and two together, and everyone knew to be careful with me. Or else my four big scary boyfriends would make them disappear.

"The boss wants to see you in the big top. Wants to go over expectations he has for your act." I smiled sweetly at Roach, the lie falling easily off my tongue.

The mothman's eyes almost bugged out of his head. "Again? Shit."

His wings stretched out from the holes cut into the back of his jacket, and he launched himself into the air. It was a wonder he could stay airborne with all the metal rings and gauges decorating his wings.

"You didn't have to do that," Mollie said dryly. "But thanks, I guess."

"Hey, um. Larry really likes you." I hiked a thumb over my shoulder, gesturing to the giant a few booths down. "But I think he's under the impression that your night together didn't mean as much to you as it does to him," I said, remembering what Lollie had told me about seeing them together.

The gorgon's cheeks flushed. "Oh..."

"If you get a chance tonight, maybe you two can hang out together. Like, on a date or something." Jesus. I was really bad at this wingman shit. Thank fuck my best friend had come pre-loaded with a boyfriend.

Mollie and all her snakes blinked at me. "A date?"

"Yeah, like playing some games together. I don't think he can fit on any of the rides, but you can share some cotton candy or something?"

She considered the suggestion and, to my surprise, agreed. "Okay. Tell him I'll meet him by the carousel in an hour."

I made my way back to Larry but not before catching Lollie scolding a clown in line, who was holding up a flaccid piece of flesh with a pout on her face. "Pleeeease, Loll?"

"I'm not going to tell you again, Daisy. I'm not putting a severed penis in the deep fryer. It's for Twinkies and funnel cake only."

I got back to Larry, practically bouncing with excitement. "I think you have a better chance at sprouting wings than her getting together with Roach. Oh, and she wants to meet you in an hour at the carousel!"

His eyes lit up. "Really? Thank you, Meg."

"Sure thing, Larry. Wait." I spun around, scanning the crowd for blue and green hair. "Where did the twins go?"

"Oh, right. The clowns told me to tell you to meet them in the Tunnel of Sin."

Unshockingly, Alistair's version of the Tunnel of Love came with a hellish twist. It was still a slow-moving dark ride, but without the schlocky romance theme with the classic swan boats and cardboard cutouts of cupids. The water was red to simulate the River Styx, and I was pretty confident that it was actual blood. There were angels decorating the outside, but they were biblically accurate, with clusters of feathers and countless eyes that tracked me as I approached.

The girl operating the ride leaned against the podium with a bored look on her face as she scrolled through her phone. She had a teal mohawk, a septum piercing and heavy eye makeup. A black body con dress hugged her shapely form, which was decorated with tentacles that wrapped around her hips and coiled around her breast.

I always thought she was hot, and the fact that she was the troupe's contortionist made her even more appealing. We'd flirted on occasion, but it never went further than that. There was no magnetic pull between us like there was with Daemon, Alistair and the twins. Which was a good thing.

Any more mates and my vagina would probably hand in its resignation.

"Sorry, the ride is closed." Her voice was monotone, and she didn't bother looking up. "Come back in an hour if you're still alive."

"Wow, Zoe. You got assigned to the ride that's mostly blood? At least you don't have to leave for lunch."

Her attention lifted from her phone, and her painted black lips split with a shit-eating grin. "Eh, I prefer my blood a little fresher. Plus, I know better than to consume anything from the boss' illusions. Damn, girl. Look at you." She unlatched the rope blocking off the entrance and gestured me through. "The twins are waiting for you inside. I'd say see you when you get out, but looking the way you do, they're going to eat you up. Maybe they'll let me have their leftovers."

"Doubtful. You'd have to fight Daemon and Alistair for the scraps."

"Yeah, I'm gonna have to pass on that," she said with a snicker. "Though it sounds like a fun way to die."

Heading into the dark mouth of the tunnel, I waited for a boat to float by before stepping in. It was made to look like an old-fashioned skiff that Charon, the ferryman of the River Styx in Greek mythology, might use. There was a single lantern hanging off the front of the boat, but it did nothing to penetrate the murk that lay ahead.

Red light bulbs lined the top of the tunnel, but they were so far and few between that they only added to the eerie aesthetic rather than illuminating anything.

Music played overhead, a slow and ominous tune that struck me as something Alistair would find romantic.

I started to wonder how I was supposed to meet the twins while confined to a boat when the flow of the water abruptly stopped, and the boat came to a halt, gently bobbing in place.

Shit. What was I supposed to do now?

After a minute of weighing my options, I stepped out of the skiff and onto the platform running alongside the water. It was oddly cold, and I wrapped my arms around myself for warmth.

As I headed deeper into the tunnel, the music quieted, making me painfully aware of my breathing and the little jingle of bells that were inside the pom poms on my bodice.

The sensory deprivation had me on edge.

I started to feel like I was in a horror movie, the kind Riff and Raff loved to watch, where the girls always got torn up by the psycho killers or the ferocious monsters.

My heart shuttered to a halt, and my feet froze in place when two lights suddenly appeared in the shadows ahead.

No, not lights.

Two flickering flames of blue and two green.

Heavy, barreling breaths that could only come from something inhuman and dangerous echoed through the tunnel. The creature stepped out of the blackness and into the red halo of light one of the bulbs cast on the water.

I'd seen Riff in his monster form before.

He wasn't as large as Daemon's hellbeast, but he was easily seven feet tall with stacks of muscle packed into his frame. He was large enough to snap me in half if he had the mind to, but his sheer size wasn't the most intimidating part. It was his monstrous skull head, with flame eyes and twisting horns.

My eyes strained through the murk, and I could just make out the faded clown paint stained into the bone of his face.

"Look at this, brother. Our prey actually came." Riff's voice came out guttural and grating. A voice that could only have been created in Hell.

"Walked right into our trap," another voice that was just as deep echoed from beside him.

The dark thrill of what was to come had the air buzzing.

"Maybe she wants to be eaten." Raff's words sparked a fire in my belly that chased away the chill in the tunnel.

The glow of their eyes grew strong as they slowly approached, and the bloody water splashed with their heavy steps.

"Run, Hell Bat. Try to get away," Riff growled.

"Yes. Give us a good chase," Raff said with a baleful laugh that had my pussy soaking, arousal dripping down my stocking-clad thighs. "We like to play with our food."

37

Eat Her Soul Out

MEG

I didn't want to get away, but I wasn't about to let them have me without making them work for it. So, I turned and ran back through the tunnel as fast as my feet would carry me. The rubber soles of my sneakers slapped against the metal grate of the maintenance landing, my short bursts of breath falling in sync.

The splashing of water and animalistic sounds of two predators on the hunt closed in, drowning out the music filtering through the speakers.

My lungs started to burn as I gulped in the frigid air.

Human survival instincts were the voice of reason in my head. *Yes. Run. Get away. They're going to eat you!*

My succubus thirst was louder, screaming, *Um, why are you running? You know what those tongues are capable of. Turn around so that they can eat you!*

There was no time to listen to either voice. My short legs were no match for their huge, bounding strides. They probably could have caught me before I'd gotten more than a few paces away.

I knew they liked watching me run.

They loved the struggle.

It had me wondering if maybe that was a result of their past. They liked the power, feeling like they were the ones in control.

After Walker's crumbled and I lost everything, I had to be fiercely independent and always in control. So, in moments like these with the twins, I loved relinquishing it.

A thick tail swooped in front of my legs, my foot catching on it like a tripwire that sent me hurtling off the platform and into the bloody water.

I scrambled to get to my feet, the water splashing violently as I struggled to get purchase on the slick bottom. I slipped again, managing to catch myself on my hands and knees. The water wasn't as deep as I expected. It came to chin level in this position.

Before I could pull myself to my full height, a hand closed around my tail and yanked me back. My hands flew out from under me.

My head was forced beneath the surface as whoever had hold of my tail dragged me through the water.

Booming laughter exploded around me, muffling for a second as I slipped back under the water and grew loud again as I resurfaced.

"S–st–op! Stop!" I sputtered. Water rushed up my nose, which set my sinuses on fire.

Lifting me by the tail, I was pulled out of the water completely. My head swirled as all the blood rushed to my head from being held upside down.

"You know that's not the magic words, Hell Bat," Raff rumbled as he hoisted me high enough in the air to meet his flaming gaze.

"If you want us to set you free, all you have to say is 'playtime's over,'" he said in a purr that reminded me this was all a game.

My mind grappled between human instincts and succubus lust. Only for a beat. My succubus side won like it always did, and it wasn't just my sex demon lust spiking my thirst and driving me into a frenzy.

I wanted this. Every fiber of my being wanted them so badly I could feel the ache down to my marrow.

And the twins' brand of pain was always torturous, addicting, *ecstasy*.

I'd rather rip out my wings than have them stop.

An unhinged grin split my lips. "Fuck you."

Just to ensure they'd give me a railing none of us would forget anytime soon, I spat in Raff's eye.

I was a succubus. My body produced copious amounts of fluids, so there was enough saliva to make the flame in that eye die out.

It sputtered back to life on the next breath, and he laughed. "Feisty little clown *slut*."

Before I could react, he lowered me, dunking my head into the water. A second later, he pulled me out, just long enough to choke down a breath before dunking me again.

"I love it when she's dripping for us." Riff laughed at his own joke.

They might have been terrifying sex demons, but underneath the horns, serrated teeth and giant cocks, they were silly clowns with their silly jokes.

Hysterical laughter poured from me as he dunked me again and pulled me back up again—the sound broken up with coughing as I sputtered for oxygen. But I didn't stop laughing.

Until Raff passed me to Riff, who took hold of my ankle, turning me completely upside down and splaying me open.

Raff's claws swiped at my apex, ripping a hole in my stockings.

"Our clown slut isn't wearing panties."

Raff's face shoved close, the heat of his breath fanning over my exposed center. "You're so fucking wet. Our twisted little clown likes it when we don't let her breathe, doesn't she?"

Riff dunked me again, this time holding me under the surface. When a hot, wet, slathered lick came over my pussy, I moaned, and bubbles exploded from my mouth as precious air slipped out.

Fuck.

This was so weird and so wrong on so many levels…

Which only drove my lust higher.

The tongue lapped at my center, the point of the muscle prodding at my clit before painting another lick through my folds.

When it plunged inside my pussy, I screamed, letting out the last of my air.

I thrashed, the spaded tip of my tail slapping at the hand clutching my ankle. The tongue pulled out, and Riff wrenched me out of the water.

He held me up so both of them could get a good look at me. "Look at what a trembling mess you are."

I *was* a trembling, wet mess—bloody water and makeup streaked down my reddened face, and my clothes were soaked through.

However, that's not what they were referencing.

Riff took hold of both my ankles and held me wide open so they could get a good look at what they did to me. Raff leaned in, my muscles clenching around him as his tongue slithered into my pussy.

"I love how her cunt twitches," Riff rasped as he watched his brother sink into me. "Pretty folds all a flutter as we fill up this cock hungry pussy."

The radiant heat of Raff's tongue spread through me, melting my insides. I went limp in Riff's grip, the blood in my head and the pleasure between my legs too goddamn much to do anything but surrender to the sensation.

"What? Is that all the fight that's in you?" Riff mocked as he cocked his head to look down at me. The fire in his eyes burned me up like a fever, fat beads of sweat and arousal streaking down my skin. "A few licks, and you're reduced to nothing but our whimpering whore?"

I whimpered in answer, earning me a chuckle from Rafferty, which reverberated through me and had my eyes rolling back into my head.

Riff readjusted me in his arms, securing one arm around my waist while he kept one hand clamped on my thigh, keeping me spread for his brother.

"Stho tight..." Raff couldn't fully enunciate since his tongue was shoved all the way down to my goddamn soul. There was so much saliva oozing onto my stocking-wrapped thighs and slipping down to the hole at my center.

With my back to Riff, my face was perfectly level with the bulge in Raff's pants.

It's almost like he read my mind because, in the next moment, he was tearing them open and pulling himself out.

The tattoo of the clown girl tied up shibari style with a balloon string filled my vision. My eyes slid lower to the thick, veiny cock of his monster form. As expected, it was monstrous—not that it had any odd distinctions about it. It was just fucking huge. If I hadn't already mated Daemon's hellbeast and Discord's pinky finger, I would've questioned if I could even fit them.

Raff's tongue slipped from my pussy, and he leaned back, his skull tipping downward as his attention slid down to my face.

I'd been upside down for so long, I should have passed out by now. With Alistair and Daemon's mark, I was experiencing minor human inconveniences less and less. I had more energy, and my senses were more acute. I didn't feel the need to sleep as often. And apparently, the location of where my blood was in my body didn't seem to matter much anymore, so long as most of it was kept inside me.

Gripping his base, he guided his tip so it slid along my lips as if applying lipstick. He pulled back, a string of pre-cum connecting us before it snapped. Then he was ramming himself into my mouth, uncaring that my teeth scraped his shaft as he hit the back of my throat.

It was now Riff's tongue shoving into my pussy—fucking me until I was pushed off the edge and screaming my release around his twin's cock.

"Good girl," Raff praised on a growl that raked over me, making goosebumps pebble my flesh. "We love it when your holes—" He drew his hips back and then slammed back inside me, hitting the back of my throat and making me gag. "Squeeze us tight. *Fuck.*"

He came with a low groan. Hot cum spurted from his tip, and without being asked, I swallowed it down like a good little succubus.

Raff slowly extracted his-still-hard cock from my mouth, and Riff finally turned me right side up and lowered me to my feet. My world went sideways, and my legs refused to hold me up. Both of them surged forward to catch me before I fell and propped me up between them.

With a possessive growl, Riff pulled me away from his brother. "You came in her first, so I get to be the first one in her pussy."

Raff's hands clamped over my shoulders and tugged me back against him. "That's not how it works, dick for brains."

They were like two siblings squabbling over a toy. I guess they *were* two siblings squabbling over a toy.

"Stop it, both of you. Y–you can both fit at once." The moment I said it, I regretted it. Their attention slowly veered to me. Their huge jaws parted, and their tongues swiped over their serrated teeth.

These demons were going to tear me apart.

38

Twin Flames

MEG

My heart thrashed in my chest as Raff's hand hooked in the neckline of my bodice and ripped it off my body with one swift tug. On my next ragged breath, the ruffled skirt met the same fate.

Looks like I'm walking out of here naked.

Riff loved cutting my clothes off whenever he had a chance. It was an excuse to put his extensive knife collection to use. Raff, however, was partial to tearing them off, and there was something hot about the sound of shredding fabric.

The cool air instantly had my nipples hardening, and the barbells adorning them gleamed with the green luminescence of his eyes.

"Stretch out your wings," he demanded, his tone rife with something dark and desperate.

I obeyed without hesitation, unfolding my wings from my back and stretching them to their full span. The air instantly grew heavy and heated with the intense surge of lust rolling off them.

When I first joined Alistair's circus, I'd been self-conscious about the smaller size of my wings. It's not like I knew a lot about my kind at the time, but I'd had this instinctual shame about them for whatever reason. Turned out, large and imposing succubus wings were considered the ideal beauty standard.

All my men worshiped them like they were the sexiest things they'd ever seen.

And my incubus twins were the first to let me know that, in their eyes, my wings were perfect.

Riff moved close behind me, and a delicious shiver rattled down my spine when I felt a hot tongue lick over my wing. "These are so fucking sexy, Harbinger."

His tongue continued to roam over my wing's leathery webbing as his fingers wedged between my thighs and rubbed through my folds. "She's wet enough, I think," he told his brother.

I was definitely wet enough—their saliva and arousal dribbled down my thighs and into the ride's bloody water.

"Loop your arms around my neck," Riff instructed in my ear with a soft growl, the sound of rustling fabric telling me that he was getting himself out. On my next breath, his long fingers were closing around my thighs and lifting me off the ground.

With my back to his chest, I did as he instructed and reached over his shoulders to lace my fingers together behind his neck. My breath caught at the way his hands completely encircled my thighs and slowly spread me apart.

His monstrous claws—flecked with flakes of black nail polish—biting into my flesh and ripping my stockings would make for good spank bank material later.

Raff stepped up to the cradle of my thighs, the fiery green flames embedded into his eye socket seeming to blaze hotter as he took in the way I looked in his brother's arms. His chest rose and fell with labored breaths. His jaws parted, deadly teeth oozing with saliva.

He was terrifying.

I knew the exact moment they felt the slight pang of fear permeate my demeanor by the dark glee radiating from theirs.

"Taste that, brother? *Fear,*" Raff gritted as he fisted his cock, giving it a few firm strokes as he stepped closer until he stood between the V of my legs. His heat seeped into the undersides of my thighs, and his breath washed over my breasts, making me squirm. Keeping one hand fixed to his cock, his other traveled up my thigh, his claws making a light clicking sound as they skimmed over his brother's. "Looks like we're doing our part in keeping the boss fed."

A guttural laugh shook Riff's chest, the sensation pleasant against my ultra-sensitive wings. "Any other mortal would be pissing themselves, but your fear just makes this needy little pussy wetter, doesn't it?"

I gave a wobbly nod as I flamed in a full-body flush.

"Fuck me, you're so fucking sexy, Megaera."

My breath froze in my lungs. Raff never called me by my full first name.

Hearing it on his tongue, whispered like a prayer, had my heart fluttering like a love-struck schoolgirl. As if I wasn't sandwiched between two demons.

"*Please*," I mumbled, my voice hoarse with need. "I need you both inside me."

My body trembled at the first kiss of Raff's cock against my center. He paused, the tip teasing my folds just enough to drive me into a desperate frenzy. My hips bucked in search of friction.

Riff chuckled in my ear as his grip on me tightened. "Patience, baby. We've been waiting a long time for this. We wanna savor it."

The anticipation ate me alive.

"Please," I panted. "Please. Please. We've waited long enough."

Riff's hands were full with keeping me spread, but his tail coiled around my breast—hard enough to wrench a pained moan from my lips. "We love it when you beg for us."

The spaded tip flicked the barbell piercing my nipple, and he laughed at the way my thighs started to quiver in his arms. "We're not even inside of you yet, and you're already in pieces. You better pull it together, or there'll be nothing left of you to return to Alistair and Daemon."

"I... I don't care. Fuck me to death if you have to. Al–Alistair can find me in Hell and bring me back." My lips split with a filthy smile. "Then we can do it all over again— Ah!"

My last syllable was strangled in my throat as Raff chose that moment to shove inside me.

He didn't take it slow—didn't ease himself in. One punch of his hips, and he filled my pussy to the brim. Before I could gather my tattered nerves and brace myself for the second invasion, Riff was right there with him.

He worked himself inside me with more care and a slower pace than his brother, but fuck, there wasn't a moment to take my time adjusting. They were frantic, so fucking hungry for me that I was in awe that they were managing to be this gentle.

The snout of Raff's skull settled over one of my shoulders and Riff's on the other. My hands flew to their horns—one on each.

As Riff slid in beside his brother, a series of broken curses and pleasure-laced growls tumbled from his jaws. "I... I can feel you, Rifton...Shit. Your dick hardware is making it weird, bro—*Fuck*."

They huffed and swore at one another, laced together on a string of animalistic noises.

I wasn't going to last long like this. No woman would.

I felt so full, like I could split open at any moment.

"Fuck, fuck, fuck," was all I could manage to babble.

They were not small males. The complicated network of veins wrapping their shafts made for a very textured experience, and Riff's Jacob's ladder piercings had drool slipping down the corner of my mouth.

"You're doing so well for us, baby girl," Raff rumbled in my ear. "Just a little bit more, and we'll both be all the way in."

"Relax, baby."

Their comforting words, mixed with their own little noises and mutterings as they lost themselves inside me, had me close to the edge. My head swam with the overwhelming fog of pleasure that wrapped my brain. I couldn't make sense of who was saying what anymore. We were tangled so tightly together, it felt like the three of us had melded into one.

"S–so full…"

"You can do it. If you can take three hellhound cocks in your pretty little holes, you can take us."

Sure enough, my body stretched to take them and the pain was chased with pure fucking euphoria as Riff fed the last inch of his length inside me alongside his brother.

"Fucking Hells, Harbinger," the blue-eyed twin moaned in that monstrous baritone. "You're squeezing us so tightly. Do we feel good inside you?"

I gave a drunken nod, unable to summon a verbal answer.

Raff nuzzled one side of my neck, the bone of his snout making a *chinking* sound against Daemon's spiked collar. Riff's tongue stroked along my neck and roamed lower to trace the hellhound's claim on my shoulder.

I shuddered as intense pleasure shot from the mark straight down to my core, where they were seated.

We stayed like that for a moment, the heated silence filled with our tattered breathing and Alistair's choice of music.

"Are you ready?"

I blinked. Now that they were all the way inside, they gave my body time to adjust. They had more patience and control than Daemon and Alistair, which struck me as ironic since Alistair had forbidden them from fully shifting out of concern for *their* lack of control.

Their hips started to move, one in and one out in perfect tandem.

Finally.

Sweet friction.

The pace started slow, but that didn't last long. Soon, their movements turned frantic. Our bodies clashed. Sweat and saliva, and who knows what the fuck else, made me slide and slip, my knuckles cracking as I held onto their horns for dear life.

"Where do you want them, baby?" Riff's voice cut through the haze of lust.

I blinked rapidly as my brain tried to comprehend the question. Then it clicked.

They wanted to know where I wanted their marks.

Alistair and Daemon hadn't asked where I wanted their marks. They'd just done it. The thought of them being so consumed by their need for me that they couldn't control where to bite me—that they just had to bite me—struck a twisted little chord inside me.

But the twins asking me? Maintaining enough control that my opinion on the matter was their first priority? It had my orgasm exploding through me before I could barely comprehend it.

"My wings!" I screamed, bucking against them even though I was wedged so tightly between their muscled forms that I could barely draw breath into my body, let alone move. "Mark me on my wings!"

39

Boat Ride

MEG

Sweet Fucking Discord.

First, shock rippled through the heady air at my request. Then their lust grew so palpable I could choke on it.

Riff bit down on one wing, and Raff on the other—perfectly in sync.

My climax would have been intense enough without the added sensation of their mating claim, shooting white-hot pain through my system. My muscles unwound as the blinding pain morphed into a deep, infernal pleasure that burned me up and turned me to ash in their arms.

Raff's fingers clenched around my horn, and jerked my head up to meet his gaze. "You're not done, baby. You need to bite us to complete the bond."

They were right. I wasn't finished. And neither were they.

They didn't stop fucking into me. My release only drove them in deeper, harder, the slap of wet flesh ringing in my ear, and their manic hunger electrified the dark of the tunnel.

"W–where?" was all I could manage to squeak out.

There was only one place I could reach that would make sense. Their shoulders.

Still, I asked. Knowing their past, I knew it was important to ask.

Raff hunched lower, the muscles in his shoulder flexing as he brought it close to my mouth. The air was still cold enough in the tunnel, and he blazed hot enough that steam rose off his skin.

Staring at the blank canvas of flesh where I knew my mark was about to mar his flesh forever had my tiny little fangs aching. I slammed them down into the muscle.

He jerked and tensed against me, hissing between clenched teeth.

Then he came with a roar.

I knew the twins liked doing everything at the same time, so before Raff finished emptying himself inside me, I craned my head and punched my fangs into the shoulder Riff offered.

Another wash of hot demon seed filled me.

Raff mumbled something in Infernal under his breath, and I decided right then I'd have my mates teach me their native tongue. Everyone in the troupe spoke English. It was one of Alistair's requirements for joining, but when I was with my guys like this, and they lost themselves in me—they always slipped into Infernal. Probably a curse, a prayer, something obscene. But I liked the idea of knowing their choice words when they fell apart inside me.

We stayed like that for what felt like an eternity, although it couldn't have been more than a minute or two as we collected our breath.

The whole thing didn't take more than an hour because, just then, the flow of the water started to move, and the boats began to drift through the tunnel once again.

The twins carefully lifted me off them. As soon as my feet were on the ground, they shifted back.

They looked almost just as fucked as me. Their green and blue hair was all askew, and their clown makeup smeared. Their pants were completely shredded from the shift.

"Shit. We should have taken these off beforehand," Riff said as he tore the destroyed garment from his body and tossed it into the water, with Raff following suit.

I grinned at them as I stepped into the first boat that passed. The only part of my outfit that survived was my stockings, with the exception of the claw marks and the gaping hole between my legs, the ruffled collar around my throat, and my sneakers.

"Who cares? Everyone here has seen us naked."

They stepped into the boat and settled down on the bench with me between them.

Raff grumbled, and his arm slid behind me on the bench to sling it over my shoulder. "The troupe has. But I don't want these mortal perverts looking at you."

His brother shrugged, raking his fingers through his electric blue locks. "If any mortal looks at her, we'll just kill them. I'll stab out their eyes, and you can set them on fire."

We fell into a peaceful silence as we drifted through the tunnel. When we emerged through the exit, the sounds of screams greeted us, and the Ferris Wheel's purple and red blinking lights lit up the night.

When the boat drifted to a stop, I realized I didn't want to get out. I wanted this moment to last just a little longer. Zoe greeted us halfway through, asking us if we enjoyed the ride before her words faded mid-sentence once she noticed we were naked.

I asked the twins if we could go in again to actually enjoy the ride this time, and they happily humored me.

We looped around two, three, four more times. I lost count.

At some point, Riff fell asleep, and his head slumped against mine. I winced from the way his horn was gouging into my skull. Before I could readjust him, Raff reached a long arm over me and, with a single finger, poked his brother in the temple, sending his head slumping to the other side.

"There—" He froze when he caught my look, registering the tears brimming my eyes. "What's wrong? D–did we hurt you?"

My heart fluttered at the concern in his voice. "No, I'm just having a really good night, is all. It's a nice break from all the shit that's been going on."

"Yeah," he agreed, and his eyes flickered as if to ensure his brother was still asleep. "Hey, uh, can I tell you something?"

Curiosity had me sitting up straighter. "Of course."

"Other than that first day we met you when Riff tongue-fucked you, this is the first time we've been with anyone in our monster forms since we left the Downside."

"Really?" I knew Alistair didn't like them being in their true forms because he hadn't trusted their control at the time. This was also the twins we were talking about. They weren't exactly staunch rule followers.

"Really. We told you that potential partners weren't into our monster forms because it scared them. But come on, Meg. That was a bad lie."

Thinking back on it, it had been a bad lie. I hadn't known better, though.

How was I to know the entire troupe was filled with freaks who loved fangs and claws and the constant threat of getting torn apart while getting some?

"So, what's the real reason?"

His gaze grew distant for a second, and he blew out a weighted sigh. "We've never talked about our lives before with anyone. Not even each other. Hell, I didn't even think about it, and I'm positive Riff didn't either. When you found out about us being slaves, we played it off. But..."

His voice shook, and the words died in his throat.

I'd never seen him like this before. He was being completely vulnerable, with no smiles and silly quips to hide behind.

"It's okay. You don't have to talk about it." I wrapped my arms around him and laid my head against his chest. His muscles unclenched, and he relaxed beneath me, his hand idly stroking my hair.

"I want to tell you. Back when Conquest owned us, shit was fucked up. We were forced to do some pretty horrible things. He liked having us in our monster forms most of all. I think it made him feel more powerful having control over us even when we were at our strongest."

My stomach knotted at what he was telling me. "You were never intimate with anyone in those forms because that's how you were abused by Conquest."

He grunted softly in confirmation.

Horror worked through me. I pulled myself up from his chest to meet his gaze. "I'm sorry. If I'd known it makes you uncomfortable, I wouldn't have—"

The incubus silenced me with a kiss on my lips. He held my head so tenderly in his hands, and when our lips broke apart, his forehead pressed against mine to keep my gaze captive. "It doesn't, Meg. Not anymore. And that's because of you."

The tears I'd been holding back rolled down my cheeks. "I should have been there with you. I want to go to the Downside and find his soul so we can have Alistair destroy it for good."

"Baby, he's gone."

"What? You didn't send him back to Hell?"

Raff shook his head. "We tortured the ever-loving shit out of him. It was Alistair who made the final blow since..."

"Since he's the only one who can completely destroy a soul."

The corner of his mouth tugged into a smile that had his green eyes sparkling. "Yup. I guess that's kind of a cool perk of being one of Discord's favorites, right? We can do all the fun parts, and our shadow daddy will be there to make sure they never come back."

Raff's voice trailed off again as he seemed to get lost in his thoughts.

Riff stretched his legs out in the boat, making it cramped.

I climbed into Raff's lap with my knees clamped around his hips. "Speaking of shadow daddy, what do you really think of him?"

The way the incubus looked at me was intoxicating.

"Rafferty."

"Hmm?" He lifted his attention to my eyes. "Oh, uh. I've always liked Alistair. He's sexy, if tall, dark and creepy is your type. I mean, the guy is weird as fuck, but he saved us. And he keeps good company. As cheesy as it is to say, Sinner's Sideshow is the closest thing to paradise any of us freaks will ever get to actual heaven. The circus might have started as just a means of feeding his magical powers, but I don't think that's why he does it anymore."

"And what about Daemon? Have your thoughts on him changed?"

At the mention of the hellhound, Raff's brows furrowed. "Riff and I have never hated him, even though he probably thinks that we do. Have I thought about orchestrating his murder? I mean, yeah." The incubus laughed again, this time the unhinged laugh that paired nicely with the melting clown paint. "He's also the devil's pet, so it's not like it's *that* big a deal if I'd gone through with it."

My tail coiled around Raff's throat, and his bare cock thickened, nudging against my center. "Okay, now give me the zero-bullshit answer."

He licked his grinning lips. "I like getting under his skin. It gets me hard."

He was fully erect now, and arching his hips off the boat's bench to make sure I knew it.

"*And?* Do I have to fuck the answer I want to hear out of you?"

His eyes lit up. "If that's an option—" he choked when my tail cinched tighter around his neck, squeezing him so the cords of his throat strained against me, a vein ticking in his jaw. "Jesus, okay. *And* I'm thankful for what he did for us. With Conquest, and getting our revenge. He didn't have to care so damn much about us healing from shit, and he did."

I unwound my tail from his throat and kissed him on the lips. "Good. Now that you've admitted that, you and Riff need to thank him. And just saying thank you isn't going to be enough, but it is a start."

The tattoo over Raff's eyebrows wrinkled with his scowl. "What are we supposed to do? Get him a fucking Hallmark card? Pop out of a cake and suck his dick?"

"Are those really the only two things you can come up with?"

Oh, his smile turned *wicked*. "No."

I gave him a stern look. "Behave."

"Do I have to?"

His hands shoved down on my hips while he surged up, filling me with one swift motion. My yelp of surprise woke Riff up with a start. "W–wha?"

Half of his blue hair was plastered up from where it had been smushed against the boat's siding. He shifted out of the way just in time as Raff flipped me on my back.

Riff knelt on the floor of the boat, wide awake. His mouth crashed down over mine, feasting on my lips as his brother fucked me. The boat rocked violently, and someone from the boat behind us whistled.

We ignored them. We were in a world all our own.

40

A Week Later

Meg

"What do you think, Pet? Should we put him in the main show when all this carnival business is over?" Roach stood in the center of the ring with dozens of fifteen-gauge needles stuck into every inch of his body, the metal glinting ominously in the spotlight. My stomach churned at the sight. Sinner's Sideshow had always been on the grisly side, and the carnival was even worse. Hell, a couple of days ago, I'd strangled a prisoner guard—known for forcing himself onto female prisoners—with his own intestines. And it was needles that unsettled me.

Getting my nipples pierced, and the tattoo on my thigh had been fine, but Roach's act was slow and painful to watch.

Especially when he'd gotten to his genitals.

While the carnival went on outside, "entertaining" the mortal scum lured by Alistair's magic, there was still a nightly show in the big top for the local supernatural populace. The show was shorter, the acts weren't as grand, and Alistair wasn't even ring-leading. But it didn't seem to slow ticket sales.

It was probably out of curiosity for the carnival that they all came.

I turned to Alistair, who held me in his lap with an arm around my waist, his other hand stroking Daemon's head, who was seated by his feet in his smaller hound form.

"Aren't we going for more scary acts moving forward? This one's kind of gross," I answered his question after a moment of thought. "You feed on fear, not disgust."

His eyes slowly turned on me, glittering like emeralds in the dark. He lifted his hand from Daemon and slid the back of his knuckles gently down my jawline. "Fear and terror are more effective when balanced out with other things, Little Demon. Why do you think I put you and your beautiful body on display, hmm? You are beauty and bliss incarnate."

He leaned in, and his death-cold lips brushed over mine in a dark kiss that sent a chill down to my bones. "They imagine having you. Fucking you. I sell the fantasy that they *can* have you. And I dash all their hopes when they're ripped apart by hellhounds the next moment. That is fear with the best flavor..." His tongue flicked out, tasting my lips. "The kind served with a dash of sugar on top."

His words had my blood icing over and my pussy molten hot all at once.

He leaned back, and I chased his mouth. He laughed, capturing my chin between his long fingers before my lips could find their target.

Alistair's devilish teasing drove me crazy.

I still hadn't given him my mark. The half-forged bond sat heavy on my soul, like a missing piece of myself that was right in front of me and I wasn't allowed to touch.

Seducing him wasn't the same as it was with my other men. He loved watching me pull out all the stops to get him in bed. It was as if he found the tension and pent-up frustration just as pleasing as sex.

So, different tactics had to be deployed.

What I knew about the enigmatic demon was that he was most responsive to me when I stood up to him, when I refused to take no for an answer. It was the only reason I'd gotten into Sinner's Sideshow in the first place. When I'd charmed him, he'd flown into a rage.

Yet he touched me. He made me his.

Behaving with him never got me anywhere.

"Alistair," I said, my whisper mischievous as I twisted in his grip to plant a kiss on his finger.

His eyes narrowed as he likely sensed my tactic. "Megaera."

I took his hand, laid it on my thigh and slowly guided it up under my skirt. His lips parted on a soft breath when his fingers brushed his mark. "Do you regret this?"

"Never."

"Do you like the things that I do to you?"

"Always."

With a smile on my lips, I climbed off his lap and knelt on the floor between his knees. I felt Daemon's eyes on me, but I didn't look in his direction, fearing I'd lose my nerve.

I rubbed my hand over the bulge in Alistair's pants, and when he didn't stop me, I flicked up the buttons on his fly and pulled him out. His cock would have been normal if it wasn't for the fact that it had fine stitching running all over it. My fingers curled around his girth and with the first stroke, wisps of shadows spilled out. It made me wonder what that would feel like inside me.

Slowly lifting my eyes to his, I found him staring down at me with a look of dark awe on his face. He didn't tell me to stop, so I spit on his shaft and started to stroke him at a steady pace.

His reaction to my touch had my confidence swelling.

His jaw set, and his knuckles turned white as he gripped his chair's armrests. "Meg—"

He sucked in a low hiss when I drew him into my mouth and traced his seams with the tip of my tongue. He tensed beneath me, and I was afraid he'd make me stop, but he relaxed a few beats later, his long fingers tangling into my hair between my horns.

My charm powers had gotten so much stronger since he'd marked me.

It was a stupid fucking idea to try and use them on him again, considering what happened last time. Still, I was curious to test my new limits. Curiosity did kill the cat, or, as the twins would say, curiosity destroyed the pussy.

In this case, it actually might. I wanted him so badly I couldn't bring myself to care.

I painted a long, wet lick from his base to his tip, and his head fell back on his chair, a masculine noise escaping from his throat. I pushed him all the way inside me until his tip hit the back of my throat, swallowing as much as my greedy mouth could take.

His fingers flexed in my hair, and his thighs trembled as I sucked him at a pace that had him melting in seconds. "Slow down, damn you..."

I released the smallest bit of my charm magic, and his cock twitched against my tongue in response. Growing braver, I released more. Daemon whined, but I ignored him.

"I–I won't last much longer," Alistair gritted, his eyes burning down at me.

I pulled back and climbed into his lap. His hands slid under my skirt, taking hold of my hips. I tried to line us up so I could finally take him inside my pussy, but he held me in place.

"Master..." I leaned into him, my lips planting a series of hungry kisses along his throat. "Please. Our bond isn't complete. I haven't given you my mark yet."

"I'm fully aware of that, Megaera."

"I want my mark on your skin so everyone knows you're mine." Feeling bolder, I released another wave of my succubus charm. His eyes flashed, and his nostrils flared.

I'd fucked up.

His hand seized my throat over Daemon's collar, and he jerked me close so his cold glare filled my field of vision. "I know what you're doing, darling. The last time you did this, you got tied up, ass fucked, and that tight little pussy destroyed on the only part of my true form you could fit. Do you really want to go down that road with me again?"

I bucked my hips against his hands, straining for more friction. "Yes."

A dangerous smile slowly spread his lips. "You little slut."

There was movement further down our row. A man approached in my periphery and took a seat two chairs down from us. It struck me as weird. No one ever dared sit next to Alistair. Even if a monster living under a rock came to the show, not knowing Alistair was a powerful demon, you could taste the violence and the dark magic eroding the air around him.

I dismissed it as some overly brave peeper, probably wanting to get a look at me.

Ever since I stopped performing on the stage, there had been monsters sneaking around the carnival and the circus, looking to get something signed. Sometimes, it was merch. Sometimes it was their penis. There were a lot of reasons the guys hadn't let me out of their sight in over a week. Evil mothers, traitorous demons and perverted fans could be hiding behind any popcorn cart or clown-shaped garbage can.

I pulled back to look at him, my eyes pleading. "Since I'm just giving you mine, your monster form doesn't have to be involved. We can do it like this. Right here. No one's gonna notice."

At some point, Roach had wrapped up his act, and Riff and Raff had taken the stage to perform their old act. Their knife-throwing, fire-eating and aerial tricks held the audience captive.

Only Daemon and maybe the creeper next to us would watch, especially since we were in the last row in the far back.

"Please, Master? I want to make you feel good. I want to mark this skin so everyone knows it's mine."

"Megaera." He lifted a hand from my hips to cup my flushed cheek. His cool palm felt like heaven against my burning skin. "This is mortal flesh I wear. So easily bruised. So easily ruined. When you mark me, I'd like it to be on something more permanent. Something worthy of being with you. Something that feels a little more...me. I've been through so many skins, but none of them have felt like my own."

A frown bent my lips. "You need an archdemon's skin."

He nodded, his gaze softening as his attention slipped to my mouth. "Yes. So please be patient with me."

The next series of events happened all in the span of a second.

Daemon jumped over us and exploded into his human form midair—naked and smoking, his tattoos all aglow—landing in front of the stranger a few seats down.

Daemon's hand snapped out, seizing the man by his throat.

My mate's chest heaved, his eyes as sharp as daggers as he released a low and furious growl. "What in the fuck are you doing here, Famine?"

41

Famine

MEG

I wasn't sure what I'd imagined the other Horsemen to look like. Conquest had been handsome, but what were the chances of Famine looking anything but gaunt and sickly? He wasn't either of those things.

His half-monster form was tall and thin. He had a thick head of dark brown hair that fell a little past his ears. He had deep bronze skin that had a metallic sheen to it. His amber eyes met Daemon's golden ones without so much as a flicker of emotion.

"Do you have a message from the other Horsemen?" Daemon spat.

Famine's eyes slivered, saying nothing.

A wave of heady anger poured off my hellhound, so potent it almost knocked me off Alistair's lap. His arms tightened around me, and I felt the presence of Al in the seat behind us, protecting me from all angles.

Daemon's knuckles cracked as his fingers squeezed Famine's throat with a neck-breaking grip. "If you're a messenger, that's bad news for you. I tend to kill messengers if I don't like the message it sends."

Famine, like Alistair, was a dead zone for my emotion-reading powers. But it didn't take succubus magic to read the irritation on his face. He wasn't the least bit phased by the naked, solid wall of muscle looming over him.

"You and I both know you aren't powerful enough to kill me. Even if you were, you'd only be doing my fellow Horsemen a favor."

He opened the brown duster jacket to reveal an obsidian amulet of Discord. "I am their enemy, just as you are, hound."

Famine's amulet, marking his loyalty to his god, wasn't the only thing of note beneath his jacket. On his throat was the faded scar of an old mating claim.

"Daemon, release our guest," Alistair commanded.

The hellhound obeyed and released his hold on Famine. Alistair lifted me off his lap and passed me off to Daemon, who carried me to the seat where Al was, dismissed him with a wave of his hand, and lowered us into the chair.

"Megaera, darling," Alistair said in a silky drawl. "Please use your charm to direct our other guests' attention back to the show."

I directed my attention away from Famine to see the Horseman's appearance, or rather Daemon's reaction to him, had caused a stir. Every monster in the house was turned in their seats, watching us. Even the twins had stopped the show, staring up at us.

"That's one of the Horsemen of the Apocalypse!"

"What is he doing here?"

"That's Famine!"

"Is he on business for Discord?"

The audience's whispers had Daemon bristling beneath me, but I patted his head to soothe him as if he was still in his hound form. "I got this, baby."

I stood up, my tail lashing like a whip and giving a tiny crack. "Listen up, you fucks. This isn't the show you came here to see. Turn around and forget what you just saw and heard unless you want to join the pile of bodies building up outside."

My magic slowly spread through the house, and row by row, the monsters turned their attention back to the ring.

Daemon's arms banded around my middle and tugged me back into his lap. "That was beautiful, Pup."

Twisting in his arms, I pressed a kiss to the edge of his jaw, earning me a soft growl. I shifted my attention back to Famine to see him staring at Daemon and me.

"Is that Lilith's half-blooded spawn?"

"It is."

I could tell by Alistair's curt response that he didn't like Famine looking at me. He tucked his cock into his pants and leaned back into his chair, steepling his fingers. "Why are you here, Famine?"

"Lilith is coming, My Lord. She thinks you're too weak to fight her and the remaining Horsemen. She intends to secure a mating bond, but she can't force you to shift and mark her. Plus, she wouldn't be stupid enough to get anywhere near your hydra form."

"No, but she can claim me. Even a half-forged bond with her would be devastating." A grave look took over Alistair's face. I had never seen him so...weary. The carnival, the magic masking it, the constant pressure of keeping his troupe safe, it was draining him.

"When are they coming?"

"Tonight."

Tonight? Were we ready? An arctic chill swept over my skin and filled me with ice despite Daemon's radiant heat.

The grave look on Alistair's face said it all. "One more night. One more night of the carnival is all I need. One more night of terror, and I'll have the strength to slay them."

"They are coming tonight, My Lord," Famine repeated. "I'm...sorry. You will always have my loyalty, no matter what happens."

"Will you help us fight?" Daemon asked, his voice sharp and scathing like he was warning Famine not to refuse.

"I..." For the first time since he showed up, emotion was stark on his bronzed features. "I can't. Death and I—"

It clicked. Whose mark it was on his throat.

"My loyalty to you has cost me greatly, My Lord. I believe you will win and that you will shatter his soul this night. But I cannot raise a hand against him. Famine's gaze slid to my thigh, where my mark was just visible under the hem of my skirt. "You understand."

"I understand."

"I haven't given you much other than to assure you of my loyalty and perhaps a chance to prepare. I don't have the right to ask you for a favor."

Daemon bared his teeth. "No, you fucking don't."

Alistair's expression darkened, ignoring Daemon. "Famine, I am weakened. I am not the demon you once knew. Whatever you need, there's a chance I cannot provide it."

"You can do this for me. Death has been my mate for ages. Countless civilizations have risen and fallen in the span of our relationship. We are done, though. The end of an age."

There was so much pain in his voice. I pitied Famine. I couldn't imagine losing any of my mates. The thought alone filled me with a desolate ache that disturbed me to my very core. And I hadn't even been with them for a full two months. I couldn't imagine losing them after being together for so long.

"I cannot preserve his soul if that is what you're asking of me."

"No, My Lord. I wouldn't ask that. I'm asking you to…"
The Horseman's eyes cut to us.

Picking up on the fact that Famine was not wanting to speak his request out loud, Alistair leaned down so his request could be whispered into his ear.

My curiosity heightened when Alistair's fingers tightened on the grip of his cane. He leaned back, his brows gnashing into a scowl. "I don't know. Your request is...Unconventional."

"He has betrayed you, yes. For that, Death will finally meet his namesake. But for all the lifetimes he was loyal, please consider my request. I beg of you."

Wow. Famine was one stoic motherfucker, looking more dignified than I thought was possible for someone on their knees, begging.

I felt for the Horseman. Knowing Alistair, so did he. Whatever it was he was asking, I had a feeling the shade was going to agree.

All attention to the conversation at hand was obliterated by an earth-shattering explosion sounding from outside, like an otherworldly thunderstorm.

Dark, vicious energy bled into the big top. It smelled of electricity and death—of Doom.

"Kill them all!"

Dread wound tight through my body. That voice. It boomed from the heavens like a cry from God, if that god was a vengeful, power-thirsty woman.

I swallowed thickly.

My mother. She was here.

This was going to be one bloody family reunion.

"What do we do?" Daemon growled, his words laced with something that had me shivering in his arms.

Nothing screamed "you're fucked" more than the traces of fear in the hellhound's voice.

Famine rose to his feet. He looked as though he was about to address Alistair again, and thought better of it. What was there to say? Good luck? Hope you don't get raped by a psychotic succubus so she can steal your magic power and end the world? If you win, have fun railing her daughter in my ex-mate's skin?

Yeeeah. Literally nothing was appropriate to say in this situation. So Famine simply bowed low to his lord. Alistair sat back in his chair with the most disturbing look I'd ever seen, his eyes glowing with malice. He dismissed the archdemon with barely a nod and a glance.

Famine disappeared in a burst of smoke and magic that left my belly feeling hollow.

Monsters climbed over seats, pushing and clawing and ripping out throats to get to the exit. The metallic tang of blood saturated the air as the mob turned savage. All the while, Alistair drummed his nails on his armrest, his brows knitting in deep thought. "One week of terrorizing and slaughtering thousands of sinners should have been enough…"

"*Alistair*. What are your orders?" Daemon repeated on a roar over the din of panic rippling through the big top.

The ringmaster finally looked at us, first at Daemon, then to me. Gone was the rage, and in its place was something far more haunting. Then I saw that strange twist of shadows behind his eyes, and I knew what he was planning to do.

Alistair was going to kill every soul in this room.

42

The Face of Death

MEG

No sooner than I'd guessed Alistair's intentions to kill the audience, shadow tentacles shot out from him in every direction, wrapping around throats and snapping necks—though only a few died that way. Most died of horrible deaths meant to wring out as much fear as possible. Shadows plucked screaming monsters out of the crowd by their ankles and bashed them against seats. Other tendrils were rammed down their throats, yanking out their insides and flinging them across the room into the tangle of bodies fighting toward the exit.

All I could do was stand there, numb to all the carnage, as Alistair did what he said he'd never do again.

"Some of these people are innocent, Daemon." My voice was hoarse with horror, to the point where I could barely hear myself speak.

Daemon's hound ears must have picked up on it because a moment later, his arms folded around me and tucked me against his chest. "There's no luxury for morals tonight, Pup."

The most unsettling part about the mass slaughter unfolding before me wasn't the sight of broken bodies slumped over the theater seats or the look of pure terror contorting their faces as Alistair's shadows ensnared them. It was Alistair's steel composure. The way he remained in his seat with his elbows on his armrests, glaring over his steepled fingers. Sometimes, it was easy to forget what kind of monster lurked beneath his human disguise.

A wall of shadows that looked like brambles grew in front of the exits, blocking off all hope of escape. Eventually, the screams died down until the only sounds came from beyond the big top.

It was all over so quickly. The shadow demon had massacred everyone in a matter of seconds.

The scent of blood in the air was overpowered by the stench of fear. I slapped a hand over my mouth, not daring to drink so much as a drop.

Alistair pushed to his feet, adjusting his top hat and taking his cane in hand. He moved to step over a body that had fallen between the seats, blocking his path to us. When he noticed the monster was still alive, he brought his cane down, puncturing its eye socket. The poor creature twitched and screamed, and

Alistair leaned down to breathe the creature in and savor the fear bleeding out of his victim.

He tugged the cane free to bring his foot down on the skull, crushing it beneath his shoe. "There…That should do the trick."

I barely had a chance to process the reality of the situation. The dark shit Alistair had to stoop to in order to save us from Lilith and the remaining Horsemen had my stomach heaving. Still, it was the lesser of two evils. Better to murder a few hundred innocents than watch the entire world burn.

"Hurry and shift, Alistair. They'll find us soon," Daemon urged his master. The alpha was still naked, and his bare skin against my wings had a way of keeping me calm and relaxed despite everything.

The shadow demon started to shift just as he had in his caravan the night he'd claimed me.

Riff and Raff bolted up the stairs toward us, hopping over dead bodies as they skipped several steps at a time. By the time they got to the top, they nearly fell backward at the way Alistair shifted into his hydra form in a cloud of pulsating shadows and dark magic that stunk of ozone.

Something was wrong.

It felt different than it had last time.

"Shit." Daemon must have sensed it, too, because he was passing me off to the twins and diving for Alistair, who shifted back to his human form and fell limp into his hound's outstretched arms.

His cane clattered to the floor. Somehow, the ringing sound it created was more unsettling than the cracking bones and ragged screams that had filled the tent minutes ago.

Alistair's eyes snapped open. He pulled himself to his feet and pushed his hound away with a curse when he tried to keep him down. "Master. You're not strong enough—"

"I fucking know!" He snapped around, his eyes wild with green fire, the rage unguarded on his face. "It wasn't enough. All that effort…The carnival, the sinners…all those monsters slain, their souls permanently shattered…all *for nothing*."

His voice was reduced to something small that I barely recognized.

"So, what's the plan now, boss?" Riff asked from behind me.

Alistair shook his head. "The plan is that you all run."

His words launched my nerves into overdrive.

I crouched to the ground and wrestled out my pink guitar case I'd shoved under the seat. Thank fuck I'd been working a shift at the carnival right before the show. I'd wiped my makeup off, but I was still dressed in a slutty clown costume, my sword in tow for the non-consensual sword-swallowing lessons I'd been giving the sinners.

I set the case down on a chair, flipped the latch and brandished my father's sword. "I can fight. All of us, we can gather the troupe and—"

Alistair sidestepped Daemon so fast his movements were a blur, and he was standing in front of me in a blink, grasping my arm that held the sword. "And what then, my little demon? War and Death are dragons. Do you know what that means?"

My heart fell. It meant that even if he did shift and could hold his form, he'd be in the air alone. Two against one. Roach and Daisy Doom were the only two members in the troupe who could fly, and it's not like they were going to be anything close to useful backup against two dragons.

He spun me around, pulling my back against his chest with his hands clamped tight on my shoulder. Bowing his spine, he pressed his mouth to my ear and hissed, *"Listen."*

My ears strained to hear over the chaos coming from outside the tent. Sure enough, the flap of great wings beat the sky. I went rigid against Alistair when a cavernous roar that could only belong to something monstrous tore through the sky.

"They are here," he rasped. "And if I can't shift, they're going to take everything they want and more from me. I can't protect you anymore. So, what you're going to do is run."

I spun around and lifted my chin, my eyes sparking with defiance. "Run? No. *No.* Fuck that."

He ground his serrated teeth. "Now isn't the time to be a stubborn brat, Megaera. I'm trying to protect you the only way I can."

"Didn't your contract with my mother specify that she can't harm me? I'm not afraid of her!"

Daemon and Alistair looked at each other, and I knew they were doing one of those silent exchanges the twins always did.

It was Daemon who turned back to me and said, "It's not her that we're worried about, Meg. It's Death and War. They'll…" His voice broke. What I saw behind his eyes raised the small hairs on the back of my neck. "They'll hurt you, and we can't take them in their dragon forms. So, Alistair is right. You have to leave."

Silence fell between us as the rest of our world went to shit. The scent of something burning singed my nostrils, and smoke started to fill the tent. Had they set everything on fire? Would the troupe members get to safety?

My pulse roared. "No."

Alistair's jaw tightened. "Don't be reckless, Megaera."

He was normally a dead zone for my powers, but lately, our half-forged mating bond allowed me glimpses into his emotions. They were complicated, a tangled mess of thoughts and feelings that someone as old as him would have. But there was no mistaking the look on his face now—the look of someone who was about to lose everything they had, who'd rather throw their toys out than let someone else have them.

His gaze cut to the twins, who were just dumbstruck. "Get her out of here, now."

"We'll come back when the fight is over. Right?" I looked to Daemon, whose gaze had hardened to stone.

My stomach flipped. "Right?"

"The three of you need to leave now," Alistair told the twins, all while refusing to look at me. "You are not bound to me anymore. All contracts of service, all deals struck, are now void."

"Alistair…" I hated how thin and vulnerable my voice sounded. "What are you saying?"

It was a dumb fucking question. He wasn't mincing words. There was no clearer way of saying it.

This was goodbye.

Yet, I still couldn't accept it. "I'm not leaving you."

Alistair met my eyes, and the coldness in them struck me in the heart like a knife of ice. "Yes, you fucking are. You don't have a monster form, and I can no longer protect you. You're free."

Riff and Raff sucked in tiny gasps behind me. "What?"

"You're free," Alistair repeated. "You're pets of mine no longer. So, go. As far as you can."

I reached out for him, but Daemon stepped between us. Blocking my path to him.

"Go, Pup."

Tears pooled in my eyes. "I— I don't want to be free. I love you. I love all of you. I don't want us to split up."

Pain etched Daemon's features while Alistair's remained cold, his mask snapping back into place. "I told you half-bloods don't belong here."

Tears slipped down my cheeks and burned my flesh like acid. I hated how I could fight tooth and claw to make this circus my home, and at the end of the day, I had to leave, not because of anything I did. I had to leave because I was a half-blood. Too soft to survive the hell that followed these men wherever they went.

Scalding tears streaks down my cheeks. "I fucking hate you."

If there was something Alistair had to say, anything at all that would subdue this raging ball of contempt knotting in my chest, he didn't say it. He turned abruptly, his coattails whipping behind him as he descended the stairs without looking back.

"Daemon, come."

The taste of ash filled my mouth.

Daemon loved me. I knew that.

But he wasn't going to abandon his master.

Not for me. Not for anyone.

His hands balled into fists at his sides, his knuckles cracking. His tattoos were all glowing, blazing that same golden hue as his eyes. "If they win, if the world burns, I'll come looking for you in the ashes."

My pulse detonated in my ear as one of the incubi—I wasn't sure who as I couldn't make sense of anything in the wake of the wreckage that was my fucking heart—hauled me over their shoulder. They shifted, hard muscles rippling beneath me and lifting me high in the air. I gripped one of their curling horns for purchase as they carried me out of the circus tent.

Through my blur of tears, my brain struggled to process the sight that met us outside and that this was really happening. That my life was burning down to ashes all over again. This time, literally.

The carnival looked like something straight from the Downside. Everything was up in flames.

Then, it was flickering like static between channels on a TV.

Alistair's magic was failing.

Swaths of smoke rose into the sky, turning it black as death.

Mortal sinners still under Alistair's hypnotic magic wandered mindlessly through the fire, unaware of where they were and unable to control their actions but fully aware of the pain. Some walked at a slow pace through the blazing carnival while they were consumed in flames. Charred bodies lay in the grass.

It was a fucking nightmare.

I tried to skim the grass, praying—I wasn't sure to whom since Discord had forsaken me—that my friends weren't among the bodies. We were moving too fast, the remains too burnt, and the smoke too thick to make out their faces.

A roar shattered the sky, jerking my attention to the heavens, and my heart plummeted to my stomach at the size of the rust-red dragon circling the sky.

War.

We made a break for the parking lot where the troupe's trailers and the cars were parked. When my yellow Volkswagen bug came into view, my insides twisted into a thousand little knots.

I held on tight to my father's sword, which was clutched in my hand like a lifeline, even though the little blade was useless in the face of Death and War.

I guess there was nothing to do but run. Not that running away would save us...

If my mother succeeded in stealing some of Alistair's power and authority through a forced mating bond, she'd end this world.

There'd be no escaping the apocalypse.

I was wrenched from my thoughts as another roar sounded. This one was so much closer, too close to have come from the red dragon.

A brutal chill slid up my back when the sky above seemed to shift, and on the next hammer of my heart, a pale dragon swooped down from the smoke.

Death.

There was no time for the twins to react. By the time we realized what was happening, he was on top of us. Giant claws, almost the size of Alistair's hydra form, closed in around me and plucked me away from the twins.

My arms shot out, reaching for them. Our hands brushed, but I was wrenched away and pulled up into the smoke. The twins' voices, screaming my name, were ripped away by the roaring wind in my ears.

This was how I was going to die.

It was funny how little fear I felt all of a sudden. Probably because there was no room to feel anything else when liquid fury pumped through my veins, taking over every inch of my body.

When I'd joined Sinner's Sideshow, there'd been a part of me that had already come to terms with my eventual death because I knew, one day, it would kill me.

I always thought it would be by getting choked to death on clown cock, or burned to death around the three flaming cocks of a hellhound alpha.

Still, I'd made peace with my death. So, when he swooped out of the sky, there was no time to throw a pity party. My tears dried, and my anger flared into something dangerous.

Something reckless.

Lifting my sword, I brought it down on his claw, hard enough to completely sever one of his talon-tipped digits. Blood as black as rot splattered across my face, some of it rushing up my nose. A screech of pain shattered my ears.

My heart slammed into my throat as we fell, and I was jerked up again when his wings caught the air, managing to keep us airborne enough for him to make a clumsy descent.

The moment I felt the solid ground beneath me, I snapped to my feet with my sword raised. The dragon's form morphed into that of a man, and I plunged my weapon in his direction before I even had time to parse his vague shape. A boot slapped into my chest, knocking me off my feet.

My back slammed into the ground, knocking the wind from my lungs.

I blinked up at the sky, and a moment later, the boot pressed down on my throat.

A man loomed over me, and I found myself staring into the face of Death.

43

Death Incarnate

MEG

In the flickering light of the fire, Death's features were wrapped in shadow and flame.

He was a tall male, with hard muscle packed onto a lean frame. His skin was the color of ash, pale with the slightest gray tinge. His black hair was long, reminding me of Alistair's, minus the shadowy movement to it. He had a sharp jaw, high cheekbones, and a nose with the slightest arch that set my pulse on edge.

He was handsome. On second thought, handsome wasn't the right word.

Death was panty-obliterating *hot*.

Maybe not in a conventional way, but for anyone who had a thing for ancient, evil demons, which I did, he was dark perfection. The only thing I didn't like was his black, bottomless eyes.

They bore into me, stripping away my flesh, and whatever he saw in my deepest depths had him licking his lips.

"Do you know who I am, girl?"

I feigned a confused look, knowing it would get under his skin. "Should I know you?"

He pinned me with a tyrannical glare that filled me with an unsettling numbness.

"I am death incarnate. One of the oldest and most fearsome archdemons to ever live."

He was fearsome. His power was so devastating it washed over my tongue and filled my mouth with its acrid flavor. Any other person in my situation would think about something tactical to say.

Before I could stop myself, I flashed him a grin too tight. "Wow. So, like, you're famous? When you're finished killing me, will you sign my corpse?"

I could almost hear Daemon in my ear, scolding me for mouthing off in a situation like this.

Surprise looked unnatural on his face like he'd never worn the expression before. He recovered a beat later. Then, his lips contorted into a smile that disturbed me to my core. "There have been rumors about your bratty mouth and the things it can do."

His boot applied more pressure to my throat, slowly crushing my windpipe.

This was the part where I needed to shut up and save my precious air. "J–just so you know, I'm super into this."

Fuck. Daemon was right. My mouth was a menace, and I needed to be muzzled.

The Horseman of Death grinned down at me, but it didn't reach his colorless eyes. "A masochist, are we? Maybe we're a match made in Hell?" He held up his hand for me to see the bloody stump where I'd cut off his thumb. His four remaining fingers curled into a tight fist, and black blood oozed from the wound, dripping onto my face, my throat, and the toe of his boot. "Because it gets me hard seeing you drenched in my blood."

The air in my lungs crystallized. He was creepy as fuck, yet he had a dark charm to him that reminded me of Alistair. The Horsemen were supposed to be birthed from the devil's shadows, right? So, the resemblance made sense.

"If it turns you on so much, I can always be covered in more." My grip tightened on my sword, and I swung it, aiming for his leg since his boot on my throat limited my mobility.

Shadowy tentacles exploded from the ground, wrapping around my wrists and ankles and pinning me to the cold grass.

He had shadow magic, too.

Sinews tensed in his neck as he leaned closer, delight making his eyes spark like steel striking flint in the dark. "What the rumors about you failed to mention is that you've seemed to inherit your mother's vicious nature."

I snarled beneath his boot. "I'm nothing like my mother."

He cocked his head, his raven hair spilling over his shoulder. He lifted his boot from my throat for an unobstructed view of my body. My skin crawled as his eyes scraped over my skimpy outfit, slithering over every exposed curve and patch of flesh.

"No..." he mused. "You aren't, are you?"

I shuddered, and goosebumps rose across my skin. His gaze was as palpable as a physical caress. "Why are you looking at me like that?"

"Like what?" Death licked his smirking lips. "Like you're the most beautiful woman I've ever seen?"

Uh oh. This fucker was actually coming on to me.

I didn't like him even looking at me. It sent a chill down to my marrow. The idea of his hands on me made me want to vomit.

Suddenly, all my marks were on fire, chasing away the ice in my bones. Somehow, death sensed their heat and crouched beside me. His hand skimmed up my thigh, pushing my skirt over my hip to reveal Alistair's mating claim.

Death raised his brows. "Well fuck me in my grave. Discord has a mate."

I swallowed thickly, straining uselessly against my shadow restraints. "Yes, we're mated. So, you can forget your plan to force Lilith's mark on him."

The demon's shoulders shook with a laugh. "Oh, you are *adorable.*"

His hand traveled up my belly and smoothed between my breasts.

I jerked against my shadow bonds. "Get the fuck off me."

Ignoring me, his fingers hooked in my shirt's plunging neckline, and with a movement so quick I could barely follow it, he tore my shirt clean down my middle.

I yelped in surprise, and with a chuckle, he tugged the destroyed fabric from my body, dropping it in a pile beside my head. My body went stiff as his fingers smoothed over my breast, his claw-like nails plucking at my nipple piercing before continuing their accent to my shoulder. The pad of his index finger rubbed the scar from Daemon's mating mark. "You know as well as I do that a demon can take more than one mate."

He wedged a hand beneath me and pried my wings out from under me, splaying them across the ground. I hated how exposed I felt. This bastard didn't deserve to touch any part of me, especially the scars my men had left.

"Four mates," he marveled as his index finger stroked over Raff's mark, then Riff's. "Busy girl."

He leaned back, pulling away from me to open his black duster jacket and expose his chest. There, exactly where Famine's mark had been, were twin bite marks. Faded. They'd forged their bond a long time ago. But it was there all the same.

"See? I have one, too." He tapped the column of his neck, opposite of where Famine had bitten him. "Wouldn't your claim look so pretty right here?"

I gaped at him, completely lost for words.

His suggestion was soft as velvet, but it didn't disguise the cruelty behind the dark pools of his eyes.

"At this point, you might as well lift your leg and piss on me since that's as close to marking me as you'll ever get."

"Bold words coming from a woman who's tied down."

Fear bubbled up my esophagus, but anger rose inside me like a tsunami, drowning all other emotions. "Oh, you better not be implying what I think you are. I have this little thing where I like to chop up rapists and feed them the body parts they don't know how to keep to themselves. You could say it's even a fetish. You want to get me going? Eat your own dick, Death. Better yet, choke on it."

The demon's smile fell some, but the cold mirth clung to the corners of his mouth like shadows. "Half-blood bitch. I can see why you have so many male cocks wrapped around your finger. You're so alluring, it's obscene."

He paused, then added, "Once all this is over, I was planning on throwing your corpse to War. He doesn't mind cold pussy. But..." Death's lips pursed with what I was sure was genuine contemplation. "I think I *will* take you as my own. My old mate is gone, and I'm not used to an empty bed."

His gaze grew distant. He was a dead zone for my aura reading powers, just like Alistair, but the pain was so obviously etched into each of his syllables. Famine leaving him had left Death wounded.

Famine had seemed like a half-decent demon. Why would he stay with Death for so long if there wasn't something good buried deep beneath his ashen skin?

"You don't have to do this," I blurted. "You don't have to betray your god like this. You actually think you're helping him, don't you? You think you're doing the right thing for your kind by sending him back to the Downside. Well, you're wrong. He's become a different person, but that doesn't make him weak. And Famine would probably take you back if you—"

His hand—the one missing the thumb—struck me across the cheek. He'd packed so much strength into the motion that the loud slapping sound rang in my skull. It seems he must have grown tired of our conversation, or at least, how I contributed to it.

"What would you know about demonkind? We all have a purpose. Mine is to destroy this world."

I gasped, reeling from the sting of his strike. "What kind of purpose is that?"

"A great one. This trash realm has poisoned the mind of a great demon I once idolized. Now, I know why my purpose is to burn this world to ash. So he'll return home and go back to being Discord."

Death hauled me over his shoulder and rose to his full height. Before I could stab him in the back, a shadow tendril slapped the sword out of my hand and sent it skidding across the grass. More shadows wrapped around my wrists and my ankles, forcing me still as the demon moved toward the burning carnival.

"He won't go back."

"Which is exactly why we're here. To help your mother mate him. With the power she gets through their bond, she'll be able to charm him into doing whatever she wants. If you're good, I'll let you watch her fuck him." He laughed, cold and cruel. "Now *that's* going to be a show."

I hated him.

No, hate wasn't strong enough to describe what I felt for this demon. I hated Alistair for sending me away, for thinking I was too weak to help him and Daemon in the upcoming battle.

But Death? All I could muster for him was deep, black contempt. A contempt so pure and unadulterated that it was almost intimate in how it wound so tightly through me.

"Fuck. You."

His hand slipped beneath my skirt and squeezed my ass so hard it brought tears to my eyes. "Oh, you will. As soon as I help secure your mother's mating bond with Discord. And I'll have to kill your other mates, of course. I'm not one for sharing my toys."

"What in the world did Famine ever see in you?"

I knew I'd struck a nerve before the words even passed over my tongue.

Death froze in place. Not being able to see his face to pick up on clues to what he was thinking unnerved me.

"We both have a thing for pain," he answered after what felt like a short eternity later. "We liked making each other hurt. Sometimes, it's the only way demons like us can feel. You're like that too, by the way your mouth keeps running. Don't worry, little half-blood..."

I bit back a whimper as his nails dragged down my ass cheek—hard enough to leave angry welts—moving inward toward my most tender place. "I'll make you hurt."

The ice in his voice was so cold that it sunk into my bones and chilled my marrow.

His touch was devastating to my system. I couldn't exactly explain it. Like my body knew what he was. Even the whisper of his breath against my skin had my human cells shrinking away while my succubus side lit up at the contact.

Arousal dripped from my center, streaking down my thigh.

I clamped my eyes shut and prayed to Discord, or whatever god was listening, that Death didn't notice my body's betrayal.

He cursed under his breath, his finger moving to the crease where my ass met my thigh and swiped up the bead of arousal. By the smack of his lips, he was tasting it. "Who knew a half-blood could taste *so* good? No wonder you're covered in mating marks. You're delectable."

My eyes frantically scanned the flaming campgrounds, desperately searching for any trace of Riff and Raff. We were clear on the other side of the camp. It would take them a while to find me, and even if they did, what were they going to do?

They'd attack Death and get their souls shattered for the trouble.

My mind turned into a cyclone of frantic thoughts and half-cobbled plans. What was I supposed to do? How the fuck was I supposed to get myself out of this situation?

I tempered myself against the panic rising in my chest.

There had to be a way out of this.

Cold dread worked through my body when I registered two sets of glowing eyes in the distance. One pair green, one blue.

The twins had tracked us down.

They were heading for us.

44

The Devil is a Dragon

DAEMON

The second we left the tent, I grasped Alistair by the shoulder, and when he turned, I smashed my fist into his jaw. There was enough force behind the blow to send him staggering back a few steps, his shadows spilling from the stitches in his skin.

The bastard had better reflexes than me, with eyes in the back of his head. He could have easily dodged the blow. He didn't. He knew he deserved it. Hell, he deserved a hell of a lot more than a punch in the face.

He'd sent Meg away with her heart in pieces, and he'd barely given her a second glance.

What pissed me off most was that I knew it was an act. He could play the part of the indifferent, cold-hearted demon, but I wasn't buying it.

His recovery from the blow happened in such a small measure of time that he was reeling one moment and standing at his full height, as imposing as ever, in front of me the next. His demeanor was cool as ice and just as jagged as if I hadn't hit him at all.

"Are you finished?"

"*Fuck you*, Alistair. Fuck you for what you did back there."

The sinews in my stomach pulled tight at the look he threw me. "I did what I had to."

"Bullshit," I snarled.

The shadow demon squared his shoulders, and with both hands on his cane, he placed it between his feet and stood tall and imposing, glaring at me as if he was intent on setting me on fire. The flames of our world were burning around us, along with the screams of dying sinners, making for a dramatic background to our stare-down.

"What should I have done? Let her stay? This is a hopeless fight, Pet. We're going to lose."

I ground my teeth so hard that pain shot through my gums. Sometimes he was so goddamn clueless. "You were right for sending her away. The reason why I want to rip that mortal flesh from your body strip by strip is for the way you did it. You broke her heart. You were so callous and cold. That was orchestrated."

Alistair's nostrils flexed. He tipped his head so the shadow that normally concealed much of his face was cast away by the bright light from the fire raging all around us, and I could see the anger so clearly drawn by the sharp lines of his face. "She wouldn't have gone if I was soft with her. Better she hates me from safety than have her love me while trapped in the arms of Death or War as her world burns to ash in the apocalypse."

"If we fail, the apocalypse happens anyway. They'll find her eventually. Better she be here with us and help us fight."

His glare narrowed on me. "How can she possibly help? She's capable, yes. But these are the Horsemen we're talking about."

My fists clenched as fury flared through my veins. "I don't fucking know! That's for her to figure out. You just have to trust her to do it."

A dozen different emotions flickered behind my master's eyes, yet he allowed none of them onto his face. He shrugged, feigning indifference. "She's better off far away from this mess. The twins will keep her safe for as long as possible. That, I trust."

He turned away from me, but I moved so fast I was standing on his other side. "So, what's going to happen? What's your plan? Put up a good fight with the expectation that you'll lose? Just lie back and let Lilith force her mark on you? Watch them kill me? And you know Death will do it, so you won't be seeing my soul in Hell. You'll lose me forever, too."

Still, not so much as a twitch of emotion.

I hated how he kept his feelings locked inside that fortress of armor he wore.

Even after all this time, he was still afraid to show me his true emotions. In a way, it was my fault, too. I'd been afraid as well.

Up until now.

I'd been with Alistair for so long, I'd lost track of the years.

Our relationship was complex and infuriating. I'd hated him. I'd loved him. There were times I'd wanted to get away and… And yet I couldn't live without him.

And I was sick of pretending that wasn't the case.

Before I could decide against it, my arm snapped out, and my hand closed around his throat—something I'd *never* done outside of sex. It was a power move, one that demanded attention.

His eyes flared hot. His lips twisted into a sneer.

But he didn't try to free himself from my grasp when he could have easily done so. "You're lucky I need your hands in the upcoming fight, or I'd rip them off, hound."

I smiled tightly at his threat. "No, you wouldn't. You love me too much. And I fucking love you too. I'm tired of pretending that we don't. You know what else I'm tired of?"

Keeping one hand clamped around his throat, my other dropped to his hip and pulled his pelvis close to mine. "I'm sick of this cold flesh you hide behind like armor. Pretending you're not kind. Pretending you're indifferent. Pretending we're just favored pets instead of the loves of your freakishly long life. Do you think it protects you? It doesn't. Meg's taught us that."

Alistair's brows pulled together into a deep scowl. "You never used to be this sentimental. It doesn't look good on you."

I shook my head with a scoff. "Why do you insist on hiding behind your armor? Are you afraid to feel real mortal feelings?"

The air buzzed between us, hot and filled with smoke.

Around us, the fire raged, consuming everything, even Alistair's carnival illusion. The games, the food stalls, everything went static until the spell shattered completely, leaving nothing but the burning circus.

If only that were an illusion, too. But no. Our home really was burning to ash.

Alistair swallowed against my hold. "I'm not afraid."

I pushed my face into his until my golden eyes reflected in the green pools of his. "You lie. You want to hear my theory?"

I paused, but only to let him know that I was on to him, not to give him a chance to argue. "You came to the surface originally to punish Astrid for killing all those people. When you told me you were going, I was surprised you cared. You're the demon who was so fucking evil that your very existence had woven its way deep into human stories. Stories they tell one another to elicit fear. But you're the devil. You're also chaotic. I didn't question it...Until you didn't want to leave."

Alistair's upper lip peeled. "I didn't want to leave so I could personally oversee the circus to keep my magical power strong on the Upside."

"Another lie."

A tendon in his neck fluttered against my hold on him, but he didn't silence me or command me to shut up.

He listened.

He never listened.

That's how I knew I was right. He needed to hear this, and he knew it too.

"You stayed on the Upside because you desperately wanted to know what it was like to feel human. It's why you've tasked me to help you create these macabre human appearances when you were perfectly content floating around in your shadow form before. And you know what actually happened?"

He blinked. He never blinked.

"Enlighten me."

"You grew something akin to humanity. It stopped being an act, where you were just playing dress up and ringleader with all your pets to act as your dolls. At some point in the two decades we've been here, it stopped being an act. You actually grew a goddamn heart and feelings. I think you realized that once Meg came into our lives."

I pressed my forehead to his so he couldn't look away. "And that *scares* you."

There was a flicker in his eyes.

Then, for the first time, I saw the man I loved, completely unguarded. "Daemon..."

I pressed my finger to his lips. "You love me. I know you fucking do. You've been so desperate for my mark. It was easy to brush it off as another form of possession, but it's because you fucking love me."

He shook his head slowly, his lips parting on a softened breath as realization took root inside him. "No..."

My thumb stroked the edge of his jaw as I kept his gaze firmly chained to mine. "Tell me why you want my mark. Say it out loud."

His lower lip trembled, and his eyes flared so wide I could see my reflection in his green pools. "Because I love you."

"That's right. I know you do. And you know what else I know?"

He pulled back just enough to drop his attention to my lips as if he was so riveted by the words coming from them that he couldn't stand to look away. "What else do you know?"

"I think your being unable to shift has less to do with you feeding than we thought. Fear keeps you connected to what makes you Discord, but there's more to it than that. You started to lose your connection to your hydra form because that's what your disciples recognize as their god."

My hand dropped away from his throat, and he took a step back, rubbing the collar of bruises in his dead flesh that was now there to stay until we found him a new skin. "What are you saying?"

"I'm saying that you don't want to be a god."

I stepped toward him, closing that little bit of distance he'd put between us and pressed my mouth to his in a devastating kiss.

The connection was stiff at first, but his lips started to move against mine as shock ebbed away and realization slowly sunk in.

When I pulled away, he chased my lips and pressed another kiss to them and then another. My hands found his hips, and I pulled him close, sighing against the subtle heat of his mouth. "You don't want to be Discord anymore. You just want to be Alistair."

And that was that.

He opened his mouth to reply, but whatever he was going to say, the words were lost beneath the deafening roar that shook the sky above. The red dragon of War descended from the dense blanket of smoke and started to circle overhead.

He'd spotted us.

I strained my eyes against the haze, noticing he had something on his back.

Fucking hells. Lilith was riding him.

As per her arrangement with Alistair, they couldn't harm each other. That meant he would have to take down War in the sky in order for me to get to her.

My grip tightened on Alistair. "You have to shift. *Now.*"

He looked away, taking in his ruined kingdom. I couldn't bring myself to look at all the destruction. All I could look at was him and how devastating he looked with his profile bathed in firelight. Looking every bit the handsome devil he was.

"Your theory is that I haven't been able to shift simply be-cause I associate it with something I don't want to be anymore? That everything I love is being ripped from me because...I'm too cowardly to play the part of god anymore?"

He spat the words like a curse, and oh, how they oozed with self-loathing.

"You're not a coward. You're just tired. Tired of being what you stopped being years ago. You have to stop associating your true-form hydra with Discord. Think about it. The last time you shifted was when you mated Meg. It had nothing to do with being Discord and everything to do with just being with her."

I grasped his chin and leveled him with a softer look that had him relaxing in my arms. "You're having trouble shifting because you have it in your head that going up there is about you protecting your throne in Hell. It's *not*. It doesn't have to be. Fuck the Downside. Kill Lilith and the Horsemen and let it rot without a god and king."

Slowly, troupe members started pouring out from their hiding spots to gather around us in a circle. Lollie and Sinclair. Daisy Doom and Roach. Mollie and Larry, hand in hand. The clowns and the stagehands. Even Alistair's shadow stood among the crowd.

It didn't matter that the dragon of War was burning everything to the ground and could, at any moment, swoop down and breathe fire down on us all. They saw Alistair here, and they came flocking to him, drawn in by the magical energy that started to teem from him in powerful waves.

"Alistair—"

The shadow demon was already hurriedly throwing off his hat and his jacket. Ancient, primordial arcana coiled around him. Then his hands tangled in my hair, and his lips smashed into mine in a kiss like we'd never shared before.

Normally, we kissed like we were going to war. Two apex predators fighting for dominance.

Not this kiss.

It was frantic but tender. *Loving.* Vulnerable. Like all the walls that had been erected between us for years were now blown open.

When the kiss broke, we stared at one another, chests heaving. "Damn you," he whispered.

"Go."

Alistair took several steps backward. The magic around him pulsated. The air crackled with electricity.

He grew, his skin expanded, shadows rippling.

Alistair's shadow shot out from the crowd and formed the second head of the scaled black hydra, taking shape before our eyes.

He was stunning. It always struck me as funny that human legends called him a serpent. He was a snake in a lot of ways. At his core, though, the devil was a dragon.

Whispers spread through the gathering of troupe members. They knew. There was only one black, two-headed dragon.

Alistair, the ringleader of Sinner's Sideshow, was Discord himself.

After today, he'd be their savior, sure. But he was our god no longer.

45

Goddess of Vengeance

ALISTAIR

I launched myself into the air, feeling more alive than I ever had outside the dead flesh I hid behind.

Daemon was right. I'd been hiding. Using the stolen flesh as armor—a disguise. Pretending I was something I wasn't as an escape. I'd done it for so long that somewhere along the line, it stopped being a game of pretend.

I didn't have to be human. And I didn't have to be Discord. I'd just be whatever the fuck I was going to be. A shadow demon that would take on whatever form or vessel I pleased.

Right now, all I wanted was to rip War's throat out and spill his blood onto the ground below. With any luck, the fall would kill Lilith.

That wasn't against our contract.

Then Death would have no reason to raise a claw against me since his only means of dragging me back to Hell would be dead.

Since I wasn't killing her directly by my hand, her soul would eventually find a new form. That was a problem for several decades from now. Or several centuries, if we were lucky.

I launched myself at War, taking pleasure in the way his fiery eyes crackled with fear. Lilith was in her full succubus form, crouched low behind his neck, clutching onto his spines for purchase.

"Discord! My Lord." Her screams were almost lost in the wind as I rammed into War, my weight outclassing his and sending him hurtling through the air. "Witness my resolve! Am I not worthy to stand beside you as your mate and queen?"

Stubborn to the very end.

Like her daughter.

War spread his wings, catching himself on the wind. Smoke billowed up around him, making him look like a worthy adversary.

He wasn't.

Before he could correct his course, I lunged at him, both sets of teeth bared. I ripped out his throat, tearing the softer underbelly and unleashing a torrent of red that rained down on my troupe below.

Al's head tore at War's wing, shredding the leathery webbing keeping him airborne.

Even as he bled out, his arms and tail wrapped around me, caging me against him as we hurtled toward the unforgiving ground.

I twisted him around, holding him below me and folding my wings so we'd plummet faster, harder, knowing he'd break my fall.

He thrashed, but with one more savage bite to his throat, he went limp.

Dead. His soul shattered just as we collided with the ground.

The earth quaked and caved in, a crater forming around us instantly at the impact. I shot up, grabbing War in my claws and hauling his limp form up, hurtling it over the ground and into a flaming tent in a gust of ash and cinder.

Lilith was passed out at the bottom of the crater. War had landed on top of her, knocking her unconscious. I tapped her bony snout with my claw, ensuring she was out cold. There was a magical field of energy protecting her, preventing me from striking her in any manner.

Pity the fall hadn't killed her.

I turned to command Daemon to finish her off, but he was already bounding over in his hellbeast form.

Everyone watched with bated breath as he loomed over Lilith. Astrid, as I'd named her when she went to the human realm, so her troupe members wouldn't suspect who she was.

I'd given her the human name at the same time I'd come up with mine. Alistair and Astrid. I'd loved my mortal name. She'd always hated hers. She hated everything that we'd shared, even though she'd pretended for so very long that she didn't.

I'd known her longer than I'd known anyone else.

Yet, as I looked down at her, lying helpless in the dirt, I felt nothing but relief.

"Alistair!"

I whipped around to see the twins shoving their way through the crowd. *Meg wasn't with them.*

I lumbered over to them, and at my approach, my troupe crumbled to their knees in fealty.

"Discord!"

"My Lord!"

I shifted back to my human form and grabbed Riff—the closest one to me—by his horns and shook him. "Where the fuck is she?"

Before either of them could respond, another voice answered. One that chilled me to the bones I didn't have. "She's right here, My Lord. Safe and sound in the arms of Death."

I turned to see the row of troupe members part. The fact that most of them were dressed as clowns had my anxiety spiking, even though clowns never once bothered me. Slowly, they shuffled out of the way to reveal Death standing behind them.

His long dark hair and the tails of his duster jacket billowed in the acrid gusts of hot air tearing through the burning camp.

And on the ground before him, on her knees, topless, bruised and bleeding, was Megaera. He had his scythe out, the curved blade caressing her throat and forcing her chin up.

It took everything within me to keep me from lunging at him. There were a hundred other ways I could hurt him. Strangle him with my shadows. Fling him into an illusion that would give Death himself night terrors.

I didn't act on any of that. He could slit Meg's throat in a blink. Since he was the Horseman of Death, he could shatter her soul, too.

There'd be no bringing her back.

Daemon prowled toward him and stopped when Death held his scythe closer to Meg's throat—enough to draw a single drop of blood.

"Down, boy. One paw closer, and I slit your mate's pretty little throat. Don't forget, if she dies by my hand, she dies forever."

His eyes dropped to Meg, and if I wasn't mistaken, I saw the flicker of something akin to fondness there. "It's a shame. I wanted to keep this one for myself. But the mission comes first..." His soulless gaze cut back to me. "So, *My Lord*, you're going to forge a mating bond with Lilith. Right here—" He pointed to a patch of grass in the center of the crowd that had gathered. "Where everyone can watch."

"You're a twisted psychopath," Daemon growled.

Death grinned at that. I'd always hated his smile. It was made worse by the fact that I liked his face. I more than liked it.

I envied it.

"I am what I was created to be. A perfect creation born from Discord's darkness. And it's out of love and loyalty for the god he once was that I drag the shadow of what remains back to the Downside by any means possible."

The Horseman hauled Meg up to her feet, bringing her back snug against his bare chest. She didn't so much as flinch as he dropped the blade to curve beneath her breast. "When you're done, I think to celebrate, I'll be claiming Lilith's little offering to you as my own."

Daemon and the twins tensed. But the fear that bled into the air, twining with the smoke that started to cover everything, came from the entire troupe.

We all loved her.

Death smirked. He knew that he had us all balanced on the edge of a tightrope. And there he was, with his scythe at the ready, threatening to cut it at any moment. "What's her name again?"

No one answered. The bastard didn't deserve to have her name in his mouth.

It was Meg who broke the silence. Up until now, she'd been quiet. Death probably mistook that for weakness. But no, she'd been calculating.

Our little demon was plotting something.

"It's Megaera."

"Megaera..." he drawled. "So, your mother named you after the Greek Goddess of Vengeance. Cute."

"Actually..." She grinned. "My father came up with the name."

A strange sound filled the air. Something snapping. I looked around and back at Meg to realize it was the sound of bones breaking and fusing back together.

She was shifting.

Meg was finding her monster form, the one none of us knew she was capable of summoning.

And by my depths, she was a dragon. Like me. A huge dragon with pink pearlescent scales and black spikes that ran along her back and down a tail tipped with a spade just like her half-form.

The tail wasn't the only similarity she shared with a traditional sex demon's full form. Her skull was that of a dragon, but it was fleshless, with two pink flames blazing bright in her eye sockets.

Megaera had found her monster form.

She was magnificent.

Goddess of Vengeance indeed.

46

The Pink Dragon

MEG

I wasn't sure what was happening to me. The anger snaking through my veins was so potent that it tore apart my nerves and fused them into something new. I was shifting. Becoming something...*demonic.*

I had a monster form.

Now, power surged through me, dulling the pain from my breaking bones and stretching muscles. I screamed, but it came out as a roar, inhuman and terrifying.

Everyone was staring up at me, craning their heads to meet my eyes. So tall. Everyone looked so small from this height. I held up my hands to see giant claws. Pink shimmering scales.

I fanned out my wings and twisted my head to see they weren't tiny in this form. The webbing was shiny, too. I caught my reflection in them and gasped. Only, it didn't come out as a gasp. A deep, guttural growl rumbled from me instead.

I didn't just have a monster form. I was a fucking *dragon.*

My mates all stared up at me with something akin to dumbstruck awe on their faces. Even Alistair. Especially Alistair.

Death's expression was the best of all. He seemed scared, only for a moment, but I saw it there all the same before anger etched his pale features. The archdemon started to shift, but Daemon's dogs appeared from thin air, and all latched on to keep him from shifting.

Death screamed as six angry hellhounds attached themselves to him. Biting and growling and fighting to keep him rooted to the ground at all costs. A tentacle made of shadows sprouted from his back and smashed into the hound, who was latched onto the arm wielding his weapon, sending the animal flying.

He swung the scythe, and the blade sliced into the hound on his other arm. Cutting her clean in half.

It exploded into ash before she even hit the ground.

"Kali!"

Daemon's tattered scream shook us all to our core. He leaped through the air and shifted back to his human form the moment he hit the ground, grasping the pile of Kali's ash in his hands.

The scar on my shoulder seared my flesh like a fresh brand. I could feel his pain as if it were my own and as if it had been my pet Death had mercilessly cut down.

The demon before me exploded into the dark visage that was the black dragon of Death. He shook the other five dogs of

Daemon's pack, but when they snapped back to their feet for another attack, their master issued a command in Infernal to keep them from meeting the same fate as Kali.

Death took flight, and without fully processing what was happening, I followed my instincts and launched myself into the air after him.

Holy freaking shit. I was flying.

After learning that if I were a full-blooded succubus, I'd be able to fly, I'd imagined it. It was mostly how I imagined, minus the wind in my hair part. Also, the part where I was a pink dragon with The Horseman of Death clawing at my wings.

"The little half-blood is full of surprises," Death rumbled as he dove at me from above. I managed to lurch out of the way just in time, but there was movement from behind me. I whipped my head around to see the shadow of another dragon sailing straight for me.

Death had a shadow, too—a shadow of his dragon form.

I dipped sharply to the right, bringing my wings perfectly vertical to miss its blow as it passed. I summoned the fiery ball of tension that had been knotted tight inside me since I'd shifted and blew an Infernal blast of pink fire into it.

The shadow evaporated in my flames, and Death laughed as he soared over me. I was close enough now to see his soulless eyes reflecting the fire in mine.

Another shadow fell over us, and I looked up to see the two-headed hydra circling overhead.

Why wasn't Alistair helping?

My mind went back to the night he'd rescued me in the haunt tent from the four men in masks who'd planned to attack me. I'd told him the damsel in distress thing wasn't my bag. Was he allowing me to take care of Death while staying close enough to intervene if shit went south?

That had to be it.

He was giving me a chance to prove that I could handle myself. That I didn't need to be sent away when all Hell broke loose.

Death was just as fast as I was and stronger. What could I do that would give me the upper hand? What was an attack he couldn't deflect?

I could charm him.

"Death," I rumbled, my voice cavernous and not at all like my normal voice. "You want to be my mate?"

His only answer was a guttural purr that called to some animalistic side of me. I steeled myself against it and continued. "Then you're going to have to prove yourself worthy of me. My mates would *die* for me. I expect you to do the same. So go on. Kill yourself."

We were passing over the big top, and miraculously, it was still standing. For a beat, I was afraid my magic hadn't managed to sink its claws into him.

Then, he started to dive right for the tent's center pole.

The pole's tip wasn't exactly sharp, but the dragon's body was so large and heavy that it ran him through. Spearing him straight through the chest.

I landed on the top of the pole, shifting back to my half-form just as my feet made contact so as not to put too much weight on it. It was easy to keep my balance, thanks to all the tricks I'd learned from the twins as part of their aerial act.

Any other creature would have died at the way the pole had maimed his chest. Torrents of blood gushed from the wound and slipped down the tent's canvas. However, since he was Death, he kept breathing. He lifted his great head, eyeing me with one of those hollow dragon eyes.

On impact, my charm magic had worn off.

His great jaws parted, blood and saliva slipping off his vicious teeth in rubbery tendrils. "You fucking bitch…"

I wrapped my tail around the pole to keep myself steady as I leaned toward him. My clothes had ripped and fallen off in the process of shifting, but my nakedness just had me feeling more powerful than ever. "Still want to mate me after I kicked your ass?"

His eyes gleamed with violence, and to my surprise, he panted, "Yes. Especially now. But you're going kill me instead. I can scent death before it arrives. Even my own."

"Any last words?"

His eyelids drifted shut as he seemed to accept what was coming. "Maybe you do deserve to be his queen instead of Lilith after all…"

I held out my hand, and a ball of shadows culminated in the palm of my hand. I'm not sure what compelled me to do it. Maybe the same urge that had me bursting into a dragon. I'd been capable of harnessing charm magic since puberty hit, but this new arcana was different. Far more potent.

It felt like Alistair's magic. It *was* his magic.

The shadows shaped into a sword and turned to that dusky pink color. I jumped down onto his skull, shoving the tip of the shadowy blade into his eye socket. I'd killed enough demons to know what it was like to take their life.

This was different, though. Something gave way inside him, something fracturing.

The demon screamed and violently jerked his head, throwing me off. I bounced down the canvas, sliding down the side. I was too close to the tent to shift. My wings would catch in the canvas. So, I slipped down, my tail slicing through the material to slow my fall instead.

Strong arms captured me.

I looked up to see Alistair. He had tears in his eyes. *Tears.*

"That was beautiful, Little Demon."

I blinked several times as my brain attempted to parse what had just happened. "I think...I think I shattered Death's soul."

Alistair glanced up at the big top where Death's body hung limp, speared on the center pole like some fantastical shish kabob. His lips thinned into a frown, though he couldn't hide the flicker of adoration as he returned his attention to me.

Maybe he wasn't trying to hide it anymore.

"You did, darling. You absorbed some of my power through my mark. Much more than I ever thought possible. You can turn into a dragon, and you can now wipe souls from existence."

I summoned the blade of pink shadows and gave it a wave. "I can use shadows, too! This is going to be awesome to use in the show..."

"Meg..."

I tapped the blush pink blade to his lips. "Don't."

I didn't want him to say it. I knew the words he was going to speak next, and I couldn't stand to hear them. I refused to hear them. "I'm not going fucking anywhere. I've proven myself, haven't I? I'm not some weak half-blood, and I don't want anyone to accuse me of being one ever again."

The ringmaster looked so sad, so ashamed. "I'm sorry for not thinking you were capable of handling yourself. But...I'm talking about your freedom. Everyone's freedom. I'm releasing everyone from their contracts with me. No more pets."

If everyone left, that would mean no more Sinner's Sideshow. My mind balked at the notion. "They'll stay. We'll all stay. Everyone is loyal to you. It doesn't matter if you're Discord or not. You're a good boss."

"They won't stay. They have no reason to."

I smoothed my hand over his cheek, feeling the fine stitching in his cool flesh. "Yes, they do."

Before he could argue anymore, the twins ran up to us. I smiled when I saw they'd found my sword, but it fell the moment I registered their expressions. "What happened?"

"It's Lilith," Riff panted as he thrust a claw in the direction they'd come. "She woke up and flew away. We know you can't kill her, boss. Should we send Daemon? Should we go?"

Alistair considered the twins before setting me to my feet. "No. Meg should go after her. She'll be able to handle her."

My attention pinged between all three of them before settling back on Alistair. A strange peace settled in my chest. I knew what I had to do.

"Will you come with me?"

The shade stared at me for a quiet beat. "I won't be able to help you kill her."

"I don't need help with that." I hitched a thumb up at the tent where the dragon lay limp. "I just...I don't know. I don't want to be alone. You know her better than anyone. I'd like it if you were there."

The twins took notice of the dragon for the first time. Riff let out a low whistle. "Damn. Look who's the new Harbinger of death now."

Alistair nodded. "Alright, Little Demon. I'll go with you."

47

Mother Dearest

MEG

We followed my mother's trail to Alistair's caravan. It made perfect sense that she'd come here since, back in the day, it had belonged to her.

I glanced at Alistair as he opened the door, old hinges announcing our arrival. "Does she think it will hide her since it used to be hers?"

A frown crested the shadow demon's mouth. "I don't know...The caravan can be unpredictable."

We moved inside, cautious, every step slow and purposeful. There were so many books and trinkets and piles of odds and ends to hide behind. On closer inspection, it seemed the first room was just like we'd left it. A total mess, but harboring no evil mothers.

We opened the second door, and instead of a hallway, we were greeted with another room.

A church.

The walls were made of crumbling stone, the pews old, worn wood so blackened with wear I couldn't begin to guess their age. There was a stained glass window of a black two-headed dragon. Crimson light poured through the glass, bathing the church's stone floor in hues of black and red.

At the front of the church was an altar—a black obsidian obelisk similar to the one in our chapel tent, only the one here was three times larger.

Lilith knelt on the floor before the altar with her head bowed in prayer.

I would have written it off as an act if it wasn't for the emotions bleeding into her aura.

But she really was devoted to Discord—so much so, that it had turned into something warped and obsessive over time.

The demoness didn't raise her head as we approached. "It's been twenty years since you've been home, My Lord. I've never understood your hatred and distaste for our realm."

Her voice froze the very blood in my veins. So chilling. Unfeeling.

"It's Hell, Lilith," Alistair said simply as he strode behind one of the pews, running his finger along the back and rubbing the dust between his fingers with a grimace. "What's there to like?"

The demoness rose to her feet and turned.

Ever since I was little, I'd tried to imagine her face so many times. I'd never been able to decide on a mental picture that felt right. The woman before me was so beautiful. Every likeness I'd imagined for her didn't even come close.

My mother was tall and queenly, with long, flowing hair the color of lavender. Even tucked into her back, her wings were easily four times the size of mine. Her horns sprouted upward, with a slight inward curve at their points.

I picked up on little emotions from her, but the only thing I could get a solid read on was ice-cold contempt. Her eyes flicked over me, and there wasn't a shift in her aura.

Knowing what I did about her, I wasn't surprised. Still, I was disappointed. I was also annoyed that Daemon and Alistair had kept the fact that she was alive from me for weeks.

Yet, it made sense.

They were just trying to protect me from getting hurt. Silly them for thinking there was any way of avoiding that.

"You used to like Hell." Her words were spoken so calmly, yet they were doused in arsenic. "You used to like me."

Tension thick enough to cut stretched through the caravan's illusion of the church. The silence shattered as Alistair threw his head back and laughed. "I forgot you were so funny. Then again, you were one of the world's first clowns. Your jokes are a bit dusty, but you can still make me laugh."

Oh, she did *not* like that. She bared her teeth in a poisonous sneer. She looked like a coiled spring, ready to leap. She didn't.

Even she had to know she'd lost, and any struggle was just a waste of energy. "You're the joke, Discord."

"And you're fucking delusional if you think I ever felt anything close to affection for you. I merely tolerated you." His smile fell away, leaving an expression that would have a weaker woman flinching. "Until I didn't. Why do you think I sent you to the Upside to harvest terror for me? I wanted you gone."

"Don't forget, you're in love with this stupid fucking circus. *I* created it. For you!"

He hummed, his fingers drumming the grip of his cane. "Hmm. Yes. Sinner's Sideshow is the second best thing you've ever birthed."

Lilith's soft lavender eyes gleamed. "And what was the first?"

"You're daughter." The devil lowered himself into a pew. "Aren't you going to even acknowledge her?"

The demon scoffed as her gaze jerked to me, the resentment carved plainly into her otherwise flawless physiognomy. That's when I flinched.

I didn't mean to—I hated that I did.

What I hated more was that she noticed. She brandished a venomous smile. "You are beautiful. You got that from me."

When I struggled to find words for her, Alistair filled in the space. "She also got your stubbornness. She wears it better, though."

Gods, the pride in his voice somehow made this whole confrontation worse.

Because she caught that too, and the loathing bleeding into her aura only spiked.

That's when she noticed his mating mark. Her lip curled in disgust. Like I was nothing but a cockroach, she'd like nothing better than to squash beneath her shoe. "You know why you're so compatible with him? Because I made you for him. You were forged from dark magic, girl. I intended to kill you in a blood sacrifice, but your blood is still his, even if it remains unspilled."

It took all the fucking effort in the world, but I forced a saccharine smile to my face, knowing it would piss her off. "Is that all you have to say to me?"

Her eyes slithered down to the sword in my hand. "I recognize that blade. It belonged to your sperm donor."

My smile slipped in an instant. "You mean my *father?*" My voice shot up an octave. I was almost screaming, but I couldn't bring myself to care. "He died thinking you loved him, you ice harpy!"

She shrugged as if she'd heard the insult a million times before. "He wasn't so bad for a human. He served his purpose. I chose him well. You turned out exceptional. You should be thanking me."

Of all the things she'd done, that was what pissed me off the most. Everything I'd worked hard for was because of me. Not her.

That was it.

My composure snapped like dry spaghetti.

I lunged at her, moving so fast that it shocked all three of us. There was no dodging me. No running and hiding. In the sliver of a moment, I had her pinned to the ground with my foot on her chest and my father's blade to her throat.

And just like that, her composure snapped, too. She didn't cry, even though a small part of me wished she would. I didn't think Lilith could cry. But she did sob, dry, ugly, weaving breaths as she looked to her god. "M–My Lord. Please. Just let me go back home."

Alistair got to his feet. His face was unreadable as it was cast in the shadows created by his top hat. "The decision on whether you live or die lies with your daughter, Lilith. Perhaps you should have given the whole mother thing a shot. Then maybe you wouldn't be on the wrong end of her blade."

"Megaera."

She said my name for the first time.

And I felt nothing.

"Why should I let you live?" I asked, my voice flat, bearing no trace of mercy because there was none. "Your mad pursuit of Alistair and his power has poisoned everything about you. You were so desperate for his mark that you convinced three of the four Horsemen to betray him. You were going to go as far as to rape him to secure your bond."

Her lips twisted into a snarl. "You make it sound so heinous. I was made for him."

"No, you weren't. You even said it yourself..." I paused for dramatic effect. "*I* was."

With a twist of my wrist, the blade slid through her throat as easily as a hot knife through butter.

I thought I'd feel something close to remorse.

Instead, nothing but numbness spread through my system as I watched her slump against the church's cold floor, her blood spreading beneath.

It was hard to say how many minutes I stood there staring at her body, knowing her soul was shattered and gone. Alistair stood with me in the silence. If I wanted to stay like this for all eternity, I knew he would be right there, standing with me.

"What now?" I whispered.

"Now...? Now, we go and see if your theory is right."

I finally turned to look at him. "What theory?"

I expected a smile on his face. He was always smiling that devilish, off-putting grin. Instead, I saw him looking at me with nothing but stark reverence and adoration. "I'm going to free everyone in the circus. We'll see if they stay. If they do, Sinner's Sideshow will live on."

48
Two Weeks Later

MEG

“A real carnival,” I beamed. “No magic. *Real* rides and games.”

Alistair frowned as he watched the sledge gang—the team normally responsible for assembling the big top—piece together the carousel. “It’s so much equipment to haul.”

“That’s how it’s supposed to work. The perk of a good old-fashioned human carnival is that you don’t have to eat people to keep it going. Though I’m sure you’ll still munch on some fear here and there as a snack.”

He cocked a brow. “Speaking of snacks, I have a surprise for you.”

“A surprise? Does it have anything to do with why you disappeared for the entire day today?”

"No, actually, that had more to do with a surprise the twins have for Daemon."

"The twins have a surprise for Daemon?"

Before Alistair could respond, Daemon rounded the corner. He was covered in grease and waving a metal bar—probably to one of the rides—over his head. "There you are. Where the hell have you been? I've been trying to put this shit together all day. Are we supposed to have screws left over?"

Lately, every time I saw the alpha, I couldn't stop myself from staring at the new mating mark on his arm.

Two weeks after we'd killed Lilith and the Horsemen, everything was starting to feel right with our world again. Alistair's identity was out in the open. Everyone accepted him for who he was and honored his wish to no longer be regarded as a god. They stayed at Sinner's Sideshow of their own accord.

All new equipment had been ordered to replace what had burned down during the attack. We decided to keep the carnival going for monsters. Meanwhile, we'd resumed the shows in the big top—which had remained untouched by the fire, though it was now streaked with Death's black as night blood. The infamous black and white striped canvas was just a little more stripey now.

And Alistair and Daemon were finally mated.

The only mark that needed to be given was mine to Alistair. We still hadn't done that deed, and it was driving me crazy.

"I've been away from the campgrounds, running some errands," Alistair explained with an aloof smile while examining his nails.

Daemon took the last few steps to close the distance between us and leaned close to Alistair, his nostrils flexing, and he dragged in a deep breath. "You smell like rotten eggs."

I blinked. I didn't pick up on that at all. The hellhound's acute senses never ceased to wow me. I turned to Alistair, crossing my arms over my chest. "Yeah. Where were you today?"

Daemon cocked his head, his eyes narrowing. "He smells of the Brimwastes. I think he's been to the Downside."

By Alistair's growing smile, Daemon had guessed correctly.

"Holy shit. What were you doing down there?" I asked, my eyes rounding.

Alistair shrugged. "Checking up on things. Making sure no archdemons rise to power in my absence. And, as I said, I was running an errand."

"What kind of errand?"

"Ask the twins. They're the ones who sent me."

A vein ticked in Daemon's brow. "You're running errands for the twins now?"

"I'd call it more of a favor, actually. A surprise. For you, actually."

Daemon's brows shot so high on his face, they looked like they might pop off. "Well, color me fucking curious. Where are they?"

Alistair's gaze moved to something past Daemon's shoulder. The hellhound twisted around to see the twins approaching, painted up in their classic clown faces, even though there weren't any shows tonight.

Riff held a box in his arms. It was wrapped up like a gift—they'd opted for children's wrapping paper judging by the cartoon character illustrations.

"Oooh, is that for Daemon?" I asked, bouncing excitedly on the balls of my feet. This was as much news to me as it was to Daemon. But I was also shit at keeping surprises like this, so it made sense why I'd been kept in the dark.

Daemon's eyes narrowed in suspicion as they slid over the wrapping paper. "*Blue's Clues*?" he asked, reading the logo on the paper.

Raff shrugged. "It was one of the few options the store carried, and it had a dog on it, so we figured it was perfect. Go on. Open it."

The hellhound hesitated. I didn't blame him.

Whatever was in the box had come from the Downside, according to Alistair. Plus, this was a present from the twins, who were notorious pranksters.

When the contents of the box gave a whimper, Daemon tore into the paper and ripped the top off. Pure joy rolled off him in strong waves as he pulled out a squirming animal.

A hellhound puppy.

"We know it doesn't replace Kali. But we figured it would at least fill a bit of the hole she left," Riff said with a shrug.

Daemon said something in Infernal as he hugged the dog to his chest. Whatever it was he said, it had the twins exchanging one of their *looks* as they beamed at one another.

Raff flashed me a huge smile and a wink. "See? Told you I could come up with a good way of saying thank you for the whole Conquest thing that didn't involve jumping out of a cake or sucking his dick."

Some of the troupe members working on the setup of the carnival took notice of the new puppy and surrounded Daemon and the twins, welcoming the new addition to the family and all chipping in suggestions for new names.

I turned to Alistair. "So. You said Daemon wasn't the only one with a surprise tonight? Do I get a puppy too?"

"If you want one. Anything you want that's in my power is yours, darling."

I leaned close to him. "You've given me everything...Except for one last thing. I want to mark you. I don't care if you don't have a new skin. I want you, no matter what you're wearing or what you look like."

Alistair reached up, his thumb tracing my bottom lip. "I thought as much, so you'll be happy to learn my surprise is something along those lines. Specifically, it's something I've been working on for the last week."

A smile pulled at the edges of my mouth. "Do I get it now? Should we slip away?"

"Not quite yet, love. Let's wait until the rest of the troupe is in bed. Meet us at the carousel in three hours."

"Us?"

I glanced through the small gathering around Daemon and the twins. "The other three?"

Alistair's jeweled eyes heated as they dropped to my lips. "I figured all four of your mates should be involved."

I couldn't keep the giddy grin off my face. "Oh. It's *that* kind of surprise."

Three hours felt like an eternity when you knew what was waiting for you. Okay, so I didn't exactly know what kind of surprise was in store for me. But if all four of my mates were involved, and Alistair was making such a big deal about it, it was safe to bet that we were going to be fucking.

I sat on one of the demonic carousel horses, idly thumbing through my phone to pass the time. The carnival was grave-quiet. It was late—It had to be about three in the morning when everyone turned in for the night.

My phone buzzed with a text from Lollie.

Lollie: Giiirl. So are they, like....all going to show up and fuck you? Isn't that a lot of dicks? Where are you supposed to put them all?

Meg: I'm a sex demon. I'll get creative.

Lollie: All I know is that you're gonna be wishing you still had those metal panties on with how sore you're going to be tomorrow.

Movement out of the corner of my eye had my attention jerking up. My eyes strained through the dark. All the carnival lights were off, so I could see nothing but vague shapes and shadows. I shivered, finding myself wishing that I'd opted to wear more than a pleated mini skirt, fishnets, and my busty ghost shirt.

Every cell in my body crystallized when a man who wasn't one of my mates emerged from the haze of night.

High cheekbones. Long black hair. Ashen skin. A jawline so sharp it could cut a girl.

Death.

No. No. No. I'd killed him!

I stumbled off the carousel horse and turned, bolting off in the opposite direction. I'd killed him once. I could do it again. But there was a voice in my head telling me to run and not look back.

Run. Run. *Run.*

I wasn't sure where I was running to. Where was there to go? The twins' RV? Daemon's trailer? Alistair's caravan? No. I didn't need any of them to protect me. I'd already proven that I could protect myself. I could turn into a freaking dragon, for fuck's sake. I could harness the power of shadows to create deadly weapons.

Still, I followed that instinctual voice in my head telling me to flee.

Whatever Death had become, he was far more dangerous by his erosive demeanor that seemed to thin the air, making my breaths come out in short, sharp huffs. What had he become? What had I done to him?

I could feel him close behind me. He'd catch up to me out in the open like this.

I had to hide. There was no way that was the logical choice, but there was no time to stop and think of my next move. I didn't dare stop to pick apart the dark little hope that bloomed inside me, wishing he'd catch me.

I detested my attraction to the Horseman. It wasn't right. It wasn't natural. It made no fucking sense, and now that he was dead, it wasn't relevant.

Only... He wasn't dead, was he? It hadn't been a figment of my imagination.

Death was really chasing me.

Without pausing to think, I threw myself into the first ride that seemed like it would be a good hiding place.

The house of mirrors.

Yes! They'd just finished putting this together earlier today. I'd seen them fit the pieces together. Dozens upon dozens of mirrored panels that created confusing paths. And in the dark, it would be next to impossible to navigate.

I picked a path at random and flung myself into the dark.

49

House of Mirrors

MEG

My heartbeat thrashed in my ears as I stole through the darkened ride. It was just light enough that I could see myself in the mirrors, my reflection fractured into a hundred identical images.

This place was creepy.

If I got out of this alive, I had to remember to bring the guys here after dark to fuck. The twins would especially like it.

My heart froze in my chest when Death's reflection appeared in the mirrors. He'd found me. He surrounded me. In hindsight, the house of mirrors had been a bad choice.

His image was everywhere. Any of them could have been real. I didn't know where to turn or what to do.

Then, I registered his eyes. Green and vibrant like polished emeralds—not black and bottomless like Death's had been.

"Your fear tastes like cotton candy. Did I ever tell you that?" a familiar voice spoke from the dark.

"You took his corpse," I said in a breathless whisper.

Alistair's new face grinned back at me through the mirrors. "I've been working on it for the last week. You did quite a number on his chest."

He'd come shirtless, leaving the brutal scar between his pectorals on full display. Countless stitches had been made to close up the place where he'd been run through on the big top's center pole.

"Oh, and this is your handy work, too, I presume?" He held up his right hand, giving four fingers a wiggle. He smiled at the stump where a thumb had been. "No matter. It gets me hard, knowing that all the scars are your doing. Knowing it was you who provided this new body for me."

Realization slowly sank in. "Famine overhead us talking about how you were on the hunt for an archdemon skin the day he'd come to warn us about my mother's attack. When he whispered in your ear, he was asking you to use Death's skin, wasn't he?"

By the way Alistair's reflection grew larger in the surrounding mirrors, I knew he had taken a step closer. "He saw it as a great honor for Death. Frankly, one he didn't deserve. But I can't deny my affinity for his face. It suits me, no?"

All I could manage was a wobbly nod.

"Does it make you uncomfortable, Megaera?"

Yes, it did. No—It didn't. *Fuck!* I wasn't sure how I felt about it.

It was intense. None of this was normal. I'd only just gotten used to the fact that one of my mates was a full-on supernatural equivalent of Leatherface from the *Texas Chainsaw Massacre* movies the twins loved watching.

I think the thing that made me the most uncomfortable was that I was very much into it.

And somehow, wearing the corpse of the monster I'd murdered—knowing what he was going to do to me with it—had me heating with excitement.

So, was I comfortable with it? No. And that's exactly why I was so fucking into it.

Jesus, I was fucked in the head.

I hadn't been able to deny my attraction to Death. He was hot. Especially now that the rotten soul that had once lived inside this flesh was gone, replaced with a man I loved. Deeply.

"Green eyes suit this skin tone better," I said with the ghost of a smile tucked at the corner of my mouth.

Alistair's new face lifted with relief. "So, this is okay? If you don't like it, I'll scrap it and find something new."

"I like it. I *shouldn't*. But that can be said for most of the shit I'm into."

"Tell me about what else you're into. Tell the devil your deepest desires."

"I like...I like feeling like a toy. I like knowing that I'm your pet." My cheeks flamed. "I like it when you own me."

His many reflections tensed. "I don't own you anymore."

"I know. But it gets me wet feeling like you do...even if it's just an illusion."

One of the reflections—the real him—stepped forward. He held out his hand, and a chain made of shadows appeared. He held one end and attached the other to Daemon's collar around my throat.

He gave it a testing tug. It felt so real. It even made a clicking sound as if it was forged of real metal.

"Crawl to me, Pet." He brandished his cane in a swirl of shadows and slowly wound the chain around the shaft, pulling the makeshift leash taut. "Crawl to your master."

I lowered myself to the floor and crawled toward him.

His eyes banked with hunger as he took in the sight of me on my hands and knees. "By my own depths, I love seeing my hound's collar on you."

The way his words dripped with lust had me woozy with need.

His hand—the one with the thumb still attached—hooked into the waist of his pants and shoved them down his hips.

Jesus Christ. Death was fucking *hung*.

I sat up on my knees, my hands making a slow ascent up his legs. This body was more muscular than the last. Still leaner than Daemon, but his frame had more sinew than Riff and Raff.

He sucked in a breath when my fingers traced that mouth-watering V between his hips.

The hand holding the chain sank into my hair between my horns. The other gripped his base and gave a pump. A pearl of pre-cum gathered at the slit in his tip and started to ooze. I leaned forward to catch it on my tongue.

"Fuck yes," he rasped in a voice that had my nerves sparking with anticipation. "Taste me."

I moaned the moment he hit my taste buds. He tasted electric. Forbidden. Like something I definitely shouldn't be putting in my mouth.

I tipped my gaze upward, locking eyes with him. My heart fluttered in my throat at the dark creature lurking behind those pools of green. On the outside, Alistair was an enigma wrapped in shadows, dark magic and stolen flesh. On the inside, he was a dragon of a man.

I licked my lips in invitation.

He took the cue, his fingers flexing in my hair, and with a push of his hips, he filled my mouth.

Oh fuck. Death had been one arrogant son of a bitch. But with a cock like this, it made sense. It was long and thick and had a weight to it that pressed down on my tongue in ways none of my other guys did in their human or half-forms.

I closed the seal of my mouth around his base and sucked while my tongue painted firm strokes along the underside of his shaft.

There was no sign of stitching anywhere around his groin like with his last skin suit. It was all smooth and perfect flesh.

Testing a theory, I scraped the points of my manicured claws over the seam of his balls.

Tendons in his neck strung taut. His head tipped back, and thanks to all the mirrors that surrounded us, I could see his eyes roll back in pure euphoria.

Just as I expected. The ringmaster was a switch, and even though he preferred to be dominant with me, he loved it when I hurt him.

My next wicked idea was inexplicably stupid.

And there was no chance my sensible human side was going to talk me out of it. Especially knowing that my bratty side turned the shadow demon on.

I leapt to my feet and swiped my claws at his face. His reflexes outmatched mine by a mile, but he didn't move.

My claws sliced into his flesh at an angle, tattered marks stretching from the corner of his hairline down to his jaw.

Instead of blood, shadows leaked from the wound.

His cock twitched as it thickened. Jeez. What was with my men and their thing with letting me cut them?

Not that I was complaining.

The skin started to fuse back together right before my eyes.

His jaw set. Anger flared to life behind his eyes, but I didn't buy it for a second. The phantom smile lurking at the edges of his mouth gave him away.

"This is the human form of an archdemon. Unlike my mortal skins before it, this one will heal on its own. Lucky for you."

Before I had time to react, his hand closed around my wrist, and he spun me, pushing my chest against one of the mirrored panels so hard the glass cracked.

I cried out in surprise, and he laughed.

He snatched my wrists and pinned them behind my back, bringing them together with a few loops of the chain leash.

He tested the bindings with a tug and hummed when I whimpered at the way the shadowy links bit into my skin.

"You know what to say if you want our game to end."

I never wanted this to end, and he knew it.

"Eat a dick," I blabbered. Okay, so it wasn't my best bratty line, but the way he was pulling my hips back, forcing my spine to arch so that he could line himself up with me, had my brain turning to puddy.

He chuckled. "How about I just feed you mine instead?"

Before the last syllable left his tongue, he punched his hips forward and filled me with one brutal stroke.

Thank fuck I liked the sensation of being split in half because, mother of *God*, was this man huge. I mean, he had nothing on his dragon form, but no man had any right being so damn big.

The mind-shattering pleasure, coiled tight with pain, was pushed higher by the display the mirrors provided.

In every direction, his reflection had mine bent over. His pants slung low on his hips, his ass flexing as he started to pump into me, the muscles in his shoulders shifting beneath the screen of his long hair—the image broken up by the fractured glass.

He draped himself over me, his hands pressing against the mirror on either side of my head to cage me in.

"Be a good little demon and take what your master gives you," he growled against my ear.

I angled my head to look at him, my cheek pressed against the cool glass. "Is it in yet?"

Obviously, it was fucking in. I'd be lucky if I could walk without a limp tomorrow, but I couldn't resist provoking him.

When it came to my men, there wasn't such a thing as too rough.

Alistair's fingers grasped one of my horns and wrenched my head back so I could catch his infernal glare out of the corner of my eye. "I've had enough of her bratty mouth. Gag her."

I blinked. Who was he talking to?

Movement in the mirrors dragged my attention up to see Daemon stepping out of the dark, his many reflections joining ours. Fuck. Had he been here the whole time, watching us?

Alistair had said to meet him and the other guys at the carousel. Had they all chased me in here? I strained, trying to see if Riff and Raff were here too, but the world around me blurred as Alistair pulled me off the glass and spun me around.

He pushed me to my knees, and Daemon was right there with us, kneeling in front of me. He caught me by the horns, forcing me to bend at the waist so my mouth was level with his pelvis. He must have come here in his hound form because he was already naked.

A hand curled around his shaft, slotting the tip into my parted lips.

I gaped at the hand wrapped around his girth. Black fingernail polish, chipped at the tips.

That wasn't Daemon's hand at all. It was Raff's.

On my next breath, a head of green hair appeared over one of the Hellhound's shoulders and a head of blue a beat later over the other.

The twins looked more terrifying than ever in their makeup tonight. They'd combined the classic clown look with their new favorite—the skeleton paint. Undead clowns.

Add in the dozens of mirrors, and this was something I'd have nightmares about for many nights to come. The kind of nightmares where I'd wake up wet and not from sweating.

"Good choice of location, Harbinger," Riff snickered as he watched his brother guide Daemon's cock into my mouth. "Now we can watch you get fucked from every angle."

50

Sated

MEG

All my mates were here now.

What were the chances I was going to survive all four of them?

Fighting dragons was one thing, but taking all four of my mates at the same time was an entirely different matter. I was strong. Stronger than I'd ever felt before. Yet I felt so weirdly fragile in their hands.

They were firm and rough but oddly careful with me as they positioned me exactly the way they wanted. Like I was their little doll to play with, one they weren't in any hurry to break.

The shadowy chain tying my wrists together disappeared, allowing me free use of my hands. Riff and Raff had both tugged their cocks out. I took one in each of my hands while Daemon filled my mouth at a slower pace than Alistair had taken with my pussy.

The shade's cool fingers dug into my hips as he resumed his rhythm, taking me with steady, hard strokes.

Daemon pulled from my mouth to peel my shirt off and discard it on the ground behind him before filling me again—using my horns as handlebars as he fucked my face.

One of the twins captured my nipples, rolling the tender buds between their fingers and tweaking my piercings while the other gently tugged my wings open and traced the mating scars mottling their thin webbing.

I moaned around Daemon, and my pussy clenched, making Alistair groan behind me.

There was so much sensation, so many different fingers on me that I could barely tell them apart. Pure pleasure surged through my veins as my mates stroked and fucked and felt me out until my nerves started to sizzle like an overloaded circuit board.

Daemon's thighs shook, and his muscles clenched. He throbbed on my tongue, and I knew he was moments away from detonation. Instead of pistoning inside me harder, he stopped all motion and wrenched himself from my mouth.

I blinked up at him.

The sight of him pushing his lips to Riff's in a frantic, feral kiss was the final push I needed to send me hurtling over the brink. I came with a whimper. My grip tightened on the twins.

Riff hissed against Daemon's lips as I spit on his length, adding more lubricant so I could stroke him fast.

Daemon's mouth ripped away from Riff's, his head turning to smash into Raff's.

They kissed like they were trying to eat each other. Starving predators, battling for dominance, each motion bruising and full of teeth. Riff's hand wrapped around Daemon's cock while the hellhound feasted on his brother's mouth.

I had gone from feeling like a delicate doll in the hands of boys just learning how to share their playthings to a piece of meat in the middle of a pack of wild animals.

It was glorious.

Daemon came with a grunt, thick ropes of seed spurting over my face. Before I had time to recover, hands were repositioning me.

Raff lay on his back, his grip clamping over my hips as I was lowered onto his dick.

I gasped when he started to fill my ass. The tight muscle stretched around him, pain and little bolts of bliss shooting through my system.

"Relax, babe. It will feel good in a second." His purr had my muscles easing. Once he was completely inside, Riff knelt between our legs. Lining his dick up with my pussy.

Thanks to the mirrors, I didn't have to crane my head to see Daemon kneeling behind Riff.

It was just like how we'd been in the ring the first time the four of us had shared one another, only with the twins swapped.

Daemon held his hand beneath Riff's chin and, in the silkiest growl I'd ever heard, commanded him to "Spit."

Riff balked. Probably just to rile Daemon. The hound fucked better when he was a little irked, and we all knew it. Sure enough, his tattooed fingers tangled in Riff's blue hair, shoving his head toward his upturned palm. "Come on. I know sex demon saliva is better than any other lubricant out there. Spit, and this will hurt a lot less."

"Don't make Leather Daddy mad," his brother snickered from beneath me.

Riff flashed his twin one of his unhinged, too-wide smiles. "Our girl gets so wet when he's rough with her. Maybe I want to see what the big fucking whoop's about—*unngh*."

While the incubus was running his mouth, Daemon shoved his fingers into mine, scooping out a gob of my saliva. His hand wedged between him and Riff, coating himself quickly before shoving inside the sex demon with one sharp thrust.

When Daemon thrust inside Riff, Riff was forced deeper inside me.

My heart pulsed in time with their motions. Beating so hard I thought it might explode out of my chest.

I could barely breathe.

They were so big—I was too damn full.

And fuck me, I never wanted it to end.

Just when I thought I couldn't feel any fuller, Alistair knelt over my head and pushed himself into my mouth.

All four men devoured me as if they were intent on leaving not a crumb behind. The twins came almost in perfect succession. Alistair followed a few strokes later. It took Daemon another minute or so since this was his second round.

And who the fuck knew how many times I'd orgasmed? I'd lost count after the third.

As everyone fell apart, I was vaguely aware of red eyes watching us in the mirrors. Al stood by, appreciating the show.

If I had another hole for him, I'd gladly offer it up. But I was completely spent, leaking so much cum I thought I might burst.

We all fell into a limp and tangled pile of sweaty limbs. Even though I had four demons on top of me, I felt so light. Like I could just float away.

The peace was disturbed somewhat when Riff jerked against me. "What the fuck is happening?"

I didn't have to lift my head to see what he was talking about. I grinned. "A hellhound is knotting your asshole."

The incubus cursed, and Daemon laughed. "That's what you get for getting blood on my carpet, imp."

"Careful," Raff snickered. "If that's the punishment for dirtying up your floor, we're going to be fucking in your trailer *all* the time."

I wasn't sure how long we stayed like that. Long enough for the twins and Daemon to fall asleep. I was just starting to drift off, too, when gentle hands untangled me from Riff and Raff's arms.

I sleepily blinked up at Alistair as he carried us deeper into the house of mirrors. He stopped when it was only our reflection in the glass panels and lowered us onto the floor with me in his lap and his back propped against a large "fun house" mirror that warped our images.

"Wanted me all to yourself, hmm?" I teased.

He remained silent, his actions answer enough as he repositioned me in his lap so that I was straddling him. His palms smoothed over my back, and in a sexy, lust-drunk whisper, he said, "Ride me, Little Demon."

I lowered myself onto his cock, deliberately taking my time. Watching his face twist with pleasure as I speared myself onto him had me chasing yet another orgasm.

His head tilted, exposing the slender column of his throat. "Bite me...Claim me."

My gaze clamped to the faded scar of Famine's ancient mating mark. Suddenly, the need to cover the old claim Famine had left on Death was just as strong as my need to mark Alistair at all.

My fangs punched into his throat. His body gave a little jump. Not a sound of pain escaped him, only a low, swollen moan.

We stayed like that for what felt like a short eternity, yet it wasn't long enough. I pulled my fangs from his throat, but he didn't remove his hands from my thighs, keeping his cock locked inside me.

Even as golden light from the incoming sunrise bled into the ride, chasing away the dark, we remained in one another's embrace. Unmoving.

"Can I ask you something?" He nuzzled my neck, his voice so low I barely heard him.

I was so tired I didn't even have the energy to lift my head from his shoulder. "Hmm?"

"How did your father die?"

My breath hitched. I wasn't sure what question I'd been expecting. Not that.

This was the first time any of my guys had asked about my dad's death. In fact, we'd avoided the topic of my father in most conversations. I knew it wasn't because of a lack of caring.

It's like they'd known it was a sensitive topic for me. And just like he'd known to avoid the subject, Alistair somehow knew I was in a place to discuss it with them. The trust had been formed. Our bonds were stronger than ever. And the pain from my past was healing as rapidly as Alistair's fresh mating mark.

"Cancer," I mumbled against his skin a few beats later. "Lung cancer. He smoked like a chimney. Most of the guys at Walker's did. After all this supernatural shit, dying of lung cancer seems kind of silly, doesn't it?"

Alistair pulled me back in his arms to pin me with a look. "It's not silly at all, Meg."

Despite the dower topic, I found myself smiling. "He would have hated you. Probably all of you."

Alistair mirrored my smile. "As your father, I'd expect no less. You know, I saw him once."

My mouth dropped open. "Wait. *Really?*"

The demon hummed in confirmation. "When I tracked your mother down and found her hiding out at Walker's. He was charmed by her, of course, but I couldn't shake the feeling that he was a good man. I pitied him...Until I met you."

My brows pulled together with my frown. "What do you mean?"

"Lilith may have charmed him into loving her, but his love for you was completely authentic. She gave him you, which was probably one of the few good things she'd ever done with her long life. Even if her intent was self-serving."

"I guess I never really thought of it like that."

He reached up to idly twine a lock of my rosy hair around his long index finger. "I'm sorry for your loss. And I'm sorry I didn't tell you that sooner. I understand it's a human formality meant to invoke comfort. Though, it should come as a consolation to know that I don't believe his soul is in my realm."

"Really?" I reeled back in his arms. The motion had him groaning since he was still lodged tight inside me.

He nodded, his Adam's apple bobbing in his throat with a swallow. "Yes. Really. When I was down in Hell getting Daemon's hellhound pup at the twins' request, I checked. He's in the other place."

My heart squeezed. *The other place.*

"You mean Heaven?" I bobbed excitedly up and down in Alistair's lap—partially because I was excited and partially because there were few things I loved more than watching the devil squirm in pleasure beneath me.

"Something like that, yes—*By my depths*, you feel so good..."

"Will you tell me about the other place?"

Another nod. "Yes. But it's a story for another time, my pet."

His arms banded around my waist, and he started to pump inside me, chasing yet another release. Unholy pleasure tore through my body, and a torrent of sinful sounds clawed up from my throat.

I pressed my forehead to his and clung to his shoulders, holding on as I let him take complete control this time. "W–will I go there when I die?"

Those eyes—so hot and full of hellfire as they locked with mine. "Not a chance, Pet. You're mated to the devil and his three favorite sinners. Even if a fleet of seraphim try and wrench you away. We'll start a fucking war with the heavens if that's what it takes to keep you." He laughed. "Hell, the humans already think I did that."

I sighed happily against his subtle warmth as my demonic ringmaster made love to me.

If it wasn't angels, I had a feeling we'd have some kind of supernatural enemies waiting for us down the line. Monsters like us had a way of attracting trouble like that.

Regardless of whoever or whatever they were, I'd just have to distract myself with what made me happy in the meantime.

My mates and their marks on my body...

And our twisted little sideshow of creeps I'd come to call family.

THE FUCKING END!

Author Note
THANK YOU FOR READING CARNIVAL CREEPS!

When I started this duet I had no idea where it was going to end up. I let my batshit muse take full control on this one and honestly, I'm **thrilled** with how it turned out. I hope you loved reading Meg and her creeps' story as much as I loved writing it. I see myself potentially returning to this world later down the line, but for now, it's a wrap!

Thank you, thank you, thank you for picking up the Sinner's Sideshow Duet. Thank you for trusting me to take you on a smutty, crazy adventure. It really means the world to me.

Until next time,
Aiden

About the Author

Aiden Pierce is a writer of dark paranormal romance and erotic horror. Her love stories are on the spooky side and usually end up with the monster or the villain getting the girl.

She lives in the Pacific Northwest with her husband and their three fur babies. When she's not daydreaming about the characters that live in her head, she can be found curled up on the couch with a black coffee and a dark romance novel.

You can find Aiden on any of these platforms:

Instagram —> @aidenpierceromance
Tiktok —> @aidenpierceromance
Her Website —> www.authoraidenpierce.com

www.ingramcontent.com/pod-product-compliance
Lightning Source LLC
Chambersburg PA
CBHW061501120726
48001CB00004B/1165